Please feel free to send me an
publisher filters these emails.

S.A. Cross- sa_cross@aweson.............

Sign up for my blog for updates and freebies!
http://sa-cross.awesomeauthors.org/

About the Publisher

BLVNP Incorporated, A Nevada Corporation, 340 S. Lemon #6200, Walnut CA 91789, info@blvnp.com / legal@blvnp.com

DISCLAIMER

Lady and the Wolf

By: S.A. Cross

BLVNP

ISBN: 978-1-68030-861-7

Table of Contents

Matt, Brett and Poppy

"Goodbye isn't forever, goodbye is just until we meet again."
There's always a story after goodbye, and I can't wait to tell you
everything.
This one is for you.

FREE DOWNLOAD

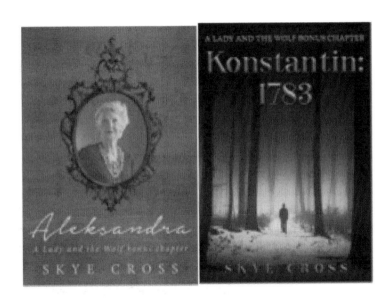

Get these freebies and MORE when you sign up for the author's mailing list!

http://sa-cross.awesomeauthors.org/

Chapter One

"Daddy, what is this?" she asked, bright eyes wide and curious as she poked the grasshopper with her pudgy finger.

Charlie laughed as he moved towards his daughter, wondering just how the little six-year-old saw the world around her. Everything to her was an adventure, and he was proud to go along for the ride. Having two older children who saw traveling to other countries as an adventure, it was nice to relive those days where the front yard was as far as his little girl wanted to go — for now, anyway.

With a chuckle, the graying man knelt beside his youngest child and answered, "It's a grasshopper, sweetie. Touch it and see what happens."

Her little face wrinkled up in disdain. "That's icky, Daddy!"

Charlie smiled and pulled her into him in a big bear hug before sitting her in front of him and winked. "Watch this."

He went on and poked the little bug, sending it hopping away into the thick brush of trees. With a shrill, delighted scream, she threw her arms around her daddy's neck so that if the bug glanced back at her, her daddy would be able to pick her up and fight it off.

"Aira, why are you screaming?" came an exhausted voice. A mother was truly never far away when her child screamed for help. She looked over the situation, and after staring at her husband with her cautious blue eyes, she eventually put two and two together. "Charlie, stop antagonizing her," she warned.

Charlie Blight smiled at his tiresome wife before looking at his daughter — who was still clinging to him — and laughed along with her. All Vivian could do was sigh as she watched her husband act like a child.

Vivian tread carefully towards the two, trying not to wince as sticks and other things stuck to her feet. It seemed flip-flops weren't the best option for camping out in the wilderness. With a swift flick of her hand, she tugged at her daughter and smiled, "It's time for dinner and bed, pumpkin."

Aira shook her head defiantly. "No!"

Vivian rolled her eyes and grabbed the little girl, gently pulling the screaming child towards the campfire Charlie had set up earlier. Aira tried to pull away from her mother, but the struggle was futile. Her mother always won in the end.

"You spoil her too much, Charlie. What's she going to do when we're not around anymore?" Vivian snapped, her blue eyes lucid and glaring at her husband from across the fire.

Charlie glanced at his wife of twenty years, still shoveling cooked fish into his mouth as he answered, "She'll be thirty by the time one of us kicks the bucket. We're not *that* old, Viv."

Vivian had always used the same rule while raising her older children — teach them how to be independent and strong-willed. Aira, although only six years old, was incredibly clingy and had no desire to be without her parents for more than five minutes. Since the day Aira was born, her parents had not had a single outing alone for fear that Aira would choke to death from screaming so loudly once she realized they were gone.

"She hasn't even started school yet. The principal at her school told us she can't go back there, not after what happened to her teacher."

Charlie tried to stop himself from laughing, but a few stray chuckles still left his lips. "How many stitches did the woman need again?"

"Five," Vivian snapped, glaring at her amused husband. It wasn't a laughing matter and was far less humorous than her husband made it out to be. "Plastic scissors should come with a warning!"

Getting over his fit of chuckles, Charlie glanced to the side where his older son, Ian, was still working out how to pitch up the tents. His first-born daughter, Avery, was trying to get Aira into her pajamas but the child wouldn't have any of it. It was a fairly funny sight.

"Mom!" Avery screamed, struggling with her little sister who simply refused to wear the garments the older girl was slipping on to her. "Come deal with this demon child!"

Vivian sighed and got up from the fold-out chair she had snuggled into earlier. With her cup of coffee still in hand, she narrowed her eyes and snapped, "Avery, you're *sixteen* for heaven's sake! Can't you handle a six-year-old?"

She sighed as she moved to join the scuffle and convince Aira that her clothes were fine and not too big.

Charlie laughed. This would probably be their last family holiday before Ian went off to college. It had been a struggle to get Avery away from her friends for even a minute, let alone three days, so he was positive this was the last time his older daughter would come out with them again willingly. Aira would be a teenager before he knew it and wouldn't need her daddy to fight off a grasshopper for her anymore.

He would even fight off a pack of wolves for the safety of his family.

"Dad, can you help me for a second? This pole's giving me some problems," Ian called as he bent over to hold the steel pole in place, grinning sheepishly. "Unless you want it collapsing later and you know how Avery and Aira *love* their sleep."

"Sure, bud." Charlie nodded and went to help his son with the tent that was just as difficult as the three arguing girl's not even three feet away from him.

A howl in the distance stopped any other noise being made in the wooded terrain. Having camped in this particular spot before, Charlie was used to the beautiful sound of wild wolves calling out to their pack, but this was different. He wondered why the sound was so close to their campsite.

They've moved closer, he thought, bewildered as to why they would move their pack closer to a human campsite. The scent of previous campers should have deterred them.

Vivian glanced at her husband, trying to hide the obvious concern that shadowed her face. Her children weren't fazed by the noise, having heard it many a time before, and Aira was too preoccupied with stirring up her big sister to care. Vivian, however, had chills running down her spine.

"Charlie..." she murmured.

"It's okay," Charlie responded, his face all smiles as he secured the large family tent. "They're wild animals, but they won't come near our site. Don't worry, hon."

Vivian could only give her husband a curt smile as she glanced at the other campers situated around them. It was a popular camping ground, so, of course, they were safe. No wolves came near them in the past.

We're safe.

Her eyes were clamped shut, her upper lip trembled, and her little hand clung to her mother's as they ran. In her half sleep state, Aira could not determine what was happening, only that every other person around the campsite with her family had awoken her with shrill screams and cries.

She wanted her daddy. Where was her daddy?

She whimpered when she heard her big sister, Avery, cry out and a loud thud followed. Her mother, who had been dragging Aira as she ran, abruptly halted, sending Aira smashing into her back.

Vivian let go of her youngest child's hand as she ran to the aid of Avery. Aira could only watch as her mother roughly pulled her sister to her feet, screaming at her to keep running. A tear slipped down Aira's little red cheek as she watched her scared mother slap her sister across the face, trying to get the poor girl to stop screaming.

"Daddy…" she whispered. She had last seen her father fighting with those giant dogs before he yelled at her to go with her mother. Ian had also been fighting with them, and his arm had been bleeding.

"Mommy, Ian needs a Band-Aid," she muttered, watching as her still frightened mother was trying to help Avery as she walked.

Her mother's head spun around and Aira, although only a child, instantly noticed those big tears rolling from her mother's beautiful eyes.

Something wasn't right.

"Aira, come over here and walk beside me. Do not leave my side! Do you understand?" she snapped.

All Aira could do was nod as she ran to her mother's side. Her own blue eyes shifted to her sister who was leaning to her mother's opposite side. Her hands, knees, and clothes were covered in mud from the rain that had hit earlier. She was also limping, and her face looked panic-stricken and strained. At that moment, Aira knew that something was horribly wrong.

They walked for a good while, and by this time, the rain was coming down so hard it stung Aira's skin. Thunder and lightning weren't far off, and when the two cracked down, Aira let out a shrill scream.

Her mother's breaths were coming out hard and uneven as she looked around for something. As she neared a steep, rocky hill, her mother gasped as a shimmer of hope showed itself. There in the center of the hill were rocks and a little crevice, big enough to huddle into but too high and steep for a wild animal to get to them.

But deep down, a terrible feeling told Vivian that these weren't normal wolves.

Why are they here, of all places...?

She gently sat Avery down onto the muddy ground and pulled Aira towards her, lifting the small girl up until she had a steady hand on one of the rocks.

"Okay, baby, you need to climb to where that opening is, okay? See it?" she pointed to the opening in the rocks, only a short climb up, while she held on to her daughter's tiny waist.

"Mom-Mommy, you said climbing on rocks is dangerous," Aira whined back, her eyes watering from the wind that was slapping against every part of her body. The rain that had started up again was making her shiver terribly in her mother's grasp.

Vivian closed her eyes for a moment, squeezing them shut as she thought of a way to coax her scared little girl to safety. "Think of it as a game, honey, and the floor is lava. Keep climbing until you get to that safe point."

Thinking that the floor was lava didn't ease the situation the least. In fact, it made Aira tremble in fear and freeze against the rocks. She was so frightened and confused.

Vivian was starting to get restless as she tried to push Aira up the steep rocky hill. Just as Aira shook her head no, as always, Vivian could hear the low, gut wrenching sounds of growls and branches crunching in the distance.

Looking down, she noticed Avery clawing away from the breach of trees and sit on the rocks. "Mo-Mom!" she cried. "They're coming!"

"Go!" Vivian shouted, shoving Aira so violently upwards that a sharp rock went straight through the little girl's palm.

In her shock, she stumbled and turned her head to look down. Her mother had let go and had picked up a large tree branch, trying to fight off the big dogs she had seen her brother and father hitting earlier. Avery was whimpering just under Aira, screaming "*No!*" again and again.

"Avery, follow Aira! Go!" Vivian screamed as she thrashed the large stick she held around in hopes it would deter the snarling animals.

Avery shook her head, her damp sun-kissed curls bouncing around her shoulders as she did so. "I can't stand up!" she cried. Her cheeks, even through the rain, were stained with dried blood and tears, perhaps from when she had tried to help an elderly woman at the campsite who was being torn apart by these animals.

All Aira could do was stare down at her shivering sister, her eyes wide and horrified at what was happening. She clung to the rocks about a foot from the ground and contemplated jumping off to help her mother. Avery shifted her identical blue, bloodshot eyes up towards Aira, almost pleading the little girl for some kind of miracle.

It was all too much.

"Aira… don't be scared…" she heard Avery whisper, her teary eyes staring up at Aira pleadingly before it was all over.

The giant dog lunged at Avery, but their mother jumped in front of her. Aira's breaths were jumpy as she stared, unblinking, at her mother screaming and flinging her arms around wildly while trying to shield Avery. Aira was taught that when someone was bleeding, a Band-Aid could always fix the wound, but there was so much blood coming from her mother that Aira was certain a Band-Aid wouldn't help her.

A tear slipped silently down Aira's cheek, mixing in with the harsh rain that continued to pelt down. The dogs had silenced her mother and sister, but they were invisible to Aira as she stared down at the unmoving bodies of her family.

She found her voice when one of the dogs leaped up and snapped its giant jaw near Aira's foot, trying to get her down to the ground. Her scream echoed throughout the dense forest, reminding her she was now all by herself. There was no one to protect her.

"Mommy, wake up!" she screamed as more tears rolled down her cheeks. Her hand that she had injured earlier was starting to sting as she clung to the rocks for dear life, and the jagged rocks that her tummy was leaning against were starting to dig into her torso. "Avery, wake Mommy up!" she tried again, her cries growing more desperate. "Daddy, Ian, help me! Chase the animals away!"

"I'm scared!" she screamed out with all her might, gut wrenching sobs following close behind.

Chapter Two

"Mr. Volkov, call on line three."

Van Volkov sighed as the shrill voice of his secretary came over the line. He didn't want to answer the call flashing on his desk phone. There was just too much work to be done, too much covering up to be made and too many distractions. It was bad enough that a pack of rogue shifters was running wild throughout forests in California and some in Colorado. Now, there were human bodies on his head.

Van ran a hand through his dark, thick hair, readying himself for the news that was to come. Although alpha of centuries-old pack, Van still had his troubles while living in the human's world. He had adapted, as he was asked too many years ago, and still, a problem that should have been left to those silly humans became his.

"Talk," he growled as he picked up the landline.

"One family dead, two people dead from another family, and ten survivors with a pretty tale to tell."

It was official. He would have to call in a few pack subordinates to help clean up this horrible mess. That was the only way to keep his pack and his domain safe. It was a frustrating decision, but he did not intend to let the police know about any of this. For now, the few subordinates he had at the scene were posing as park rangers, trying to quiet down the survivors and clearing out the bodies.

"Van, he's coming into our territory and killing humans. He wants a fight."

Van growled quite viciously before slamming the phone down onto its hook. Standing up, the chair skidded from under him and smashed into the wall as he wiped everything from his desk, glasses smashing onto the floor and papers flying everywhere.

From the outside, all workers could do was stop and stare through the plain glass door as their boss and chairman destroyed everything in his path. He had a short fuse, everyone in the building knew that much and never dared say anything that could spark that fuse.

He stormed out of his office, car keys in hand, and started to unbutton his shirt. He was so angry his body was actually heating up quite a bit. His personal secretary, Emma, was fast to catch up as she grabbed onto his arm. He dragged the smaller woman along as he thundered down the hall and towards the elevator.

"Van, where are you going?" she gasped, already under the impression he was going out to hunt down the rogue's that were becoming an annoyance to the shifter's very existence.

Although a strong Lycan, Van could not take on an entire pack of rogue wolves. It was suicide.

"Cleaning up their mess," was his only response as those elevator doors closed, leaving Emma staring in disbelief.

It had taken at least an hour to reach the camping ground where the incident had occurred. As soon as Van stepped out of his Cadillac Escalade, the smell of blood, sweat, fear and dirty mongrels wafted through his nose and invaded his senses. This was going to be a long day.

Even before he saw the destruction of tents and camping equipment, his inner Lycan was jumping around and growling something to him. His golden eyes that he had covered with contacts earlier that day were narrowing as he looked around. Something was off.

"Van…"

A slap on the shoulder brought him back to his senses. He twisted his mouth and turned towards the assailant, a scowl shadowing his features.

"Drake." He nodded.

The man sighed, his hand never leaving his best friend's shoulder. "Bit of a mess, isn't it?"

Van looked around at the humans covered up in emergency blankets. Some were crying while some were tending to their wounds. It didn't make sense.

"Why didn't they kill all of them?" he asked.

Drake clucked his tongue as he thought of an answer that would satisfy his leader. "No one knows what goes through the mind of a rogue shifter, Van. There hasn't been a group attack aimed at humans in centuries."

Van nodded as he glanced around, his sight moving towards the deep neck of trees. As soon as he focused, his wolf — the Lycan that owned him — started to growl fiercely, crying out, *"Danger, help, mine,"* all at once. Before Van could stop himself, his legs were moving towards the brush. With one fell swoop, he had crouched down and jumped to the top of a tree, landing on the branch before jumping to another.

Van glided from one tree to another; the thinner branches breaking after he had jumped to the next one. He normally wouldn't allow his Lycan to control him in such a way, but it interested him about why it was so disobedient. He hadn't felt this sort of adrenaline since he was a pup and enjoyed the feeling of complete freedom, although he knew as soon as he found what was causing his mind to go rogue, he would leave it be. This was out of pure curiousness, nothing more.

It wasn't long before he zoned in on what was causing his inner disturbance, and as soon as he did, he wished he hadn't. He had thought the scents he picked up when he had first gotten out of his car to inspect the campground were bad, but this was making his nose turn up and his eyes, flare. Urine, blood, fear, infection and the utter stench of rotting flesh were filling his senses rapidly. Whatever his wolf was looking for, it was near death.

"Save... Must save..." it called out to him, a more desperate tone ringing through his ears. If to at least stop that terrible whining, he would go and investigate before leaving and washing his nose out with bleach.

As he neared the steep rocky hill, Van found the "thing" that was filling his senses with rotting flesh. Two bodies lay at the bottom of the hill, one on top of the other, both female from their apparel and hair. He could often determine females by their scent, but once dead, the female's egg's that let off that certain scent died with them. These women were unrecognizable with all that blood covering them. Even Van, who was used to death, had to turn away.

He jumped up the hill with ease, using the rocks to tread on as leverage, and made his way to where a new scent was drawing him in. Whatever this new discovery was, it could have most certainly smelled as bad as the two dead humans below. As he got further up, he noticed an opening in the rocks and stepped onto the ledge. He leaned back and grabbed hold of both sides of the opening, peering in carefully. Although dark, he could see perfectly fine, and ultimately found the source of his reckless abandon earlier.

At first, it looked like a dead animal huddled up towards the back. Humans were strange creatures, and despite the smell of urine and other such things, Van could tell this girl was still alive.

"She must have survived the attack," he muttered, trying to let little emotion taint his tone. He could not have cared less if a human lived or not, but since these humans were in his domain, he had sworn to watch over shifter, creature, and human alike. It was a position he begrudgingly accepted the day he was born.

Its breathing lingered for a moment before inhaling, almost gasping for breath. Even though he could smell nothing, her being a child and her skin so raw she was unrecognizable, he could still tell that this child was a female. Van could hear her forced breaths from where he was balancing and knew he was this human's link between life and death. This far out in the woods, no one would find her, and death was unavoidable even with medical help. There was only one thing he could do.

He moved into the shallow cave before kneeling beside the broken human. He pulled back his hand, concentrating the Lycan within him, and with a loud growl, his nails grew longer, his teeth sharpened into razor fangs, and the hues of his normally calm eyes turned to slits. This was a far cry from his full wolf form, but that would take out a lot of his energy. This child only needed a quick cut, and it would all be over.

"I'm doing you a favor, human," he growled as his hand flew towards her chest.

"Dad-Daddy?"

The little whimper caught him off guard. His hand had stopped its onslaught millimeters from her chest, not expecting the human to be able to breathe for much longer, let alone speak. His eyes narrowed dangerously as he inspected the odd creature before him.

Her gap-tooth smile caught him further off guard. Despite being near death, she smiled at him and uncurled her arms from around her legs. "You didn't... You didn't hurt... the doggies... did you, Daddy?" She coughed and spluttered everywhere as she said this, making Van edge back.

The doggies... did she mean those mutts from last night? Is she worried about the shifter's who slaughtered her own kind? He frowned as he thought it over, confused and disturbed with the odd human before him. However, the child couldn't have been more than six years old, so, of course, she still had an ounce of innocence left in her after the horror she may have witnessed.

"Save... Save... Help her!" his wolf cried out. This sort of reaction had never occurred before, much less towards a human. The almost deafening thump that rattled throughout his mind was getting to be too much. It seemed the only thing to placate his temperamental Lycan was to do what it wanted: help the human child.

He felt the bile rise in his throat as he edged closer and gently lifted the child into his arms. It was awkward. He had held a child once before in his life, and after this, he never wanted to do so ever again.

She did not squirm or even wriggle from her obvious infected cuts. She seemed almost content as she nuzzled her face into him. How this girl could confuse him with her own father was beyond Van as he glared down at her, growling low at the thought of anyone catching him in this situation.

As he jumped out of the cave and bounded the trees, he held her a little tighter, protecting her from the coming onslaught of loose branches and leaves.

"I won't be responsible for any fresh injuries," he tried to convince himself. He swore this would be the last time he helped a human like this, and it would be the last time he ever saw this girl again.

As soon as he made it back to the camp, he handed the child off to his beta, and went about brushing off any dirt she may have left on his suit. Drake checked the little girl's pulse, timing the rhythm with his Armani watch. She was sweating and running a high fever among other complications. Her hand, which had a deep gash in it, was starting to swell with infection, and her legs were covered in claw marks. She had been out there for two days in the blistering cold with nothing but rain pelting down and wind prickling her tiny body. She didn't have much time left. Van could instantly tell it was slowly breaking Drake's heart to see this little girl's legs covered in sores from sitting in moisture and her own urine for two straight days.

As the ambulance turned up, Drake ordered the paramedics to make the little girl top priority and told them he'd be at the hospital shortly to give her treatment. The two men nodded as they wheeled the child into the awaiting ambulance, wrapping her in an emergency blanket and giving her an oxygen mask.

Van stayed to the side, idly watching his brother work on the child before sending her off.

"It's not like you to be this worried about a child. A *human* child, no less," Drake said as he casually stood beside his alpha.

Van grunted as his eyes narrowed in the direction those medics had taken her. "Unlikely; I just didn't want any more problems concerning humans."

"You do realize that getting her medical treatment means this is going to be all over the news, right?" Drake looked concerned.

Van shook his head. "Would you have preferred I put her out of her misery myself?" God knows he tried to.

Drake chuckled as he took off his medical gloves. "Her name's Aira Blight. It was written on the tag inside of her night shirt."

Van's nose crinkled up in disdain. "And this means something to me because…?" he muttered.

"The family that was killed. Their names were on the registry at the forest entrance ranger station. They're all dead. She's the only one that got away, and even I'm not sure if all that fighting is going to be worth it." Drake frowned as he said this, a sympathetic glint in his eye as he stared in the direction the ambulance had sped off in. "She might die tonight from all that exposure."

Van frowned. "Well, save her Doctor."

And with that, he made his way back to his Escalade, too proud to explain himself to his baffled kin.

Chapter Three

Emma Volkov marched down the halls of the Los Angeles Children's Hospital. Nurses halted what they were doing and nodded to the wife of Drake Volkov, the hospital's surgical director. She nodded her greetings to the staff but never stopped for a moment.

Drake had called his wife earlier and told her to meet him at work. Being the wife of her boss's brother, she had no qualms about leaving her own work without notice. She was the only human who knew Van's secret — the moody Lycan often needed her help when it came to special situations inside his business.

As she was beeped through the door of the intensive care unit, Emma was shocked to find none other than her cold brother-in-law sitting in the waiting room, casually mingling amongst worried parents of other children and family members.

Whatever she was called here so urgently for, Emma knew she should brace herself for quite a shock.

"Van, why are you here? What's going on?" Emma asked, slightly puffed out after her mini jog from the hospital's parking lot.

Van never even acknowledged the leggy blonde. His only answer was a swift flick of his chin towards the window to the left. Emma was confused, at first, but gathered her senses and waltzed over to the window. Her only child, Aiden, was tucked away safe in bed by this time of night. A woman from Drake's pack came to take care of him while Emma rushed to the hospital after her husband's bewildering call. What could be so important that even Van, a man who only cared about the safety and solidarity of his pack, would be sitting in this stuffy waiting room?

Gripping her clutch purse to her chest, Emma made her way to the window. Could Van possibly have a child? Was that the reason he was waiting so patiently? So many questions ran through her head, but when she came to the window and stared through, the situation only grew more mysterious.

Inside the plain white room was a tiny girl. Her legs were propped up, airing the sores that cascaded down her skinny little legs. Her right arm and hand were bandaged and propped up by a belt and a pole. She was connected to so many wires; Emma couldn't help but gasp, take a step back and cover her mouth with her dainty hand. She couldn't think. She just stared, completely horrified.

The girl was obviously human for even wolf pups healed faster than human children. Her adoptive son, Aiden, had almost completely severed his finger off at one point, only for it to completely heal two days later.

There was not a single flower, card or present sitting in that room and waiting for the little girl to wake up. Emma's thin brows furrowed as she looked around the waiting room. There were parents catering to their own sick children in wheelchairs, family friends who seemed to be laughing and chatting, and then there was Van who simply sat there, out of place as usual. Where was this little girl's family?

"Where's your mother, Angel?" Emma whispered as she gently touched the glass when what she really wanted was to go in there and stroke the little girl's pained face.

"They were victims of the rogue attack Drake and I investigated earlier today. They're dead," came Van's stoic response. The lack of care in his voice didn't deter Emma but only made her curious as to why he would even take notice of this situation, to begin with. Van despised humans, and it had taken almost five years for him to even acknowledge her by her first name.

Emma didn't respond to Van, however. She was still watching the child's round face, observing her chest rise and fall with the help of the breathing tube down her throat, concentrating on how her little nose crinkled ever so slightly, most probably a bad dream of some sort.

Emma's heart broke in half.

She continued to stare, Van watching over her shoulder, as her husband walked in. He had a surgical gown, a mask and surgical gloves on. He seemed to notice his wife staring in almost instantly, and even through the mask, Emma could tell he was smiling as he gave her a big thumbs up, a signal the girl would be okay. Drake knew her too well. He knew she would be worried the moment she laid her big blue eyes on the little girl.

Emma smiled and gently chewed on her lower lip, contemplating over the entire situation. The raw need to comfort this child as her own mother would was overwhelming. Emma never had children of her own for human women can't produce offspring with their Lycan partners; but once she and Drake had adopted Aiden when he was only a small pup, her maternal instincts had been set on fire.

She looked at Van, who was staring adamantly at the girl with a piercing look. Emma couldn't help but notice his normally dapper attire was lost, his shirt a mess with mud and other things she couldn't name right off the bat. His jacket, which he kept ironed and in immaculate condition, was carelessly crumpled over his shoulder. His normally neat dark hair was falling into his eyes, and his face looked worn and tired.

"Van, have you been here since early this morning?" she timidly asked. It was near seven in the morning when he stormed out of his office, and judging from the pitch darkness outside and the clock she checked before rushing over, it was near ten at night.

He let out a grunt and turned away. "Drake coerced me into sticking around. Don't think about it too much," was his gruff reply.

Emma blinked as she leaned against the glass, watching, as his shoulders seemed to shake as if he were having a battle within himself. Emma had never known Van to complain about his Lycan, but it seemed it was giving him a little bit of trouble these days.

"Are the elders still giving you problems about finding a mate, Van?" she asked, and when she did, she noticed immediately how Van seemed to stiffen. His whole posture straightened up instantly, and his long legs carried him away from her.

"I'm going to get a coffee," he muttered as he almost ran towards the stairs instead of taking the elevator.

Emma sighed. Van was an unopened book. She knew deep down he didn't want to find a mate because that would mean a weakness for him. Rival packs often aimed for the mate of an Alpha because once your mate dies, you will slowly die with them. It was an enchantment going back hundreds of years. Having a mate makes you stronger, faster, invincible almost, but once that mate is gone, their significant other dies shortly after. It was unfair in Emma's eyes. Even Drake was far stronger than Van all because she was tied to him. Their energy was one with the other. When he bled, she bled, and if they ventured too far apart for too long, it would be like their flesh was ripping from their skin. A male shifter should never venture too far from his mate, be they a human or a wolf.

"Emma, hon, you okay?" came that smooth, velvety voice Emma loved so.

The vivacious, young blonde turned around just in time catch her husband's delicious smile. In Emma's eyes, Drake was the most gorgeous man she had ever laid eyes on. In the beginning, it had been like a dream to think he had chosen *her* amongst the many beautiful and talented women chasing at his heels. It wasn't until she found out his secret did she understand he wasn't just in love with her, but it was their destiny to be together.

Drake wore a smile as he disposed of his surgical gloves, walking quickly towards his wife. Emma had always thought that Drake and Van looked very similar with both dark, wild hair and those amazing natural golden eyes when they didn't wear contacts, anyway. But when she had gotten to know Van, it was obvious he and Drake were in no way, shape or form alike. Drake was kind, considerate and loved human affection. Van, however, was curt, rough and hated the idea of showing any form of emotion. That was a weakness to him.

Emma wondered what sort of mate could turn Van into a good man, but she had also wondered if it would take a woman twice as blunt and toxic to tame him.

Drake circled his wife, wrapping his arms around her waist as they both stared through the window at the little girl still on the brink of death. She seemed stable, but Emma could tell that Drake still had his concerns.

"She's a fighter," he whispered into her ear.

Emma smiled. "She's a little angel…" she whispered back as she took one of Drake's hands from around her and entwined her fingers with his. "And she's all alone now."

Emma sighed as Drake squeezed her just a little tighter. She came from a broken life. With no parents to speak of, he and Aiden were the only family Emma had left. Drake knew as soon as Emma saw this little girl, she would sympathize. She was a kind woman, maybe too kind at times.

"Yes, we tried to contact any family member, godparent, anyone to try to come and see her. She's had a few visitors today, but they all said the same thing. 'I wish I could take her, but I can't. Sorry' and left." It was a sad situation. "They didn't want anything to do with the hospital fees, either."

Emma's eyes widened as her head spun around to look up at her husband in disbelief. "Then, she'll be taken away and put into a home, won't she?" she asked, a little hysterical at the idea.

Drake nodded. "Yeah, as soon as she has recovered."

Emma bit her lip, her eyes wide and pleading as she thought seriously about what she was going to say next. Drake had never been one to say no to her, but she didn't want him thinking she was treating this poor girl like a puppy she wanted to take home. If for a moment, she wanted to give this little girl a good head start in a world that was far too cruel to her.

"Drake, we have more than enough room at home, and Aiden always wanted a little friend to play with. I mean, we can talk about it. It doesn't have to happen now... but, what I mean is, can we...?" She was sputtering and mumbling as she tried to ask her husband if they could take the child home with them. Her words and sentences were everywhere, but she wasn't surprised when Drake knew exactly what she meant.

His smile was more than enough to tell her he was more than happy with the idea. "I thought you'd see it that way. We'll talk about it and wait until she pulls through. She may not like us when she wakes up. She'll need to adjust, Em. She lost everything she had ever known."

Emma nodded as she tried to hold herself together. *Lost everything she had ever known,* his words resounded throughout her mind. When the child woke, would she wonder where her mother was? How would she react?

After a brief kiss, she stared at Drake and smiled as best she could, given the situation. "Will our insurance cover her injuries?" she asked.

Drake chuckled as he gently brushed the side of his hand against his wife's cheek. "It's already been taken care of."

"By who?" she asked, confused. "I thought no one wanted anything to do with her medical bills?"

Drake couldn't contain it much longer. "Ask the insurance king himself," he whispered, smiling as he glanced towards Van who was making his way towards the loving couple, coffee in hand, and a dark scowl on his face. Someone must have gotten under his skin in his brief walk to the cafeteria on the second floor.

Emma's eyes widened. "How did you convince him?" she gasped.

"I didn't," was his only reply as he continued to watch his brother, that knowing smile never flinching.

Emma realized that in the end, the girl would need a lot of therapy after she recovered. Throwing her into a home wasn't an option. She would need extensive, costly therapy to help her overcome the trauma of watching her family be torn apart right before her eyes. Drake knew Emma's love and his guidance would help the child recover. They just needed the chance.

"Mrs. Volkov?"

Emma, who was in the middle of reading out a paragraph from a children's book to a still-sleeping Aira, looked up to see who was calling her. She recognized the person standing at her door as a night nurse and smiled. "Hmm?"

"There's someone here for Aira." By this time, the staff in the ICU ward had come to learn the name of the child brought in three days prior and adhered to the wish of Doctor Volkov's wife that whenever they addressed the girl, sleeping or otherwise, to use her name. It was now commonplace, and the nurses enjoyed speaking to her as she slept, finally having a name to a face.

Emma nodded and quietly sat the large Peter Rabbit children's book beside Aira. She gently brushed her hand against the sleeping child's cheek and whispered, "I'll be right back," before following the nurse outside.

As she was led to the waiting area, she immediately spotted a rather young woman with pale skin and dark hair. Despite Aira being slightly tanned, this woman resembled her. Emma's stomach dropped.

"You're here for Aira?" Emma asked. She was hesitant, scared, and felt sick to her stomach all at once.

The moment the woman noticed Emma she stood up and smiled. Her mouth was perched open as if wondering what to say and instead poked her hand out. "Yes, yes! I-I was Aira's pre-school teacher from a couple of years back. My name's Loretta."

Emma let out a sigh of utmost relief. Although thrilled that, perhaps, a family member of Aira's had come to take her to a home she was familiar with, she couldn't help but feel saddened. She was by the little girl's bedside every day, for almost every second she was asleep and couldn't imagine what she would do if those days by the girl's side were gone.

Her smile was radiant as she gently took the younger girl's hand. "Nice to meet you. I'm Emma. I'm taking care of Aira until she wakes up."

The woman seemed nervous, but that nervousness quickly turned to turmoil as she clutched a large duffle bag to her torso. "She hasn't woken up yet? Oh, that's terrible. They were an awesome family."

Emma's lips formed a straight line as she watched sadness wash over the girl's face. "You were close to her family, then?" Her mouth was moving before she had a chance to think about what she was asking.

The girl's big brown eyes seemed to brighten as if recalling a sudden memory. "Oh, yes, I, um, used to go over to their house a lot. My mother and Vivian, I mean, Mrs. Blight, ran the school PTA meetings, and when I got a job at the local pre-school, they sent her to my classes. She was a daddy's girl, so she only ever stayed for an hour or so before Mr. Blight came and picked her up," she explained. "I attended their funeral the other day. There were people lined up all the way outside the church."

Emma smiled sadly, nodding as Loretta explained. Drake had told her Aira's comatose state was probably brought on by extreme shock, and from what she had just learned, the shock of Aira's parent's sudden death must have hit the child harder than they originally expected.

"Oh!" Loretta gasped as she dug her hand into the duffle bag she had been clutching onto. "I brought pictures Mrs. Blight gave to me for the school Easter banner two years ago. I thought you could stick them up for her, so she sees her family when she wakes up."

Emma let out a light laugh as she took the pictures and looked them over. Many the pictures consisted of Aira smiling with her pre-school friends. The rest of them were of Aira and her family at home. A sad grimace graced Emma's face as she looked at them carefully, placing Aira's features to her parents. She hadn't even heard the girl's voice but could imagine her as a light, bubbly child. She just hoped that light hadn't faded from all of this horribleness.

"Thank you. These are perfect," Emma said, her eyes lighting up as she glanced at the now nervous girl.

"Also." She dug back into her bag and pulled out some large pieces of paper. "The kids at the elementary school Aira used to attend wrote some get well letters and pictures for her."

Emma's smile brightened as she took some of the letters and drawings, looking them over adoringly. She had thought Aira had no one, but it seemed she was a beloved friend to her peers.

"Um," Loretta fidgeted as she stood in front of Emma, trying to get out her obvious question. Emma raised a thin brow, urging the girl to carry on. She took a breath and went for it. "Are you by any chance related to *the* Van Volkov?"

Emma blinked as she tried to work out what the girl had just asked. "Can you ask that again but slower, this time, sweetie?"

The girl fidgeted as she asked again, "Are you by any chance related to Van Volkov?"

Ah, now, she understood perfectly. Emma nodded once. "He's my brother-in-law." Well, technically he wasn't related to Drake in any way, shape or form, besides having

Lycan blood connecting them, but this girl didn't need to know the nitty-gritty details of that.

From the reaction displayed across Loretta's face, all grievances seemed to disappear. Emma had to admit that although he was the owner of one of the most influential insurance companies in America, Van was still popular amongst girls of all crush-worthy ages. He was on Forbes top ten list of America's most eligible millionaires for goodness' sake. She supposed being Russian was also quite appealing.

"Can I meet him?" she suddenly asked, eyes wide and hopeful.

Emma was taken aback by Loretta's sudden outburst. This wasn't what she had expected from a grieving family friend, but Emma, in her kindness, had to acknowledge that this was a young girl before her and of course, Van was a very handsome man. It didn't excuse this sort of behavior, but Emma, as always, pushed that fact aside and smiled that oh-so-pretty smile, the one Drake had told her she could get whatever she wanted with.

"Why don't you tell me a little more about Aira's family, and I'll see what I can do."

Chapter Four

"Okay, sweetie, this might feel uncomfortable for a little bit but keep still, okay?" The strange doctor gently cooed as he pulled the breathing tube from Aira's throat. Aira was still too drowsy to really take in what was happening, and when the doctor pulled that horrible thing from her throat, she coughed and spluttered everywhere.

Tears came to her eyes when the itching in her throat wouldn't disappear. It was a horrible feeling that Aira had never felt before. No matter how much she wanted to speak, her voice would just not come out. Oh, how she wanted to ask where her mommy was.

"Mo-mo…" she choked out, trying desperately to get out the word "mommy," just so they would understand what she wanted. In the end, she gave up.

The pretty blonde woman that had been by her side the moment she opened her eyes was on top of her in an instant.

She was rubbing Aira's throat attentively and whispering soothing words of encouragement. Aira wanted to ask who this woman was and why she was there in her mother's stead, but since that was impossible, she just let the strange woman carry on.

The doctor was to the side of the room, on a phone that looked like what her daddy used to use, and the man didn't look happy at all. She didn't understand where she was or who these people were, but what she did understand was that they were here to help her. She wondered what had happened to her. Her only memory was camping with her mommy and daddy. She couldn't remember anything beyond that, only that something terrible had happened and a hero had rescued her.

Her mother would always scold her about her dreams and how they weren't real. Maybe that wasn't real, either.

He didn't have time for this. Reports had to be filed for potential investors, applications had to be filled out for reputable clients, and there was still the trouble of covering up the carnage of the campsite massacre three days before. He hadn't even checked in with his scouts in Moscow about the progress of his pack still located in his native homeland. He didn't have time to scratch his own ass let alone do tricks like a monkey for Jillian Wright.

However, Van smiled and played coy as always. Jillian was the daughter of Lucas Wright, the Alpha leader of the Ochao wolf clan. They had been native to America for centuries, and Van had been having a power struggle with them for over sixty years since a third of his pack had migrated here from Russia originally. However, when Van had taken up his position as Alpha almost forty years before the migration, he had made a promise to the pack elders that he would protect the domain in which his pack called their home including the humans and creatures within it. Already covering the area from Moscow to Krasnoyarsk and small areas of Poland, Van had already taken leadership of the largest wolf pack in Russia. It didn't help that he had also taken up the role of protector for the whole of California to Wisconsin, as well as twelve other states in-between.

He supposed Lucas only gave up in their battle to see if Van could live up to being a leader of a pack that size. He had been doing fine up until recently when the rogues moved in and started to hunt down humans. In the end, Van had succumbed to only stretch his domain as far as Nevada and ultimately relinquished his sixty-year reign over the other territories between California and Wisconsin. Lucas hadn't complained and moved the members of Van's pack to California. The majority hated the idea of their Alpha weakening his resolve and returned to Russia. No one would ever know the pressure of having to scout an area of that size, all for the sake of humans.

"Father still refers to you as 'that dirty Russian wolf,'" Jillian quipped as she lounged back in Van's leather two-seater couch. She had thrown her Dolce and Gabbana heels off as soon as she sank into the heavenly chair. She tilted her head to glance at Van who seemed to be stuck in his own world as always.

The corner of her pouty lips twitched. "I didn't think you'd listen to me, anyway," she muttered, running a thin hand through the tresses of her black-as-night hair.

Van had been listening, but the words that fell from those ever-red lips of hers were always the same trash. "Is there something you wanted, Jillian?" His tone was laced with annoyance, but he knew Jillian took what she could from him without a complaint. Her smile was proof enough.

"I heard through the rumor mill that some rogues have been giving you trouble. I came to see if you were all right."

The she-wolf oozed with that seductive femme fatale aura Van had grown accustomed to. She slinked from her place on his office couch and made her way towards his desk. The way she glided, barefoot, across his office didn't affect Van in any way. He had his way with many women but stayed at a safe distance when it came to Jillian. She was trouble he just didn't have the patience to deal with.

Van never said a word to her, but Jillian's mouth seemed to keep running on pure determination. "Have you thought about my offer?" she purred, lazily draping her upper body across the dark wolf's desk.

Ah, so that was it. She hadn't been worried, as he had already suspected; she had wanted an answer to the question she had constantly been on his tail about for three years now. He wondered if she ever grew bored with his answer.

"No," was his only response as he continued to read over stray documents.

The enchanted smile she had just been parading around moments before quickly disappeared. Van could say with utmost honesty that he never grew tired of that rejected look on her face. The way that fire in her eyes quickly turned to heated anger gave him a sick sense of amusement. He disliked women like Jillian though she would never know that fact.

"If you were my mate, my father would hand over our pack to you, Van. With so many members, those rogues would not dare step into your territory again!" she yelled. Van could tell Jillian had enough of his constant rejections. He also had enough of her proposals.

His mouth seemed to twitch as he dropped his documents and snapped his head up to look at Jillian, raw annoyance obvious even through those silly contacts he wore. "Jillian, does your wolf call out to mine?"

She had heard this too many times to count. "No, but I, as my own person, call out to you." Her desperation was starting to show as her small hands pressed firmly against his black marble desk.

Van's brow tilted upwards at her bold declaration. That was something he had never heard her say, but still, he did not waver in his decision.

"I need a mate who is strong, dependable and fierce. I do not wish to be like Drake and have to watch my mate with constant worry something may happen to her. You should know better than I that once we mate, your heart beats with mine. If you bleed, I bleed. Your thoughts are my thoughts, and your death is my downfall," he growled. His Lycan was growling at hers, and Van knew she could feel it as she took a timid step back.

Her face said it all before she even opened her mouth. "I am no disgusting *human*."

His smile threw her off. It was frightening.

"You may as well be. Now, leave." And with that said, he went back to his paperwork, trying to pick up where he left off.

The slam of his office door never even caught his attention. However, the cracks in his marble desktop were more alarming than the angered she-wolf that just stormed out of his office. He had Emma call someone to replace the damage Jillian had done once she returned from fawning over that human child.

He refused to believe he had been too hard on Jillian, but those fickle emotions of hers were weakness in Van's eyes. The Ochao clan were a pack of weaklings to him, not only because of their mixed human blood but because the years of diluted DNA had left them mere humans with the ability to morph into animals. Unlike his wolf ancestry, the American Wolves could interbreed with humans, which ultimately weakened their primal blood. Jillian had told him she was no human, but the human blood of her mother that ran through Jillian's veins told Van a different story. Jillian could not call out her wolf in her human form as he could, allowing him to jump from towers and land on his feet unharmed, nor could she grow claws and sharp teeth to ward off threats without shifting fully.

He needed a mate on the same level as he if not stronger. He would never lower himself to his brother's level and take on a human as his second soul, only to fear each day could be her last.

The buzzing of his cellphone ripped Van back to reality. As he looked at the caller, he was tempted to just ignore the flashing screen altogether. He answered, though, to satisfy whatever Drake was interrupting him with.

"She's awake, just thought you'd like to know."

Van growled as Drake hung up. Drake knew he hated to be hung up on. Van supposed that was the only way to distract him from ripping his own eyes out as his wolf whimpered and panted in his mind as if reverting into a pup.

For the first time in his life, Van Volkov was confused with the monster that ruled over him.

He didn't come because he wanted to. He didn't come because he had to. He most certainly *did not* come because his Lycan told him to. He was here because if he didn't show up, Drake would not let up about how heartless he was for a very long time. He had had that conversation before and grew tired of the same pointless arguments.

He moved through the buildings different areas with a swift stride. Emma had discreetly messaged him the room number the girl had been moved to since her recovery a day before in the ICU. According to the message, she was out of any immediate danger and was on her way to a complete recovery. Van doubted the girl would completely recover, not after witnessing the deaths of her sister and mother. He had gotten word a few days ago that two male corpses had been found twenty meters away from the campsite. They were identified as Charles and Ian Blight, the girl's brother and father from the looks of it.

He eventually found the room where the child had been moved. As he looked around, he noticed she was in a room with two other children and their parents. The stench of antiseptic and other horrid smelling chemicals hit him like a punch in the face. He held back his nausea as soon as he smelled out the girl he had originally come for.

A doctor loomed over her, an unknown presence, as they checked her IV and throat. Van's brows furrowed as he tried to contain his Lycan's threatening growls.

Van let out a loud cough to gain the man's attention. From his scent, Van could already name the man who spun around in panic. This was a doctor Van had met once before but hadn't caught the name, or he might have but didn't bother to remember it. He was one of the newer physicians his brother had taken on board at the hospital.

"Can I help you, sir?" the young doctor asked as if Van were a customer shopping for a new dress shirt and not a visitor at a hospital.

His answer was blunt. "I'm here to see the child. Where's Drake?"

Yes, where were Emma and Drake, the people who had been fawning all over the child not a day before? He expected Emma might have gone out to get clothes for the girl, but Drake was nowhere in sight. From the smell of it, they had been in the room not long before he arrived.

It seemed the young physician didn't have a clue on who Van was, either, as he replied, "Drake?" It seemed his brother wasn't on a first-name basis with his staff.

Van had to control his twitching hand from springing out and ripping this man's face off. "Doctor Volkov," he spat.

His beady burgundy eyes seemed to flash with recognition. "Oh, he's in emergency surgery at the moment, so I'm here in his stead. I'm Doctor Barlow."

Van nodded. He didn't need any more information and simply brushed passed the clueless doctor, grabbed a chair from the corner, and sat by the human child as she slept. Van had to admit; the human looked like an average enough child without all those tubes, drips, and catheter in her.

"Um..."

Shit, what did he want now? Van never even glanced at the pathetic human. He was too busy thinking of ways to drag the idiot's body to the mortuary without being noticed. He supposed he could just shift into his Lycan form, but that would most likely take out the whole building with his size and weight. Though, with one bite, he wouldn't have to worry about hiding the body. Uh, human flesh did taste so bland, though...

"There's a problem with the child's insurance claim, and Doctor Volkov isn't here," he muttered, handing Van a clipboard with the necessary paperwork. The Russian Lycan simply glanced at him but didn't bother touching the object the moron tried to shove into his hands.

"*Chert*," Van muttered, cursing in his native tongue. "Just charge it to the Volkov's direct finances." When he had filled out the form to claim for Aira Blight, he had used his name, but it seemed there had been a problem with the claim. He didn't want to deal with this fool for any longer than necessary.

He heard the nervous gulp the doctor took. "Well, would-would Doctor Volkov mind that? I heard his brother has a bit of temper when it comes to charging funds to his account..."

Who *was* this idiot on about?

"Doctor Volkov's brother?"

"Yes, Van Volkov. Everyone knows he checks those finances. I wouldn't want to annoy him without Doctor Volkov here to confirm everything."

The tangible sweat that was forming on Barlow's forehead was quite amusing. It was interesting how some humans would sweat when they were nervous or frightened.

"I don't think you could annoy him anymore than you already have, *Doctor*," the irritable wolf growled. Oh, but he was going to enjoy massacring this fool when no one was around.

The noticeable surprise on the doctor's face was evidence enough that he was now aware of the person sitting before him. Van had to admit that it was quite entertaining to watch that horrified expression wash over the doctor's already pale face. Recognition had almost instantly flashed through Barlow's eyes, as he looked Van over.

"I-I'm sorry, sir. I'll do it right now," he stuttered before scattering to exit the room.

Van smirked, trying to hold back his chuckle as he demanded, "And get this girl a private room."

Throughout the whole discussion, Van could make out the silent glances he was getting from the two mothers fawning over their own children in the room. With the lack of funds for the hospital, children were put into rooms with other sick children. It was disgusting in his opinion only because he had to be in the same room as the child he had saved.

"Yes, sir," Barlow confirmed as he all but ran down the hallway.

His initial annoyance seemed to instantly melt away as he glanced at the small child sleeping soundly in the steel bed. Her little face seemed pained; however, as she moved her head from side to side, Van repelled the sudden urge to rip out the IV's that were causing her pain. He couldn't understand why. If his Lycan simply liked children, why it was only focusing on this child and not the two others in the room.

"Ex-excuse me, sir, here are some flowers for the little girl..."

Van turned around, only to come face to face with one of the children's mother's holding up a bouquet. It seemed this woman didn't recognize him either as she pushed the flowers into his chest.

"Thank you," he muttered grudgingly. Humans and those fickle emotions of theirs...

She smiled, nodded, and went back to cleaning her own snot-nosed brat. Van held on to the flowers as he looked around the separated areas, coming to realize that each wall the children "owned" was covered in "Get Well Soon" cards, pictures, photos and other such useless shit while their side tables were filled to the brim with flowers and small trinkets.

It occurred to him that those flowers weren't gifts out of sympathy but because the stupid female couldn't fit any more of these weeds onto her son's bedside table. She had seen that the girl's side was completely bare and wanted to get rid of them.

Van growled as he crushed the flowers in his hand, ignoring the way the patients and visitors looked at him, mortified. He stormed out of the room, dumping the flowers into a passing wastebasket, and pulled out his phone. He couldn't contact Emma for this matter; he would never hear the end of it if he did. He went to the next best contact, which was a supervisor in one of his most established departments, and growled out his demands.

"Tell everyone to sign a card and get a gift by this afternoon. Tell them to send it to the hospital where my brother works. Direct all gifts to Aira Blight. If I find out anyone hasn't done this, throw their shit out onto the street and have security escort them from the building."

With that, he hung up the phone and sighed. The supervisor barely had a moment to respond, but Van barely had a moment to think of a response himself. This wasn't something he was doing out of kindness or pity. This was about pride. If Emma and Drake didn't care to fill that girl's room with all of those silly items, then he would do it.

After all, he knew what it was like to wake up in a cold, lonely room with only your thoughts to keep you company.

Chapter Five

"Aira, are you awake?" Emma dropped the three bags full of clothes she had been lugging throughout the hospital onto the floor, her hands covering her mouth in surprise. She was shocked to find out Aira had been moved to a private room when she knew her or Drake had asked for that. But this — *this* was just insane. "Who-who? What? Aira?" She gasped.

Aira was awake and already playing with two Barbie dolls she had unwrapped. The rest of the room was filled with brightly wrapped boxes and a nurse trying to organize where to put all of them. Get well soon cards were pinned to the walls while dozens of bouquets of flowers were sitting on Aira's bedside table. The remaining flowers that couldn't fit amongst the others were stacked atop each other in a box to the side.

Did Drake do this? she thought, desperately trying to work out the situation. She looked over to Aira who was playing contentedly with her dolls before moving over to the nurse. "Lisa, who sent all these?"

The nurse shrugged. She knew as much as Emma did. "Your charming brother-in-law told Barlow to move her to her own room. Not two hours later, about a dozen or so couriers came marching through with all these cards and presents. It was a madhouse here for a second there! Everything was addressed to Aira. We couldn't even get through the door for a while. It was so packed up," she explained, her arms waving around left and right to emphasize the insanity.

"Van did this?" Emma asked, surprised. She hadn't expected him to come visit, and why would he change her room?

Lisa nodded as she picked up another box to stack onto a bigger one. "Mmm, and since his medical insurance was insufficient coverage, he charged her fee's directly to your family's fund. It's all anyone can talk about. Doctor Barlow is still in shock."

Emma was in shock herself. Van did all this. That didn't make sense. She looked over at a get-well card she had picked up off of a box earlier and read what was inside.

All the best, Emily Vincent. Emma's brows furrowed as she read the name. Was that Emily from auto coverage? Emma went on to another card which read; *Get well soon kiddo, Derek Lawrence.* This was too much of a coincidence. Derek was a supervisor for their life cover phone support. Emma had gone through about forty more cards before she came to the realization that every one of these well-wishers was people that worked for Van.

"Ah, Mr. Volkov, sir!" Lisa suddenly cried, smiling big for the man who was the center of talk around the hospital.

Emma spun around, eyes wide, and wondered if Drake would come to her rescue. There in the doorway was a less them impressed Van with Loretta, the woman who had come to visit Aira two days before, standing next to him, all smiles. Van's face said everything. What is this bullshit?

Emma was about to speak when Loretta rushed in to greet Aira. The little girl simply looked at her, stared for a moment, and then went back to her dolls. Emma was too worried about the promise she made with Loretta to care about the rejected look on the preschool teacher's face. Obviously, Loretta had come back to visit, only to catch Van on her way in.

Oh, God, Emma was going to die when Van found out the deal she had made.

"H-hero!" came tiny, strained cry.

It seemed everyone's attention was diverted to the little girl in the bed, whose eyes lit up like the night sky on July fourth as she gazed at a dumbstruck Van.

Did she seriously just call him "Hero"?

Chapter Six

"Aira doesn't seem to remember anything about what happened to her family. Over time, her subconscious might come to forget the trauma."

Emma nodded. "But she won't forget her mother and father, will she?"

Susan sighed, "It's hard to say. She's incredibly stable emotionally, but mentally… it's troubling how she can't remember. To be able to come to terms and accept something like this will be impossible for Aira considering her age and memory loss. Without that, she'll continue to live in a world where her parents are still alive. It's a common situation with children and adults but incredibly difficult to assess what will happen when they finally come to grips with the trauma."

"It could be months or years when she finally remembers, and when that happens, well… the backlash could be incredibly distressing for you and Drake." Susan crossed her arms over her chest as she stared through the door of Aira's hospital room. The little girl was on the bed playing with Drake, making him take the Ken doll and play with the Barbie Aira was holding. "I've explained this to Drake, but he assured me you both could handle it. However, I wanted to know your thoughts on this, Emma."

Emma pursed her lips as Susan looked at her for an answer. Maybe her answer was too obvious because Susan simply shook her head and smiled. "You and Drake are truly kind people, and you Emma, maybe too kind to get yourself into this sort of situation."

All Emma could do was smile knowingly. "She needs our help," she replied.

"Another human to add to your growing family. Aiden and Drake will live so much longer; doesn't that worry you at least a little?" Susan asked.

Emma knew Susan had known Drake and Van since they were mere pups and knew the hardships that came with time and the humans that had so little of it.

Emma laughed. "No, it doesn't worry me at all. I'll live until I'm one-hundred years old if that's what it will take to make sure Drake and Aiden are happy. For now, we'll just tell Aira her family has gone away for a little while."

"Bye, Aira, we'll miss you!" Lisa cried as she hugged the little girl just a bit tighter.

Since she had spoken out to Van and called him "Hero" a week before, Aira had not uttered another word since. Susan had told Emma that this was normal after everything she had been through, and while still confused about her parents, they shouldn't force her to speak if she did not want to. She would let them hear her voice when she was ready.

Emma giggled as more nurses came to wish the little girl good luck in her recovery with teddy bears, flower's and gifts at the ready. Even doctors and surgeons came to shake her hand and bid her farewell. Although unwilling to speak, Aira seemed to light up their eyes with that giant gap-toothed smile of hers. While it made others happy, that smile brought a tear to Emma's eye. She knew nothing of what sort of torture that little girl was going through on the inside.

Loretta was also there for the third time since Aira's admission. She said her goodbyes to Aira and handed Emma an envelope with the contents of their promise made over two weeks before.

"Uh, my number is also in there if you ever need me and if, well, you know, in case Mr. Volkov…" Her eyes bounced around to make sure no one could overhear their conversation. Emma supposed Loretta still had a little hope left even though Van had brushed the poor girl off and ignored her very existence their first meeting.

Emma held up the envelope and waved it around. "A promise is a promise after all."

"Are we all set?" Drake called as he came up to his wife and Aira. The crowd of nurses had dispersed, and Loretta had already run off, late for her morning shift at the daycare.

Emma greeted her husband with a short kiss and nodded. "All set."

"Great!" he shouted as he took the handles of Aira's wheelchair and ran off, wheeling Aira towards the exit doors.

All Emma could do was laugh. It seemed Drake was just as excited as she was to introduce Aira to their son, Aiden.

"Happy birthday, Aira!" Emma chimed as she brought the large cake out into the dining room.

It had taken some time and a lot of favors from Van, but the adoption had gone through smoothly. Aira had legally become their daughter three months after her discharge from the hospital. Although she was still unable to speak, Aira and Aiden seemed to communicate without the need of words. The moment Emma had introduced them they had been inseparable. For the first four weeks, it was impossible to stop Aira from sneaking into Aiden's room at night to sleep, but the little seven-year-old boy had insisted he protect his "sister" from monsters. Emma found it cute.

When the adoption papers came through, Drake had also acquired Aira's original birth certificate. Even though she had a birthday party to represent the day she became a part of their family, Emma thought it only obvious to also have a party to celebrate the day she was born. Her parents would have wanted that.

As Aiden buried Aira in presents, as well as helping her open those, Emma watched in adoration. She sat at the dining table with her cheek in her hand and a big smile on her face. "Isn't that precious?" she whispered to her husband in the seat beside her.

"Hmm, it is... did you go and get the things from her old house?" he inquired, a frown playing on that handsome face of his.

Emma looked down and sighed. "Yeah, I did. There was still a bowl of half eaten cereal on the table. The milk had curdled from being left for months, so I cleaned the kitchen a little bit. I got everything from Aira's room. The little guide Loretta drew out for me when she gave me the key in that envelope really helped." She let out a sad little laugh.

Drake smiled at his wife and leaned in to bury his face into the crook of her neck. "You did well, Hon," he whispered.

Emma's mouth angled into a shy smile as she lifted her hand to place it behind Drake's head. "She did have a good life, Drake. It's such a shame, you know; I took every picture I could find before I left. Van did say the property and house were left to Aira, but I couldn't just leave them sitting there to rot in the dust for the next ten years."

No, she couldn't just leave the smiling faces of Aira's family to sit in a dark, lonely house like that. They were packed away in a box way up in the attic, where Emma would give them to Aira when she came to remember her past. Emma cleaned them every day. Until then, Emma was contented with Aira writing her name as "Mama" and Drake's name as "Papa." Mummy and Daddy, those names were special and only Vivian and Charles Blight had those titles.

When Aira was done opening her presents with Aiden, Drake got up from his place next to Emma and pulled a box out from under the large dining table. Aira simply stared, a blank expression on her little face, while Aiden's eyes lit up at the possibility of more presents. After all, he and Aira shared almost everything besides underwear and Barbies.

As soon as Drake sat down, he read out the little card that was attached to the gift. "Dear Aira, may this day bring you all the love and happiness you deserve. Happy birthday, your Hero."

Emma's eyes bulged, and she almost spat out her coffee. Aira had a different reaction as her big blue eyes lit up with glee. Emma watched as she tore away the shiny silver wrapping paper and gasped in surprise. In the box was a basket filled with everything Superman; T-shirt, Superman doll, the lot. It took all of Emma's willpower not to burst out in hysterical laughter.

Aira had become quite the Superman addict and always connected the fiction superhero with Van — the man who had saved her. Although she couldn't remember the deaths of her family, Aira vividly remembered her savior's face. Emma knew it was Drake who had signed the letter and bought the present, but the glow on her little girl's face was worth the little white lie.

Sighing, she remembered her last conversation with Van a few weeks back. It had gone better than she had expected.

"So I'm assuming both the parent's life insurances will go to Aira?" Emma asked. *Drake had already spoken to Van who handled mostly everything that had to do with the Blight family lawyers and the adoption process. Emma hadn't expected more news after the adoption was final.*

Van shuffled some papers in front of him and nodded. "Yes, she stands to gain about five hundred thousand from her father's claim and four hundred and fifty thousand from her mother's. That includes the family home and all stock investments they had."

Emma took in what he was saying with a deep sigh. "Have you worked out where it's going to go?" she asked.

"I expected you and Drake to use it to support her?" Van inquired, his brow arched.

Emma shook her head. "We'll raise her on our own dollar. Thank you!" she huffed.

Van gave her a blank stare as he spoke. "Well, with all the bullshit I had to go through with those damn lawyers I expected a little more praise than that."

Emma calmed down a little bit and straightened up. "Van, I know nothing about how to handle that much money and Drake won't have anything to do with it. What do we do?"

Emma assumed Van expected that answer. Drake didn't want anything to do with blood money even if it was for Aira if, by the off chance, she didn't come to remember on her own. She supposed when that time came, they would shoulder the burden onto Van as well.

"I can pay for the taxes on the girl's home until she comes of age. I'll put half the money in a trust for her. When she's twenty-one, she can do whatever the hell she likes with it." By the time the taxes for the house were paid, the girl would be lucky to get out with a quarter of what she inherited, but this was the only reasonable solution.

Emma's face dropped at the thought of Aira being left with nothing. "What about the other half?"

"I'll use that to cover any extra expenses she might need. I heard she's a bright kid from Drake and she'll need a *good school to go to in the future. Therapy, school, college and all of that will be costly."*

Emma didn't know what to say. It wasn't like Van to help so openly especially when it came to humans.

"Van, thank you," Emma gushed, a bright smile spreading across her face. "Then, since that's all cleared, I should get back home—"

"Emma," Van growled before the poor woman could even get the glass door open. "Don't let the girl catch on to what Drake, Aiden and I are. That could possibly do more damage to her. Her family was killed by our kind. Remember that." With that said, he went back to scribbling something onto a document.

Emma smiled. "Her seventh birthday's next week. You should come."

He didn't reply as she left his office.

Deep down, Van did like the little girl. Emma could tell. He didn't openly help people he didn't like.

Aira beckoned Emma over with her hand, and the older woman gladly complied. She walked over and kneeled beside her adopted daughter, paying close attention to everything Aira had gotten from her Superman trove. She couldn't help but giggle.

Aira quickly scribbled something down on her little portable whiteboard. Although only just turning seven, the girl was well clued when it came to words and how to use them in a sentence. Her writing was horrid, however.

I'm Lous Lan; she wrote. The letters were sloppy, and the name was spelled wrong, but Emma had read this phrase before. Aira meant to write, I'm Lois Lane. This made Emma giggle even more.

"And Van's your Superman, I take it?" she asked with a small smirk playing on her lips. Drake wasn't as collected and almost fell off the couch laughing when Aira wrote, "Yes!" with a big smile on her face.

She went on to scribble more, which left Emma confused at her sporadic behavior and Drake thoroughly amused. All questions were answered when Aira showed them what she had written. Drake soon needed water from laughing so hard.

"Love Van," was scribbled across her whiteboard.

Emma was shocked for a moment before she swooped in and gave Aira a big bear hug. "You are just adorable, but you need to be older to be Van's Lois Lane, sweetic," she giggled nervously.

Emma didn't know why, but she had the worst feeling about this in the pit of her stomach. She held Aira in her arms and continued to smile, but inside, she was fretful.

Unbeknownst to her worried mama, Aira was silently praying she would grow bigger, just like Emma had said.

Chapter Seven

FIVE YEARS LATER

"This is lame!"

"Aiden, behave. It's just for today," Drake reprimanded as he laid out a cloth on the picnic table. "It's your mother's birthday."

Emma giggled as her only son huffed and kicked up some dirt. Being thirteen years old, she didn't think he would be too happy with the idea of a day away from all those electronics he had come to depend on, but her daughter on the other hand...

Aira smiled as she gawked, wide-eyed, at the forests around them. Emma had been a bit hesitant to come to a wildlife sanctuary for a picnic with Aira, given the trauma she had sustained six years ago, but it seemed she was still ignorant of the death of her family, a death that had happened in a park quite like the one they were picnicking in. Drake and Susan,

Aira's therapist, had both told Emma that keeping Aira away from anything that could possibly jog her memory wasn't the way to go. She would come to remember, eventually. Sheltering her would only cause more harm than good.

Aira laughed and ran to her mother, her eyes lighting up with wonder. She grabbed Emma's hand and shook it, pointing towards deer and other animals that were barely hidden by the brush of trees. Emma felt like she had been holding her breath for the majority of the car ride and finally, let it out once she saw that Aira was still herself. There was nothing to fear.

"Do you like it here?" Drake asked softly as he wondered over to his wife and adopted daughter. The smile and rapid nodding seemed to give him the answer he was hoping for.

Aiden let out a huff of air as he ran over and grabbed Aira's hand, leading her into the neck of trees. Aira obediently followed, sticking closer to the older boy as he said, "If you like it so much, let's have a closer look, you dummy."

Emma laughed and shook her head. Aiden was protective of Aira, and if something made her light up, you'd bet your life Aiden would get it just to see her happy.

"Look after her, Aiden. It smells like rain soon!" Drake called out as he watched the two walk off. All he got was a short wave from his son. "I worry that he's a little too much like my brother sometimes…"

All Emma could do was nod. "I wonder the same thing sometimes, but then, I remember Aiden knows how to show his emotions, unlike Van."

Drake chuckled and wrapped his arm around his wife's shoulder, nuzzling his chin into her hair. Emma giggled before a car coming into the park's car park caught her attention. The flashy black four-wheel drive could have made anyone stop and stare, but she and Drake knew the owner all too well.

"Speak of the devil, and he shall appear, as they say…" Drake mumbled, his chin still resting atop his wife's golden curls.

Emma gently nudged her husband with her elbow, trying not to let a laugh escape. "I can't believe he actually came." Just as Van slammed his car door shut, Emma whispered, "He doesn't look all too happy about it."

Van only nodded his greeting as he glanced at his beta and the human mate by his side. In all honesty, he could have been doing paperwork back at his office. There was the problem of investors backing out of their deals, but after being nagged to no end by Drake, Van was beckoned to the occasion. It would have at least been tolerable if not for a certain someone who had been prancing about his office the whole morning.

"Happy birthday, Emma!" Jillian yelled, a big bright smile spreading across her flush face. As she waved, she held up a colorful bag, no doubt with a gift inside. Jillian Wright never came to a special occasion empty handed after all.

Emma smiled back and shook her head before sauntering towards the two shifters. "Jillian, you really didn't have to get me anything but thank you," she gushed as she took the bag Jillian handed her.

Jillian's hair cascaded over her shoulder in dark curls while her rosy lips twitched into a nervous smile. "Oh, don't be silly! It's your fortieth birthday after all!"

Emma's eyebrow slightly twitched as she picked up the hidden chuckle her husband had tried to cover up from behind her. "I'm thirty-five today, actually. But thank you all the same."

As soon as Emma had muttered those words, Jillian was off to Drake, taking his arm and casually feeling his shoulders. Emma shook her head as Van came to stand beside her. Although Jillian was well aware that a mated wolf could and would never leave his or her chosen mate, she never failed to fawn all over the kind doctor although that morning she had professed her love to that same doctor's alpha... *again*.

"If I weren't trying to fix this power struggle with that bitch's father, I would have ripped her throat out before we came. You have no idea the headache she caused on the ride over here," he growled as he shoved his clawed hands into his pant pockets.

Emma shook her head as she went to sit the bag Jillian had given her onto the picnic table. Van knew that Emma was aware that when Drake or Van used the term "bitch" they didn't use it in the same context humans did. Bitch to a shifter meant a female of their kind although it had only started to become popular within the last decade. It meant nothing derogatory though he knew she still felt uncomfortable whenever Drake used the term.

As she started to unpack lunch, Van asked, "Where's the pup?"

Emma didn't even have to ask to know which one of her children Van was referring to. "Aiden took Aira to have a look in the forest. They should be back soon."

Van's dark brows furrowed. He smelled rain coming their way earlier that day and wondered why in these weather conditions Emma would release her grip on the girl even for a second. "You sure that's a good idea?"

Emma turned around to look at Van bemusedly. "Are you worried about Aira, Van?"

That cheeky smile that spread across her lips knocked Van's guard down. He looked away before muttering, "It could cause some problems if she remembers, Emma. Don't forget that."

It had been a good two years since he had seen the human child he had begrudgingly rescued that dreary day. He was her financial guardian on paper, but when the day came that she started to remember her past, he knew he would have to take the brunt of it. Drake and the human were weak and softhearted; they would do more harm than good when explaining themselves to the child they took in. He didn't care much for the girl, but he didn't want Drake to be a depressed mongrel when Emma was let down by the girl's reaction.

"Aiden is growing much stronger since his wolf has been coming out. Aira will be fine with him," Emma said with a bright smile. "I know as well as you do the repercussions. It doesn't make me regret my decision to take her in."

Van was about to respond when his senses started to flare. His eye twitched as his sense of smell shifted to a being that was rapidly coming their way. His nose was thrown into the air as he sniffed out the being, only to be hit with the scent of Aiden. The lingering frightened scent that hit him wasn't the least bit comforting.

It seemed Drake was already aware as he shot forward, knocking Jillian back as he met his son halfway across the neck of trees.

"Aiden, what's wrong?" Emma panted as she ran to her son, looking him over as he rested against her. "Where's Aira?"

"She-she's gone. I can't smell her out! She was behind me, but she's gone now!" he panted, his eyes tearing up. His mother hugged him before looking up at her husband whose golden eyes had turned to slits, as he looked around, trying to pick up anything that could tell them where Aira was.

"Drake... find her..." Emma whispered as she hugged her frightened son. Drake could find her. Aiden was just inexperienced to his senses. There was no doubt Drake would be able to find Aira. Van knew better, however.

After a moment, Drake shot off. Emma didn't need validation that her husband knew which direction to search. Van was sure of that.

All Van could do was stand in the clearing, watching the almost hysterical human try to calm the pup in her arms. He sensed Jillian move to his side, but anything the dark she-wolf said up until that point fell upon deaf ears. All he was focused on was the rain that began to fall from the clouds that gathered. It had been sunny prior that day, but dark clouds had begun to form. All that, however, went unnoticed when his wolf started to stir.

"Mate... mine... save..." drummed into the alpha's head like a siren. It was a feeling he hadn't felt in five years, not since that day...

He growled low as he shot forward, crouching beside Emma and the pup. "Can the girl speak?" he demanded. His gaze was towards the deep brush of trees, staring intently through the clearing, trying to pick up something — anything. Once the rain hit harder, it would wash away the trail the girl had vanished from.

Emma looked confused as she glanced up at Van. "She can say a few words, but she can't speak. She didn't take her whiteboard either."

Aiden removed his head from his mother's shoulder, gazing up at his uncle. "Is Dad gonna find her, Van?"

His growl seemed lower as it vibrated through his chest. "Not if the rain hits, pup." And with that last statement, Van took off into the trees just as his brother had, getting a running start before jumping with inhuman ability.

The rain was picking up as he jumped from branch to branch, trying to sniff out the pathetic human. He had sniffed out her scent not moments before the rain began to fall in large, heavy droplets. Now, there was nothing.

Dammit, he thought. The human could be anywhere even below him, and he wouldn't even know it. He had soon stopped wondering why he had gone out of his way to find her and reminded himself that although he had no emotional attachment towards the child, she was still under the care of his beta. There was nothing more than that.

"Van!"

His neck snapped in the direction the shout had come from, only to spot Drake directly below him, staring up with golden slitted eyes. Van knew that Drake was close to shifting and tearing the woods apart.

He dug his claws into the trunk of the thick tree he had perched himself on. As soon as he steadied himself, he growled out, "Drake, you'll tear this place apart!"

Drake was sopping wet as he stood stock still below his brother. "I'll be able to pick up her scent if I bring out Akim, Van," he growled back. The normally placid doctor was close to snapping, and Van knew he had little time to take control.

Just as Van was about to retaliate, a sharp, almost painful feeling coursed throughout his body. His inner Lycan had been going insane, but now, it was close to taking control. With a curt grunt, he was off to another tree and another, ignoring his beta's shouts from behind. As soon as he reached his final branch, he had jumped to the muddied floor below, looking around with his sharp golden eyes.

Something had drawn him here, yet he had no clue what he was even searching for… until he spotted a little human huddled up under a large old tree. The pitiful whimpering was evidence enough he had come to find the source of his rogue Lycanthrope yet again.

His dark hair that had been absolutely drenched from the rain fell over his forehead and into his eyes as he knelt to inspect the child. His button down white shirt stuck to his skin and dark dress pants were muddied, but he didn't seem to notice as the girl looked up, only to give him a wide-eyed look of pure astonishment. The smile that spread across her lips was no longer gap-toothed; her teeth had straightened into perfect pearly whites. He didn't understand why when moments before, she had been sobbing so heavily, she was now smiling as if all her prayers had been answered.

"Her-hero, you came..." she whispered. That one phrase was spoken so quietly that a human wouldn't have possibly heard her.

However, Van Volkov was no human.

It took a moment for him to recover before he noticed a small gray ball of fur huddled against the girl's chest. The wolf pup in her arms was nearly as shocking as when she had first spoken. It didn't take long for the little pup to notice him and almost clawed its way up the girl's shoulder.

Her sudden gasp was enough to send Van into action as he grabbed the pup with his clawed hand by the scruff of its neck, bringing it to his face for closer inspection. It was most certainly no threat towards the child, but a wolf pup was confusing, given the girl's circumstances.

"Vaughn!" she whispered as she jumped up to grab the pup back. However, Van was quicker as he yanked it away, ignoring the pup's cries.

"Vaughn?" he questioned with his eyebrow slightly arched.

He supposed in her moment of shock to see him appear, Aira had forgotten that she was once mute. "His name... I named him after you."

It took all his willpower not to throw the pup into the woods, take the girl back to Drake, and pretend none of this had ever happened. However, hearing her speak for the first time since that day he had visited her in the hospital sent a strange emotion running through him, something akin to happiness.

He brushed away that feeling very damn quickly.

As he sighed, he scooped the confused child up into his free arm while still holding the struggling pup in his other and started to walk towards the picnic site he had left Emma and the others in. The girl never said a word the whole way, much to his appreciation, and it wasn't long before Drake had picked up her scent and followed.

"Mo-Mom! Can-can I keep him?" Aira all but shouted, finding more strength in her voice. "Hero said he was lost, just like I was!"

Van could smell the tears coming to Emma's eyes as she stared intently at the child speaking before her. She hadn't questioned why Aira was speaking, and he supposed she was just grateful the child could remember how to speak at all. In the end, all the human could do was a nod and ask a series of questions to which the girl answered just as enthusiastically as she had the first time. She looked as if she didn't know whether to cry or laugh, maybe both.

The rain was still coming down as Emma shooed the girl and pup into their car. Van watched carefully, almost possessively, as Aira seemed to forget his very existence for the moment. That prospect did not sit well with him.

As Drake spoke with his giddy and relieved wife, they failed to notice their adoptive daughter escape their vehicle and run into the clearing, leaving Aiden with her little friend. It also took Van a moment to realize she was running straight for him or the skinny arms that locked around his waist. His senses, which had calmed down over the past hour or so, were now going wild again as she nuzzled against him.

"Thank-Thank you for finding me again, Hero," she said.

He expected to shove the girl away or at least beckon Drake over so that he would take her, but to his bewilderment, he let her carry on. His hand moved to her shoulder, ready to shove her away, but instead, he couldn't bring himself to do it.

"Hmm," he grunted, and although he would deny it for years to come, Emma and Drake could have sworn on both their children that they had seen Van — always stoic Van — smile, even for just a moment.

Chapter Eight

As annoyed as he was throughout the days following Emma's birthday, today would have to top off his list. The Russian wolf marched back and forth throughout his office as someone he had detested, someone who could make the bile rise in the alpha's throat by her mere presence, someone who he never thought he would have to see again, stood leering at him as if he had killed her damn dog.

"Mother, please sit down," Drake tried to beckon as he pushed a seat towards the elderly woman.

"Be quiet, boy. You have done enough damage." The woman's thick Russian accent was noticeable, which made her son grimace.

Aleksandra Volkov had a voice that made Van's blood run cold. It was deep, much deeper than a woman's voice should be, and had the proper authority needed to be the mate of one of Russia's most powerful shifters, the former alpha,

Van's *adoptive* father. His real father was a dark wolf that could shift into quite a huge and vicious sight and trumped any and all others when he was still alive.

"A human! It wasn't enough you had to mate one, was it? You had to go and pick up a tinier human. Do you know the whispers that are circulating? Do you know what I have seen of her, Drake?" Her big green eyes were wide as she stared up at her son. "I have seen what she will bring. That is why I am here!"

Drake's normally placid face darkened. "That's enough, Mother. She's just a little girl."

Aleksandra's brows furrowed in confusion at Drake's words. "I have seen what that *little* girl will bring. I have seen that girl soaking in the blood of our pack's *future*!"

A loud bang sounded from Van's desk, making both the woman and Drake's heads snap around to see what was happening. Their alpha had a steely gaze as he watched both carefully, his sharp claws peeling back across his desk and making a sharp screech that sent both the occupants reeling back.

Not only was Van's pack known for having such a large group but also for their most powerful asset — a golden wolf that could see into the future, near and far. Aleksandra was a she-wolf born with some blessed power centuries ago when his pack roamed free throughout the cold, barren lands of Russia, during a time where they did not have to hide their true forms. There was fear, but they were hailed as gods, and humans kept their distance. Now, only traces of their existence still lingered in bedtime tails and books, never to be believed in.

Aleksandra's eyes narrowed. "He will not stop. He will come for her, and you will be his sacrifice, Kostya. You think that day he came and slaughtered those humans was all by chance?"

"My name is not Kostya," Van growled, malice dripping from his tone. He hated that name, and Aleksandra knew that.

Aleksandra smiled. "You don't invite Riding Hood into your home and not expect the hunter to come looking, *Van*."

She clasped her purse shut and left the office of her alpha; her heels clicking loudly down the hall as she headed towards the elevator. Drake sighed heavily before chasing his mother, slamming the door closed behind him as he left.

Van frowned. Only a few people confused him, but Aleksandra and her future telling magic seemed to be filled with nothing but riddles. Aleksandra was wrong; Aira Blight was just a child that was caught in the middle of war — a war she would never be a part of. The rogues that left her family slaughtered in the rain wouldn't come back for her.

I have seen what that little girl will bring. I have seen that girl soaking in the blood of our pack's future!

If that fortune came to be, he wouldn't hesitate in killing the human himself.

Lady and the Wolf | **69**

Chapter Nine

"Mother!"

The irritated she-wolf turned her head to stare at Drake, her eyebrows creasing slightly at the delay, showing briefly the dread she had tried to mask while in Van's presence. She knew she was being doubted, and if there was anything Aleksandra Volkov hated most, being doubted was certainly in her top ten.

"What is it? I'm tired and just want to go back to my hotel," she snapped.

As Drake slowed to a halt beside his mother, he asked, "Is it true what you said?"

Her face dropped slightly. "You doubt me too, son?"

Drake shook his head. "I don't doubt you, but what you said was going too far. Were those rogues really after Aira?" His desperation was showing. He wanted answers, but Aleksandra couldn't help but notice both her son and Van both shy away from her dreaded warning of the future, a future that the human could possibly destroy their entire existence.

She sighed as she gently clutched her purse to her chest. "You know as well as I do that Van is a target, and if, by chance, he found a mate, he could possibly become a very strong leader."

Drake was confused as he took a step forward. "What do you mean?"

Aleksandra smiled. "They came looking for the mate of the Konstantin that day they attacked the humans. It's too bad the seer they have on their side is not very accurate for they came a few years too early. It's ironic. Their attempt at changing the future really did set everything in stone, yes?"

Drake was in shock and trying to take in what his mother had just revealed to him. Her smile never faltered as she gently touched her son's face, her perfectly manicured nails gently grazing his cheek as she said; "You're just like your father, so compassionate. But sometimes taking in strays only leads to trouble." As she said this, her eyes shifted down the hallway towards Van's door. "I sometimes thank the spirits Van took over when he did. I wonder if this girl reminds him of himself, after all, a child that was raised from murder and misery is bound to lead a lonely existence. The nightmares still rip him apart."

Drake never said a word as his mother left the building.

Chapter Ten

"Emma!"

She had heard the screaming long before her name was shouted so desperately. She couldn't believe that the nightmares that plagued Aira so viciously could actually hurt her during the day. When Aira had first been plagued with these horrible night terrors, Emma was convinced it was simply at night, but during the day, they seemed to be just as frequent when Aira went to sleep. She was exhausted from being kept awake for most of the night, fearing her dreams above all else.

As Emma reached her daughter's bedroom, the sight of the dark-haired child huddled up in the corner, shivering and sobbing, no longer made her frantic with worry. This ritual happened day and night like clockwork. Emma even knew the dream that plagued her child; of wolves chasing her through a dense forest, biting at her heels and murdering strange people who tried to protect her. Aira would never remember that those same people she often dreamt about were her own family, people who had given their lives protecting her.

"Shush, it's okay, honey. Emma's here," she cooed as she cradled Aira in the corner of her pink bedroom.

Aira nuzzled her head into Emma, sobbing quietly as she said, "There-there was so-so much blood..."

Vaughn, the pup Aira had rescued in the forest on Emma's birthday, whimpered as he licked the shivering girl's arm. Emma had decided to let Aira keep him despite the puppy eventually growing into the size of a small horse.

Emma seemed confused. Aira had never dreamt about blood before despite her dreams involving death. She had never told Emma anything like this before. "Blood?"

Aira nodded. "I-I was covered in blood, and those wolves, they were everywhere. They were growling and-and one—" she began to sob harder as Emma cradled her.

Emma was shocked she could hardly speak. "And what, sweetheart?" she stuttered, afraid of Aira's answer.

Aira's bright blue eyes shifted to look at Emma's pale face. "Hero was a giant wolf."

Chapter Eleven

"Aira, you haven't been coming to our sessions. Is everything okay?"

A curt nod from the twelve-year-old girl was all Susan expected to receive. Having been in Aira Volkov's life from the time she was only a small child, Susan Balk was used to the growing girl's awkwardness. The she-wolf knew that Aira was growing wary of her routine appointments with her and wanted nothing more than to be free from these sessions. Susan thought Aira was ready to stand on her own two feet, but Emma was worried. Susan knew Emma too well; she knew the time was growing closer to tell Aira the truth.

The room was quiet as Aira stepped outside, giving Susan a chance to speak with Emma.

"Has she been doing her voice exercises?" Susan asked flippantly as she shuffled some papers around.

Emma smiled. "She's very articulate now, but she still has trouble saying certain words... but no, she hasn't."

"It's okay to be scared, Emma. There's no possible way you can keep her in the dark forever. One day, she'll have to know the truth…"

Emma nodded, as she always did. She knew Susan was right, and that the voice exercises would help her adopted daughter overcome some of her speech impediment, but Aira just seemed so adamant that there was no use in the voice exercises Susan laid out for her.

"She speaks of Van quite a lot lately. Have the dreams been continuing?" Susan asked as she shuffled some papers around.

Susan could tell that Emma was gulping back the memories of that horrible afternoon, six months prior when Aira awoke, screaming and shaking her head. "No, she seems to be able to sleep a lot better these days, but her mood is down."

Susan looked up at the younger woman, a coy smile playing across her lips. "Oh, perhaps it's because she hasn't seen her *hero* in such a long time?"

Emma visibly paled. "No, no," she laughed lightly, "maybe it's something to do with school."

She crossed her arms over her chest as she edged towards Susan's office door. The she-wolf could sense Emma's out-of-character anxiousness and jumped in with, "Maybe you and Drake are taking the silly fortune telling of a senile old wolf to heart."

Her smile never faded as Emma all but shouted, "Who? No! Of course not!"

Susan's smile never faltered as she said, "Van would never take a human as his mate, much less a little girl taken in by his beta and only true friend, Emma. Aleksandra's fortunes are never set in stone. Remember that. Van is ignoring her crazy talk. Why can't you and Drake do the same?" She sighed as she continued. "He will never admit it, but the distance Drake is showing him must be confusing especially because he *is* Drake's leader."

Emma couldn't retaliate; all she could do was stop and stare.

"There have been some problems with our pack back home. He's going back to Russia, Emma. Van could be gone a long time; I wonder how Aira will take it when she finds out."

Emma gulped back whatever was troubling her and nodded. "I know; he has offered to take Aiden for training. Drake thinks it's a good idea to take Aiden back to the place he came from."

Susan bit her lip, trying to contain a sly smile. "There was some information that leaked out about the rogues that killed Aira's family venturing back to their homeland. Although he still says to this day that he's not going after them because of their fruitless slaughtering; I think he still feels compassion for the little girl he saved all those years ago."

Emma's face couldn't have dropped any lower. For the first time in the many years she had known Van, she had never expected him to go out of his way for a human child. Perhaps her worst fears were coming to life.

"Perhaps, Van should be the one to tell Aira?"

Chapter Twelve

Her eyes followed him as he went to and from each bedroom of his apartment, making sure he had what he needed for his long trip away. This hadn't been a spur of the moment decision; it had been an idea lingering in the back of his mind for some time now. He needed to go home and work out the problems he had left behind when he had ventured to American soil.

"My father says you are weak," she snapped, her eyes flaring.

Van did not stop what he was doing as he replied, "Oh? I suppose he has agreed to my offer, then," he said matter-of-factly.

Jillian let out a soft growl. "Six years, Van. That's all he can spare to take care of your territory here."

His curt laugh didn't go unnoticed by the irritated she-wolf. "Six years is all I need, my dear."

Jillian's temper was rising by the second. She just wanted one moment of his attention solely on her. Even for just a second, he could tell. She needed him to know how much this hurt that he was just *leaving* without a second thought. These little emotional guilt trips were beginning to bore him.

Without even thinking her actions over, Jillian reached out her clawed hand and grabbed hold of Van's arm. Her eyes flared like wildfire as his cool golden eyes stared back at her with little more than an annoyance.

"At least promise me you'll come back, Van," she growled. "That you won't just abandon everyone you have standing behind you *here*, in America."

His face faltered for a moment before he finally just gave in. Ripping his arm away, he straightened his shirt and nodded. "I'll come back when I win this fight."

Jillian smiled. "Thank you, Van."

He was sure she wanted to say more, but the ringing of his cellphone halted whatever words were ready to spill from those lips of hers.

Van's face contorted into an annoyed scowl as he answered. "What?"

He recognized the voice on the other end of the line almost immediately.

"Are you going to miss us, Van?"

Van sighed heavily. "Aiden and I will only be gone a few years."

The tremble in Emma's voice was evident. "Just 'a few years' is a long time to humans, Van…"

"By the time Aiden returns, he'll be a young adult. His feelings won't change. You accepted this the moment you took him in, Emma." Van knew Emma was still trying to accept the fact that her son would be gone for such a long time. She was aware she would have to let Aiden go sooner than she would have liked, but this is what she had agreed to the moment she took him into her home.

"What about Aira?"

He frowned and ignored the strange stares he was receiving from Jillian as she paced around. "What *about* Aira?"

"Susan suggested you tell her what's happening."

Van's eyebrows shot up. "And why would that silly old cow suggest that?"

There was a silence on the other end of the line for a moment before Emma spoke. "To this day, since she was a little girl, she still thanks her Hero for saving her life. She doesn't thank anyone else. She thanks you for the good day she had or when she goes to sleep and wakes without nightmares. She adores you, Van."

Van growled. This was just like the human to try to give him a ride on the proverbial guilt train. It didn't help that his inner Lycan was giving him quite an annoying headache.

"Fine, send the girl over here tomorrow night."

He stared at her from across the table, eyeing the child as if she were a wild animal ready to attack. God forbid she would have if not for Emma holding her back and reminding her about manners and such. Van remembered there was a time where small children would run from him and avoid his presence at any cost. But not this child, no, she was the one human child who could look the alpha right in the eyes with that big dopey grin plastered across her face. It irked him to no end.

"Uh, Hero—" his pointed look ceased her from continuing that sentence, "Mr. Van, why do you have such a big table?"

It had taken time, but it seemed she had finally learned to drop that horrible name she had come to call him. However, once the child had learned to speak, she just wouldn't shut the hell up. Another reason why he disliked humans, they spoke to him as if he were on their level, unlike the wolf pups of his clan that grew up knowing their alpha was God to them and that he should be feared. However, Drake's pup, Aiden, had grown up with humans and was still reluctant to treat his alpha as an alpha should be treated. Van reasoned that the pup would be beaten into shape soon enough if Emma stopped coddling the boy long enough for Van to get to him, that is.

Van went back to cutting his raw meat, ignoring the child's earlier question. The meat was only slightly cooked with blood still dripping off his fork, but that was the way he liked it. Hunting was becoming a problem in recent years with many grounds as non-hunting areas, and those damn Rangers were becoming a nuisance. He supposed he should just buy some land, herd some cattle, maybe sheep. Lamb was a particular favorite of his. It tasted much better when it was a fresh kill.

"Mr. Van?"

His head snapped up as he heard that little voice address him. He had to hold back a growl just so he wouldn't have to deal with Drake if he should so happen to frighten the child.

"Yes?" His reaction was cautious. There was no telling what the girl wanted next.

She wore an expression he had never seen before. "Are you real-really leaving?"

It was a simple enough question. He could answer "yes" and leave it at that. He could shrug it off and simply go back to eating his food or tell her a little lie. She would forget him soon enough.

However, his lips started to move without him even registering to what he was about to say. "Yes, I'm leaving, and Aiden is coming with me."

That odd look on her face never faltered. "How-how long will you be gone?" she stuttered.

"A long time."

Her head dropped as she looked down at her food, poking at her steak as if trying to pick up a piece. Van huffed lightly as he stood up and moved silently behind the child, taking her small hand in his larger one as he showed her how to cut the tough meat. Van's actions weren't out of kindness, as he tried to make himself believe, he did it to stop that annoying clanking sound she was making with her fork against the plate. That was all.

"Mine… mate…"

Van's eyes, which were concealed with colored lenses, shot open almost instantly as he heard his Lycan. Even through the contacts, the hues of his eyes had noticeable slits from the agitated Lycan inside of him.

Van ripped his arms away and took a step back, trying to control the monster inside of him. Whatever had set it off had riled his inner Lycan up so much that it was hard to control.

Aira twisted in her seat and glanced at the man behind her. Van couldn't help but notice her confused stare, and as quickly as it had first happened, his Lycan suddenly calmed itself.

"What?" he growled out as the human stared at him profusely.

"Hey-hey, Mr. Van, a-are you okay?"

His low grunt was all the confirmation he would give to her. "Why are you stuttering, girl?" he asked. He needed to change the topic.

Her face quickly flushed red. "Em-Emma says I do it when I-I think too hard about what I want to say, so my-my words don't come out right."

He didn't respond as he strutted back to the other end of his dining table. It confused him a great deal as to why he felt such... *Guilt*, was that the right word for it? Yes, guilt for embarrassing the human. It was an emotion he hadn't felt for decades. It was a shame he had lost his heart a long time ago. There was nothing in his soulless chest to even hold a soul if he even had one. If he had one, to begin with, that is.

If his emotions weren't confusing enough, the little human child's next question only intensified his already buzzing mind.

"Will I be able to call you on the phone like-like Emma does?"

Van sighed heavily as he refilled his Scotch glass. "Yes, you'll be able to contact Aiden every now and again."

Her frown only intensified. "I know. I-I wanted to know if I could call you-you, Mr. Van."

By all that was mighty and cursing all the spirits of his pack, this girl really knew how to confuse a poor wolf.

His answer was sharp and straightforward. "No, I won't have any service where I am staying."

Of course, for the majority of his stay in his homeland, he wouldn't be under the warm glow of a lamp while he sat around and read the daily news. Van would be going back to his roots while he searched for the rogues with his scouts. Truthfully, he enjoyed reverting into his Lycan form, free to roam the icy terrains as he pleased. However, he couldn't explain that to the human in front of him.

She looked deterred for a moment before that bright, *irritating* smile snapped back onto her face like a rubber band. "Can you receive letters?"

His eyebrows furrowed. "Yes, I suppose someone can bring me any mail I receive while I'm away. *If it's important.*"

"Can we write to each other, Mr. Van?"

Those big blue eyes of hers widened as if pleading with him. Van couldn't understand what sort of fascination she had for him. It was simply ridiculous, silly, and moronic. He would not give in to those eyes.

Taking another sip of his scotch, Van grunted, "We'll see."

He would not cave to this worthless human. He wouldn't.

Chapter Thirteen

She didn't understand, not really, anyway.

Emma had told her that being a teenager was tough, that a girl at her age would experience new things, new hopes, dreams, and romances in the future. She had the world at the tip of her fingers but knew there had always been something holding her back.

Maybe it was *him*. Maybe he, the man she never knew, but always held on to in her heart, was the reason she stood there and smiled so happily when all she wanted to do was cry. Maybe he was the reason she held such a tough front while she watched the only friend she ever had, Aiden, walk away. She would miss him terribly, even if she knew he was safe with Van watching over him.

She never let that one word slip until the very end. "Goodbye…"

It sounded so rough like they would never see each other again.

Aiden smiled as he slung a heavy arm around his sister's neck. At thirteen year's old, he was a big boy and would only get bigger. Aira knew they wouldn't be together forever but had hoped they would be by each other's side for as long as forever would allow.

Without thinking, Aira wrapped her skinny arms around Aiden and let a few tears fall from her eyes. "Will-will you call?"

Aiden chuckled and threw her that little boy grin she and Emma loved so. "Every day," he promised.

That was enough to keep Aira from going into a fit of hysterical sobs. Although Van had made up an excuse not to receive phone calls, Emma had assured her Aiden would have his cellphone with him every single day.

"Vaughn, you take care of her, 'kay?" Aiden said as he eyed the almost fully grown wolf behind his little sister.

The wolf behind them made no sound. He only nudged Aira's arm lightly, which made the girl smile as she scratched behind his ear. Normally, animals that weren't boarding the planes with their owners weren't allowed to roam freely throughout the airport, but the influential man that stood off in the distance quickly changed their minds. Van still visibly cringed from the name Aira had given the animal, which made her laugh quietly.

Aiden petted Vaughn's head. "Watch my sister, okay? She's a bit of a flake," he laughed.

Aira huffed. "Who's a flake?" she muttered disdainfully.

The large wolf simply stared at Aiden as Aira continued to pet behind his ear. Aiden winked and with a last goodbye to his sister, moved over to his mother.

"See ya soon, Ma," he whispered as he gave Emma a great big bear hug.

Emma wasn't as subtle as her daughter and let the tears fall freely, squeezing her son as tightly as she could. Aira knew that Emma's only wish was that this day would end and Aiden would just come home. However, that was impossible. Aiden's homeland called him — the place where he was born, and in order to mature, as her father and Van had explained, he needed to leave. It would be a long time, and he would be a man when he eventually came home, but it was a sacrifice Emma had said she accepted the day Aiden came into her life. Whatever that meant.

"Take care, my darling boy. If you ever need us, no matter where you are or whom you are with, your father and I will find you. There is no place too far, remember that."

Her face, although stained with tears, forced a ready smile. Emma finally let Aiden free from her hold but continued to hold his hand. Six years, that was a long time. "We'll be big and old like they are when we meet again, Aiden," Aira joked, ignoring the glare her mother threw at her.

Aiden chuckled lightly, trying to cover the soft cry that was threatening to spill out. "I love you, Mom," he said, turning back to his mother.

Emma smiled a smile that showed all the pride that welled in her heart for Aiden. "I hope you find what you're looking for."

He pulled her in for one lighter hug, and before they broke apart, he whispered in her ear, "No matter what I find, you're my mom, and no one could ever change that," and kissed her cheek. Those words made a tear spill down Aira's cheek.

As Aiden wondered over to Van and Drake, his knapsack casually draped over his shoulder, Emma gently touched her cheek. If not for the little hand that tugged at her own, Aira knew that Emma could have stood in that airport for hours, just staring.

"Mom, we'll be okay," Aira whispered, "We still have each other."

Emma looked down at the little girl, her mouth opened in an "O" shape at how mature she sounded right at that very moment.

Aira mimicked Emma's smile, trying to lighten the mood. It was all she could do to try to ignore the livid expression of the older lady standing by her father and Van. It was as if she were trying to stare straight through the little girl's soul. Aira didn't want to upset her mother any further so didn't acknowledge the women's keen eye zero in on her. She just had to ignore it.

Chapter Fourteen

Van eyed the boy as he casually waltzed towards them. His gaze strayed, but he made it a point to not even glance at the child by Emma if, by some off chance, she was giving those sad pathetic eyes.

"Ah, Vnuchek, you've grown," Aleksandra gushed. She grabbed Aiden by the shoulders and looked him up and down, her mouth twisting up into the only smile Van had ever seen his adoptive mother make. Van simply assumed that if the old bitch had made a real smile, her wrinkled face would have cracked and fallen right off.

Aiden stiffened as he looked at his father for any sort of reassurance. All Drake could do was watch in amusement. Aiden had met the woman once before when Drake and Emma had first brought the shifter pup back from Russia, but he was far too young to remember the former Luna.

"Hey… Baba…" Aiden greeted, a little hesitant.

Van and Drake almost fell over themselves. If there was anything their mother hated above all else, it was being reminded she was much older than most of the elders in their pack. Aiden had basically called the she-wolf *old* grandmother, and he knew it.

Van could have sworn he saw the bitch's eye twitch ever so slightly.

"*No...* its babushka, darling. Drake, why aren't you teaching the child his native tongue? Have you forgotten your heritage since you've been in America?" She struggled to find any sort of mercy for the boy, and all who stood witness noticed it; so naturally, she redirected her irritation towards Drake — the son with the least backbone in her eyes.

Aiden let a sly smirk make its way across his face. "Right, sorry, *Baba...*"

Van mentally groaned. It was going to be a long flight, a *very* long flight.

Just as the time came to board the plane, and Drake had said his goodbyes to Aiden, Drake pulled his brother aside. He kept an eye out to make sure his wife and Aira didn't notice him and gently tucked a letter into Van's hand.

Van looked confused for a moment. "What's this?"

Drake smiled. "A letter from a little girl too shy to say a proper goodbye."

Van had arched his brow before Drake slapped him lightly on the shoulder. "Take care, Van. Remember to call us from time to time. Say hello to the *family* for me," and with that, waltzed back towards what remainder of his own family in America, leaving Van to wait and wonder.

He glanced down at the letter in his hand. It reeked of the human child, and Van found this sort of tactic rather... smart. It seemed she wanted to remind him of the conversation they had had prior to his departure.

As he walked towards the terminal, he sliced the letter open with a single claw. What he read made his mind race. It was hard to make out the messy handwriting, but from what he could read, he realized the child was a lot brighter than he had originally thought.

Dear Hero, (Mr. Van)

I hope we can write each other. Dad told me you would be in a place where not many people will get the chance to talk to you. I think that's terrible because I like talking to you very much. You don't have to write back, but it would mean a lot if you did. Mom is helping me write this letter and she said you like trivia. I like trivia as well. My teacher says I'm really good.

 So, here's my question:
 What's the capital of Russia?
 I hope Dad remembers to give this to you.
 I'll miss you and Aiden.
 - Aira

"Boy, why do you have that look on your face?"

Van ignored his mother as he sat down and folded the letter into his front pocket. "What look?"

Aleksandra frowned. "You know what look. Don't get too attached to that child; heed my words, *Kostya.*"

"Call me Kostya again, and I will throw you off this plane," Van threatened with an eerie smile.

Aleksandra huffed and glared daggers before turning away.

Van simply muttered a sly remark before getting comfortable in his seat. He hoped the old she-wolf next to him would shut the hell up relatively soon. Before he changed his mind and cut her throat.

Chapter Fifteen

He hated flying. Between the screaming children — why they allowed children in first class was beyond him — and his mother's constant complaints, he wondered if going full frontal lycanthrope on the plane would be a good escape to this otherwise hellish experience.

Aiden seemed to be doing quite splendidly with that little iPod thing he had blasting into his ears. The rest of the world appeared to be just a distant figure whenever Aiden would listen to that trash. To any other passenger, the music that vibrated through his earphones was just a soft murmur, but to Van and any other shifter, it was like a bass loudspeaker at a concert placed right beside your ear. He wondered how the pup could tolerate that torture.

"Attention passengers, we'll be landing at Domodedovo International Airport in approximately thirty minutes. Please fasten your seatbelts, and I hope you enjoyed flying with Delta Airlines."

Aleksandra sighed. "Thank God, I couldn't bear another moment on this God-forsaken human contraption. Aiden?"

Her attention soon turned to her grandson. With a swift hand, she yanked the earphones out of Aiden's ears. The wolf pup seemed to be in a state of shock for a moment. Aleksandra smiled.

"It's rude to ignore someone when they're talking to you, boy."

Van sighed. It looked as if Aiden had no idea what he was in for with this woman.

Let the torment begin... Van thought disdainfully as the plane began its descent.

His Lycan was already calling out with an emotion he had never felt before. The beast inside him knew where he was, the place Van was born. Although Van himself was not a person who felt excitement or joy or was even overly eager for such trivial matters, he still felt almost happy to be back in the place he had once called home.

Aiden looked lost as he, Van and Aleksandra moved into the Mercedes limousine Van had specially imported years before. Even now, in the many years he had been absent from his homeland, it still carried the scent of memories long lost.

"Van! It has been a while," came a cheery, gruff voice from the front of the limo. His English was still rough but understandable, nonetheless.

Van knew this voice well and chuckled. "Ivan, how have you been?"

The red wolf grinned cheekily, a sharp pointed fang just overlapping his lower lip as he did so. His sharp Russian accent made it almost impossible for Aiden to even understand him, so the young pup simply gazed quizzically between the driver and his uncle.

"I've been well, sir. The house is so alive today! Everyone's glad to have you back home." The grin never left his boorish face. "And who might this young pup be?"

Aiden knew he was being referred to when the Russian wolf's eyebrow raised and his bright blue eyes seemed to avert directly onto the boy.

Van was in the middle of a much-needed stretch and answered, rather casually, just as he cracked his neck. "Aiden, my nephew," he grunted.

Whenever he returned home, it was as if a hundred blocks of steel had been relieved from his shoulders. He felt free to relax. Maybe that was why he rarely returned to his homeland. The more comfortable he became, the more he felt obliged to stay.

Ivan leaned over the front seat to shake the boy's hand, but his effort of kindness was quickly diverted as Aleksandra slapped his hand away.

"Drive, Ivan. It was so sticky hot on that damn plane that I now need a bath," she snapped with a rigid expression playing on her aged face.

Ivan took the hint and pressed a button to roll up the window dividing the back passenger seats and himself. Van could sense that Aiden couldn't help but feel a little guilty for the man. He had just been so cheery a moment before, but that happy spark had died out in a matter of moments and replaced with a steely expression. Van knew that Ivan disliked Aleksandra, as many others did, but she still demanded respect.

"Mother, your authority ceases when we get back to the pack," Van growled. His posture, a moment ago slack, had now stiffened as he made his dominance known.

It took all of Aleksandra's will not to cower. Now that they were back in their homeland, Van's law was back in order, and she was just another lower rank.

Her face hid nothing as she replied disdainfully; "You can order me around when you've been home for more than ten minutes, *son.*"

Van didn't reply. His attention had been stolen by the fast moving landscapes outside the limo windows. His Lycan rarely tried to command him, but at that very moment, all his spirit wanted to do was run.

It had been such a long time since he allowed himself to roam freely in his Lycan form. If he could, he would have probably jumped out the window right that very second. However, there were certain things he had to take care of before he even thought of letting his Lycan out to play.

"Promise me something, pup."

Aiden's head snapped to the side, giving his uncle his utmost attention. "What is it?"

Van had waited a moment before he spoke, wondering how he would word this. "You're going to meet a lot of different people in your stay here. *Certain* people may try to put things into your head, and you may learn things you do not wish to learn. Some information may upset your mother and father, so keep it to yourself." He turned to face the boy, a coldness washing over him Aiden had never seen before. "Are we clear, Aiden?"

Aiden could only nod as he took in what Van had told him. That was the first time in years Van had actually called him by his name, which gave Aiden the impression what Van had just told him was very important.

"I won't tell..." he whispered.

It seemed the "Devil-May-Care" attitude Aiden showed back in the US had quickly changed since they left the Airport. Van knew the pup was feeling the overwhelming aura of his pack mates, and by his withdrawn behavior, a rarity for the young wolf, he was in no way comfortable with the change in his inner self.

"He will learn just how far you and his father have fallen from your status. Is that what you're afraid of, Van?" Aleksandra snapped. She never turned to look at Van; she just continued to glare ahead at the window separating them from Ivan with her arms crossed over her chest.

"We all fall, *Aleksandra*; some just fall harder than others," Van replied.

Van could feel the link between him and his pack growing stronger the closer they got to the house. It was a feeling he would often have to get used to whenever he returned home. He only had a few hundred shifters under his leadership back in America, but here, in his homeland, he had thousands of shifters linked to him and his thoughts.

From the way the energy shifted, Van could only guess they knew he had landed in Russia hours before Ivan was given the call to come pick them up in Moscow. They were a long way from the bustling city, and that's just the way Van and his family liked it.

The car suddenly came to a standstill. The only noticeable feature surrounding them was the multiple cascades of snow. It covered the thousands of tree's surrounding them, and the little bit of snow that fell from the clouded sky made Van remember the first snowfall he had seen on the grounds of the wolf pack's Volk mansion. Hundreds of years had come and gone since then, but the scents and sights were still the same. It was as if time had stood still for the house and all that surrounded it.

Aleksandra had already exited the car, and Ivan had come to her beck and call. It appears some things never changed.

Aiden was still snoozing from the long car ride, and Van didn't have the patience to wake him and answer the millions upon millions of questions that must have been bouncing around in his head.

"Welcome back," Van whispered to himself as he gently closed the car door, so as not to wake his nephew up. Perhaps, he wanted to get the reunion out of the way so that Aiden wasn't too swamped with everything all at once. Van knew, maybe a little too well, what it was like to be a new pup in a big pack.

He stared down the giant mansion as if expecting a herd of elephants to come running out and pounce on him. The colored glass of the giant windows shimmered as they usually did, and he could see the silhouettes of his pack mates bustling around the main entry, possibly trying to pry out and get a glimpse of him.

"Interesting." He let out a soft chuckle and made his way up the cobblestone steps, heading towards the mansion's large stone veranda that surrounded the property. It looked like it had been well-kempt since his last visit, and the snow that fell a good percentage of the year seemed to have been swept off.

There was a moment of hesitation as he gently placed his hand on the giant wooden door. He couldn't help but think how memorable this was. How he had walked through this door millions of times without a second thought; it confused him why he was so put off by the idea of walking into his own home now of all times.

He didn't have to think very hard about it as the door was flung open for him, and a small figure emerged quite timidly, he noticed.

Short bright red hair filled his vision for about half a second until the girl looked up. Her vision was momentarily impaired by Van's broad chest, but after a moment of relative shock, her gaze finally met her Alpha's. Her eyes were a deep, beautiful ember — no, not really, perhaps, more of a burning bronze. He really couldn't tell under that big tuff of fire red hair.

If not for the distinctive scent this little female was displaying, Van might not have even recognized her. His eyebrow arched up, and he took an immediate step back.

Her eyes seemed to widen ever so slightly. "Van?"

His expression showed little more than an annoyance. "Elina, hello," he nodded. "You've grown."

It took a moment before the red she-wolf realized what he had said, and immediately, turned her head to the side. "I-ah... well..." she stuttered, not quite being able to form a coherent sentence.

Van hadn't meant the comment as a polite gesture. He was merely pointing out the fact she was no longer the runt of the pack although she was still quite small.

"Elina," he muttered, darkness falling over his face. She reminded him too much of someone, and that was irritating enough as it was.

"Mate... far... mate."

He growled low, and it took all of his strength not to slap himself in the face if to shut his Lycan up. It had been a while since his Lycan had started with that bull crap. He didn't know what it wanted, but he did know it was beginning to get damn near impossible to ignore.

Besides the constant nagging of his Lycan, he was being bombarded with thoughts and emotions from his pack. Everything was centered on him, and although having your alpha return would be something to celebrate, he just wished... for damn sakes... that they would all shut the hell up. He was starting to get a headache.

The last thing Van Volkov expected was a fist, coming full force, into the side on his face.

Chapter Sixteen

Van never even flinched. The fist sent a strong hit his way had indeed hit its target, but Van simply stood his ground, unmoving, and unflinching. It was like a Ping pong ball had just tapped him on the cheek; but still, it was an annoyance he didn't want to deal with. The owner's clenched fist was still lodged into the alpha's cheek, but that was only because Van had his wrist clenched in a bone breaking hold.

Van didn't have to look at the assailant to know who it was. "Nikolai, if you want to punch your superior and make it effective, you should throw your full weight into the punch." He turned his head to face the other male. The hues of his eyes turned to slits under the contacts he used, and the corner of his mouth twitched. "Like this…"

The younger man didn't have a chance to even defend himself as his alpha twisted his wrist, the bones making a sickly crunch, and without warning, landed a punch to his cheekbone with his free hand, crushing any sort of bone and cartilage. Van had a bored expression strewn across his face as the shifter grunted in pain. He only let go of Nikolai's wrist when he heard the gratifying pop of his shoulder dislocating. It seemed Van had forgotten to let go of his twisted wrist when he landed the punch. The force of the hit would have sent Nikolai hurtling a few feet away, at the very least *if* he had let go, that is.

It had taken a moment before Van realized Elina was still standing in the doorway, eyes wide and horror-struck. He wasn't quite certain if she was concerned for the mutt he had just knocked around or the fact Nikolai had actually had the gall to pop him one in the face.

"I just cleaned up the veranda this morning!" she shrieked, both rage and terror echoing through her shrill vocals. "Goodness."

Well, Elina's English had certainly improved, he noticed.

As for the shifter writhing in pain next to him, it was clear his native tongue had only become even more vulgar.

There was a great amount of contempt in the man's eyes as he stared up at Van. He was trying in vain not to writhe around in pain, but the tormented look that washed over his face like a giant tidal wave showed everything clearly. He despised Van, and Van had little like for his pack member. After all, Nikolai saw it as abandonment when Van had left.

Nikolai grunted, "Why are you back here?"

For what it was worth, Van felt something tug at his Lycan — the feeling of disappointment was slowly washing over his very soul. Van had grown up with the angry shifter writhing in pain before him. They had hunted together, been there through each other's first shift, and Nikolai had been the only one allowed near Van when his adoptive father passed away almost a century ago.

Van smiled with a disdainful edge. "Still cannot speak a lick of English, can you?"

Nikolai's scowl showed some truth. "Is it your business?" His sentence came out forced and slow as if he were thinking about the words before he spoke them.

"I suppose an idiot only needs a lick to get by," Van said after a moment of thought.

Van was vaguely aware of his nephew's presence in the distance, but he couldn't back down as an Alpha. He needed to show Aiden just what happened to wolves that broke the rules. "Nikolai..." His voice sounded tormented, but he never wavered in his stance.

Nikolai grunted as he got back up to his feet. His arm was hanging down from his shoulder, but that didn't seem to make him flinch, not even a little bit. His eye was slowly turning a blackish purple, and his cheek was swelling up. However, he never let Van know just how injured he was as he said, "My apologies, Alpha..."

This placated Van for the moment. *"I'd like you to meet my nephew, Aiden."* It had been so long since he had spoken in Russian. He knew it would come back to him. English wouldn't be needed here.

The pup was standing further towards the car now as Van flicked his hand, telling Aiden to come closer. He seemed frightened after witnessing the encounter between Van and

Nikolai, and after a moment of coaxing, Aiden finally ventured towards the stone veranda.

"This is Nikolai, Aiden. He is an old… *friend* of mine."

Aiden, knowing little of his family's native language, simply greeted Nikolai with a curt, "Privet. *Hello.*"

Nikolai immediately recognized the young pup, and his eyes bulged. He looked Aiden over for quite some time before curtly nodding his own hello. "*He is weak. He will need to train.*"

Van didn't expect anything less from Nikolai. The man was a brute force when it came to regular shifters and would shape Aiden into a fine future Alpha. Van had made plans many years before for Aiden. He would take on the pack Van had served his life to protect when the Alpha was ready to step down.

"Elina, where is everyone?" he asked as he sniffed the air. He could sense the hustle and bustle going on inside the house, but his pack was large, and he couldn't account for even half his pack until he had been home awhile longer. The link was still frail, and only time would reconnect him to his pack fully.

Elina smiled, while Nikolai simply looked on in apprehension. "It's a full moon tonight. Everyone's getting ready for the little one's first shift."

Ah, how could he have forgotten? Tonight, for wolves, was like Christmas morning for humans. Tonight, the pups would come into their wolf forms, and the excitement was only intensified to find out which pup was above the rest. So far, only he and Drake had that curse.

It all made sense now. Aleksandra wanted Aiden to come to Russia for the new moon. It was only unfortunate Drake and Emma weren't here to witness Aiden's coming of age.

Van let out a curt, cruel laugh. "Get this mongrel to Artyom. I'll take Aiden in to meet his… *family*." It felt odd to refer to anyone other than Drake and Emma as Aiden's family.

Elina nodded once before walking over to Nikolai and taking his good arm gently. "Since I was a child, you have not learned your lesson," she reprimanded as they headed towards the back of the large building.

Van looked down at his nephew and placed a hand on the pup's shoulder.

"Van…?"

"Hmm?"

"What if they don't like me?"

Van chuckled, amused by the boy's self-consciousness when the day before, he was so full of pride. "You are their future, pup. Rather than judge you, they will watch your every move. The future may scare them, but remember that one day these wolves will be under your law, your eye and your strength."

Aiden didn't understand. "What about you?"

Van's eyes seemed to take on a mist of something Aiden couldn't quite make out as if he had just stepped into a world made only for him. "Me? I already know my future. I have nothing to run to anymore, as I have nothing to run from. My future is dark, and I have accepted that."

The house was indeed alive and buzzing with a cheerful aura. Pack members gathered around Van, welcoming him home and asking how Drake was. No one asked about Emma, and Van knew the reason — Drake was dearly missed, and the females blamed Emma was taking him away.

Males chuckled and chatted with Van about their training and how Nikolai had been working them to the bone. Some were even boasting about their pups and the ever-anticipated new moon later that night.

Van relaxed as he sipped his cocktail. *"And how is your family, Kasimir?"* he asked. Kasimir had been loyal to Van's family for centuries and one of the few wolves alive that had served next to his late alpha.

The old wolf grinned from ear to ear. "My boy, I *can* speak English!" He laughed. "Valentina is well and expecting her fifth child. Can you believe it? Fifth! I was shocked, but Darya and I are as excited as we were when Melor was born."

Van listened to every word Kasimir rambled. The alpha didn't know many as proud of their grandchildren as Kasimir, perhaps, because he only had the one pup. When Kasimir's eldest grandson, Melor, was born, the celebrations seemed never ending. That had been the last time Van was home. It had been ten years since then.

Kasimir's amber eyes shifted as he finally stopped talking and looked towards Aiden, who was being coddled by two she-wolves in the corner. The older wolf's eyes suddenly turned somber, and a soft smile graced his worn face. "I wish Samiul were alive to see your return, my boy. Aiden has grown into a fine young man. Emma and Drake did a fine job, a fine job indeed."

Van nodded. "They worked with what they had. Aiden will become a strong alpha. I just hope you will teach him everything you taught me, Kasimir."

Kasimir's eyes widened. "What are you on about, boy?" he snapped. "What about your pups? When you find your mate, you'll—"

Van anticipated this argument and cut his old friend off. "I have no interest in finding a mate. A mate is a weakness. If Darya were to die, so would you, Kasimir, and who would protect your daughter and her pups?"

"You would protect them if anything were to happen to me, pup. I know you would," he said with a determined nod of his head.

Van frowned. "The elders are determined, and now, I think I know who has been pushing them on this issue…"

Kasimir scoffed and placed a large, calloused hand on Van's shoulder. "I'm only thinking of you, boy. I don't want you to find your mate and reject her because you're scared. You, I, and the elders know the repercussions of you rejecting your mate."

Van's eye twitched. He was becoming irritated very quickly with this topic. "I fear nothing."

"You may not fear death, but you do fear losing something of true value. 'Tis why you resent Aleksandra, because she fought to live when Samiul passed on. Is that what scares you — the torment or the fact when you find your mate, you will love no one, trust no one, and live for none other than that one person?"

Van was done with this conversation. "I prefer being alone, and as for Aleksandra, I resent her for one reason only, and you damn well know what that reason is. Excuse me, Kasimir." The ice that dripped from his voice told Kasimir to back down, and so he nodded and watched idly as Van walked away.

Kasimir sighed as he ran his fingers through his graying hair. "No one prefers to be alone, pup. When you find your other half, I pray to the spirits you do not let her go even if the past still haunts you."

Van escaped quietly out of the large dining hall. His mood had been relatively placid only minutes before, and now, he felt like ripping something apart. Kasimir had a way of stirring Van, but today, something about their topic of conversation had just given him an unruly itch.

He sighed heavily as he stood on the first-floor balcony. "I'll find a mate when I damn well feel like it," he growled. "And if I reject her, it's because I want to die on my own terms."

And yet, in the back of his mind, a little voice was pestering him to reach into his pocket. There was only one thing he had been holding onto since he landed in his homeland, and the battle within himself waged on whether he would give in and reply to Aira's letter or not.

With a tormented sigh, Van jumped onto the balcony rails like a wild animal and leaped to the nearest tree. It was time, after ten years of being subdued, to let his inner Lycan out to play. He had subdued Konstantin for far too long.

Chapter Seventeen

"When we got the call from Mr. Volkov, we were very surprised. Van told me you were very bright, and that our system would suit you perfectly, Aira," the woman smiled and slipped a bit of paper across the desk. "These scores are outstanding. It's hard to think you're not even in middle school yet, which is why we are excited to offer you a place here in Newport."

Aira fiddled with her hands as the school administrator beamed at her. "Thank you..." she muttered. Calista could tell the child felt uncomfortable being praised.

"Tell me, Mrs. Volkov, where did you think of such a pretty name? I've never heard of it before. Aira, I mean," she asked, her eyes bright and curious. Something about the way the administrator asked this question didn't sit right with Aira, but she continued to ignore the itching feeling that was slowly creeping across her skin.

Emma smiled as if she had known all along why Aira was given her name. "It means 'Of the Wind' because my husband and I knew that one day Aira would spread her wings and go places, meet people and do good things with her life." Her eyes were filled with love and adoration as she looked at Aira. "Aiden really enjoyed it here."

The administrator laughed. "Keeping with the As, I like it. Aiden was such an... *active* student here, will he be returning?"

The light in Emma's eyes seemed to vanish almost instantly at the mention of Aira's brother. "No, unfortunately, we sent him away with my brother-in-law so that he can... *study* and reach his full potential — potential he might not otherwise achieve here in the States."

Calista's smile instantly vanished when Emma finished her sentence. "Right, well then, we look forward to seeing you here in September, Aira. Your class sheet and information booklet will be sent out to you in the mail in about a week or so, and orientation is September 2nd. Welcome to Newport, Miss Volkov, and call me Calista from now on, Mrs. Volkov. Feel free to look around and meet some of Aira's teachers."

The conversation ended quickly, and Emma graciously shook the administrator's hand and told Aira to thank the woman. Aira visibly blanched and quickly mumbled a thank you. By the end of the conversation, the girl looked as if something were wrong. With a quick goodbye, Calista's smile fell instantly from her face.

"It's done..."

Calista's face fell in a grimace, and her seemingly innocent charm had vanished. Her shoulders tightened, and her neck cracked as she twisted it from side to side. "The smell of that girl is putrid. It took me back to the day I could have ripped her apart."

A loud grunt came from behind her. "In time, Calista." He jumped through the window and moved to a drawer under her desk, where he pulled out a packet of cigarettes.

Calista clenched her fists and was only holding onto her wolf by a mere thread. "I could have had her that day, Erik. I could have ended this and saved our future. The older she grows, the more chance we take that… that… Van will find his mate and banish us for what we've done!"

Erik sighed and ran a hand through his thick tangled mass of hair. "She's a little girl, still. Volkov is in Russia with his mutts. The problem will be only if he returns before we can take care of the *problem*."

Calista folded her arms over her chest and sighed heavily. "This wasn't supposed to happen, Erik. He wasn't supposed to find her yet, if at all. Noah warned us, and you didn't take his warning seriously!"

Calista huffed and undid the first two buttons of her blouse. The office was hot and stuffy, and she could feel the sweat dripping from her forehead just thinking about what that girl had in store. "Pups, elders, our brothers and sisters, Erik, because of *her,* they all die. Volkov will be stronger than anyone could have ever imagined, and then Ronan will throw our asses to the vampires!"

Erik, already aware of this, sighed. "Yes, I know. Everyone knows."

Calista looked out the window, spying down on the girl as she walked with her mother. "She doesn't know the harm her very existence will do to our kind, not until it's too late. We are stronger than these humans. We should be ruling over them, and *they* should be the ones in hiding!"

Erik thought for a moment, taking in what Calista had just said and shifted uncomfortably as he took a long drag of smoke. "One way or another, she will die, Calista, and then we will roam these lands free once again. I only hope her death doesn't anger Volkov, or we'll all be as dead as those bloodsuckers."

"They haven't mated yet. Her death will mean nothing." At least, that's what the golden haired she-wolf had hoped.

Erik grunted. "In time, all who have been hurt will thank us for what we've done. They will never know the good she brought or the destruction." His grin was wide as he thought of a future where wolves ruled over the humans. "Ronan has promised the vampires never-ending feasts for their assistance. We can't lose even if Volkov catches on prematurely."

"I hope you're right, Erik…" Calista eyed the child who smiled and laughed while Emma talked to her about how great the school was, thanks to Calista's heightened senses. "I hope you're right."

Chapter Eighteen

He wasn't certain where he was headed. All he knew was that his Lycan would bring him back. After all, he was only half in control when he shifted. It had been ten long years since he had last let his Lycan out. It was too dangerous to let him out in the States only because there was no place big enough where he could roam without being noticed. In his homeland, however, his territory was safe and so was his pack.

"Konstantin, I know you're there!" he called, his pace never wavering as he took a giant leap, catching the tail of a tree and jumping to the next.

"Free..." was the only thought he could get from Konstantin. Van chuckled, knowing his Lycan, Konstantin, was pacing to and fro, just waiting to be released.

Van took another giant leap and landed on his knees in the snowy terrain. The ice shifted and swirled around him as he kneeled down and slowly raised his head. Van could barely take it as the blood vessels in his eyes seemed to explode, and his amber irises glowed a bright gold. His Lycan, also known as Konstantin from his life in the other world called Altholo, growled low in excitement. He had not been to this clearing in so long that Van was eager to search for new intruders.

His neck snapped to the left with a sickening crunch that echoed throughout the distant plains. His shoulder popped, and his left arm twisted outward. His bones started to snap and break, only to realign and grow. His face contorted, and no longer was he even recognizable. A snout of some sort of beast began to grow, and his body flew forward as his size tripled.

Growls and snarls left his throat as his wolf took over. In a matter of minutes and for the first time in almost ten years, Van had released his Lycan. No longer was the businessman from Washington in control but the ancient wolf that lived inside of him.

Konstantin howled to the skies. He took his time to get readjusted to his own form and reveled in the scenery. He easily toppled the giant tree's that his master had just leaped through, and his paw prints left in the snow reminded him of the scared local humans who used to worship the ground he walked upon. He was revered as Konstantin, the Wolf God, because of his size. But that was years ago, and those humans had been dead and buried. He ignored the pang of hurt that struck through his soul.

His howl echoed for miles as he called out to his brothers and sisters. The howls that riveted back were haunting and beautiful all at the same time. It was his way of telling every creature that was within his domain and under his law that he had returned. Despite not for good, it left a peaceful silence, knowing they were safe while Konstantin watched over them. While Van was a protector of shifters and humans, his wolf was the protector of creatures of all types — be they mythical or not.

"*Are you having fun, pup?*"

Instantly he recognized the voice and huffed. "*New Moon is near, Kasimir. Are the young one's ready?*"

"*Well, you've certainly gotten everyone in the mood. I think we startled Drake's pup.*"

The black wolf seemed amused by this. "*He will learn in time.*"

"*Don't break anything on your way back here, Alpha,*" Kasimir joked.

It seemed it was time to go celebrate with his family. It had been a long time after all.

Chapter Nineteen

Aiden shifted from one foot to another awkwardly. He had been here less than five hours, and already, he was being swarmed by one member of the pack after another. It was as if he were some sort of new toy to be passed around.

The howls he had heard earlier were very new to the young wolf. He had never been around any wolf other than Van and his father. He heard wolves often had to be initiated into a pack, which could be quite painful, but he had an instant connection the second he got off the plane. He heard so many voices in his head that it was driving him completely insane! It was like a party was going on in his mind, but he wasn't invited. Elina had explained to him that he would get used to it and learn to tune out some of the voices.

"Konstantin's coming!"

"It's been so long since the land felt Konstantin."

Konstantin? Aiden was confused. Who was Konstantin?

"Pup, you seem lost," came a gruff voice.

Aiden turned around, surprised. He wasn't sure if that was a voice in his head or not. "There are so many voices in my head! Kasimir, who's Konstantin?"

Kasimir laughed and gripped the boy's shoulder. "Oh, are they on about that?" He gave a pointed stare to some of the closest males, which quickly shuffled away. "Konstantin is Van's lycanthrope — his spirit, my boy. Once you find your wolf, you'll know if he's special or not if he has a name. Of course, Van's Lycan was named many years before he was even born."

Aiden's brows furrowed. "Does my dad's wolf have a name?"

Kasimir looked shocked. "You've never seen him shift?"

Aiden shook his head. He had never seen his uncle shift or his father. "They said it was too dangerous."

"And it is with them being Lycanthropes and all."

Aiden was now even more confused, "What do you...?" He couldn't finish his sentence for a soft tremor caught his attention, and everyone seemed to be fascinated by the clearing just outside the house.

Before Aiden could ask, he had his answer. A wolf, the size of a house, trotted through the clearing. He looked monstrous with his teeth gaping forward and his fur looking like razor sharp spikes. Although he was sure that if he touched the fur, it would be as soft as a feather.

The pack members seemed happy and were flocking. The males were gathering in groups while the females fluttered about putting food on the outside tables. No one seemed the least bit fazed when Van sat himself down on all fours and simply watched.

Aiden leaned against the stone veranda railing and stared, fascinated. "What is he doing?"

Kasimir leaned beside him and grinned, the crow's feet around his eyes deepening. "He's watching over us. Our wolves are most vulnerable now, which is why the new moon is so rare. If there is trouble, Konstantin will protect us. That is his job as our watcher."

Aiden continued to stare, fascinated by his uncle. "Does my dad look like that, too?"

"Not as large but yes, he does."

Aiden was so enthralled by the giant god-like beast that he didn't even notice when Kasimir ushered him towards the stairs. "Well, it's time to find out which of the pups will shift tonight."

"Some don't?"

The old wolf chuckled and shook his head. "It's very rare — very rare indeed. You will soon find out, my boy."

Aiden found himself being ushered towards the clearing his uncle had just trotted through and studied four older males who stood around some kids his age. "Where are we going?"

Kasimir shook his head. "So full of questions. Tonight, the pups shift for the first time. This is why you came, boy."

Aiden was frightened and tried to hesitate but was continued along. The pups that were around him looked just as nervous as he did and he couldn't understand a word they were saying. Kasimir stood close by and winked when Aiden looked at him for some support. It was then he wished he had his father with him. He had thought when this time came he would have Van for support, but it seemed his uncle had been replaced with his wolf.

The elders began to speak, and still, Aiden didn't know what they were saying. It wasn't until Kasimir spoke to him through their link did he have a clue to what was going on.

"They're saying to close your eyes and concentrate. Feel the wolf inside of you and release its full potential."

Aiden looked around; noticed Nikolai had surfaced and was standing to the side, watching the boys, and girls do as they were told. Aiden followed and closed his eyes, feeling for anything inside of him. All he got was silence besides the voices of all the pack members. As he opened his eyes, however, he was greeted with a sight that even terrified him.

The children around him were shifting. He could hear the snapping of their bones and the awkward way their bodies tensed up. Fur sprung out, and their jaws misaligned. They were shifting while he was not. Furs of red, black, white, gray and assorted variations came into vision. The newly shifted wolves whimpered as their parents came to their aid, and the elders smiled in gratitude.

Aiden looked to Kasimir for any sort of reassurance, and all he got back with a lopsided frown.

Kasimir watched on, and Aiden continued to look at him in pure terror. His stomach was doing flips. He was frightened and just wanted to run and hide. The only sort of guidance he received was when he looked to Konstantin. The giant wolf seemed to calm him, and Aiden took in a deep breath.

The elders gathered by Aiden and patted his shoulder, giving him their congratulations. This was something that hadn't happened since Van and Drake, and they were almost yelling in joy. Pack members smiled and said things Aiden couldn't understand.

"Kasimir, what's going on? Why didn't I shift?"

Kasimir sighed. "Well, pup, it seems you're a Lycanthrope with Lycan blood. You won't shift for a long time yet," was all he could say. "When you do shift, it will be because of something that brings your wolf out. Something that is so emotional it can't stay dormant."

Aiden blinked and stared at Kasimir as if he were insane. "I'm... I'm going to look like Van?" That was crazy. Van was massive! He didn't want to look like that!

Kasimir chuckled. "You have a lot to learn, young man."

His old and tired smile seemed to light up as he looked over and noticed his grandson, Melor, running about in his wolf form, his father by his side.

Gulping back his concern, Aiden stared up at Kasimir sadly. "I'm sorry you couldn't be with your grandson tonight."

Kasimir looked down at Aiden, a bright smile washing over his face. "No, son, I'm happy I was here with you. A confused pup needed me more tonight. Van isn't the best at being very fatherly, and that's where I come in. After all, I owe it to Van and Samiul."

Chapter Twenty

Konstantin looked on and studied Aiden. Kasimir was doing most of the work, and he knew his master was thankful for that although his master was dormant and couldn't hear or see what was going on. The moon was already high, and his pack members were shifting to join the pups on their first run. Van was right to trust his Lycan. Aiden was a lycanthrope and would lead them when Van could no longer do that job, but unlike Van, Aiden was pure Lycan, not some reincarnate with a monster inside his soul.

"Are you contented, son?"

Konstantin growled low in his throat. *"Hello, bitch."*

Aleksandra folded her arms over her chest and gave the giant black wolf a look of pure distaste. "That's no way to speak to your mother," she snapped back. She turned and watched the festivities with little to no interest.

"You are my master's step-mother, not mine," he snapped back. A wondering pup that came up to him and jumped on his chest momentarily diverted his attention. Konstantin leaned down and used his massive nose to nudge the pup back to his apologetic parents. He knew them and mentally congratulated them on their pup's shift.

Aleksandra paid no attention to the pup and continued, "I am his mother. Be it by blood or not, I raised him."

"What do you want, mate of Samuil?" he asked, placating Aleksandra by referring to her as Van's father's mate. Her name had never left his tongue nor would it ever. It would be like swallowing poison.

"You cannot blame me for that girl's disappearance forever, Konstantin."

"I will hold you responsible until your death. You made my master miserable, and so I shall make your time on this earth miserable as well."

Her lips twisted as she looked up at him. "The human child... you know what she is to you. Stop pestering my son with it. You are the reason he found her."

He ignored her, but Aleksandra continued, "She will kill you, Konstantin, maybe not by her own hands, but she will kill you and therefore, kill my son. Listen to me; do not continue to blame me for the past."

Konstantin growled, his anger rising. *"If that should happen, so be it. I live for her. She is mine."*

"Heed my warning, Konstantin. That child will be the destruction of everything we hold dear. And you know Van will kill her before he lets that happen."

The black wolf huffed and continued to watch over his pack. *"He will learn to cherish her just as I have."*

Aleksandra shook her head. "She is your mate, not Van's. Van will never let her take what's his to protect. He's fighting you, *Kostya*, and he will fight you until he dies."

"And I will protect her until I die."

His master may not know it yet, but he will continue to protect her because she is his and always will be. Aira was his calling, and he saved her once. He would save her again — even if his master denied his own feelings.

Chapter Twenty-One

She couldn't. She shouldn't. But she had to. She took a leap, and she finally gripped it by the neck and shook with all her might. She was going to do it... she was going to ask the dreaded question.

Aira bounced on the balls of her heels and smiled that ever gleeful smile at her mother. She prayed to all that was holy and divine that Emma wouldn't shoot her down again.

"Mom... can I ask you something?" *Please, God, Zeus... Santa, anyone! Let today be the day Emma finally caved*, were the fleeting thoughts that crossed her mind as her mother turned around from the cooktop and smiled back.

"Hmm?"

It was now or never. "I want to wax my eyebrows... and shave. Please, Mom! I'll be thirteen soon. I'm old enough!"

Emma stiffened for a moment. Aira had been asking the same question for weeks now, and each time, the answer was no. Emma didn't want Aira to be ruled by vanity like most teenage girls; Aira knew this. She wanted her daughter to be happy with the way she was, and besides, her eyebrows were as light as anything. The girl was tanned naturally, of course, and you could barely even notice her eyebrows as it was. Shaving, however, was a big step Emma just didn't think Aira was ready to take, but Aira knew what she was ready for, and shaving was certainly on that list.

Aira kept her hopes up, as her mother turned around, that smile still bright and sparkling. For a moment, Aira was adamant Emma would say yes. That is until she sighed and repeated that dreaded word, "No, Aira."

Her posture instantly slumped, and her head went limp. "Whatever…" she muttered under her breath.

Emma's eyes widened considerably. "Hey, what's with the attitude lately?"

Aira's pouty lips twisted into a sulky frown. "All the other girls are allowed to, and I don't see why I shouldn't be—"

Emma cut her daughter off as she held her hand up in the air in a "stop" motion. "Aira, no. Your eyebrows are fine. Leave it."

Aira spluttered and gawked. "I'm nearly thirteen years old. I'm not a little kid anymore!"

Emma rarely, if ever, lost her temper. The woman was a saint in her own right and tried to do the best she could, but Aira knew her behavior was starting to get on her mother's nerves. The girl didn't know why she was becoming so dramatic over something so little, but she was tired of being treated as if she were still a mute — never being heard, just spoken down to.

"After what happened at school yesterday, you don't deserve anything," Emma grumbled under her breath but instantly regretted the words that left her lips.

Emma saw the look of hurt that washed over Aira's face, but before she could apologize, Aira was shooting up the stairs, tears racing down her face. Emma sighed as she watched Aira fly off.

It wasn't fair! She never got to do anything her friends got to do. She was never allowed to go to the mall with her friends alone, she wasn't allowed to catch the bus like other kids her age, and she most certainly wasn't allowed to use makeup or shave.

She stomped straight passed Vaughn, who watched after her, obviously confused. Aira had never ignored her pet without at least patting him on the head or giving him a treat. He trailed after the upset girl but instantly backed away out of fright when Aira ripped the ladder down that lead up to the attic.

She climbed up the ladder and once situated in the attic, Aira pulled the ladder back up with a loud bang. She had hoped she made the house rattle and maybe even topple down. Ugh, why had Emma said that?

"One... two... three..." she counted, as she always did when she was upset. Normally, by the time she reached one hundred and a sixty, she had calmed down. However, this time was different. This time, it had been Emma who had hurt her.

Aira knew deep down in her heart that she wasn't a normal child. Normal kids didn't wake up screaming in sheer terror from a dream, only to forget what she had been scared of, to begin with. Normal kids didn't see a therapist twice a week or have a speech impediment so severe sometimes you would have a stuttering attack. Most kids weren't adopted, either…

She paced back and forth, just thinking. She continued this for quite some time before finally falling to the floor with her knees to her chest and her head in her hands. She tried not to cry, but the tears slipped down her cheeks as if they had a mind of their own.

It wasn't Emma who had set her off. It was something completely different. *She* was different, and that was the problem. Aira wanted to be normal… so normal that it killed her.

It didn't help that something was eating her up inside, something she could never tell Emma or Drake. Something that scared her so much, she would rather cover it up than be looked at as anything other than normal. It wasn't her fault! Something had just snapped, and before she could bring herself back, it was too late.

"I'm busy. Can't you think of anything else besides calling me ugly?"

Mackenzie laughed haughtily. "Have you looked in a mirror? Your eyebrows are like caterpillars crawling along your forehead!"

Aira chewed at her bottom lip nervously, contemplating how she would react to the older girl's harsh words. "I-I like the-them."

"She forgot how to talk again," laughed Nathan, a boy who was always at Mackenzie's beck and call, as of late. It was no secret boys liked the pretty Mackenzie Reed, but it hurt that they continuously harassed Aira simply because Mackenzie didn't like her. It was like she was being lynched because of the way she looked and spoke.

However, Aira held her head high and continued to pull her books from her locker. Her only friend, Miranda, stood off on the sidelines pretending like she didn't even register to what was going on. Aira was used to that. She didn't want Miranda to get involved, but she sometimes wished someone would stick up for her. It was sad how sometimes Aira would dream that Van and Aiden would miraculously return and put these kids in their place.

But that's all they were; dreams. She could keep dreaming until the cows came home, but it would still be the same.

"Ugly."

"Weird."

"Loser."

The names still hurt even after two months of continuously hearing them spat at her. She suddenly didn't like middle school anymore. She learned the rules pretty quickly, and after two weeks of sitting by herself and talking to teachers on lunch break to pass the time, Miranda had said hello to her in English class. It wasn't a very verbal friendship, but it was a friendship all the same. Miranda was the first friend Aira ever had. Aira was awkward, and Mackenzie took advantage of it.

She didn't deny it when Mackenzie took a stab at her self-worth. Aira continued to smile because she knew out of all those hurtful comments, no one could tell her she was worthless. That was something she would never believe.

Before Aira knew it, a couple of more students had crowded around. Some were Mackenzie's friends, and some were just people walking by. The onslaught of hurtful comments continued, but she ignored it.

"I have to go to class…" She tried to divert their attention. All she had to do was get to her third-period class, and she would be safe. Then she could go about her day hiding. It was the same routine day in and day out.

Mackenzie wasn't about to let her just slip away as she jumped in front of Aira. "You know, Aiden used to call you 'The Freak,' right?"

Her eyes widened and without a hitch, replied, "Don't lie, Mackenzie, it looks uglier than I ever will." It took all of her concentration to say that without stuttering.

Aira turned around to walk the other way, but Nathan was behind her with two other students. Every time his mouth opened, she swore she would pass out from his breath.

She was lucky because her math's teacher, Miss Holt, came stumbling out of her classroom just in time to see the spectacle. "What are you all doing out here? It's class time!"

Miss Holt was too distracted with Mackenzie to notice Nathan reach out and try to grab hold of Aira to knock her books down like he usually did. However, today was different. Today was very, very different.

Just as Nathan reached out, Aira's head began to thump wildly. Nathan didn't even need to slap her books out of her hands because she dropped them onto the floor as she brought her hand to her forehead. Everything seemed to slow down as Miss Holt rushed to Aira's side, holding the girl steady as she wobbled around. She felt like a sack of bricks had been tipped on top of her.

Miss Holt's words faded out as Aira looked around in confusion. It was blurry, and she used the teacher to steady herself. She could faintly hear Miss Holt telling a student to get the nurse before everything changed right before her eyes.

The students around her were no longer human; Aira's heart thumped madly in her chest, almost as loud as the thumping in her head earlier, and all she could comprehend were the wolves.

The wolves that surrounded her.

Aira gasped and covered her mouth. The halls changed, and she was no longer in her school. She was in pitch blackness. All that could be seen were the big, black wolves snarling at her, and the woman who kept her steady. Aira stepped back as the wolf closest to her snarled. She let out a frightened sob but couldn't step back anymore. Looking to her right, Miss Holt was no longer there. In her stead was a taller woman, with long sandy curls and big doe blue eyes. Those eyes stared down at Aira.

The woman didn't seem phased by the rogue animals nearing them and simply smiled.

"Honey, you need to climb."

Aira's brows furrowed. That voice… she knew that voice.

"Pretend the ground is lava… don't be afraid."

Her voice was hauntingly beautiful. Pretend the ground is lava? What did that mean? "I don't understand. What is this?"

The wolves were foaming at the mouth, but they kept at a distance. Something was keeping them back. The strange woman seemed to glow as she squeezed Aira's arms reassuringly and turned her to face the demon dogs before them. The woman leaned down, and her chin rested on Aira's shoulder. The gesture was warm; loving... she remembered that feeling of safety.

"I love you, my darling girl."

And just as quickly as it had happened, there was a flash, and in that flash, for just a moment, Aira had seen two decaying bodies lying below a steep cliff. The image was enough to make her scream, terrified by what had just happened. She didn't even realize whom or what she was pushing away before it was too late. A loud crash was the first thing she heard when everything returned to normal, and Nathan lay unmoving against the steel lockers.

She didn't mean to push Nathan. Honestly, she didn't. An ambulance had to be called after that. Nathan had broken a few ribs, and from what Emma had told her, he had two purple hand marks on his chest from where she had pushed him. The lockers where he had fallen had to be replaced because of the large indentation he had made when he made contact.

Looking down at her hands, Aira wondered if she were some kind of monster or maybe if she were crazy. She didn't tell Drake or Emma about the weird blackout she had had. They had been upset enough when the school called them. Aira wasn't allowed back for a week or so — not until everything calmed down.

Aira sniffled a little, trying to hold back tears. She was so consumed in her own thoughts she didn't even realize someone had pulled down the ladder and climbed up into the attic with her.

"Aira...?"

She didn't reply and simply turned away from the voice.

Emma sighed when she had finally found her daughter. "Oh, Aira, I'm sorry... I'm just a little bit confused about you lately." She crawled up to the sniffling girl and sat beside her. "You know I love you more than anything, don't you?"

"I love you, my darling girl."

Aira finally turned to look at Emma and shook her head. "I didn't mean to do it."

Emma smiled reassuringly as she took Aira into her arms and kissed her cheek. "I know, sweetie. You wouldn't hurt anyone purposely. You should talk to Susan about it."

How could she? Susan told Emma everything. Aira couldn't trust anyone with something like this.

Emma looked around and after a moment of contemplating, decided to show Aira her surprise. "I have something for you."

"What is it?"

And for a fleeting moment, Aira thought Emma was going to hand her a waxing kit. However, something even better landed onto her lap. Aira's smile lit up the dark attic when Emma told her whom it was from.

"Van kept his promise." Emma's smile was almost as bright as her daughter's — *almost.*

Although the last few days had been hectic, Aira's hero came thundering through the storm and made everything better. Somehow, she knew he always would be there for her when she needed him even though he might not know it.

Everything would get better. It just had to.

Looking over the letter, Emma and Aira couldn't help but giggle as they cuddled and read the hasty writing. Even in letterform, Van was as serious as ever, but that's what Aira loved about it.

Aira,

I hope you're doing well. Emma told me about Newport. Congratulations! I hope you get settled in. The answer to your question is Moscow, my home. I may not be able to write you after this, but I hope you take your studies seriously and work hard. Tell Emma, Aiden is doing well, and that a phone line should be accessible soon.

Best Regards, Van

Yes, everything would get better in time.

Chapter Twenty-Two

He knew the feeling of complete abandonment. He knew the sensation of abandoning and being abandoned, and yet, he couldn't change a thing about himself. However, he could hang on to what little sanity remained. He hoped Aiden would never turn into what he had become. To become insane, he had to have been sane at one time. He laughed at the irony.

Sighing, Van shook his head to try to clear the fog around him. If he hadn't opened that Goddamn drawer, he wouldn't be thinking these mundane thoughts. It was possible he had opened the drawer to just catch a glimpse of it; it had been so long after all. As soon as he spied the object in question, all the memories came flooding back of that night centuries ago when he was just a child left on the doorstep of the Volkov's, the night *she* left and never returned.

Van growled and stood from his seat. Whenever he was in a decent mood, something always crushed it. Something always pulled him back to that time. He hadn't thought much of her existence since his last return to his homeland. That night usually came in brief memories; the most vivid one was when he had realized she caused his insanity when she saved his life. He had spent much of his adult life looking for her, wondering if she had died of old age or just floated from one life to another.

He could feel them getting closer, but the crunch of snow that seemed to be right beside him made Van jump back, frightened and trembling.

"It's okay. I won't hurt you."

Her voice was soft and caring. He looked up to take her in against the misty flakes that had previously blurred her out.

He let out a small growl, the kind an animal made when cornered. This didn't deter her as she used one hand to gently brush against his arm. "Don't be scared. I'm here now. I won't let anything happen to you, Van."

"Van?"

Van, momentarily distracted with the memory of *that* night, jumped slightly. He was rarely caught off guard but bounced back to reality quickly.

Van hadn't heard that voice in a long time, but the familiarity of it brought back good feelings. "Valentina, how are you?"

Her smile was that of sadness. "Today is a happy day, Van. Why are you sad?"

Van's brow arched a mile high. He had meant to block himself off but remembering the girl that saved his life as a child had left him open, and so his pack had felt his emotions. "I don't get sad, Valentina. How is Anton?"

She stepped closer, and Van averted his cold stare. The closer she got, the more she noticed the open drawer that always stayed locked. Staring at the trinket inside the drawer, she understood what Van had been thinking. She had almost forgotten it was *that* time of year.

"We have not forgotten, but we do not wish to remember—we forgot for your sake, Van. I know your mother and father are watching over you, and they would be so proud of the man you grew up to be." Her eyes were downcast and staring intently into that stupid drawer.

Van knew as soon as Valentina realized he wasn't at ease, she would be at his side. That was just the kind of woman she was. She was one of Van's closest and only friend, and through her, Anton had become one of his best allies. However, he treated them no differently to the rest of his pack.

"It was good to see Konstantin again, but I was slightly hurt that I was able to see our protector before our alpha. I was so busy trying to wrangle in Melor that I didn't have much time to talk." She paced the office, looking it over carefully as if it had been decades since she had stepped foot in there. "I had to apologize to Anton for making him babysit the pups. It was quite funny, however."

Van chuckled. "Melor must be a handful himself. He would be ten, wouldn't he?"

Valentina suddenly stopped pacing as she faced her leader and placed a protective hand over her slightly protruding belly. "He was born a month before you left, Van. A lot changes in ten years."

She laughed, taking away that sad note in her voice. "Oh, but how difficult it was to get you to even hold him. It took me years to forgive Anton for that stunt."

Yes, that was a memory he didn't wish to go back to. Throwing a newborn pup at him wasn't the most conventional way to get him to hold it. As soon as Melor was in Van's arms, he instantly returned the pup to its mother. Kasimir and Valentina spent the next few days making Anton eat out in the snow. After that, Van had sworn off holding any of Valentina's pups.

Van shook his head and stood up from his desk, closing the drawer as he did so. "I heard you are having a girl this time around."

Valentina's face lit up brighter than the night sky. "Yes! Can you believe it? Four boys, but finally, I will have my little girl. Someone who can finally understand what it's like to live in a house run by little men." She laughed.

Van shook his head but never cracked a smile. He was sure he had forgotten how to by this point in his life. It was troubling him how his thoughts always shifted back to things he never wished to remember. Maybe that is why he stayed away.

"How are Drake and Emma?" she asked with that same pleasant smile plastered on her face.

Valentina was the only shifter to accept Drake's relationship with Emma, other than himself. Even Kasimir had been hesitant to welcome a human into the pack, but after meeting her, Kasimir instantly fell in love with her charm and kindness. It was a trait Emma never even knew she had.

"They are well."

Her next question made Van stiffen considerably. "I heard they adopted again quite some time ago."

Van simply nodded. He knew exactly where this conversation was headed. It was a topic no one had dared bring up until now; however, Valentina was not hesitant to ask the questions others squirmed asking.

"Is it true… you saved a human?" Her question was blunt and left no room for excuses. Van never made excuses, to begin with.

His face seemed to darken as he answered. "And what if I did?"

Valentina's face dropped, and her pleasant tone seemed to take on an edge. "Emma was the exception because she is Drake's mate, but I will not accept another human. What they did to Samiul is unforgivable!"

The emotion that settled in the pit of Van's stomach confused him. He didn't think twice about his reply, however, as he said, "And what makes you think I care about your acceptance towards Aira, Valentina? If I don't remember that child killing Samiul."

"You're even using *its* name. How cute."

This conversation had become unsettling. Van was aware that Valentina's trust in humans was nil, but to even bring this up was made him think there was more to what she was saying. "I would appreciate if you did not call the girl *it*."

"And why is that?"

"Because we have a debt to pay to the human. Her family was killed by Ronan and his pack of rogue mutts. I just happened to stumble upon her when Drake and I were securing the area." He looked up and gave Valentina a hard stare. "Her mother and sister were torn apart in front of her. They were unrecognizable when I found them."

Valentina shook her head although her ashamed look said it all. "Do not try to sway me with pity. Aleksandra has told me everything, and it does not give you the right to say to me that I owe that human anything. I owe humans nothing."

"Who implied I wanted you to pity her?" Van snapped, which sent Valentina reeling back. Van had never snapped at her before.

It had seemed this reunion was turning into a war very quickly.

"Do you know what is being said? Aleksandra has seen that girl's future, and her future is to destroy us... to destroy *you*! Is it because she reminds you of yourself? Did you save her to repay a debt because you were saved by a human?"

Van chuckled darkly and shook his head. "I thought you had better sense than this, Valentina."

She shook her head slowly. Van already knew Valentina couldn't believe what she was hearing and quite frankly, neither could he. "You have changed, *Alpha*. Once Markus hears about this, he'll—"

"He'll *what*, Valentina?" Van interjected, his voice filled with anger and annoyance, "If Markus so much as lays a finger on that girl's head, I will rip his throat out." It wasn't a threat. It was a warning.

Valentina's soft face seemed to drop, and as she took a step back, Van ignored the tear that slipped down her cheek. "I'm sorry to have bothered you."

All Van heard was the soft clicks of Valentina's shoes as she made her way out of his office. What had begun as a friendly chat had quickly turned into something that made the dark alpha incredibly uncomfortable. In that one conversation, he had shown rawer emotion than he had in centuries. It disturbed him.

But to bring Markus into this... why would Valentina bring *him* into their conversation? Van hadn't spoken to Markus in years, not since his last meeting with the elders.

A loud knock at his door stirred Van from his deep thoughts, but without even looking up, Van already knew who it was. "What is it, Ivan?"

Ivan's constant grin irked Van. It was as if the red wolf didn't know how to pull any other expression. "A letter for you, alpha."

Van nodded towards his desk, and Ivan sat it down. As if the man could sense his leader's incredibly unstable mood, he said his goodbyes and hastily left the room. Van was grateful because, at that point, it would have taken an army to calm him down if aggravated further.

His head was reeling with thoughts. Everything Valentina had said just kept making loops in his head. Growling, he slammed his fist down onto his desk, creating a large crack in the ivory. It didn't bother him; it matched the numerous other cracks that covered his desk. His temper was still that of an angry bull — unpredictable, volatile and dangerous when pushed.

Grabbing the letter, Van ripped it open with one of his claws. He hadn't even realized his sharp teeth and claws had started to show but wasn't surprised. That tended to happen when he was angry enough.

Opening the letter, he was surprised to find it was from the human. Before he could even think about it, he was already reading away, scanning the letter. It was amusing, the things she rambled on about. However, once he finished reading, three words stuck out to him: flashes, dreams, and *wolves*.

She spoke about these flashes she had, the nightmares that plagued her, and the wolf-like dogs that chased her in every scenario. Van knew this letter was different from the others. Emma had obviously not helped her write this.

And as if something had taken over his motor skills, Van had already sat down to write a letter back to her.

After all, a promise was a promise.

Chapter Twenty-Three

FOUR YEARS LATER

There were three things she detested more than anything in life — thunderstorms, dishwashers and birthdays.

Well, *her* birthday to be more exact. Aiden, however, couldn't stop twitching as he grinned from ear to ear on the computer screen. Aira sighed heavily as she attempted to shut the laptop, only for Aiden to cry out and frantically wave his arms around.

"Hey, come on, you're sixteen and act like a cranky old lady!"

Aira's eyebrow perked up as she assessed what he had just implied. "You're an idiot, Aiden."

His lopsided grin quickly turned into a frown. "Hey, ouch?"

"What would you know? You haven't visited once since you left."

Oh, now, he understood. "Hey, Air, you know I can't. This is the best I can do for now." His frown was depressing, but Aira huffed in acceptance.

Aiden smirked as he suddenly recalled an incident previously that month. "This wouldn't have anything to do with Van not sending you any replies to your recent letters, would it?"

The mortified look that crossed the sixteen-year-old's face was all he needed.

"How-how did you… *who* told you?" she shrieked. If Aiden hadn't already anticipated this outburst and turned down his speakers, his ears would still be ringing.

He laughed, and that was it. She had had enough. Aira slammed the lid of her laptop closed before Aiden could let out another bellowing laugh and rolled her eyes. He used to be such a serious boy when they were kids, but it looked like his time away had turned him into quite the joker. Aira was grateful that they could at least Skype each other, but even that wasn't enough. Sometimes, all she wanted was a hug from her big brother, not a comforting smile from behind a computer screen.

She had sent countless letters for over a year now asking, well, more like begging, Van to come home with Aiden for a few days since her seventeenth birthday was only a month away. A year ago when she first brought up the subject, she was more than hopeful Van would come around. Her hope quickly diminished when Van blatantly told her no and stopped responding to any letters even mentioning the matter.

It wasn't fair! She hadn't seen her brother in person since they were twelve years old. This wasn't normal, and

Emma and Drake could never convince her otherwise. She understood Aiden was going back to the place of his birth and finding his roots but did that really take four years? She was getting tired of empty dinner places, Christmas's with no family, and birthdays with everyone but the people she cared about most. Everything just seemed so *wrong*.

Aira always had a hunch that Emma and Drake were keeping something from her but never questioned what it could be. However, she never understood why Emma and Drake could go and visit Aiden in his homeland, but she couldn't. She was always placed in the care of two or more people when her parents left and locked down tighter than Fort Knox until their return. She couldn't help but notice these people her parents surrounded themselves with were... well, strange.

However, Aira also wanted to meet Van again. Through their letters over the years, she had found in him a very close companion. Emma even hinted that Aira was starting to talk like Van and that her attitude lately had started to sour. Aira admitted she was being a pain in the butt lately, but that had nothing to do with her emotions towards their family situation. She was a practical girl and realized quickly that even though she hated birthdays, she wanted to become an adult as quickly as possible. Maybe then, Emma, Drake, and Aiden would trust her with whatever secrets they harbored.

"Oh, there you are. Any messages?" Emma asked as she quickly discarded her work jacket.

Aira's smile didn't quite reach her eyes. "No," was her nonchalant response.

Aira had been asking Emma for some time now if, after she had graduated, she could work with Emma in Van's wwwwÉÉÉÉww

ÉÉwwÉÉwwwwÉÉÉÉw

ÉÉwwÉ

ÉÉÉÉÉÉÉÉ

company since her mother was basically doing Van's job in his stead while he was away. Although Van did some paperwork from his current location, Emma took on all the heavy stuff. Emma always hit back with a solid "No" and told Aira she wanted her daughter to go to University and become her own person with her own aspirations and goals.

Emma had been working more and more lately, which didn't bother Aira. She liked to be alone with her thoughts. At one time, she used to love being surrounded by people and family, but after that incident in her first year of middle school, she preferred to be by herself.

Aira looked up from the homework she had started after slamming her laptop shut on Aiden and gave Emma an apprehensive look. The woman was dancing around the kitchen putting some dishes away and seemed to be skirting around something. The odd glances she was giving Aira didn't exactly ease her wary glance.

"You wanna ask me something?" Aira asked. She couldn't help the edge to her voice.

Emma froze as she placed a dish on the counter. Her sigh was deep and riddled with uneasiness. Aira could tell. "I got a call from one of your teachers yesterday. You're skipping classes again, Aira." She turned around to stare at her daughter, but all Aira could do was smile.

"Oh, yeah?" was her flippant reply.

Emma's eyes widened in shock, and she scattered to find a response. "What has gotten into you lately, Aira? Just a year ago, you were still the sweet, caring little girl I always cherished. I know teenagers go through a stage where everyone's the enemy, but I am not your enemy, sweetie."

Aira rolled her eyes as she went to grab her work from the bench and make a run for it. "I need to finish this."

"No! You are going to talk to me, and you are going to explain why you're doing this to yourself. You're so smart, Aira. Smarter than many kids out there, and yet, you want to throw all that away, for what? Because you're angry? What are you angry about?"

One after the other, the questions kept flying out like poisonous knives, but Emma wasn't done yet. "Even Van has noticed the change in your personality from your letters, he's concerned and—"

Emma was abruptly cut off when Aira spun around on her heel and glared. "What would he know? He left and took Aiden with him. You told me it wouldn't be long! You tell me every year that they won't be away much longer. They just left, mother. And do you know who else just left me? The people who gave birth to me. So right now, everyone's the same. Everyone leaves; I'm just readying myself now before I'm dropped like a sack of potatoes. Until you can tell me the truth about everything, I'll continue to treat others and myself this way. You told me I'm smart, so don't treat me like an idiot."

With that, she turned around and hurried up the stairs to her bedroom. This argument became almost a weekly ritual, and Emma had to realize she wasn't that little girl they humbly took into their warm embrace. Aira was growing up, and yet, after being with Emma and Drake for so long, she knew next to no one from her adoptive family. She didn't know who her grandparents were. She didn't know if she had any cousins or close relatives besides Susan and Van. She knew she was adopted, but did that mean ostracizing her away from everyone? Aiden knew his family; Aiden knew where he came from — Why did Aira know nothing about herself?

Why was she locked away from a world she knew nothing about? Drake would tell her it was for her own safety. But what the hell were they protecting her from?

Nothing made sense, yet they sat on their high horses wondering why she acted the way she did. It was a cycle she didn't want to continue going through.

Groaning, Aira opened her laptop and stared idly as she ignored the Skype calls from her brother. She would not talk to him right now, not until he started giving her the answers she wanted.

Chapter Twenty-Three

Aiden sighed and rolled his eyes as he shut down the computer. His sister was becoming more and more difficult with time. Her stubbornness was a surprise, considering the timid and happy little girl she used to be. He had noticed her begin to change when she was thirteen, months after his departure and her first week in middle school. Van knew what had happened to her but refused to tell Aiden. It was odd how Van almost protected that trust she had in him.

Ugh, girls, they confused him, well, human girls at least. Aiden sometimes forgot Aira wasn't like the rest of them. Aira was human, and Aiden had almost let the secret slip quite a few times. Aiden, a shifter, was naturally drawn to his pack and other wolves and did not even realize how this must have affected his sister. He missed his mother and enjoyed seeing her whenever his parents came to visit, but he most certainly wasn't homesick. In fact, leaving Russia and returning to the

States would leave him feeling more homesick than when he left almost four years ago. However, his mother and father could not be apart because of their bond. It was too dangerous.

However, he and Aira were almost inseparable as children. Wherever one was, Emma was sure to find the other. It was hard leaving her, but over time, they had both grown and changed. Aira had become a beautiful young lady and found her voice whereas Aiden left behind his pre-teen angst and became a confident young man. Perhaps, this place changed him for the better. He found he was wiser and more in tune with his wolf. He could even communicate with it sometimes.

The only issues he ever had were with Nikolai. The bigger wolf, in size and order, seemed determined to kill Aiden when it was time to train. Winter was easier than the warmer months because even though he didn't have fur, his skin was still much thicker and almost heavier than humans. Kasimir told Aiden that would cease once he shifted.

He had made friends quite fast, but no one extremely close. He had taken Melor in as a little brother of sorts, as he was three years younger. Being fourteen and already so in tune with his wolf, Aiden was a little bit jealous of him. Melor's mother, Valentina, and Van seemed to get on quite well, but things were tense there for a little bit in the beginning. Kasimir explained it was because Valentina had made a remark about Aira, and so, it had taken Aiden a while to warm up to the she-wolf. Even though he had accepted her, Aiden was still uneasy when in her presence. She had had a daughter a year or… three back… maybe.

Jeez, he couldn't even remember when Valentina had had her daughter. Melor would talk about her, but she was born a sick pup and was rarely allowed to leave Valentina or Anton's side. In fact, Aiden didn't think he'd even seen the girl with him being away on hunts and scouting missions so often. Practice makes perfect after all. It dawned on Aiden he knew more about his pack than he did about his own sister or mother.

"Heh, maybe she has a point..." he huffed as he leaned back in his chair.

"*Who* has a point?"

Aiden jerked back as he heard the familiar voice by his bedroom door. Van was good at that — sneaking up on people. Aiden could hear so many of his pack's thoughts and voices, but Van was good at keeping everyone else in check, but no one could sense his thoughts.

Aiden grinned after getting over his initial shock. "Yeah, Aira wants us to come home."

Van's eyebrows etched into an annoyed expression. "We have two more years before we can leave. Until Ronan's left, I can't leave, but you are welcomed to return, pup."

Aiden seemed to think this over. Van had never given him the option to leave before, but Aiden supposed it was due to a certain human's incessant pleading. "I'll think about it. You never know, I might invite her here."

Van didn't seem pleased with this answer as he turned to exit, muttering under his breath, "I have better things to do than protect that girl from wolves all day," and left.

Aiden chuckled as he did so. "Sure, you do."

Chapter Twenty-Four

Van cracked his neck as he trudged down the hallway.

Bring that girl here? *Here* of all places? That was like bringing the lamb to Sunday dinner. She wouldn't survive here with Ronan still lurking around, causing him trouble. If what Aleksandra said was true, Ronan wanted the girl dead. He'd rather not have saved her life only for her to be killed in his own domain. Still, Van was curious as what threat that little girl could have possibly held against Ronan.

Ah, but she wouldn't be a little girl anymore. Time didn't seem to exist in his world, and the human would have been nearly seventeen. He tried to pretend he didn't remember, but it was a hard task. He remembered her birthday was nearing. How could he forget after all those heartfelt pleas she had made for him and Aiden to return for this one day?

He growled low as he contemplated the idea. No, he would not have that child sway his decision. However, his resolve was wavering quickly as he remembered Emma mention a change in her personality. He would never admit it out loud, but he had formed a... friendship of sorts with the human he had rescued. Although he found that ever present smile of hers irritating, he did not want her to become cold and bitter over a situation she did not have any control over in the first place. His influence in his words alone seemed to rub off on her, and he argued within himself that the letters they exchanged had to stop.

He didn't have to think for long as Ivan, disheveled and noticeably irate, stormed up to Van and spoke so fast Van had to grab hold of his shoulder.

"*Say that again, slower, this time*," he snapped in his native language. Ivan was still learning English, a language Van preferred, but could not make coherent sentences even in Russian when obviously panicked.

"*Alpha, th-there are dozens of shifters in the courtyard! They want to speak to you.*"

Ivan was sweating and obviously psyching himself up for a fight. Van swore under his breath and cursed the human girl for taking away his attention to his pack and the woods around him. Van had felt an uneasy presence drawing closer earlier that day but ignored it as he had thought it was a pack simply passing through and moving on. With the strange weather and ever growing human towns and cities, it was nothing new.

But why did they stop *here*? Although known far and wide as a God and protector, Van made it clear to all shifters not from his pack that he would not shoulder their squabbles and fights among each other. As he made his way towards the front porch, he made a note to bellow that very thought out and make it clear.

The crowd that was gathered at the windows was mainly females. They gawked outside as if it were Armageddon. As Van moved closer to the door, they moved aside to let him through. Van nodded as they did so and threw the door open, letting it bang against the outside. His fighters and scouts were already trying to calm the chaos that was happening in his front yard. However, what Van saw was a very different scene to what he had imagined.

For the first time in a long time, Van was lost for words. Complete and utter horror stood before him, and all he could do was stand there, mouth agape, and stare. It seemed the dozens of shifters could already sense him because they all looked towards him in pain and fear.

"Ronan did this…"

Van tilted his head, already knowing the voice. "How many?" was his only question.

Kasimir sighed. "It may not look like it, but several packs were attacked over three days. Borya explained that they tried to send help to Konstantin, but the Taiga meant death if they came. Ronan had scouts and rogues ready to kill on sight everywhere."

"Borya…" Van whispered.

"Dead."

Van could feel a rumbling in his chest. He knew Konstantin was ropeable at this point, and there was no going back if he shifted. He would tear this whole place apart to find Ronan. If he wanted a war, then by God, Van would bring him his damn war.

Looking at the mothers and pups that trembled with claw and bites marks and even burns, Van chuckled almost insanely. "We wasted too much damn time! All this to secure my pack when there were others dying," he ranted as he jumped the veranda and made his way towards the injured. "He dies today."

Kasimir's eyes widened as he tried to form a sentence to stop his leader. He could see Van's claws sharpen and his form tense. "Van, do not do this!"

Kasimir looked up and noticed Aiden come up behind him, looking just as wide-eyed as Van had. It looked as if Aiden had overheard their conversation. "Aiden, talk some sense into him!" Kasimir pleaded. However, Aiden simply jumped out after his alpha, following him and growling menacingly. "That's not what I meant!"

As Van made his way towards the forest, he quickly scanned the injured souls around him before his gaze landed on a young woman cowering with a group of pups towards the end. He stopped to get a better look, and as she looked up to stare back at him with her pale blue eyes, Van's own eyes widened in sheer astonishment.

Whatever plan he had for Ronan would have to wait because his whole world, and his pack's, came to a complete standstill as he uttered, "You…"

She looked confused as she stared up at him. "What?" she whispered. She was obviously injured and frightened.

The air tensed up as they stared at each other. Memories flashed through Van's head as he remembered a time long forgotten when he was a pup, and his world crashed down around him.

Chapter Twenty-Five

Her accent was strange as if she didn't know how to speak properly. His father had once told him that there were many other languages in the world and that their language was just one of thousands. Did she not speak his language, or was she speaking slowly to calm him down?

It was then that he noticed her right arm was missing from the elbow down. His golden eyes widened as he stammered, "Where-where is your arm?"

It was quite frightening to see. He had never met anyone with a missing limb before. He didn't even know that was possible.

Her eyes seemed to dart down to her missing arm, but instead of taking offense, she simply smiled. "Oh, this? I was in an accident."

Memories he had pushed to the very back of his mind came flooding back almost instantly. Emotions he had kept bottled up — both hatred and love — were blazing throughout his body. The very reason for his contempt and compassion towards humans kneeled before him, and he stood petrified at the sight of her.

Her smile lit up her entire face. She gently patted the back of a weeping pup as she asked, "Is that my name?"

And just as suddenly, everything that was flooding back seemed to just disappear in an instance. But the girl before him had the same aura of the girl who had saved his life when he was just a pup, running from the slaughter of his pack. But the thought at the back of his mind told him that the girl from his past would never forget him so easily. Through time and space, he was sure that she would never forget who he was.

"You have both arms," he muttered without even thinking.

Maybe the resemblance is what startled him. There had been many girls who had resembled the girl who saved him, but none that stopped Van Volkov in his tracks, none that made him look twice and question if the human was still alive.

"I do have both arms," she replied. "Is that a problem?"

His eyes turned steely as he sized up the smaller female. "No... I suppose not."

His response made her frown as if disappointed. Van didn't pay any mind as he readied himself to deal with the chaos around them. That sudden flood of emotion completely wiped away his blinding rage at the current situation, leaving him to think about what he would do next.

"Your clan holds, what happened to them?" he asked. It wasn't so much a question as it was a demand. He wanted to know what had happened and when.

Her face dropped, and all color drained from her previously flushed cheeks. "I— They were burned to the ground, sir. We fled before the humans caught on and came to investigate the smoke."

The way she sneered the word humans made Van uncomfortable. Van was also curious as to why she could speak perfect English. Native shifters knew little English, as they preferred to keep to their traditional tongue, all except the few packs that had migrated to the States for safety.

"What's your name?"

Her eyes seemed to light up when he asked this. After a moment of thought, the girl grinned and quipped, "*You*, apparently."

He couldn't contain the low growl that rumbled through his chest at that sly remark. "Don't get smart, bitch."

She seemed to let his crude sentence roll off her back as she shrugged. "Borya named me Innochka."

Van couldn't help but arch his brow. Borya named her, which meant she was a stray that came into his pack. Innochka — one of innocence, the name seemed to fit her. It was a strange name, however. He'd never heard of it before.

Grunting his acknowledgment, Van nodded towards the main house. "Take those pups into the house. The females will know what to do. Can you mend wounds, girl?"

Her eyes were wide with wonder as she nodded vigorously. "Yes! Yes, I can, sir."

"Good, get to it then. There are a lot of wounded people, not just from your pack." He turned to leave but paused for the moment before turning back and saying, "And stop with that sir crap. My name is Van."

He faintly heard her say his name as he walked away, heading towards Aiden who stood waiting in the clear. Aiden had an expression of pure hate etched across his face as he looked around at the chaos.

"Is this what you brought me here for, Van? To watch people die by that-that bastard's hand?" Aiden growled out. Van knew this was the first time Aiden had seen something like this, and the alpha guaranteed this would not be the last time.

All Van could do was nod as he tried to hide his unease from his meeting with the girl. "Yes, Aiden, this is the problem I'm training you to help me take care of. This is what it's like to watch everything you protect and hold dear be destroyed right in front of you."

Aiden let out a soft grunt as his sight turned downcast. "We can't leave, not with things like this. I'm sorry, Aira," Aiden whispered that last sentence and kicked at the dirt with such force a large chunk went flying. "God fucking damn it!"

Time indeed did stand still for Van. Aiden had also grown up and with that came heavy responsibilities. Aiden had the burden of shouldering not only his own pack's safety but also every pack that was within Volkov domain.

"Stop acting weak, pup, and get the men in order. We need scouts to keep an eye on the outskirts to make sure that mutt doesn't head towards Taldom. It's his only direct route away from this land. Get the trackers out there and find whatever rogues are left feasting."

Van's posture was stiff, straight and alert. He needed to become the beast he had been before he boarded that plane four years ago. He was becoming too comfortable in his home that he forgot about the seriousness of the situation at hand. Ronan was out for blood — the blood of everyone who ever went against him, and Van would sooner lick a human's dirty shoe than lay down and die like a dog for that filthy mongrel.

It was time to take back the lives Ronan stole.

"There were three packs involved, all under your law, Alpha."

Van nodded as he crossed the room to look at the map Kasimir had laid out. "Names?"

"Vadim, Kirill, and Matvei, as you know, they were under Borya's protection in your stead. Borya held down Matvei until he had no choice but to evacuate, and his remaining scouts were sent out to warn our brothers who were still unaware in Vadim and Kirill." Kasimir sighed heavily, saddened by the whole situation before saying, "Unfortunately, we were too far for them to send a wolf call or get to us without being caught. Alpha Mikhail of Vadim is currently recovering from his injuries, but our brothers of Matvei are…"

"I get it," Van snapped as pushed his hair away from his forehead in frustration. With a low growl, it took all of his self-control not to rip out his own hair. "I'll head out there with Aiden come sundown when my scouts return with news everything is clear, not that I wouldn't like a run in with one of those dirty mutts. However, the faster we get to any survivors, the better."

There was a moment of silence as everyone in the room either quietly burned with absolute hatred or sighed out of grief. Aiden, however, stood to the side and stared out the window, looking at the wounded as his pack mates tried to find space in their homes or the main house for them to rest. He tried to keep his mind preoccupied when he noticed more than several bodies laid out with a sheet or coat covering their faces. He, as well as everyone else, knew what that meant. They were just more notches in Ronan's belt of carnage.

His trance was abruptly broken when Van growled, "Aiden, are you keeping up?"

Van watched as the pup nodded his head, but the Lycan knew better than to take Aiden's half-assed answer seriously. They were speaking Russian the majority of the time, and although Aiden was now semi-fluent in the language, Van knew the boy still found it hard to keep up with certain phrases and words.

"We're going to look for survivors from Matvei and Kirill, I know. These clans lost their alphas and betas, so they didn't have anyone to lead them here," Aiden answered.

Van nodded. It was an unfortunate situation. Borya and his beta stayed behind and sacrificed themselves for their pack mates. Van could only hope to go out the same way once this was all over.

"Why not go to Matvei as well?" Aiden asked, curious as to why Van rarely ever ventured out towards that clan.

"It's too close to Dimitriev domain, pup," Kasimir answered.

Aiden scoffed, "That domain is dead. There's nothing there anymore. For all we know, that's where Ronan is hiding."

"There are still human towns and farms out there, boy. Any shifter under Dimitriev law and protection might be dead, but the humans that reside there are still well alive. We have no claim over that."

Van rubbed his left temple as he thought about what they were going to do with the bodies of his brethren. It would take days to get them back to their land for burial, lest, he face the wrath of any God watching over them at that very moment.

The look Kasimir gave his alpha could have struck down Katia, spirit of time and fate, herself. "Listen here, boy, you were born on Dimitriev land. That claim is your birthright and so help me—" Kasimir paused as he sighed, annoyed by everything at that very moment. "Yet, you refuse to even step foot on that land. You wanted that land back once and now—"

The old wolf was cut off as the table between them was hurled over, causing a loud crash. The room was left in silence all except for the low, hostile growls of Nikolai from the other side of the study room.

Van ignored him as he snarled, "Sorry, old man, I couldn't hear you. Can you repeat that?"

Yes, this was the alpha Kasimir had come to know. This was the once angry pup that would have happily slaughtered anyone who didn't show respect. This was the man who showed anger first, rational thinking second. Kasimir knew his alpha's good mood was too good to last.

Kasimir had to hold out his arm to keep Nikolai from charging. "He'll have you dead before you take two steps, Nikolai," he warned. Kasimir knew Nikolai would take the warning more seriously if he spoke in his native language.

Van chuckled darkly before he kicked the already turned over table. It made a horrendous squeal as it slid across the hardwood floor before crashing into the wall. Van was already out the door and stalking towards the courtyard before the table hit the wall. They could hear his grunts and yells as he stalked further away.

Chapter Twenty-Six

Aiden sighed as Kasimir muttered, "Maybe I went too far there."

"*He was never good under pressure. He's a bomb ready to blow*," Nikolai grunted as he took a step back. He had psyched himself up for a fight although he knew full well he didn't stand a chance against their Wolf-God, Konstantin.

"He met a girl today. She made him stop in his tracks, and he was muttering something about her only having one arm. Is that what you were implying earlier when you mentioned Dimitriev?"

Aiden had been standing back and watching the whole encounter with a shocked expression. He had seen Van blow up many a time, but today, it had been far worse than usual. Today, it seemed like Van had lost all sanity because Aiden had never seen his alpha show that sort of disrespect towards Kasimir.

Kasimir seemed to know the reason behind Aiden's shocked expression almost instantly. "Get ready for a whirlwind, pup, because that is why they call Van a beast. When he is angry, he loses control. That is the boy I've always known, especially when his past is involved."

Aiden gulped back his nervousness as he nodded for Kasimir to carry on. Nikolai seemed to have lost interest as he snorted, "*I may not know much English, but it does not mean I am stupid. You can talk until your beard falls off, but she's never coming back. He should forget this imaginary savior at some point. It has been going on for far too long.*" And with that, Nikolai stormed out of the room.

Kasimir sighed and shook his head, "Those two are still children, no matter how old they get."

Aiden mimicked his mentor with an equally exhausted sigh. "I felt like I knew everything about Van by now."

Kasimir chuckled. "No, lad, you still have much to learn about Van's tough history, as well as your fathers. But, if you wish to know more, then I will tell you."

Aiden's brow arched up in almost the same way as Van's. "Yeah?"

Kasimir paused for a moment, probably thinking if this was a good idea. After a moment of debate, he looked to have concluded something inside of his head, and whatever battle was waged, the side that wanted to tell the story won over everything else.

"Van was born to a different pack many years ago. When he was just a pup, about ten years old, some rogues caught wind that he was the reborn Konstantin. His pack was powerful and was held at a higher power than even the

Volkov's, but overnight, they were slaughtered. Van's father managed to get him out in time but unfortunately, passed on to the other world before he could get his pup to safety… that's when Van was saved by a human girl."

Aiden stared in complete amazement. "Van was saved by a human? But he dislikes humans?"

Kasimir shook his head sadly. "To this day, no one knows if she was human or Lycan. She fought off the shifters that were hunting him down and brought him to Samiul, your grandfather, and Aemilius, a head elder. Van begged her to stay because, at that point, she was all he had, but she left him. Since then, he had a chip on his shoulder regarding her. No one ever knew who she was or if she ever even existed. All we know, for sure, is she had one arm, wore strange clothing and had a strange accent."

Kasimir smiled sadly as he gripped Aiden's shoulder. "Van created a wall that no one can penetrate, friend or otherwise. So don't blame him for the way he is. He can't show his sadness any other way. He covers his emotions with anger and a stone face. He sees a mate as weakness and an opening to destroy him when really, he is afraid of love in any form. None of us want to see him lose his mind again. To Van, humans will only ever look out for themselves."

Aiden's face contorted into a mixture of confusion and anger as he shifted his gaze back to the window, watching as Van gave commands and checked on the wounded. "But she saved his life. Doesn't he owe her that much?"

Kasimir's eyes went to where Aiden was staring. "Van was scared, weak and had just lost everything. As Samiul and I had gathered, he just clung to her, seeing her as protection.

Whatever connection they had, he saw her leaving as abandonment. He was inconsolable and just shut down. He would demand we find her, but we looked for months, and nothing ever showed up that she even existed. Perhaps, he created her in his mind to replace his father. Some say she was a powerful L'ightat that was called on to protect him. Whatever the case, she's either dead now or was a figment of Van's imagination."

"I've heard of L'ightats," Aiden muttered. "I was told they don't exist anymore."

Kasimir placed his hand on Aiden's shoulder. "No one really knows, son. Maybe they're just hiding — scared and confused just like us. But if they ever came back, it would be a very dangerous war if Ronan got his hands on one."

Kasimir removed his hand from Aiden's shoulder and walked towards the exit. "If that girl was real, I pray she never returns. Van does not need more blood on his already stained hands." Kasimir was aware Van already had enough blood to cover every wall in this large old house. "Van's anger towards her outweighs his gratitude. Maybe, he wishes she had left him for dead."

Aiden continued to study his alpha as he shouted orders and was becoming increasingly more agitated. Aiden could tell just by his face. "Not all humans are bad, Kasimir."

Kasimir chuckled as he turned to look at the boy. "Yes, your mother is a good soul, but she is the exception."

Aiden turned to look back at the older wolf with a small smile spreading across his face. "Not just my mother, there's another human that I know would never betray Van, and I think he knows that as well, and that's why she scares him."

Kasimir gave Aiden a confused look before shaking his head and exiting the room to help with the chaos still happening around the property. Aiden simply sighed and leaned against the wall, deep in thought.

Even if Kasimir didn't understand it; even if he didn't understand it; maybe, his mother and father didn't even understand what was happening, but Van and Aira's friendship was something not even this mystery girl could ruin. Even when Aira eventually found out their secret, Aiden knew her heart would always accept them for who they were, and deep down Aiden was sure Van knew that just as well as anyone.

Chapter Twenty-Seven

"Vaughn, if you don't get your big fat butt up this ladder, I will personally put you on a diet."

The wolf whined as he sat just under the attic opening. Aira could threaten to throw him outside, chain him up or even send him to the pound, but the second she mentioned cutting off his food supply was when she got results, fast.

Aira giggled as Vaughn huddled up the ladder just as she'd taught him when she was younger. Although the wolf was getting much too big to even still be allowed inside the house, she didn't mind. He couldn't fit in any dog bed, so she was happy to share her own with him. She didn't even mind cooking him up a feast every night for dinner. Emma kept reminding Aira that Vaughn was a wild animal and explained the dangers of keeping a wild animal contained.

Even though she did have a wild animal in her backyard, Vaughn never dug holes, he never tried to escape, and he had jumped on her only once in his adult life. She had fallen and hurt her arm, and Vaughn never did it again. Aira believed wolves were the smartest animals in the world. She had her friend to prove it. She even showed her teeth to greet him sometimes, which he licked and sniffed with a wag of his tail. Emma would often stare in shock and ask Aira to stop doing it. Her father, however, seemed to approve of it and even encouraged her to know more about wolves.

Aira gave out a strained groan as she pulled Vaughn up the ladder. When he was finally up and safe, Aira gave out a wheezing laugh. "This was so much easier when you weren't so... *big*."

Vaughn seemed to give her a contented look before licking her face. "Okay, big guy, don't slobber all over me and be quiet. Aunt Susan is downstairs with Mom, and I don't want her to ask me about school." She rolled her eyes and crawled to the back of the attic. "You know how hard it is to lie to her. It's like she does some sort of voodoo-hoodoo stuff on me."

As soon as Aira found her spot towards the back of the attic, she pulled out her mini flashlight and switched it on. Light shone through the little arch windows that surrounded the top floor, but even that wasn't enough to calm her fears of the darkness. She got herself comfy on the pillows she had hauled up there over the last few years and covered herself with a wooly blanket. Vaughn moved closer to her and rested his head in her lap although Aira was sure all he wanted to do was explore.

She smiled as she massaged his head. "You know what, Vaughn? I should probably apologize to Mom. I mean, I've been a bit of a brat, right?"

His little whine seemed to prove what she already knew.

With a soft giggle, Aira shook her head. "My parents mean the world to me, but sometimes, I wish... I wish I knew who I was. There's this giant piece of me that's out there somewhere, but I'm too afraid to go and find it. I'd say Aiden knows how I feel, but Aiden knows where he came from. I mean, Aiden's biological family and Dad's family have close ties whereas my own parents don't even seem to know where I came from."

Her smile slowly started to fade as she added, "I sometimes wonder if they want that little girl back. I didn't think about this sort of stuff back then, but now, all I want is that piece of me back so that... so that I can move on and let people in wholeheartedly instead of just using what's left. Do you get it?"

Aira huffed when she realized she wouldn't get an answer, at least, not an answer in human terms. "Yeah, well, maybe you understand a little. You don't remember where you came from either. But then again, you're not the one talking to an animal."

Aira pushed a strand of her dark hair behind her ear and closed her eyes. Up in this cold, dark place, she could dream and wonder all she liked without having to explain herself. She could wonder freely if she looked like her mother or if she had any siblings and not feel guilty. She could even go back to when she was younger and remember how many days she and Emma spent just talking about nothing. She could even wonder about Aiden and how things would have been different if he were still here. Would they still be close? Or would they fight like other siblings?

Aira wanted to believe that school wasn't a problem. Honestly, she did. She didn't want to be embarrassed by the fact she had no friends. That people were watching her every move, just waiting for her to mess up. She didn't want to believe that she was such an awkward person that she couldn't even make friends without spilling something or saying something wrong. She didn't want another birthday with no friends there to give her a punch for every year she was alive…

Uh, she hated being a teenager. She hated it, hated it, *hated it*!

Her grades didn't suffer, so skipping classes every now and then didn't really matter. In all honesty, she only skipped the classes that required her to do presentations and speeches. The teachers didn't seem to say much when someone would cough in the back and make insults like, "Fatso" and "Gross."

Maybe if you were born rich, you were born pretty. She wasn't born either one. Her mother was probably a teenager or maybe a prostitute or even sickly when she gave birth to Aira. Maybe that explained it. But Aira always wondered… if her mother didn't want her, why did she give her a name? Aira always thought that once you named something, you liked it enough to keep it. Perhaps, her biological mother did keep her at first and then decided to give her away, and Emma and Drake were just too kind to change Aira's name.

Aira was suddenly broken from her thoughts when Vaughn started so wriggle around. He wanted to play. Aira giggled and, in an attempt to keep him busy, threw an old pillow across the floor to give to him as a chew toy. Vaughn took the bait and skidded around to "kill" his prey.

"Woah, woah, woah, Vaughn, stay!"

Just then, Aira really did wish she had put him on a diet because his butt smacked up against a pile of boxes stacked up high. Before Aira could let out a scream, the boxes toppled on top of her.

With a pain-filled grunt, Aira shoved the fallen boxes away from her and glared at Vaughn. He didn't look sympathetic in the least as he shook the pillow in his mouth. Ugh, she had taught him how to sit, shake and even how to balance a treat on his nose, but she never taught him how to *stay*.

He was still none-the-wiser as Aira shakily got to her feet and prayed Emma and Susan didn't hear the commotion. As she bent down to pick up some of the spilled contents, she silently cursed her bad luck when she realized a picture frame had cracked.

"I hope this wasn't important…" she whined, a little distressed at the impending reaction of her mother when she found out. "Maybe there's an empty one in here…"

She sat the dust ridden picture frame aside and fumbled through a couple of boxes before she felt something nudge her leg. Looking down and praying it wasn't a rat, she noticed Vaughn had left his chew toy and ventured over to lick at the dust on the frame. After a moment of panic, Aira pushed the nosy wolf away and picked up the frame.

"Ew, don't lick that! Ugh, Vaughn, sometimes I feel like putting you in a… muzzle…"

She had looked down at the picture just as she finished her rant and, eyes wide, couldn't believe what she had found. Frantically, she pulled the sleeve of her jumper down and wiped away at the remaining dust.

Her mouth was watering as she felt the contents of her stomach making its way north. Her hands were shaking so badly she had to sit the frame on the floor just to get a better look at it. Without even realizing it, her eyes were welling up with tears of shock, confusion, and betrayal.

The picture was of five people. A woman with lightly tanned locks and big, almond-shaped eyes stood in the back, she was beautiful, elegant, and had a face that could even be compared to Emma's. Beside her was a man, possibly in his late thirties, early forties, grinning big and wide for the camera. He was obviously being silly.

A girl and a boy stood in the front. The girl looked around her age and none too happy. Her smile wasn't very big, and she looked awkward. Aira could instantly see the similarities between this girl and herself. The girl had a lighter shade of hair color, but her eyes, mouth, and nose made her look like a mirror image. Aira knew those eyes. She could almost remember…

"Aira… don't be scared…" she heard Avery whisper, her teary eyes staring up at Aira pleadingly.

"Ah…" Aira gasped and shook her head as a sudden flash crossed her vision.

Avery… Was that someone she knew?

Without giving it a second thought, Aira continued to study the picture. The boy next to the pretty girl looked a little more at ease as he laughed, probably from the face the man was pulling. He was darker than the woman and girl with dark eyes, possibly green or brown, and a handsome face. His hair was the same color as Aira's, and he looked to be very tall. Aira instantly knew she cared about this boy. She didn't quite know why.

Ian, her big brother, had also been playing with those dogs. But why was his arm bleeding? "Mommy, Ian needs Band-Aids…" she muttered, watching as her still frightened mother was trying to aid Avery as she walked.

She blocked out that flash as best she could. Her head ached as she carried on to the child in the man's arms. She refused to look at her, but Aira knew she had to know. She took a deep breath as she finally studied the little girl who latched herself to the man as if her very life depended on it. She had dark hair that curled at the ends. She obviously didn't like the hat she was wearing because she tried to pull it off just as the picture was being snapped, and the woman had noticed. The child had big blue eyes that were prominent in the sunlight, a great contrast to the other two kids in the front. She had a big gap in her front teeth from where her tooth had previously come loose but grinned without worry, copying the man.

Aira knew that that little girl loved these people very much, so much that she forgot about them to hide the hurt…

A tear slipped down Aira's cheek as she started to remember her parents, her brother and her sister – her life before darkness. Looking down, she had unknowingly pulled something else from the box. Whatever had fallen out, it was light and would have gone unnoticed.

It was a laminated newspaper article. The title read, "Six People Dead in National Park Wolf Attack." Below were pictures of the scene and the faces of the people from the photograph all except one — *her*. The ending of the article read, "*Local girl, age 6, was the only survivor from her family of five. She is in critical condition having major flesh wounds and suffering from exposure after being out in the cold for at least forty-eight hours.*"

As soon as she finished reading, all those lost memories came flooding back as if someone had just opened the floodgates.

With a chuckle, the graying man kneeled beside his youngest child and answered, "It's a grasshopper, sweetie. Touch it and see what happens."

Her little face wrinkled up in disdain. "That's icky, Daddy!"

"Mommy, I don't want Avery to dress me! I want you to!"

The tears were coming out, and she had no control over it. "Daddy…" she mumbled as if she expected something to happen.

Something did happen, however…

"Daddy…" she whispered. She had last seen her father playing with those big dogs before he yelled at her to go with her mother.

Her mother's breaths were coming out hard and uneven as she looked around.

"Okay, baby, you need to climb to where that opening is, okay? See it?" she pointed to the opening in the rocks only a short climb up while she held on to her daughter's tiny waist.

"Go!" Vivian *shouted, shoving Aira so violently upwards that a sharp rock went straight through the little girl's palm.*

"Avery, wake Mommy up!"

They didn't move. They would never move again. They were both dead, and she was left on the edge of a cliff to stare down at their lifeless bodies for two days.

She remembered.

"I'm scared!" she screamed out with all her might, gut-wrenching sobs following close behind.

Blood started to gush from her nose as the flashes came and went. Aira started to shake uncontrollably as she fell to her hands and knees, trying to calm herself down. It wasn't working, and she could feel her throat starting to close. It was getting harder and harder to take a breath of air. She tried her hardest to stay awake before finally collapsing into a convulsing heap on the floor.

Chapter Twenty-Eight

Emma laughed at some corny joke Susan made about the coffee at the hospital. Emma liked these times where she could be herself and talk about anything whether it was human or shifter related. She had confessed her worries of Aira to Susan, but the woman reassured the tired mother that Aira was just a teenager. It was healthy, and it was great she was speaking out instead of always smiling. Emma always knew that smile was too big to be true.

All through Aira's childhood the girl had never spoken out of turn or spoken back for that matter. She never even asked Emma or anyone for a drink when she was thirsty. It was as if she was trying to gain acceptance as if she thought she was a guest and not part of the family. Emma had also admitted to using Aira as a shoulder to cry on after Aiden's departure.

"Oh, don't be silly, Emma, I'm sure Aira wanted to comfort you just as you comforted her through those horrible nightmare stages," Susan reassured. "Children can be a lot more in tune with a parent's emotions than you think. She grew into a beautiful girl, mind you."

Emma smiled and took Susan's hand. "Thank you, Susan, for everything you have done for Drake, Aira and I. Without you, I'm sure Aira would have had a harder time adjusting. I mean, every night, in her sleep, she would cry either for her mother or for her hero. It broke my heart every time."

Susan giggled to cover her tears. "My pleasure, dear—"

A sudden, loud, thumping noise suddenly pounded from upstairs. Susan had heard it first and instantly looked up. Being a she-wolf, Susan could instantly pinpoint where the sound was coming from. She could also hear Aira's pet, Vaughn, yelping and making distressed sounds. In his own way, he was trying to call Drake for help.

At that very moment, just as Susan was about to launch herself out of her chair, Drake walked in with their dinner Emma had sent him out to get. It seemed he had heard the noise from out in the driveway. As soon as he heard their pet making those horrid sounds, Drake and Susan knew what was happening. Something was happening to Aira, and he was frightened.

Drake was the first to bolt up the stairs with Susan and Emma close behind. As soon as he reached the opening to the attic, he just about ripped it off its hinges before jumping up with little effort. What he found was something even a shifter couldn't handle.

His little girl, the daughter he loved more than his own life, was sprawled out on the floor convulsing and foaming at the mouth. Her face was covered in blood, and Vaughn was whining and jumping around her as if trying to get some unseen force off of her. As soon as he noticed Drake, he stopped whatever noise he was making and ran to him.

Drake, skidding to his knees, moved quickly as he seized Aira and held her still so she wouldn't hurt herself. He couldn't move her onto her side for fear of her banging her head against the hardwood floors. As he concentrated on his daughter, he ignored the horrified scream Emma let out when she came across them.

"Susan, grab her legs, so she doesn't hurt herself. Emma, call the hospital and tell them it's an R56 and to dispatch an ambulance. Make a bed available in emergency and ICU."

Emma tried to take deep breaths as she pulled out her cell phone and made her way downstairs to wait for an ambulance.

Drake grunted as he waited for Aira to stop convulsing. With all his strength, it was difficult to hold her in place without breaking any of her bones in the process. Although he worked in a children's hospital, he wanted to be the one who was there to help her in an emergency. He didn't trust someone he didn't know with his daughter's life.

As Aira's convulsions started to calm down, Drake stroked her damp hair out of her face and whispered, "It's okay, sweetheart, we're going to get you help."

He saved her life once; he'd save her again. Only this time, Van wasn't here to help them through it.

"Drake…" Susan whispered.

Drake looked up, confused before he realized what Susan was motioning to. Down beside them was the newspaper article released two days after the incident at the park and a photo of Aira and her family. Now, he knew exactly what was wrong with his daughter.

"Shit, she's in shock."

This was bad. They needed to move her soon to find out what sort of shock she was in. It could have been her heart or even a ruptured blood vessel from the looks of it. Anything could have happened to trigger this.

For the first time in his life, Drake Volkov didn't know what to do.

"Mommy, I don't want to go back to that place," she whined.

Her mother laughed and asked, "Why not, baby? Are those kids mean to you?"

Aira shook her head. "No." She pouted for a moment before finally explaining herself. "No, I have friends, but I like you more… and Daddy. I love my daddy."

Her mother laughed and kissed her on the forehead. Aira could feel the smile in it. "Of course, you love daddy more, what did I expect. Are you excited about camping this weekend? We haven't been camping since you were a little baby!"

Aira scrunched her face up. "Is Avery coming?"

Her mother nodded. "Mmm-hmm, of course."

"Yay! I can put worms in her bed! But shhh, don't tell," she quipped with a wide grin. "But… wait!" She waved at her mother with her hands, almost frantic. "How will the tooth fairy know where I am?"

Vivian laughed harder before giving her daughter a hug. "Mommy's a bit short this week, so I'll be borrowing that money."

Aira's face dropped almost instantly before she screamed and ran into the living room after her daddy. She explained what had happened and her Daddy grinned. "Dad needs some money too, sweetie."

Aira pouted and folded her arms. "You're both meanies!"

Her daddy chuckled. "Meanies who love you very, very much. We love you and Avery and Ian to the moon and back, and this weekend will be very special. It could be the last weekend we spend together as a family."

Chapter Twenty-Nine

Darkness is the best way to describe someone who feels so very alone. It's what most people feared, being alone in the dark and not knowing what was in front of you or behind you. It can be either incredibly debilitating or empowering. Aira didn't know which one she wanted — to be immobile and depend on anyone willing to help or to take control of her own soul slowly being sucked into darkness.

She admitted that she was weak, and her weakness was what controlled her, at least, her weakness for upsetting the one person who would have gladly given her the moon if she had asked — her mother.

Aira had been awake for some time but continued to lay silent as her parents stood by her bedside in a never-ending vigil. She didn't know how long she had been out for or what even happened for that matter. She remembered the pictures and finding secrets she wished had stayed just that — secrets. It was funny how, however, many days ago, she was so adamant to find out about her biological parents. She never imagined she would find something so sinister.

It hurt — it hurt so bad she almost she wished she had never woken up. It wasn't the fact that Emma had lied to her or even finding out she had indeed once had a beautiful, *normal* life. What hurts the most was finding out that they were dead. They were all dead, and they were never coming back.

The endless sobs continued as Emma filled the room with tears. "I-I should have hidden them better. I should have... I should have been watching her. I didn't know, Drake, I didn't *know* she still went up to the attic to be by herself!"

Aira cracked her eyes open ever so slightly. Besides the wave of dizziness that washed over her, she could still see her sobbing mother. Emma was hunched in a chair in the corner with a tissue box almost glued to her side. Her father, Drake, was kneeled down in front of her, rubbing her arms up and down in comfort while whispering some sort of gibberish.

She didn't know what exactly had happened to her, but she knew that what her parents found when they came and rescued her must have horrified them. She didn't blame herself for what had happened, but she did blame herself for digging deeper. Maybe this is why they lied to her. Maybe the reaction she had had was exactly what they had been afraid of all along. She could remember bits and pieces of those horrid flashes, but there were still things missing. What she could remember didn't make a whole picture.

Right now, however, she couldn't think of that. She needed to help her mother before she tried to remember anything.

Slowly, Aira opened her eyes. She had been awake for hours, awakening in the middle of the night while Emma snoozed beside her on the hospital chair. It took close to forever for Aira to calm herself down. Emma never even budged. She had had hours since then to think about things and weigh her options of what to say when she was ready to face Drake and Emma.

She wondered if this was what it was like to be a grown up. She didn't like making these sort of decisions, but she knew that their emotions were on the line. If this were what it took, she would keep this secret until the day she died.

Drake was the first to notice Aira's eyes flutter open. He raced over to her and cupped her cheek, "Sweetie, it's Dad, can you hear me?"

Aira didn't know why she giggled inside her head. Maybe it was the fact she could hear them perfectly this whole time, and yet, her father was making sure she wasn't deaf or blind. Truthfully, Aira wouldn't have minded that much. She had been a mute through most of her young life after all from what she could remember, anyway.

Emma came shooting over next. She grabbed Aira's hand and squeezed her so tightly Aira was sure she felt pins and needles start to spread throughout her hand and lower forearm.

"I'm not deaf, Daddy," she smiled as big as she could. For some reason, from the way her voice was all croaky and scratchy, this seemed like déjà vu like it had happened before. Perhaps, she simply recalled her time in hospital after the... accident.

Aira blinked as she remembered her hysterical mother by her side. Emma cried into Aira's hand — deep, heavy sobs — and repeated over and over, "I'm sorry. I'm sorry. Thank you, God."

A tear slipped down Aira's cheek as she used her free hand to touch Emma's head. "I'm sorry if I scared you, Mom."

For the first time since she regained consciousness, Aira saw her mother smile. That one smile made Aira realize that her decision to keep what she had found a secret was indeed the right choice.

It was like a whirlwind after that. Drake and a herd of nurses examined her and made her as comfortable as possible. She received gifts from friends of her parents and was holed up for hours while her mother finally went home to sleep. It was in the eighth hour that Drake finally came back to talk to her.

Aira grinned. "Hey, Doc."

Drake chuckled as he took her hand. "No dizziness or nausea?"

Aira was sure he had asked that nearly fifty times already. She shook her head, though. "Nope!"

He seemed happy with that answer for the moment. She was certain he would be back in an hour or so to ask the same questions again. That made her want to laugh.

It seemed like an eternity before Drake finally spoke, "Aira, honey, do you remember what you were doing before you collapsed?"

The million-dollar question she had been dreading. Aira had always been bad at lying especially to her parents. It had taken her months of practicing in the mirror and holding her breath so she wouldn't break down into tears just to lie with a straight face about her school issues. Right now, she had to be strong and say the lines she had rehearsed over and over in her head since earlier that day.

"I think… I was talking to Aiden about my birthday. Then, I had a little argument with Mom. It was silly," she smiled as big as she could to get her point across.

Although Aira knew her father was trying to pull an equally straight face, she couldn't help but notice his obvious sigh of relief.

Yes, now, it was clear. Her knowing the truth would surely break their hearts.

Drake let out a small chuckle before he squeezed her hand. Aira realized he wasn't any less worried than Emma.

"Sweetie, when someone's brain is… shocked, it can sometimes cause a very bad reaction. Something like that had happened to you, and so, your brain temporarily shut down to repair itself. Your heart's fine, your blood pressure is a little high, but everything else seems to be in perfect shape. Whatever happened, you can tell me," he urged.

Aira forced a hearty laugh as she kissed her father's cheek. "I'm fine, Dad. I really can't remember anything besides talking to Aiden about my birth—" Aira suddenly gasped as she recalled her brother. "Mom hasn't told Aiden about this, has she?"

Drake's brow arched up in confusion. "I don't think so. We haven't heard from Aiden in a few days since we've been here the whole time."

"A few days?" Aira asked, shocked. She hoped this didn't cause another nosebleed…

Drake sighed and patted her hand reassuringly. "You were asleep for four days, hon."

Aira groaned and shook her head. "Can you ask Mom not to tell Aiden, please?" She didn't want him to worry, and she didn't want to guilt him into coming home, not this way, anyway.

Her father looked hesitant but nodded. "Sure, no problem…"

She let out a sigh of relief. "Did I get any letters from Van?"

She remembered she had sent at least four letters the week before, and it was about this time Van would have sent a reply even if he did ignore her pleading for them to come home.

"You should get some rest," Drake smiled as he stood up. "And I'll go get you some dinner."

"Dad…" Aira tried to argue, but Drake shook his head.

"Just stay put, okay?"

Aira watched as Drake left the room. As soon as the door closed, she let out a deep sigh. This wouldn't stay a secret for long. She and Aiden had a strange bond. She knew he would know something was wrong, and she dreaded the outcome that would have.

Chapter Thirty

Emma let out a large exhale of breath as Drake explained Aira remembered nothing of that day. She could have screamed with joy, but instead, she simply hugged her husband as tightly as she could. She felt Drake's smile as he nuzzled into the crook of her neck. Emma knew that Drake was just as thankful.

They knew that if Aira remembered what had happened, she would have hated them for their lies. They didn't mean to lie; they just told her stories when the topic was brought up. Emma knew what it was like to lose a family, and she didn't want Aira to feel that grief even if she *needed* to grieve.

She sighed. It had been a very long four days. "Oh, I have to call Aiden back… he's been trying to call the house while we've been at the hospital."

She smiled as she pried herself away from her mate, only for Drake to keep hold of her hand. She gave him a questioning stare.

"Aira asked that you... *not* mention what's been going on."

It took a moment for Emma to comprehend what Drake had just said and her eyes widened. "What? But Drake, Aiden would never forgive us if we didn't tell him! What — this is ridiculous. Why?" She was sputtering so much she completely forgot what she was even talking about.

Drake squeezed her hand, and she knew he was thinking about his answer, given her reaction. "I don't think she wants him to worry."

Emma's mouth contorted into a sullen frown as she snatched her hand away. "Drake, I need some things from the store for dinner. I'm making Aira some pasta, so would you mind...?"

Drake gave his mate a skeptical look before nodding his head. "Sure... just, make sure you think about what I've asked about what Aira had asked." And with that, he left.

Emma sighed again, this time, her sigh consisted of sadness and defeat. She was conflicted within herself — respect the wishes of one child or faith the wrath of the other. It was a horrible situation, and she was horrible at hiding any sort of distressed emotions from Aiden. He knew when she was upset.

It seemed luck wasn't on her side as the phone began to ring. She let it ring out, not sure if she could hold in her tears until the message machine beeped and Aiden's distressed, almost frantic voice came over the speaker.

"Mom, are you there? Dad, pick up the phone, I've been trying to call for days." It was silent for a moment before

Emma heard Aiden talk to someone as if arguing and then a sudden chill ran up her spine as a deeper voice suddenly spoke.

"Emma, answer the phone now."

Emma was not a shifter nor would Drake ever try to turn her into one — it would kill her in the end as with any other human. But as Drake's mate, she felt a sudden pull. Van knew she was there; she knew he knew she was there. As he was Drake's Alpha, he was also hers. She couldn't stop her arm from reaching out and grabbing the phone from its charger. When she hesitantly pressed the call button, she was aware Van already felt her unease.

Chapter Thirty-One

He had felt it for days now. It was a feeling of dread as if something had happened. He had ignored it and pushed this feeling down as deep as he could, but as an alpha, it was his duty to protect all within his pack, including those he had left behind.

He knew Emma was listening to her son plead for her to answer as he felt her energy spike with nervousness. When she finally answered, he felt his annoyance turn to rage almost instantly with her hesitation.

"What happened, Emma?" he growled. Something had happened; he had felt it days ago. It was as if his head had been split in half. He had ignored the strange sensation but quickly realized something was not right. His brother had even blocked him out, which caused the alpha to raise his concern with Aiden.

Normally, he wouldn't bother using control over his brother or his brother's mate, but when Van Volkov wanted answers, he would need to turn to such means. He would *not* be lied to.

"Everything is fine, Van," she chirped with what sounded like a forced response.

He almost felt his eye twitch. "Do not lie to me, *human*."

He ignored Aiden's low grunt, feeling the pup's anger rise at Van's blatant disrespect for his mother. Van didn't have time for this and gave Aiden a curt glare. Something was most certainly *not* right, and he would find out what was wrong even if the pup hated him by the end of it. He was a hated wolf throughout most of the world, anyway.

He knew Emma couldn't go against him any longer when she quietly said, "Aira collapsed... She's in the hospital recovering."

It was as if his vision was clouded in red. He could feel his muscles spasm as if he were about to turn. His claws sharpened. His fangs grew as if he were about to go into battle.

His eyes turned to slits. All he could see was a glimpse of that human, only a child, back in that hospital with tubes running each and every other way keeping her alive.

"Van…" Aiden said as he moved towards him. He had heard what his mother had said, but before he could properly voice his concern, he was obviously taken aback by his Van's sudden aggressiveness.

"When?" he all but shouted. He could feel something close to dread rising in his gut. He didn't stop to think about it too much. He was too caught up in something he, himself, couldn't even explain.

Van could sense the shock and fear in Emma's voice as she replied, "Four-four days ago, on Monday night."

Emma and Drake were about a day behind him. He had felt that overwhelmingly terrible sensation early on or around Tuesday. It didn't make sense to him, and he was far too stubborn to see that it could have possibly been his link to Aira. He had no link to that human.

His anger seemed to take control of him, and before Emma even explained what was going on, Van had hurled the phone at the wall. The wall cracked, and the phone smashed to pieces as he turned and marched towards his office, leaving Aiden to deal with the situation on his own.

As soon as he made it to his office, he unleashed what he could only explain as an emotion he didn't care to feel again. He needed to calm himself down, and the only way he knew how to was to wreak havoc on whatever was in his way.

However, before he could take out his anger on his desk, Aira's face flashed through his mind for a brief second. It was a face that looked much older, but it was that girls face. He hadn't seen her since she was a child and couldn't have possibly known what she would have looked like now.

He leaned against his desk with his arms steadying himself. He dipped his head down and took a deep breath. He needed to calm whatever was making his wolf want to come out and tear the house down. He knew this wasn't he; that this was his Lycan's reaction. Konstantin was riled up about that human girl.

"Mate! Hurt... Help!"

His lips pulled back into a feral snarl as he took the edge of his desk and hurled it into the adjacent wall. The sudden crash caused the room to shake, and Van grabbed his head with his hands, hoping to get his Lycan to just stop.

"Ugh..." he grunted and then exhaled slowly. The absolute need to run as far away as he could was overwhelming. He needed to concentrate. He needed to stop this assault Konstantin was displaying.

Breathing in and out in an even motion, he pushed Konstantin to the back of his mind, bringing his rational thought and energy back to the forefront. The pressure began to take hold as he collapsed to his hands and knees as if begging the Lycan to just stop this onslaught of pain and emotions.

Just as suddenly as it had happened, it stopped mysteriously. Van panted hard as he gathered his wits and tried to make sense of the whole situation. He never had that reaction to anything. Van Volkov didn't lose control. The only time he had remembered losing any sort of control over Konstantin was when...

Van snarled as Konstantin tried to come back through as if trying to shift his thoughts elsewhere. After a moment of struggling within himself, Van finally found the strength to lift himself from the floor.

He took a moment to collect himself and after picking up his desk chair, sat down with his head in his hands. Konstantin was never a Lycan one could easily control, Van was well aware of this fact, but after decades of peace with his inner demon dog, he had thought himself the dominant of his own body.

Van's eyes, glowing gold, slowly dimmed as he calmed down. He tried to think of what could have caused this and if it would happen again.

A light tap at the door was what initially broke him from his thoughts. He didn't have to sniff twice to know who was at his door.

"What?" he barked.

The door creaked open slowly as Innochka popped her head into the office. "Sir…?"

His growl could have made the floor rumble. "I told you to call me Van…" He paused for a moment before sighing. "What is it?"

He heard her gulp nervously and snapped, "Well?"

"I… I wanted to see if you were okay. I heard things crashing and—"

"—and Elina didn't tell you to stay away?" he finished.

Her mouth was agape as she struggled to find something to say. "Ye-yes, she did, but I wanted to see if you were alright."

There was something about this girl, something besides her looks that Van just couldn't pin point.

Quickly getting to his feet, Van stepped towards her. He grabbed her chin with his thumb and index finger and tilted the shocked girl's head back ever so slightly. Her eyes wide, he looked down at her face as he studied her. The heat that instantly rose to her cheeks didn't go unnoticed.

After a moment, he let her go. "Do you know your way around the areas where packs Vadim and Kirill used to reside?"

It took a moment for her to register his words before she nodded quickly. "Yes."

He stepped around Innochka before heading out the door. "Good, you can come with us to scout the area. I haven't been around those parts in ten years."

He moved to walk down the hall when her voice stopped him. "You can call me Inna, Van…"

He tilted his head to look over his shoulder. He saw her eyes were wide, and she was smiling as if it were Christmas morning. He felt the corner of his mouth twitch up into a smirk before simply nodding and continued to walk.

Inna trailed behind him. That smile still stuck on her face.

"I'm going back to the States to see if she's really okay," Aiden muttered as they trekked through the dense woodlands.

Van didn't even pay him a glance as he said, "Do what you want, pup."

"And you're not coming with me?" he asked. Aiden was annoyed with Van's curt answers. It had been this way since they started for Vadim.

Aiden could tell Van wasn't the type to go running to someone when they were ill and offer some kind words. That just wasn't him, but it wasn't fair, besides the letters Van and Aira exchanged, he still refused to even speak to her on the phone. Aiden shouldn't have been surprised with his response.

"I don't have time," was his blunt response.

Aiden eyed his uncle before letting out an exasperated sigh. "I know what you really mean to say is, 'I don't have time for the human.' Is that it?"

He could tell that one really irked his alpha, but before Van could respond, a loud cry made both Lycan's look behind them.

Aiden rolled his eyes when he noticed Innochka had fallen behind and stumbled over a thick tree stump. It seemed like they were leading her instead of the other way around. Most of the shifters that were trained or experienced in this location were either injured or dead. The ones remaining were too frightened to leave the safety of Volkov grounds.

Aiden, with a deep sigh, turned to go and help her again. She was still too weak to jump using the trees or even run, so they had opted to walk. It was slower, but Van didn't seem to mind, and Aiden just felt sorry for Innochka.

Just as he turned to go and help her find her footing, Van held his hand up, silently telling Aiden to stay. The younger wolf obliged and watched as Van went to Innochka and held out his hand. The girl smiled and happily took it, using Van as leverage by holding onto his shoulder.

The rest of the trip consisted mainly of this, Innochka smiling at Van and Van occasionally asking if they were heading the right way. It was odd not being able to sniff the air and just know what direction to go.

Although out of sight, Van knew that Nikolai and another scout, Demyan, were following closely by jumping the trees and cliff sides. It made it easier if they ran into anything dangerous so that they had invisible allies to help.

Finally, after some time, they made it to Vadim. It was quite obvious that the fires had been put out by human hands, but because Van had already contacted police, an investigation wasn't lodged in the fires, and bodies had been removed prior to any human interference. Those that passed would be buried with their native ancestors on their pack's land. It was law within their world. They deserved to stay on the land they were born and raised for fear their spirits would come back as a wondering mess and their wolves, the beasts that lived within their very being, would never be able to go on or be reborn. After all, a lost and forgotten wolf was often an angry wolf.

Innochka gasped and grabbed hold of Van's hand. Van scanned the area for any immediate threat, and when it was clear, he brushed off the easily startled girl by removing his hand from hers and moved to look at one of the homes left in complete chaos. Innochka didn't seem to mind as she wondered over to another home in search of any survivors.

Aiden took his chance to continue his discussion, but Van seemed to have already been clued in on Aiden's motives when he said, "I will leave when I feel the time is right, pup. I won't leave without fixing loose ends here. Too many lives are at stake."

Aiden looked down. "I know how it happened. Mom said Aira found some pictures of her real family in the attic and that Dad had found her up there just... shaking and unresponsive."

Van's body immediately went rigid when Aiden mentioned the girl's family. "So, she knows?"

His face never changed from that stoic mask he displayed as Aiden nodded. "Yeah, guess so... but she can't remember what had happened. Mom said that's normal for people who have seizures or pass out."

Van didn't know if that was such a good thing. However, all that played through his mind was that she knew. Somewhere, deep down, she knew the truth, but Van wasn't there to take on that problem for Drake. He refused to go running back to look after an issue he never wanted to begin with. He wasn't going to get his hands dirty a second time with the human.

Van still wondered why he had saved her. He had thought his inner Lycan knew the answers to that question, but whenever he had a reaction that stirred Konstantin, the words the Lycan cried out were gibberish and didn't make sense. He was sure Konstantin was trying to warn him or tell him something, but when Van wouldn't or couldn't listen, Konstantin would take his wrath out on the man that contained him.

He even thought Innochka had caused Konstantin to suddenly attack her, but when he touched her and stared into her eyes, he knew that Konstantin had no connection to her despite her resemblance to his past.

The wind shifted, and a scent wafted through the air, turning Van's attention in the direction Innochka had ventured off to. It seemed she had found her way into one of the abandoned houses.

Van stepped forward and nodded towards the house to direct Aiden, who had already noticed. Van saw that Aiden's energy had shifted, his posture had straightened and his jaw was tense.

"Aiden?"

The scent, which had now turned into two scents, wasn't threatening nor was it even male although, from the smell, Van could already tell that the owner was indeed frightened and panic-stricken.

"There's... something calling me," Aiden muttered as he stared directly at the burnt out structure.

Van's brows furrowed as he started for the house. "Then let's see what it wants," he growled and with one swift kick, he turned the already shaky door to splinters.

It took all of two seconds for them to head up the stairs and find the scents in question.

Innochka stood in front of a young woman who cried into her shoulder. The girl heaved and hiccupped every now and then, mumbling hysterically in Russian, "Tanas, thank you! I knew he would lead you to us!"

It seemed the girl was a pack member of Matvei for Tanas was a spirit who controlled destiny and fate, a divine that pack members of Matvei constantly depended on. Van had already suspected Borya had taken in Innochka simply because he thought Tanas willed it to happen. Though his Lycan was known as the God that protected them, Van believed in none of it. He believed you controlled your own fate and happiness, not that he would know what it was like to have any of that, anyway.

Innochka smiled though it didn't quite reach her eyes and brushed back the woman's hair gently. "Calm yourself, Olya. You're safe now."

The alpha seemed to take no time in getting to the point. "Are there any others?"

Olya's eyes, void of any appeal whatsoever, stared at the alpha, apprehensive. This girl looked very familiar to him as if he had seen her before many times.

It seemed Innochka sensed her hesitation. "No need to be afraid. This is Alpha Volkov. He saved us when we made our journey to his pack's land."

Olya's eyes immediately widened in shock. She seemed aghast and disgusted all at once as she spat, "Alpha Volkov... where was Konstantin when we needed him? Where were you when our homes were set ablaze and those... those monsters took my father's life?"

Ah, now he remembered her. Van remembered Olya very well. She was Borya's eldest daughter. The way she held herself and her overall attitude towards a wolf with power told him she was indeed the hotheaded child of an alpha. Borya did not raise his girls to bow down to just anyone.

"I didn't get word until an army of shifters made camp outside my front door, so I advise that you start teaching your tongue respect before I rip it out. I'm sure you'll find something to take the edge away from that... problem as soon as we go back." The harsh edge to his voice had certainly made that angry expression instantly disappear.

Van did not and would *not* take lip from a bitch in heat. He could smell it a mile away, which was probably the scent he had smelled earlier. During mating season was where most deaths occurred, mostly due to females such as this. The shock of her father's sudden death and the evacuation of her pack was probably what held back any aggression she may have had. It wouldn't have surprised him if the females above the age of twenty-three from Matvei were all suffering from more than just grief. He was going to have a field day having Drake import him sedatives and hormones to calm down these annoying she-wolves.

Her face instantly turned red out of embarrassment and anger. Whatever sort of garbage she was raging about next fell on deaf ears as Van seemed to have picked up something strange. The second scent he and Aiden had noticed seemed to have become sweeter, almost as if…

Being an alpha, Van had inherited a lot of traits, and knowing when a female shifter was close to her life-mate was one of those traits he rarely ever felt the need to acknowledge. He found those sickeningly sweet scents terrible on the nose and often ignored them when possible. After realizing just what was happening, Van grunted disdainfully and swore under his breath. He had never hated his heightened senses more than that very moment.

Aiden was in a trance beside Van, and it took all of the agitated alpha's willpower not to just punch the boy in the face that very second. With a low growl, Van broke Aiden from his blank staring contest with the wall and nodded towards a room to their left. "Go in there and check for bodies."

Aiden seemed to stiffen for a moment. "Wh-why?"

Van held back the urge to chuckle. It didn't surprise him that Aiden was wary of going inside; after all, his way of life would change after he found what was inside. This, however, did not please Van in the least. Aiden would be weaker and more vulnerable when his time came to take Van's place as alpha, but Van would not deprive someone of something they search for since the day they are born. He would not push his hate and fear onto Aiden.

"Do it before I drag you in there," Van sneered. The pup had moments to do it before Van changed his mind.

Olya seemed to have momentarily forgotten about the older alpha wolf as she gasped, "Lillya!"

It seemed that was the push Aiden needed as he heard his mate's name for the first time. In an instance, he barged down the door, and that was all it took. Van began to make his way down the deteriorating stairs to meet Nikolai for an update and to see if he had found any others.

Sighing tiredly, Van just hoped this would take Aiden's mind off of the *human* back in America. Deep down, he knew that, somehow, she was the cause of his unease and loss of control over Konstantin. He would no longer reply to her letters nor would he spend any more time thinking about the matter.

As soon as he got out the door, his legs suddenly gave way to his weight, and he fell to his knees. Konstantin would fight him, but he would fight back just as hard.

He would never admit to what he knew deep down was true.

Chapter Thirty-Two

For God knows how long, the celebrations had been endless. Aiden was praised and congratulated for finding his mate at only eighteen when some waited decades. Although born with an overwhelming desire to find one's mate to become stronger, not all shifters found their other half. The most common problem was the way wolves seemed to humanize themselves in a society where their kinds were merely legends. They would move on after waiting and then come to find themselves settling with humans.

Van was sure his pure blood would soon be diluted through reproduction with humans. He was certain nature would find a way to make that happen. Although Lycans from his ancestry could never have pups with humans, Mother Nature had a way of... adapting.

But then again, if Mother Nature had a way of adapting and using natural selection, he wondered why the hell it didn't kill off the mongrel standing in front of him.

"Van, brother, it has been so long!" the man chirped.

Van could feel his entire face go into an uncontrollable twitch, as he responded morbidly, "Not long enough, Savelij."

Within the world they were born in, male shifters considered themselves brothers to each other. Normally, Van wouldn't have had a problem being referred to using the old ways, but he found himself quietly gagging when Savelij used the term. He was nothing but a lapdog to Markus Perov, and Van had no respect for tail chasers.

Speaking of which…

"How is Markus?" Van flippantly asked.

Even though Van hated to admit it, Savelij and Markus were both wolves of high blood, and therefore, he *had* to ask if his ally was doing well. Though, he wouldn't have felt the need to send a well-wisher card if Markus was already six feet under. Van would probably have a party… with fireworks.

Savelij didn't seem to catch Van's bored undertone. "Yes, yes, he's doing quite well. Calista is also doing well if you haven't heard."

Van's brow arched. "Oh, yes, Calista, I owe my gratitude to her. She helped my—"

"Mate!"

A sudden familiar pain shot through his head, cutting off his sentence. Konstantin rumbled forth once more, and Van pushed him back into his place of slumber. It was becoming a normal routine over the last couple of days.

"My… beta's daughter get into the school she had wanted to attend." Van repelled the urge to groan as Savelij gave the alpha an amused smile. Although he and Drake were technically adopted brothers, Van rarely referred to Drake as his brother.

"Is that so? I heard about the human child your brother took in after Ronan went rogue in Washington. Such a waste of a talented lycanthrope." Savelij shook his head as if it were such a travesty.

Van, for just a moment, wondered how long this degenerate would live if he just let Konstantin do as he wished. The odds were in his favor — Savelij was known as a coward when it came to either war or fighting for dominance.

Van decided to get the topic away from Aira for fear his demon wolf would have some sort of negative reaction. Still confused as to why the girl triggered such a strange thing in Konstantin, he refused to even consider that she could be his…

"Yes, well, rogues are killed on sight. Ronan chose that way of life and so, all I can do is try to minimize as much damage he is doing as much as possible," Van muttered.

Savelij's face dropped as if Van had said something completely ridiculous. "Van, *please*, let's not throw Ronan in with those animals. We prefer to label him as a renegade, so you'd be getting into a tad bit of trouble if you or yours killed him before his capture." That hideous smile reminded Van of just why the shifter needed a good roundhouse kick to the face.

Van absentmindedly cracked his knuckles as his claws extended from his fingernails. He should have known those old bastards would do this. They wouldn't want their own monstrous creation dead before they got hold of him themselves. The elders and high council believed they could reform a wolf that had caused so much damage and bloodshed to his own brethren that they lowered his status from rogue to renegade. They'd rather see clans and packs rot in their own shit than have Ronan destroyed.

Van knew very well that he had no place to criticize; he was a monster of their creation as well.

However, instead of killing the messenger, Van gave Savelij a sinister smile. "Those *animals*, as you call them, stay away from lands owned by shifter and man alike. Ronan sets those lands on fire and chases *your* people from the only home they have ever known."

Van's arm extended to the window. Savelij looked outside and saw the tents pitched where the retreating packs had now taken shelter.

"We don't have enough houses to cater to the masses that sought my protection, so they're forced to live out in the open and camp outside my front door. They have no home to return to because of Ronan. Some have no family to return to *because* of Ronan." Van thought of Olya and Lillya as he said this, "Borya is dead, and I am left to find a safe haven for his two daughters."

He also briefly thought of Aira and how Ronan had hunted her family down like common dogs — he had killed humans who had nothing to do with this fight. Yet, Van still did not know why Ronan targeted a little girl and then simply left her there to die.

To die alone in a hole, Van thought disdainfully. For all the grief she would have to deal with in the future, he should have killed her the moment he found her. He was merciful, and now, she would pay with a lifetime of mental anguish.

Ugh, he kicked the girl from his thoughts. He had to concentrate on Savelij. Van didn't trust this moron as he could throw him far.

Savelij seemed to have caught on to Van's little guilt trip. "Sacrifices must be made in this waiting game, I suppose. After all, it seems he's invading *your* territory only at the moment. In all honesty, it's surprising that he let so many get away. I wonder if he was trying to shift your attention elsewhere…"

It was obvious Savelij was trying to ignore the way Van's eyes glowed gold in his anger. His head snapped to look at the moron and with a sneer, asked, "Explain, before I throw you out this window."

The normally calm lap dog's energy spiked with panic. Savelij knew from experience Van didn't make threats he didn't plan to keep, and they were very high up.

Savelij hid his fear as best he could and gulped back a lump forming in his throat. "Markus got word that Ronan returned to the States three days ago… to get a head start."

A snarl left Van's throat as his canines began to show. Things had been quiet since his return, but now, it made sense. Ronan was biding his time and letting Van become comfortable.

"And it took you *this* long to tell me because?"

Savelij laughed nervously as he backed away. Van knew he was struggling to stay upright from the sheer rage of energy seeping off the alpha. It was clear who the dominant wolf was.

"You don't react well to bad news...?" was his only excuse.

Van had just about had enough. Not only was Konstantin trying to come out but his own anger was also begging Van to *let* Konstantin out.

He chuckled darkly. Savelij didn't have time to react as Van grabbed him by the collar of his suede jacket and ripped him back, making the dopey wolf fly back into the wall behind them. While Savelij was left to get over his initial shock, Van's clawed hand was already around his throat and mouth, holding the flailing wolf in place as Van lifted him inches from the ground. The angry alpha pulled his free hand back and flicked his wrist, showing Savelij his sharpened claws and letting him see just how much damage they could do, especially to the jugular.

Van smirked before moving his hand that covered Savelij's mouth an inch to let the moron speak. "Ma-Markus, he'll send fighters out here after you!"

His smirk never vanished as he chuckled, "And why would any *puppies* Markus sends out scare me, lap dog?"

He didn't miss a beat as he struggled to answer, "Be-because Ronan's going after that human you rescued! You'd be wasting time fi-fighting Markus!"

All Savelij felt was the ground hitting him from beneath. With a grunt, he collapsed and looked up at what could only have been Konstantin taking over Van's body. His hunch was verified when Van spoke, having his own normal tone as well as a deeper tone of voice mixed in.

Konstantin had come out to play.

"How do you know about Aira?"

Savelij instantly regretted angering the dark wolf. All he could do was splutter and shake as he responded, "Everyone knows about that-that human girl you saved! Ronan wants her, he... he told Markus himself!"

Pathetic, Van thought as his face turned up in disgust.

He should have known Markus was still in contact with Ronan. Markus chose to be Switzerland in this power struggle although Van never did expect higher ups to choose sides and take cover. Ronan used to be in Van's situation, protecting humans and wolves living in peace beside each other, but then he started to have strange thoughts. Ronan started to become paranoid, edgy and unsocial until finally, he believed all humans should be destroyed or live under Lycan law. Ronan believed in the old ways of the world they had descended from. Lycans, the first wolves to leave that world and live amongst humans. Even Van didn't wish to return to Altholo, and he sure as hell wouldn't serve under Vorra.

Van Volkov served *no one.*

Van stomped away from Savelij, knowing the idiot would find his way out on his own. It was best he gave the wimpy wolf a head start before his merciful mood took a turn.

Van had some planning to do. It seemed his return to the States would be a little earlier than expected.

Chapter Thirty-Three

He didn't know he could feel this way about anyone before Lillya came along. It all happened as if it were some sort of dream. He had been terrified when he had heard his wolf rambling in gibberish and going crazy. Aiden hadn't figured out the name of his wolf just yet or even spoken to him very much, but Aiden knew something was not right. The intensity only seemed to worsen the moment he and Van entered that house in Vadim.

He had sensed the girl but refused to budge. The feelings and overwhelming need that jolted through him scared the living hell out of the poor boy. He had only been snapped out of his confusion when his uncle had ordered him to go check the room nearest to them; it was as if Van *knew*. Thinking back on it, he hadn't thanked his uncle for being so demanding. Being an alpha, Aiden couldn't deny Van and had gone to move into the room when Olya had mentioned his mate's name.

"Lillya."

That finally pushed and sent him flying into the room. When he had first seen her lying there on the ground and staring wide-eyed at him, his first instinct had been to go and inspect her for injuries. He had stayed back, however, using every ounce of self-control he could muster. He didn't want to scare her. After a moment of simply watching each other, he could feel it. She had injured her leg. It was as if Aiden's own leg had the deep slash. It was that strong.

Despite her wound, Lillya had smiled at Aiden, and everything seemed to instantly fall into place. All confusion simply melted away, and *they* just seemed to make sense. The moment Aiden kneeled and touched her cheek, it was as if he had known her his entire life. Her memories seemed to mesh with his, including her father's death, and he could feel his own memories flooding into her.

He had felt amazing afterward, and when they returned to Aiden's pack, everyone seemed to know as soon as they seen him with Lillya. She and Olya were accepted almost instantly within the pack and were as if they had never known anything else. It made Aiden ecstatic when they were reunited with what was left of their pack from Matvei, and over the next few days, Aiden had helped Van and Nikolai bury the bodies of those who had not made it to Volkov land.

Unfortunately, Borya's body was not recovered in the search, and so, Lillya and Olya could not properly say their final goodbyes. Kasimir suspected Ronan or one of his followers had thrown the body into the flames when they set the pack houses on fire. It was impossible to know for sure as all the burnt bodies smelled the same. Aiden cringed at the memory.

Aiden, shoving those unhappy thoughts away, grinned when he opened the door to his bedroom. His mate was laid up in bed with her leg elevated to let the wound heal naturally. Bandaging it would only prolong their naturally fast healing process.

"How are you doing?" he asked as he moved to sit by his mate.

Lillya giggled softly. "Oh, how many times will you ask me that? Lyubov moya, ty tak smeshno!" she exclaimed, *My love, you are so funny.*

Aiden leaned over and brushed a few strands of her golden hair behind her ear. He loved how she would speak fluent English one moment, only to falter and revert to speaking Russian dialect. It was just so... *Lillya.*

Olya, however, refused to speak English. It made Aiden laugh that this girl who held so much pride in herself felt embarrassed because she couldn't speak English fluently. It really surprised Aiden that so many packs had made their younger generations learn a variety of different languages in preparation for the future. They knew their place within this region was uncertain, and many had an emergency plan to send their kin to America with the other shifters who had migrated prior if the tensions with Ronan became any worse. As far as Aiden was aware, the pack families in this area had been under threat for more than fifteen years since Ronan's first attack on Matvei when Lillya was just a pup.

However, most of the survivors from Ronan's attack would be leaving soon. Van had made certain to secure their place in packs scattered across Europe and some in America for their safety and mental wellbeing. Those who chose to stay, such as Borya's pack, were aware of the dangers but put their trust in Van as their new alpha. The previous alphas of Vadim and Kirill chose to stay by Van, knowing the battle that was to come when Ronan finally stopped playing cat and mouse. Construction would be starting soon while they and everyone else recovered from this disaster to make more houses available for the newcomers.

Aiden respected Van a great deal. His alpha had opted to keep families together and offered his pack to them. Aiden knew Van would have to spend millions to create a township of that size. Before, Aiden was aware his uncle was able to stay low on the radar without the dozens of small houses being noticed, but now, Van would have to pay out millions more to have this land registered as an actual town. Aiden was aware this happened quite often in America with large wolf packs, but he believed his uncle was quite happy not having to deal with taxes, paperwork and human laws. He even overheard his uncle talking about "selling" the company he had built back in America to another company and put the money into a rollover account for future security.

It was only now that Aiden realized why Van had refused to go back to America this soon. Ronan had not only caused his uncle problems in their world but also in the human world. His alpha had to juggle human ways and law with his own duty to the shifters affected by Ronan's evilness — shifters who never had to deal or socialize with humans before. Aiden wondered if any of the people that were not originally from Van's pack had even met a human before. He wondered if any of them even knew the value of a dollar bill.

Aiden's stomach dropped when he realized that the pack might not even be able to shift into their wolf forms without fear of being spotted. If they couldn't shift at least once every few weeks, they would go stir crazy. It was like keeping a wild animal in chains at the zoo. He wondered if when the day came, and he shifted for the first time, he would even be allowed to have his first run.

Lillya seemed to sense his unease. "Lyubov moya… what's wrong?"

Olya, who sat on the other side of Lillya, frowned. "Is it Alpha Van?" she asked, genuine concern crossing her face.

Aiden shook his head no. It still surprised him how fast Olya had warmed up to Van since her arrival. He reasoned that maybe it was because Innochka had convinced her that Van was a good wolf or perhaps that injection Kasimir had given Olya (along with about twenty other females) calmed her urges down. Aiden tried not to laugh, cringe or show any sort of reaction to that last thought.

"No, I'm just thinking about our future here and what I can do to help Van… and you," he said as he took Lillya's hand and kissed her knuckles.

Lillya sighed happily and cupped Aiden's cheek with her free hand. "I am lucky Tanas chose you, Aiden."

Aiden chuckled lightly. He was still getting used to Lillya's talk of spirits and divinity and all that other stuff. He personally didn't understand it nor did he believe it, but if it made Lillya happy, then he was happy. He supposed that if the wolves that lived inside each of them were spirits in their own way, then it was possible Tanas and Killia and all those other "spirits" were in some way connected to them also.

Kasimir had briefly touched on the subject when Aiden had asked. Kasimir *was* his mentor after all. The old timer wolf had explained that spirits watched over them and that when Van passed, Konstantin would live on as a spirit as well. That is if Konstantin found his other half, his mate before he passed on to the *other* side. It's why Konstantin has been here so many times before, and that is why Aiden's Wolf will also be content when he dies. In the beginning, each spirit had another half, but it was lost, so they come back to this world to search. Unfortunately, they need a vassal, and that is where shifters come into play. It was all very complicated.

Before Aiden could reply to Lillya, his attention was shifted to a presence at the door. Aiden had to control the low growl that rumbled in his chest at the intruder. He was still very protective of his injured mate.

Ivan smiled nervously. "Sorry, sorry! But Alpha wants to see you!"

Aiden nodded, and Ivan waved as he left, still nervous about the young wolf's temperament. Aiden wondered what could be so important that his uncle would call him away from his mate.

As Aiden got up to leave, Lillya held on tight to his hand, preventing him from moving any further. "Before you go, I heard it was your sister's birthday tomorrow from sweet Kasimir. I didn't know shifters celebrated such a thing! But do wish her the best from me." Her smile only made her all the more beautiful in Aiden's eyes.

It was true. Although shifters didn't *celebrate* birthdays, they still acknowledged that special day as a sort of coming of age. Their kind didn't age all that much until they were at least a few decades old. But they needed some way to remember how old they were in human years, he supposed. Truthfully, Aiden did miss birthdays — now, the only thing he looked forward to was his mother and Aira singing happy birthday to him over the phone once a year.

Aiden smiled awkwardly. Lillya knew his mother was human and had accepted it because she was mated to a wolf of high blood like Van and Borya, but he didn't know how she would react to finding out his sister was human also.

He smiled, effectively hiding his concern. "I'll make sure to tell her, *Lyubov moya*," he said, mimicking her sweet words from earlier.

Lillya shook her head, grinning from ear to ear before she ushered him out. "Go, go; do not keep your uncle waiting."

Aiden laughed and followed her commands, exiting the room and shutting the door softly so Lillya could have some privacy with her older sister.

If Van were serious about Aiden becoming Alpha one day, he was sure Lillya would be a wonderful Luna. It was a sad thought, but Aiden was sure Van did not intend to find a mate despite the elder's constant worries that Van wasn't strong enough to take on Ronan without his other half.

Just as Aiden turned the corner to head up the stairs to Van's office, an unknown shifter came flying down the stairs, nearly making Aiden crash into the wall as he avoided the distraught man. Elina and a man from their pack chased after him, trying to calm him down. It obviously wasn't working from his frantic words. He was speaking Russian so fast; Aiden had a hard time catching what he was saying.

"He's crazier than ever! Wait until Markus hears of this! That stupid Volkov is no good! He's insane!" The man rambled on like this until he was out the door and running for his vehicle outside.

Stupid Volkov? Aiden wondered as he watched the scene from the middle of the stairway.

Now, he was beginning to grow a little concerned.

Chapter Thirty-Four

It had taken a little bit, but he had calmed down to the point where Konstantin was put at bay — the giant snort he had heard in his head was proof that his wolf was satisfied with Savelij's punishment… and his reaction wasn't too bad, either.

Now, he had a more serious task at hand — convincing his brother and Emma to move to Lucas Wright's compound for Aira's safety. He kept telling himself he was doing this more for Drake's wellbeing than the humans.

"So, Ronan's back our way then? This couldn't get any worse…" Drake sighed heavily on the other end of the phone-line.

"It can get a lot worse, Drake. He's been there for some time now. Anything over a day is more than enough time to get your hands on something you want," Van explained. He knew Drake expected him to tell the harsh reality of the situation.

Van heard another audible sigh from the other end. "Aira's in safe hands for now. Thank you for telling me, Van. I know this must be a problem for you since I did agree you wouldn't have to involve yourself in Aira's life when Emma and I adopted her."

Van's brows sloped downwards as he frowned from that response. "I do not *dislike* the girl, Drake. I do, however, dislike the danger she puts you and Emma in. Either way, Aiden and I will be coming back to make sure things are safe for all parties." Van didn't know whom he was trying to convince with that statement — Drake... or himself.

For some twisted reason he will never understand, Van asked, "How is the girl?"

And his resistance all went down the fucking drain from there. He growled, angry with himself.

"Aira? She's doing really well. Despite her health, she went for her driver's test a couple of days ago and passed. Emma suggested we get her a car for her seventeenth birthday, but Aira said she would rather wait a couple of years. She's not a very confident driver. Maybe when things calm down, we can make up some excuse about her inheritance money and let her use that to buy herself a car. I know she's been a little bit depressed about things lately especially school." Drake sounded like a doting, worried mother. It almost made Van laugh.

"School?" Van had asked before he could stop himself. He grabbed the nearest pen and squeezed, hoping it would distract him the next time he spoke.

He could tell Drake was nervous with the answer as if he wasn't supposed to say anything at all. "Emma spoke to

Aira's head teacher about her skipping classes and her recent absences. Apparently, Aira is having some problems with some other kids. Quite a few times, they've found her eating by herself in the girl's bathroom. The teacher offered to counsel, but with everything Aira has been through, Susan and I don't think it's a good idea."

Crack. As soon as Drake finished speaking, the sterling silver pen Van had been squeezing snapped in half. He wasn't even worried about throwing his attention elsewhere anymore as dangerous thoughts ran rapidly through his mind.

What the *fuck* was he paying that school for if that was the sort of environment she was in? Who the hell was running that zoo not to notice a student missing from classes? He had paid a large sum of money to that damn Institute to keep that girl safe when all the while she's been running around, God knows where, with Ronan tracking her... He was going to murder, no, rip apart whoever oversaw that piece of shit compound. He was going to destroy that building when he let Konstantin out for some teenage dog treats.

Van took a deep breath to keep from losing his temper. He didn't even know why he was losing it in the first place and he especially didn't want Drake asking questions that could possibly trigger his no good, *stupid* Lycan.

"Van, you there? Van?" Drake's voice cut into the middle of Van's inner rampage.

The alpha cleared his throat, "*Yes*, Drake?" He was on edge, so very fucking close to the edge.

There was a moment of silence before Van heard one of the doors open and close in the background. The sound of two giggling women could be heard and then Drake's voice asking how shopping was. After a moment of mindless chatter, Van was becoming annoyed.

The next thing Drake said made Van growl low. "Aira, there's someone on the phone for you; he wants to wish you a happy early birthday."

Yes, he was falling off the edge, and his first victim would be his mindless beta.

After a moment of hearing the phone shuffling around, a light, musical voice came from the other end. "... Hello?" she asked hesitantly. After some time, he could hear her say, "Dad, there's no one there."

"Hello?" she asked again.

He should have hung up and pretended this never happened. He should of. He swore he was going to hang up that damn phone.

But instead, he growled out, "Hello."

He heard the girl take a sharp breath. It felt like she stayed there on the other end in silence for a lifetime before Van finally snapped, "Speak."

Two seconds later, Van almost put a hole in his desk from anger when she snapped, "I'm not a dog, Mr. Van."

His growl was starting to become more feral as he sneered, "Stop running away from school like one then, *girl*."

Gone was that little girl who followed him around like he was her king. From her letters alone, he could tell that she had become quite witty, but talking to her over the phone for the first time since his departure, he realized that little girl he had rescued had turned into a snarky little teenage brat.

He grunted, trying to contain his anger. However, for the first time in two weeks, Konstantin was at peace, no growling, snarling or trying to use Van's body as a punching bag. He hardly noticed, though, as he tried not to throw his last working cell phone at the wall.

A moment of silence and Emma reprimanding Aira in the background later, Van had calmed down. This was ridiculous.

"Happy birthday, for tomorrow," he finally muttered, attempting very hard not to growl or snap.

Her voice held slight surprise before she quickly covered it up and mimicked his own bored tone. "Thank you, Mr. Van."

"I hope you're doing well after that incident."

He could have sworn on his father's grave that the snarky brat muttered, "Not that you would know."

"What was that?" he asked, a hint of irritation seeping into his voice.

Her response was immediate. "I said, you should know," she lied. "I sent you a letter about it two weeks ago and two more letters before that one."

Van could feel the corners of his mouth tug up into what could only be counted as a smile, albeit a scary one, but a smile, nonetheless. The little girl who would say sorry or thank you every three seconds, even to a complete stranger, had actually grown a backbone in his absence. Van had thought he'd be the one having to knock some backbone into her, but he could tell she had done that all on her own.

It suddenly dawned on him that she was upset he hadn't responded to any of her letters for the past couple of weeks now. He held back a chuckle.

"I have better things to do than play pen-pal," he said, hiding any emotion from his voice. He needed to stop this phone call.

It seemed that the human didn't like that response because she responded with her own little comment. "Dad says you hate it when people hang up on you, Mr. Van."

Van, for a minute, was confused... until he figured out just what she was getting at.

A tense, almost demonic, sound erupted from within his chest. He was going to kill her if she even tried it. He would have no mercy on her life this time around. He'd rip that backbone right out of her.

The next thing he heard was a dial tone and then utter silence. Van held the cell phone to his ear for all of three seconds before he crushed it in his hand, sending little pieces of battery, plastic and glass spiraling to the ground.

He decided, right there and then, he would personally find Ronan, tell him where the girl was, and then sit back and watch as she screamed for help and begged for her *hero*'s forgiveness. She had given that silly nickname him as a child if he cared to remember any of those fickle little things.

Van had a feeling she was certainly going to be the straw that broke the damn wolf's back.

As if on cue, Aiden came striding into the room, a big dopey grin plastered across his face. However, as soon as he saw Van's face, the grin was wiped off and confusion flooded in.

"You look angry," was the only comment he could think to make after one look at Van's face.

Van felt like throwing something, anything, and Aiden just happened to be in his direct line of sight after that comment. Instead, he put his hand on his forehead and tipped his head back. "We have to go back to the States, pup."

He didn't have to look to know Aiden's face dropped. "What?"

Now, looking at him after calming himself down *again*, Van's brow arched up. "You've been pestering me for months about going back, so what's with that damn face?" he growled.

"Well, that's exactly it, I *have* been pestering you for months, so why now?" Aiden countered.

Great, Van just had one smartass hang up on him. He didn't need another one doing it in his own office.

Aiden took a step back as Van's face seemed to turn steely. "Because Ronan's back in the States. He got a good head start on us, and I want to make sure he doesn't target your mother or father to get back at me," he lied. He only wanted Drake to know at this point what Ronan was after. That is if Savelij kept his damn mouth shut.

Aiden's mouth formed a straight line, and Van could tell the pup was conflicted. Van understood that Aiden's wolf was one hundred percent dedicated to being with his mate at the moment, but Van didn't want to waste time getting Kasimir or Nikolai passports. Van was sure he and Nikolai wouldn't last two seconds together on a plane without causing some sort of accident mid-flight, anyway.

Aiden didn't seem convinced. "Can't Baba—" he coughed, afraid she had somehow heard him, and continued, "I mean, Babushka, do it?"

Van had to admit that he was impressed at how hard the boy was trying to come up with excuses not to leave his newly found mate. "Aleksandra is in London, calming down our brothers who have somehow given into their paranoid delusions that Ronan will come and burn them out of the house and home next. She has been there for weeks, as you very well know," he snapped. The longer his mother was away, the more peaceful it was.

Aiden's upper lip visibly twitched. "I can't just leave Lillya," he stated bluntly.

Ah, that's what Van was waiting for. The corner of his lip seemed to lift ever so slightly to reveal an agitated smirk. "Since you were honest, I'll give you two hours to pack and explain yourself to the she-wolf."

Aiden's eyes widened. He had an "are you serious?" look plastered all over his puppy-dog face.

"But- Van... ugh," he grunted and frowned as if reverting into a young boy.

"You're not mated *yet*. She will be fine with Kasimir and Darya watching over her," Van reasoned. He was getting tired of this conversation rather quickly.

Thankfully, it didn't take long for Aiden to cave as he nodded. "When do we leave?"

Van sighed. "Tomorrow night is the earliest we can leave. We will be back in five days, so don't get too dramatic about it."

Before Aiden could make his escape, Van let out a short whistle to catch his attention. "Give me your cell phone."

Aiden, surprised, gave Van a curt glance. However, he did as he was told and threw the phone to his leader, grumbling as he exited the newly refurbished office.

Van clutched the cell phone, thinking for a moment.

"I'm not a dog, Mr. Van."

"H-hero!"

"Can we write to each other... Mr. Van?"

"I said you should know I sent you a letter about it a week ago and two more letters before that one."

He grunted, wondering just what that girl was doing to him. Van Volkov didn't feel guilty nor did he take any sort of bitching from a female — a human one at that.

However, his fingers seemed to have a mind of their own as he dialed the number to the Mercedes-Benz car dealership in Washington. After speaking to the dealer for a few minutes, he told the human what he wanted.

'If you can transfer the money by five o'clock, we can have it at your brother's door by Wednesday, Mr. Volkov,' the man explained.

Van snorted. "Not good enough; tomorrow morning... by eight," he replied flippantly.

The man sounded stunned as he tried to explain how that wasn't possible. Van simply sighed and said, "Well, if you don't want that damn commission, I'll just..."

The man, on the other end, panicked and promised the car would be there by eight the next day. Van smirked. "Make sure you add a bow on top."

After that, he called his bank to arrange the money transfer.

The things he did for that one little *human* girl...

Chapter Thirty-Five

Aira screamed loudly into her pillow, kicking her legs up behind her and strangling it as she did so. She had been so happy when she had heard Van's voice over the phone. It had been the first time in years she had actually spoken to him instead of talking through letters. She had almost forgotten what he had sounded like and then everything came flooding back when he had said that first word.

Van had sounded tired; his voice laced with wariness and unease. Aira couldn't help but notice he sounded harder, gruffer as if he had forgotten how to speak kindly. From what Aira could remember, Van had never spoken to her with such a haggard tone, granted he was never the kindest man in the world, but his voice would always soften when he spoke to her.

Sighing heavily, Aira pushed herself up and kneeled on her bed, staring blankly at the pillow she had just attacked. She always thought that when she first spoke to Van, it would be like when she was a child, mainly her babbling on and Van simply listening, commenting every now and again before he would simply grow bored.

"Hero…" she whispered, trying hard not to feel sorry for herself. Whenever Aira felt sorry for herself, she always ended up balling like a big baby.

"I have better things to do than play pen-pal."

In those last letters, Aira had poured out all her worries and frustrations to him. Every letter she sent before held her heart in some way, but those letters were some of the most personal, and he had not even opened them. He had not even bothered to even take a glimpse. He probably just threw them into a corner with the other trash.

It broke Aira's heart to know he hadn't even called to ask about her well-being. Emma had broken down and told Aira she had told Van and Aiden, and after being initially angry, Aira had waited by the phone, hoping that she could catch it when Van called… but he never called.

Aira took a deep breath as she ran her fingers through her dark curls, pushing her hair out of her face so that she could breathe and see straight. She was acting like some sort of jilted girlfriend, and that made her feel uneasy.

Aira was no idiot. She was perfectly aware that Van had always made sure she was looked after. He remembered what school she wanted to attend and made that happen. Van had even sent her flowers for a couple of birthdays after he left. The man also made sure she had the best tutors when she was home-schooled for that brief period of time. It was because of Van that Aira could proudly say she had perfect grades in all her classes.

Or perhaps, she just wanted to show Van she was worthy of his attention. There had never been a time where Aira had done something half-heartedly and pushed herself thinking of her hero. It was only in the last year she had given up trying and started skipping classes. Maybe she had just been kidding herself, and it wasn't her issues with the students at the school that bothered her. It was the fact Van would never look twice at her no matter how hard she worked.

Aira had even stopped looking at her reflection for too long. She had such a baby-face and no *real* curves to speak of. Her nose was flat and her lips fairly thin, but what really bothered Aira were her eyes. Her eyes were too close together. Other people said they couldn't see what she saw. Staring in a mirror for hours just picking out flaws in yourself tended to make your imperfections seem worse than they really were, she supposed. Aira knew what her issues were. She looked like a teenager, and she hated it despite the fact she *was* a teenager.

Aira could remember the day she started to dislike the way she looked, acted and spoke. Her mother had taken her to a high-tea event when she was fifteen with other mothers and daughters. Aira had felt out of place almost immediately when she looked around at all the gorgeous, elegant women sitting down and talking even Emma seemed to take on an air of elegance.

It was that day Aira made a wish that she would become elegant and beautiful like those women. She wanted to be a lady like those women in old time movies. She even worked with the way she spoke and walked, taking care not to swear or say inappropriate things. However, just like everything else, she had given up on that wish. She still didn't swear, though. Those words just weren't in her vocabulary since Emma never swore and Drake didn't often swear, at least not around her.

Aira groaned and held her head in her hands. For two years she had worked hard to achieve her many goals, and now, it seemed like it was all pointless. Everyone around her always had something to say — a little remark here and there about her behavior or her attitude, and it was driving her crazy. Aira was finally coming out of that shell she had hidden herself in for years, and it seemed the people around her didn't like what was coming out, everyone except her father.

Even her aunt Susan tried to put it down to some medical reason, trying to give Aira's *condition* a name. There was nothing wrong with Aira; it was just those stupid emotions and feelings floating around in her body that she didn't understand. Nothing had felt right for a long time with Aira.

Aira huffed and got out of her bed, feeling that if she stayed for much longer, she might have just gotten back under the covers and fell asleep. Today, she turned seventeen, and she refused to spend it moping in bed all day.

Vaughn was by her side in an instant. Aira smiled down at the wolf that gazed back at her. He had not left her side since she was sent home from the hospital.

She patted his head and laughed lightly. "I'm sorry, Vaughn. I didn't mean to scare you."

The animal simply chose to stay beside Aira as she fumbled through her wardrobe for something to wear. It was summer and jeans would drive Aira crazy in the heat. She threw on some shorts, and to her dismay, she realized Emma had taken most of her things to either be washed or were still packed up downstairs in her hospital bags.

"That's great," she drawled sarcastically. She would have to wear the only shirt that was left in her clothes drawer, which was a two-year-old Superman T-shirt. It's not as if people didn't stare or say something snarky at school enough already when she walked by.

After she had thrown her clothes on, Aira bent down and flipped her hair, untangling it as she did so. She didn't care about doing her hair as much as Emma insisted for her to at least make it look pretty as she felt. Aira didn't have any reason to stick hairspray or hairpins in her hair. It was just *hair* after all.

Aira was just about to make her bed when noises outside her window caught her attention. Being the first room on the second floor of the house, it was strange to hear such loud noises. She could hear men speaking and a car moving into the driveway. Aira had known her parents were downstairs all morning waiting for her to come down so that they could "surprise" her with birthday wishes, as they did every year. Sometimes, they would even pretend they didn't remember, which Aira found cute.

But right now, she could plainly hear Drake outside talking loudly to another man. She moved quickly to her window and threw it open, poking her head out to get a better view. Aira nearly fell out the window with what she saw.

A beautiful white two-door sedan type car sat in the driveway behind her father's SUV with a giant pink bow wrapped around the top. On the bonnet of the car, a banner was strapped down, making Aira's eyes bulge as she read what it said in big bold lettering, "Happy Birthday Aira!"

On top of nearly falling out the window, she all but choked on her own saliva with what the unknown man said to her father. "Mercedes-Benz, E-Class Coupe, last one in stock — I had to call in a few favors to get this baby to Washington by this morning. Mr. Volkov is certainly persuasive when he wants something…" the man said as he filled in paperwork.

Aira could tell her father was in just as much shock as she was. "Um, yeah, my *brother* is certainly something else…" he muttered disdainfully.

The suited up man ripped off a bit of paper and gave it to Drake. Aira studied them both as she all but gawked out her window.

"Hey, don't I have to sign any forms for the ownership?" Drake inquired before the man could take off to the car parked on the street.

He shook his head. "No, Mr. Volkov already took care of that yesterday," he answered, and then muttered under his breath. "Damn fax machines. If I never have to use one again, I'll be one happy man." And left.

Aira, in her state of shock, swore for the first time in her life — if you could even call it a curse word, that is.

"Dad, what the hell is that?" she screamed. She was in utter disbelief.

All Drake could do was look up, grin nervously, and yell back, "Happy birthday, hon!"

"He got her a *what*?" her mother gasped, almost dropping the eggs she had cooked for breakfast.

Aira's eyes shifted to her father who looked just as confused. "He got her a Mercedes, Em."

Emma laughed and shook her head. "I guess a simple card isn't good enough for Van. I thought you were going out there to tell them they had the wrong house, Drake, but when you came back and said it was for Aira, I felt like fainting," she joked.

Aira chewed on her lip nervously as she tried to take in the situation. Van had never once gotten her a gift for her birthday since he had left except for flowers and a card on the odd occasion but a *car*? And a Mercedes Benz no less! She was absolutely stunned. From the way she treated him on the phone yesterday, Aira expected nothing from her savior except maybe some coal on her doorstep.

Sighing, Aira got out of her chair and grabbed her bag and books. "Okay, I better get going."

Emma blinked, looking worried. "You're going to school *today* of all days? Sweetie, I think you should give it a couple of days and then—"

Aira smiled and shook her head at her mother's wary expression. "I'm fine, Mom. I missed a lot of classes, and with the ones I was already skipping, as you know, I won't graduate with enough credits to go to a decent college. I may as well go today and pick up what I missed," she reasoned. She had become quite good at lying over the last few months.

Truthfully, Aira just didn't want to stay home on a day like this, knowing what she knew about her biological family. There were too many thoughts about them running through her head like if they ever had a cake for her or if she had friends come over for a party or a sleepover and if her biological mother woke her up with hugs and kisses like Emma used to. Aira needed to get her mind on something else, just for today.

Emma looked skeptical as she nodded slowly. "Well, all right... are you taking your, uh, birthday present?" she asked, a playful smile finally forming on her still worried face.

Aira laughed and shook her head. "Nah, I'm just gonna walk today," she explained before turning and making a beeline for the front door. "Love you both." She waved behind at her parents before leaving the house.

Chapter Thirty-Six

Drake chuckled at his daughter. She was probably still reeling from Van's unexpected surprise. It was certainly out of character, but then again, Van had never been normal. Drake was starting to become a little worried that the angry, stoic, emotionless Alpha would go out of his way to make Aira smile. Drake knew that better than anyone as Van used to send out gifts for Aira's birthday and then call up a day later demanding Drake return them and to keep his mouth shut.

Sometimes, if Van sent flowers and a card, Drake would pretend they never showed up and then give them to Aira. The doctor even had some pictures of Aira smiling with the gifts to show Van later on. He hadn't seen his daughter smile like that for a while now, though.

"Are you going to tell her or should I?" Drake asked as he took a sip of his hot coffee.

Emma visibly stiffened. She knew exactly what her mate meant. "Well, I suppose we can both tell her. Tonight's her birthday. I don't want anything to make her upset," she replied, a small frown playing at the corners of her mouth.

Drake grunted and leaned back in his chair, thinking about how they were going to tell Aira about their decision. They didn't know how they were going to tell her they were leaving for her safety and would probably never return, but he knew she wouldn't take the news well.

She wouldn't take it well at all.

Chapter Thirty-Seven

That morning had been hectic. She preferred when things were quiet and people didn't make a big deal about anything to do with her. Aira hated attention of any kind that put her in an awkward situation like accepting Van's gift.

She stopped at the cake shop by her school as she did the mornings she walked and picked up coffee. She needed a kick start to what was already becoming a strange day. Aira smiled and thanked Isla, the girl working behind the counter that day, and went to pull out her wallet.

Isla, a petite girl with hair streaked with several different colors, shook her head. "It's on the house, Air-Bear."

Aira laughed before chucking the coffee money into the tip jar by the register. Isla just rolled her eyes, expecting as much. Aira Volkov couldn't take a freebie even if you threw it at her; chances are, she'd catch it and throw it right back.

Isla was nice to Aira. The girl was good to talk to when Aira just needed to get some things off her chest, but she had never told Isla she was adopted. Some things just didn't need to be known. The girls knew next to nothing about each other, but Isla knew Aira was related to Van Volkov, and Aira knew Isla made awesome coffees. That was all they really needed to know.

The door to the café dinged as someone flopped in, stumbling around until he finally found a seat. Falling into it, the young man laughed and threw his hand in the air. "Isla, I need a hit!" he shouted.

"Again, Erik? You're getting to be a bit of a drunk these days. Every morning, it's a different level of hungover," Isla complained with a sigh before turning to the coffee machine. "You better pay me this week!" she warned.

He simply let out a quiet chortle before his attentions were brought to Aira. "Ey, Aira!" he cried, waving his arm lazily.

Aira smiled and waved back. "Hey, Erik."

She had seen Erik in and out of this place for the last couple of years. They didn't really talk, just a hello and a bye then and there. Aira thought he was quite funny when he wasn't drunk. He rested his head down on the table and closed his eyes, which gave Aira the opportunity to annoy the auburn-haired man.

Walking passed him, Aira slapped a ten-dollar bill onto the table and grinned as Erik popped one eye open to glance at it. She felt a little sad that he didn't jump up in fright like he normally would have but laughed all the same.

"Breakfast is on me."

Erik simply watched her from his resting place on the table as she left the shop, smiling politely at a man standing outside with a cup of coffee of his own. As soon as she was completely out of view, Isla brought his beverage to him.

"I'm gonna miss watching her. Four years of just watching and waiting for Ronan's orders gets really boring after a while though he can't expect us *not* to talk to her," he said as he flippantly took a sip of his coffee. "I could have taken her out a lot sooner if *those* weren't watching all the damn time." He nodded to the guy standing outside the shop.

Isla raised her left brow. "Volkov's got his eyes on her, and he doesn't even have to be in the same country," Isla laughed as she sat down opposite Erik. They simply watched the *human* for a moment before he chucked his cup and took out his cell phone, obviously updating whoever was in charge. "Van had people watch her before, but I see he has updated his security to shifters now instead of humans. *That* could be a problem."

Erik snorted and slid over a nearby newspaper to his friend's side of the table. "Not according to that."

Isla unrolled the newspaper and looked at the headline, her smile turned into a frown. *"Van Volkov lands in Washington…* this morning?"

Erik shrugged. "I heard the news just before I got here. He's quite the celebrity with the humans here."

"This is bad, Erik. You need to get this done today, or we'll never have another chance. He wasn't supposed to find out this quickly," she exclaimed, trying to calm herself down. If Volkov got to the girl first, then they wouldn't get another chance. Calista already messed up on their first attempt to kill the human.

Erik huffed as he sat up straight in his chair. "Don't worry. By the end of the day, her head will be rolling right into Ronan's lap."

Isla rolled her eyes and sighed. "I kind of feel bad…" she remarked, her frown deepening. "What if Noah's wrong, Erik? What if we're killing an innocent girl who has nothing to do with that sort of future? Nothing's set in stone but—"

Erik sighed heavily as he held up his hand for Isla to stop talking. "What if he's *right*? Ronan saw it, Calista saw it, *everyone* saw it… You saw it too, Isla. So don't sit there and tell me that girl won't make us all suffer," he snapped.

Isla was about to speak when Erik suddenly stood up, his chair screeching back as he did so, and walked towards the door.

Just before he exited, he looked back and said, "I'd rather kill that girl today and see her buried with respect and people who will mourn her. Humans, shifters, vampires and Lycans alike will spit on her grave and curse her name for the hell on earth Van Volkov will cause. At least, this way, he will only make *us* suffer for her death and not the entire world."

His face looked haunted as Isla asked once more, "But what *if* we're wrong?"

His smile was frightening as he replied, "Then we'll take whatever punishment Volkov has for us, even Ronan will do that much. Ronan may see humans as pests, but he wants us to have a better future and to get that future, we have to kill Van's mate and take back our freedom from the humans who made us hide in shame."

With that said, Erik left, heading towards the high school.

Isla hoped he was right because she knew all too well the torture Van Volkov would put them through if Noah had been wrong all along.

Chapter Thirty-Eight

Aira took in a sharp breath as she stared in complete shock around the hall. It wasn't what was *in* the hall that scared her. It was what had been plastered onto the lockers. Someone, somehow, had scanned dozens of copies of a newspaper article and pasted them all over the lockers.

"*Mourners Gather at National Park on Ten Year Anniversary.*"

Aira briefly read one flyer, and her heart almost stopped. This was an article from months prior, and there was a picture of some of the people that attended to pay their respects. Among those people were Emma and Drake. Their names were also in the written article. But that wasn't all that was on the flyer. Written in big bold letters was the sentence, "God, You Fucked Up. You Missed One. AIRA BLIGHT."

She knew exactly whom they meant. It was hard not to since she was the only student in Newport with the name Aira after all. They were talking about her. Aira felt like bile was rising in her throat as she looked over and noticed that they were *everywhere*.

It wasn't until she heard paper shuffling that she looked further down the hall and saw a teacher and Mackenzie scattering to get the flyers down. They threw what they could into the box behind them and continued to pull the rest down.

"Hey."

Aira recognized the teacher as Mrs. Callaghan, their homeroom teacher. She looked stunned to see the girl and stumbled over her words as she exclaimed, "Aira! I thought you weren't coming back until tomorrow. Happy birthday, dear!"

Mackenzie didn't say a word; she just continued to rip down flyers. After a moment of Aira just staring at her, she finally snapped.

"I know what you're thinking, and I didn't do this! So just keep walking and pretend this never happened," she barked as she continued with what she had been.

"I didn't think that, Mackenzie," Aira said, a small smile gracing her face. The truth was Mackenzie hadn't bothered Aira since middle school. It was mainly Nathan and his friends and some of the other girls that really went out of their way to make Aira feel uncomfortable.

Aira turned around, pulling as many flyers off as she could. She tried not to look at them as she threw each one into the box. It didn't take very long for wondering students just getting to school to notice what was happening. Aira tried not to panic, but a tear slipped down her face as she noticed only a third of the flyers had been removed.

Aira tried to ignore the stares she got when the students who read the flyers looked at her, catching on to whom this horrible act was pointed at. Aira was lucky she got that coffee to give her a kick start to what was turning into a very, very horrible day. She was used to nasty things being said to her, but this was going way too far.

As Aira worked as fast as she could, she didn't even notice four other students come over and help out after reading what the paper said. It did have her name on it after all.

It wasn't long before more people started to drop their things by their lockers and take off any flyers taped down. Pretty soon, they were all gone, and the only traces left were the box, which was quickly taken away by the janitor to be disposed of.

The teens helping quickly dispersed as well, heading to class, but not before passing Aira and muttering a quick sorry. She knew it was mostly out of pity, but Aira was grateful all the same.

"I'm so sorry, Aira. Mackenzie told me who did this, and as soon as I see them, they'll all be suspended," Mrs. Callaghan said, a look of panic on her face. "Please don't tell your father."

Aira blinked for a moment before nodding slowly. "I won't…"

That seemed to please the older woman. "Mackenzie, can you stay with Aira? I think she needs some off time today."

Mackenzie nodded briefly. The woman smiled and quickly walked away.

Mackenzie and Aira were thrown into an awkward silence as they both leaned against the lockers. All that could be heard were teachers shouting in class or chalk writing against the chalkboards. It seemed like forever before Mackenzie finally spoke.

"Nathan and his friends did it. I saw them come here yesterday after dark when the janitor left and before security got here. I came early today to help with the dance set up and that's when I found... well, this," she explained, her eyes downcast. "I wouldn't normally care but... I lost my parents as well, and this was just low even for Nathan."

Aira looked at her, shocked. "I'm sorry." She honestly didn't know how to respond to that. "Thank you for doing what you did."

Mackenzie shook her head. "It was nothing terrible. My mother had a car accident when I was four, and my dad died before I went to middle school — heart attack. I'd ask about your parents but... I read some of the stuff in that article. You saw them die. That must have been terrible." Her tone dropped considerably as if she were about to cry.

Aira pursed her lips and tried to throw the girl a smile. "I don't really remember. I only just found out myself a week or so ago. I didn't even know my original birth name until then."

Aira Mae Blight — her name before that day. And to think, Aira had escaped her own home just to come here and think about it even more so.

Mackenzie simply threw her an unsure glance. "That day, when Nathan grabbed you, and you flipped out, I didn't tell him to do that either. I didn't mean for it to go that far, but Nathan, he's still crapping his pants about it even now. That's why he's been tormenting you since then."

"I didn't see anyone stand up for me, though," Aira replied, a little angry. No one had ever stepped in and told Nathan *or* Mackenzie that what they were doing was wrong.

The pretty blonde snorted. "You really are an idiot, Aira. You didn't work your ass off like the rest of us to get into this place. Your uncle and daddy called in a favor. It pissed everyone off. You walked in here like some little, rich, stuck up bitch."

"If I remember correctly, you were the one who picked on my stutter and called *me* out first. Newport *did* check my grades, anyway, and they liked what they saw," Aira snapped back. They didn't know a damn thing about her.

Mackenzie remained silent after that. Aira coughed lightly before continuing, "I would have come the year after, but I really wanted to go to school and make *real* friends my age. I was tired of being around adults all the time. Then, this place just turned into my own version of a living hell."

"Trying to make me feel bad?" Mackenzie laughed sarcastically, but Aira could tell she was feeling it.

The dark-haired girl shook her head. "No, just explaining why. If things were different, we could have been great friends."

It was possible if things had been different. Mackenzie could be nice when she wanted to be, no matter how rare that was.

"Aiden never called you a freak, either," she admitted. "I used to have a crush on him, but all he talked about was Aira... Aira... Aira and how great you were. I guess I was jealous of the fact you were rich and had a brother like Aiden," she said as an afterthought.

Now, it made sense. Mackenzie wasn't this evil person, but just a sad, lonely girl who could never get her emotions to come out the way she wanted, so she chose to make other people feel the way she did. Aira could honestly relate to those exact feelings.

"So is everyone still peeved I got in with my family's help?"

Mackenzie laughed and shook her head. "No, they got over it. They just think you're a prude bitch," she joked. "You don't swear, you don't stick up for yourself, and it's like you're always looking down on people."

Aira blinked, confused. "Will I be cool if I swear?" she joked and then added, "Shit... um, fuck... penis?" she asked jokingly.

Mackenzie was almost on the floor; laughing so hard she was basically in tears. Aira couldn't help but laugh with her. Her laugh was quite catchy and musical. Now that she thought about it, Mackenzie only laughed when she was making fun of someone, but it always sounded forced.

"You're an idiot, like, seriously," she giggled as she got over her laughing fit. It took a little bit, but she finally got over her laughing fit.

Just as Aira was about to respond, a loud, blaring ringing sound could be heard from above them. It was so loud that when Mackenzie said something, Aira could barely hear her. Then, to Mackenzie's dismay, the sprinklers started to go off. Both girls gasped and screamed when the freezing water hit them, immediately drenching their clothes and hair, making them look as if they'd just jumped into a swimming pool.

"What—?" Aira was about to ask what was going on when students came running out of their classrooms guided by teachers.

"I guess we should follow them!" Mackenzie yelled, trying to talk over the annoying ring of the fire alarm.

Aira nodded and moved to follow the crowds of students evacuating when all hell literally broke loose.

Students started to scream hysterically as they shoved each other to run the other way, away from the main exit. Aira was nearly flattened when one larger girl shoved her violently out of the way, screaming and crying in a panicked trance. She looked around, but Mackenzie had been swept up in the crowd. Aira stayed close to the lockers, confused and a little sore from being thrown against them.

Then, as if in a nightmare, Aira saw the reason for everyone's panic induced craze. Standing at the door like something straight out of hell were three massive wolf-like creatures. They snarled at the teachers who were trying to get the students away, and as soon as one caught sight of Aira, it was as if they found exactly what they were looking for.

The man that stood behind made Aira's blood run cold as he set his cold, golden eyes on her shivering figure.

As soon as she went running and by God, she was ready to run for all she was worth, the man was hot on her trail.

It all happened so fast. He grabbed her by the hair and pulled her back violently. Students were still screaming and running from all angles. No one paid any attention to her as they tried to escape from the wolves tormenting them. The man grabbed her throat and threw her back against the lockers.

She could no longer touch the floor as he held her up, slowly choking her, and smiled. "Hello, Aira Blight. I haven't seen you since you were at the coffee shop this morning... or that time you were running away from me with your mother. She put up more of a fight, though," he laughed, making a joke out of his horrible gesture.

"E-Erik... st-stop!" she choked out.

Aira let out a strangled scream when she recognized her tormentor. She was losing oxygen fast and knew that she was going to die today if he didn't let her go.

She couldn't die, not without seeing her hero at least once.

Chapter Thirty-Nine

"Welcome back, Mr. Volkov," the captain said as he took the CEO's bags off the hanger and handed them to another man.

Van nodded as he started walking towards the Airport's terminal, Aiden close behind. The alpha had been having a strange feeling for the last few hours — a feeling strong enough to make him call in his company plane — and had dragged Aiden out of bed, all but throwing the poor boy into the car with Ivan. He even had to threaten Aiden's life when the boy was stupid enough to snarl at Van for getting too close to his sleeping mate.

Pulling out Aiden's borrowed cell phone, Van put in the code for his brother's number and waited for Drake to answer. His annoyed growl was proof that he was not in the mood for any delays today.

"Hello, oh, glorious Alpha," Drake answered. There was amusement in his voice, and that irked the older Lycan.

"The girl, where is she?" Van snapped. It certainly wasn't the most pleasant greeting, but his patience was wearing thin.

Drake sounded confused as he replied, "She just left for school. Is everything okay?"

Van paused for a moment as he slowed his what Aiden referred to as death-march and tried to hide the deep sigh he had been containing. The girl was safe, so he found relief that this feeling wasn't connected to her. He had jumped into the car before even thinking about contacting Drake, certain this gut-wrenching feeling had something to do with the girl. He supposed it was because of his unease towards Ronan and the entire situation.

Without missing a beat, Van said, "We're at the airport. Come pick Aiden up."

"What about you?"

Van, already staring down the reporters that gathered at the terminal, let out an annoyed grunt. "I have something I need to do."

He hung up the cell phone and shoved it in his pocket, much to Aiden's annoyance, and said, "Pup, Drake's coming, so go grab the bags."

Right then, a photographer stepped right in front of Van's warpath and screamed when the agitated alpha grabbed his camera lens, crushing it in his palm. There was nothing he hated more than photographers. He had already warned them to stay the fuck out of his way many times before.

Aiden stayed back to apologize while his uncle kept walking, growling viciously at anyone stupid enough to get in his way.

Van stormed through the airport, making sure to side step any security that got in his way. He needed to see for himself that the human was indeed okay. He needed to see if she was safe. He had had shifters watching over her for some time now when she went to that school, but they could only watch her from the outside. Whatever happened on the inside was out of their limits.

He had no time to deny why he was going through this much trouble as a burning sensation swelled up in his throat. Something was not right. He picked up speed as he left the airport and called for someone to bring his car. His office was much closer than where Drake was coming from.

The sudden urge to get to Aira's school was beginning to become overwhelming.

"Mate... help... mate!"

Well, it seemed Konstantin was back to bother him, however, the voice in the back of his mind was all the encouragement he needed to go and see for himself if she was indeed okay.

Chapter Forty

Emma yawned as she held the house phone to her ear while flicking through a magazine. Her mate had rushed out so quickly that she had forgotten to ask him to pick up Aira's birthday cake from the bakery. It still shocked her that Van had gotten here so fast. It was at least a nineteen-hour flight, yet he had managed to get here overnight.

She suddenly gasped. "He took the company plane!" she exclaimed. "Oh, that dirty — uh, what happened to 'The company plane is used for business only, Emma,'" she seethed, mimicking what Van had said to her when she suggested she and Drake take that same plane to visit Aiden. He was such a hypocrite.

Finally, Drake picked up the phone. "Oh! Hon, can you pick up—?" she was suddenly cut off when Vaughn, Aira's wolf, came bolting out of the living room. This was strange since Vaughn was usually quiet. Emma had to sometimes make sure he was still in the house and had not escaped.

"Em? You still there?"

Emma gasped loudly as Vaughn ran straight through the gauze back door and jumped the fence, growling viciously as he did so. Emma held back from screaming and quickly rushed to put on her shoes.

She could hear Drake asking, "Em, what's wrong? Ah, damn wireless... Emma!"

By now, Emma was losing her patience as she replied, "The dog just jumped the fence!"

"We don't have a dog..." Drake said, sounding confused as to what Emma was talking about.

Emma fumbled with her shoes, almost falling over herself in the process, and snapped. "The wolf, Drake. The animal that's been living with us for five years!"

She could hear Drake stifle a chuckle on the other end. They both knew she wasn't very good under pressure, and Emma knew Aira would never forgive her if anything happened to that wolf. Wild wolves were shot on site if they caused any problems, and she didn't think the police would stop to check the dog tags of a wolf chowing down on a stray cat.

She was just about out the door when an emergency broadcast flashed over the television she had been watching earlier. Still, on the phone to Drake, Emma stopped to see what was happening.

"*This is an emergency broadcast coming in from Newport High School. The school is currently under threat from what students believe are 'giant wolves,' the school is being evacuated, but some students and facility members are still inside the building. Officers and emergency services have responded but cannot currently access the building. Two officers have been severely wounded and taken to St. Joseph's Hospital, along with two teachers. No students have been reported injured as of yet. We'll keep you updated."*

Emma could have fainted. In fact, she felt like her whole world was about to collapse into itself. She let out a terrifying scream as she begged Drake to get to Aira's school.

"Drake, there were wolves at the school! Oh my goodness... no, no, no!" she screamed over and over, almost falling to her knees. She should have listened to Aleksandra. Why didn't they listen?

She heard Drake curse over the other end, and then she heard the car screech and tires spinning.

"I'm going there now!" he yelled before hanging up the phone.

Emma, snapping herself out of her panicked state, grabbed her car keys and ran out the door. She sped there as fast as she could, running every red light that tried to stop her. When she finally got within blocks of the school, she was stopped by traffic and parents of students who were on a mission much the same as her own. She didn't think twice before jumping out of her car, throwing her heels off, and running towards the school yard where hundreds of other fearful parents and guardians stood waiting to get to their children.

Police and squad cruisers barricaded the area, letting no one get near enough to see what was going on inside. It was then that Emma saw a familiar face and went running to him, grabbing his arm.

"Damian! Oh, thank God. I need to get in there," she cried, shaking his arm. She knew it would take some time for Drake to get there since he was further away.

The officer looked confused for a moment before finally recognizing the woman. "Emma? What are you doing here?"

Emma let out a soft cry as she explained, "My daughter's in there!"

He looked baffled for a moment. "Daughter?"

"Yes, Aira! Can't you go in there?"

Finally, recognition flashed through his eyes. The girl Emma and Drake had adopted had been kept a big secret through the shifter community, so Emma wasn't surprised that it had taken him a moment to realize.

He shook his head as he tried to calm her down. "Emma... if I go in there, they'll know what I am. I can't risk that," he explained, holding on to Emma in case the woman collapsed. She looked frantic.

Suddenly, one of the creatures could be seen from the front of the school. People gasped and cried out, but the real chaos began when it let out a horrifying roar as if telling the humans to get back. It was then that Emma realized these were not normal wolves — they were high blood shifters.

"Those are—"

Damian cut her off. "Ronan's damn lapdogs," he finished.

Emma cried. Her sobs could have most likely outweighed the screams of the people who surrounded her.

"He's after my daughter! He'll kill her, Damian," she sobbed, nearly collapsing as she held on to the man.

Damian gave Emma a sympathetic look as he held her. He had daughters of his own, but even if one of them were in this situation, he couldn't have gone in even if he wanted to, and Emma knew that. "Emma, it's not looking good if he is after your daughter," he said sadly.

Emma sobbed hysterically before loud gasps from the people around her made her look up to see what was happening next. Vaughn, Aira's wolf that had escaped earlier, ran through the crowd as he went straight for the school's entryway. Emma stared wide-eyed as he bypassed the giant wolf standing guard, getting into the school. People were pointing and going crazy, wondering what the crazy "dog" was doing.

He's going to help Aira. That has to be it, she thought, a small, fleeting spark of hope igniting in her chest. That wolf would never let anything happen to Aira.

Screeching tires could suddenly be heard, and as if everything that was going on wasn't enough, people were starting to get more anxious in the mounting traffic. It felt like an eternity until she realized that Aira's pet wasn't the only wolf that wouldn't let anything bad happen to her daughter.

"Van," she gasped and pulled away from Damian, running to him, and grasped his shirt. "Van, Aira's in there! She's in there with those-those *things*!"

Emma looked up in Van's eyes and saw something that was more frightening than anything she had seen in her entire life. Through his golden eyes, she saw flecks of red seeping into his irises as he looked towards the building. She had seen Drake's eyes do the same once when she was in danger.

As Van gently pushed her away, he moved to cross the safety guard, and she stared as Van simply shoved an officer away and the man went flying across the pavement. Something in Van had changed; something not even she could have ever imagined.

Chapter Forty-One

Aira fought to stay conscious. She had been deprived of most of her oxygen for almost five minutes. Erik watched her the whole time, just smiling and asking if she was ready to die yet. She kicked so hard that dents were being left in the lockers, and she was sure her legs were bruising up from the impact.

Just when she was about to give up, Erik's grip loosened and she took in a deep breath of air, but that luxury ended quickly as his gripped on her neck was reinforced tenfold. She made horrid choking sounds as she tried to call to Vaughn, the wolf that currently had Erik by his forearm, snarling at the man that dared to touch his owner.

With a flick of his arm, the wolf was thrown to the other side of the hall, smashing into the lockers. His yelp was so loud Aira was sure Erik had severely hurt her best friend. This only made her kick harder.

Vaughn! Get up! she thought desperately as she seen her pet whimper on the ground. "Get away from here!"

She closed her eyes for a moment, accepting the fact she wasn't going to struggle anymore, and just let him kill her. She couldn't handle the pressure on her neck any longer, and her grip on his arm slackened. She thought that she was as good as dead until she was let go completely, making her fall to the floor in a broken heap. She immediately gasped for air. Panting hard, Aira was sure she was going to have a heart attack.

"V-Va—" she tried to cry her pet's name. She tried to tell him to get out before he was killed.

His teeth were dug into the back of Erik's neck, making the shifter take a step back before reaching behind him. The wolf let go and moved quickly to stand in front of Aira in a protective stance.

Erik's attention was pulled from his prey to the commotion happening at the school doors. The giant wolf standing guard started to howl uncontrollably as if something or *someone* were trying to get in. He seemed to sniff the air, and Aira noticed the blood instantly drain from his face. No longer was that sick smile there but instead, a look of pure terror.

Aira took this opportunity to get away. Forcing herself up off the floor, she made a bolt for the staircase. Not daring to look back, she heard Erik laugh nervously, "Run, run, Red Riding Hood! Hide if you can. The big bad wolf's here, but he'll never save you in time!"

Aira, with her wolf running beside her, could hear Erik chasing behind her before she heard the loudest, most terrifying crash she had ever heard in her life. The force shook the building and made her stumble. She cried out but quickly fixed her footing and headed for the AV room. She slammed the door shut behind her, whimpering as she looked around for something or anything to hide in.

Chapter Forty-Two

He heard the terrified cries loud and clear as he ventured towards the beast standing guard. He could feel Aira. She was right behind the door, and yet, this thing wanted to keep him away. He was slowly losing grip on own consciousness, Konstantin was wanting to come out to protect Aira. Van needed to do this quickly so these squalling humans wouldn't catch on to anything more than what they had seen today.

It was then, as he looked passed the dog growling in his face, that he saw Aira being held up against the locker by her neck and that wolf she had adopted was jumping to attack the assailant.

He saw nothing but red after that. He grabbed the shifter in front of him, and after one push, the dog went flying back into the building. In an instant, Van was inside standing over the animal, growling so low it would have been barely audible to a human. He was giving it the warning to stay down or be killed. The bastard who dared put his hands on Aira would be the first to die. The rest, he would slowly torture when he got the girl to safety.

The beast seemed to take the hint as Van moved to the staircase, following the scent. Before he could go up, however, a hand was on his shoulder, pulling him back. He looked around and there stood his target as if begging to be killed.

The look of absolute shock that crossed the shifters face made Van incredibly satisfied. He turned around, and the man paled considerably, looking as if he were half dead as Van stepped closer.

Erik shook violently from his own fright. He had tried to rip Van back to get a head start, but he was like a statue. As soon as Van had turned around, there was no running at that point. His eyes were a ghastly shade of yellow and red — a common trait in alpha's that felt their mates were threatened.

Van decided to give this idiot a taste of his own medicine as his hand reached out, his claws extended, and he moved forward. Erik had no time to react as the alpha pierced his shoulder and pinned him to the same lockers he just had the girl pinned to.

He growled as if he had lost all sanity. "You dare touch what's mine? You dare try to take what has always been *mine*?"

This wasn't him anymore. This was Konstantin's pure rage speaking.

Erik shook from pain and fear. "No… *Alpha*."

Van smiled a smile so evil it could be compared to the devil himself and leaned down so that his face was next to Erik's ear.

He chuckled, "You tried to take my heart, so I will take *yours* as payment."

Erik's whole body seized as Van's free, clawed hand went straight through his chest. He started to choke on his own blood as the substance came up his windpipe and out of his mouth and nose. Looking down for a split second, Erik saw that Van's hand had gone all the way through to his wrist. The last thing he ever saw was the angry alpha pulling back his hand, holding his still beating heart.

Van dropped both the heart and its owner to the floor, simply watching the shifter convulse before lying still.

He felt Drake and Aiden were near to deal with the rest of the rogue shifters running around the place. Knowing they were being taken care of, he turned and ran up the stairs, sniffing out the girl. If there were even a single scratch on her head, he would pull apart this entire building and kill whatever was left inside.

And then, to Van's horror, he heard four loud booming sounds, and the building started to shake.

It suddenly occurred to Van that Ronan wasn't stupid enough to send just four shifters and expect the job done. No, he had a plan B all along.

He had this place rigged to blow if Erik failed; knowing any human inside wouldn't survive.

Chapter Forty-Three

The bones of the rogue's neck cracking didn't faze Drake the least. Being only a beta, the giant wolf that had attacked him wouldn't lay down and submit. Therefore, Drake had no other option but to take it out. He didn't like killing, but his daughter's life was in danger, and he would have taken out even Van to get to her.

Drake looked back to his son who stood behind. "Aiden, go scout around the building and make sure no shifters are trying to escape."

Aiden was about to protest but nodded slowly, aware there wasn't much he could do with his limited strength and power. He ran out the emergency back exit, telling his father to stay safe as he did so.

Drake growled as he ventured further into the school, sensing something up ahead. He expected a lot of things but not a dozen or so cowering students hiding in one of the hallways. He was going to continue searching his daughter when he heard the blasts coming from either side of the main building. His eyes widened in horror as he felt the foundation give a powerful shake, quite aware of this impossibly dangerous situation.

"Everyone, *up!*" he shouted, making some of the teenager's flinch and growled, "Move it!"

They all seemed to take the hint as they ran for the main exit, sidestepping a shifted wolf by the lockers who looked dazed and confused. It wasn't until they ran to pass the bloodied body with a hole in his chest that they screamed in horror and stampeded out of the school. One girl tripped over, and Drake went to her aid, shielding her from the dozens of students who would have surely trampled her in their frenzy.

The Lycan grunted as he pulled her up and helped her walk to the door, telling kids who lagged behind to move it as the building started to shake more violently. It was going to collapse any minute. As soon as he got the last one to safety out the door, he went running back inside for Aira, but it was too late.

A great bang sounded, and the door was blocked off as bits of the ceiling caved in. The glass doors blasted open, and as Drake shielded his face, his arms were cut open from the flying shards.

Letting out a thundering yell, Drake used his strength to try to move the debris out of the way, but his attempt was futile.

"Aira!" he screamed.

He had one mission as a father: to rescue his daughter from harm's way. And he felt as if he had failed her as he dropped to his knees and slammed his fists into the concrete, putting large cracks into it as he begged whatever God was up there to let her come out alive.

It was as if his prayers were answered as he heard a dry, croaking voice call out from around the other side of the school.

"A-Aiden!"

Chapter Forty-Four

Aira clutched her throat as she tried to get the burning feeling out of it. Vaughn stood next to her, whimpering as he sniffed around and ran to one of the desks. Aira's head snapped around when she heard a soft cry and noticed that there were students hiding under their desks in the classroom. Her eyes widened as she thought for she had lead Erik straight to them. She visibly tensed when she also noticed a teacher hiding under her own desk with two other students huddled with her.

Aira didn't want these people to die because of her. She didn't want blood on her hands as she watched them die. She felt the need to do something or anything, but first, she needed water.

She kneeled down by the scared teacher and asked, "Do-do you have a-any water?" Her throat was still tight, and her voice was raspy.

The teacher, wide-eyed, nodded her head and pulled a bottle out from her drawer, still sitting on the table. Aira took it and quietly thanked her as she gulped the water down, already feeling her throat ease up just a little.

It was then that she felt the building start to shake. Her eyes widened since this shake was different to the one from earlier. She stood there in shock for a moment before a familiar voice caught her attention from outside the window. Racing over to it, she threw the window open and stared down. She could have sobbed with what she saw.

"Aid-Aiden!"

The man below her looked up, and the look on his face almost made Aira laugh — laugh and cry all at the same time.

"Aira, I'm coming up!" Aiden cried as he went to start climbing the building. Aira shook her head no, which confused her brother.

It took most of her strength to speak. "The-there are people… still up… here!"

She could have sworn she saw her brother visibly tense up. "How many?" he called back.

She did a rough head count and answered, "Six!"

It was then that she saw her father round the corner as if a bat out of hell and gawk up at her. She saw his eyes were cloudy as if he had been almost in tears and smiled at her. She smiled back, one of her own tears falling down her cheek. She quickly wiped it away, however, as she looked down at her family. They had come for her, and she was grateful.

"Daddy, Aiden… ca-can you catch them?" she asked. The students in this room were juniors since it was a mixed school and were fairly younger than she was. Their parents would be missing them.

She saw her father look down, as if in thought, and then look up with determined *golden* eyes. She didn't have time to wonder why he had golden eyes before he replied, "Send one down at a time!"

That was all she needed to hear before she went and grabbed the nearest boy, pulling him towards the window. He looked unsure and panicked as he shook his head, "I-I can't. It's too high!"

Aira smiled at him, trying to show him everything would be okay. "They'll catch you. I p-promise..." she stuttered as her voice started to lose its hoarseness.

The young boy whimpered with apprehension but put one leg on the windowsill. It was then Aira noticed police and firefighters standing below with her father and brother. She felt the building shake violently once again and pushed the boy out. Aira watched as her brother jumped and caught him, placing him on the ground where an officer took him away.

From the shaking, Aira knew something was terribly wrong, so wrong that the firefighters never even got a ladder out to get up here.

"Aira, the building's going to collapse, hurry!" her brother pleaded.

Ah, now she understood why. Nodding her head, a wave of bravery she never even knew she possessed washed over her as she took a student, one at a time, and helped them out the window. Aira felt a pang of guilt as she shoved the hesitant ones out roughly, but they had no time. Her father and brother caught each one without a hitch.

By the end, it was just she, the teacher and her pet wolf left. The teacher, under Aira's pressuring, put one leg out the window. The woman was an elderly, and although she wanted to stay and let Aira jump first, the girl couldn't let her do that. The woman looked terrified and wouldn't be able to jump on her own. With one shove, she fell with a scream and was caught by Drake.

The girl turned around and looked at her pet next. With a soft, sad smile, she tapped the windowsill so Van could jump up. She took his head in her hands and kissed him gently, and he licked her cheek back.

"Good boy..." she whispered and lifted the wolf up from behind, shouting down to Aiden, "Incoming!"

Aiden only had a moment to prepare himself as Aira's wolf friend came flying down on top of him. He caught the animal at the last minute, and Vaughn couldn't have been happier as he licked at Aiden's face.

Drake stared up at his daughter, panic lacing his calm demeanor, and snapped, "Aira, jump!"

He didn't have to ask twice before Aira put her leg over the window's ledge, but another shake of the building made her stumble back. She cried out as she lost her footing and fell to the floor, injuring her leg as she did so.

Just as she was about to get up and try again, the door to the classroom flew open. She stared, fright making her blood run cold as she expected to see Erik at the door, ready to kill her.

Instead, tears spilled from her eyes as Van, disheveled and bloodstained, stood at the door. He stared at her for a moment as recognition started to cross his face, and he all but ran to Aira. Aira got to her feet, using every ounce of strength she had left, and when her hero got to her, her arms instantly flew around his neck.

She was crying too hard to even realize his arms had encircled her waist, pulling her into him. She sobbed into his shoulder, muttering words he probably couldn't understand, and he held on to her as if he were afraid she wasn't really there at all.

"I-I didn't think you'd come for me..." she cried softly.

She felt Van stiffen under her, still amazed it was really him, and heard him murmur, "I will always come after you, whether you need me or not."

They were both jolted out of their embrace when the building shook wildly, and Aira felt the floor start to sink. Van kept hold of her as everything started to fall to pieces, and he shielded her with his own body to keep rubble from hitting the girl.

She could faintly hear her father calling her name as Van pushed her down onto the floor; covering her and pushing his own body up as both his hands were on either side of her head. Rubble fell around them and before she could comprehend the situation, the building had stopped shaking, and they were thrown into darkness.

She stared up at Van, and he stared back, his eyes holding hers for what seemed like an eternity before Aira realized what was happening. Van was lying over her, his arms holding himself up as he strained to hold the debris of the collapsed building all on himself. If he moved, she would be crushed.

Aira looked at his arms as she lay perfectly still and noticed his muscles tense with the weight he was protecting her from. They were buried beneath the building in all of two seconds.

Aira, still in shock and scared of the darkness, reached up and touched Van's cheek gently. She wiped away some dirt as more tears spilled from her eyes.

"Van..." she whispered, before quietly sobbing. All Van could do was watch her as he focused on holding up what could have been the whole roof of the building from crushing her.

Chapter Forty-Five

He heard her whimper under him and could smell the saltiness of her never-ending tears. The girl was scared; he was fully aware of that fact. He was barely holding himself up and knew that he couldn't do this for much longer. Konstantin wasn't begging to be set free; his wolf knew that if he shifted he would crush her. Between him and the rubble he protected her from, Van wasn't sure how he was going to get them out of this.

For the first time in his life, he was powerless. This was all he could do to keep her safe.

He grunted as the weight on his back started to send a searing pain through his entire body. His arms were tingling and threatened to go completely numb. He couldn't even move his head without little bits of brick and chipped rock falling onto the girl.

His breathing became heavier. He wasn't sure how long he could keep this up until he felt a timid, soft hand touch his cheek. Looking down through the darkness, he could see her so clearly as she smiled up at him, giving him the motivation to keep going even if just for a little longer.

He knew the silent question she wanted to ask. "I'm fine," he growled. His voice was deeper, huskier, fooling no one that he was indeed struggling.

"Van," she whispered as she stroked his cheek with feather-like touches. "It's getting harder... to breathe..."

He hadn't noticed it, but the air was indeed getting denser. He could keep going like this until there was no oxygen left and stay conscious, but *she* would soon pass out, and that was where things would become dangerous.

He couldn't help but snap at her. "Don't you dare fall asleep, Aira."

Van was forced to stare down as her eyes brightened. "That's... the first time you... said my name." She tried to giggle but ended up coughing.

No, no, no. "It's hard. I know it's damn hard but stay awake," he commanded. He would not be protecting a dead body. He would not let her die in a place like this.

His throat made a low guttural sound as he asked, "What's the capital of Singapore?"

Her face, pale and sleepy, was laced with confusion as she answered hesitantly, "Singapore City?"

He grunted. "Your turn."

Finally, understanding washed over her. In their letters, they would ask quiz questions back and forth. It had stopped some time ago, but Aira had enjoyed it. She had even missed it.

"If a doctor gives you 3 pills… and tells you to take one pill every half hour, how long would it be before all the pills had been taken?" she asked. She tried not to gasp in-between sentences as best she could.

His answer was instant. "One hour. If you take a pill at one o'clock, then another at one-thirty, and the last at two o'clock, they will be taken in one hour."

She smiled up at him. "Your turn…"

It went on like this for some time back and forth until eventually, Aira had stopped responding, simply giving him a gentle sigh whenever he would ask a question.

He could hear her wheezing as she said, "I… know about my real… family…"

Van stiffened as she said this but gave no reply. He simply kept silent, carefully watching her as he had been for the time they'd been buried.

"I forgot… I sat in that cave… for two days… waiting for them to wake up… but they never… woke up…" Her voice cracked as she said this, and a tear slipped down her cheek. It was amazing after all that crying earlier that she still had some tears left.

That was something he didn't know or didn't wish to know. He had never thought much about what the child went through or how long she had stayed conscious before she finally fell asleep during that time. Even knowing the torment she must have endured, he refused to pity her, for Aira didn't need pity — she needed strength.

Silence followed for quite some time before Van finally noticed that the girl's eyes had closed. On the outside, he simply stared in what could only be described as terror, but on the inside, his emotions were churning.

"Aira!" he snapped.

She didn't even flinch. Her eyes stayed closed.

"*Girl*, wake up," he growled, trying once more to get her attention. He didn't get a response.

His heart, something he thought had stopped beating a long time ago, began to beat rapidly as he stared down at the almost lifeless girl.

Van, in desperation, contemplated shifting and letting Konstantin take over, although he knew the dangers.

It wasn't until he heard the digging above them that he felt a little hope reignite within himself.

Chapter Forty-Six

Jillian Wright stood among the hundreds of shocked humans and the building that was currently demolished. Dust still clouded the air as firefighters moved in with masks to protect their lungs from the debris. It was a horrible scene especially knowing that Van was trapped somewhere under the rubble with that *human*.

"Why would you risk your life for her, Van?" she whispered disdainfully to herself.

She knew the dark alpha was still alive. She could feel him as could any other shifter in the area. His energy was weak, but he was alive. That was all that mattered. What really truly puzzled the she-wolf was what drove him to run in there to save that little girl. She had thought with Van's departure that this silly venture had been over and done with.

The humans were slowly being evacuated from the lot by her father's team. As soon as they were gone, the rescue operation could commence. They needed shifters in their wolf forms to be able to get in quickly. With all this chaos, their sense of smell was at a great disadvantage in their natural states, but if they shifted, they could find Van easily enough and remove whatever was pinning him down.

"Father, will it be much longer?" she asked as Lucas came up behind her, putting a reassuring hand on her shoulder. He knew she was worried.

He sighed, "They're going as quickly as they possibly can, Jill, but the paramedics can only cater to so many. We're moving everyone out as best we can at the moment."

Jillian's eyes swept over to Emma, who cried on her mate's shoulder. Emma knew as well as any of them that if Van was barely holding on, then there wasn't much hope for the girl. Either way, they'd both be dead within the hour when their oxygen ran out.

"How long do you think he has?" she asked, crossing her arms over her chest. It was her way of dealing with this anxiety. She had to stay calm for Van's sake.

Lucas Wright wasn't hopeful. "An hour, maybe. It depends on how deep he is."

Jillian huffed as she turned around and raised her hand to the men helping people get out of the vicinity. "Come on, move it!" she yelled. The humans seemed to usher faster from her booming voice.

At this rate, there wasn't much hope left to really hold on to.

It had taken a good hour and a half, but the humans and reporters had been evacuated. Jillian's father had managed to persuade the fire and police department that special services were on scene and that they weren't needed. Although they agreed to leave, they left one officer on location to make sure everything was in order—Damien.

Jillian knew her father would breathe a sigh of relief that it was Damien and not some human ready to go crying into a corner. They only needed Drake right now to tend to Van and Aira. No one had to know the alpha and girl were still in there. It hadn't taken Jillian very long to persuade the principal and police chief that all the students were out safely.

Now, the *real* rescue operation could begin. Jillian turned to her father and with a curt nod, gave him the go ahead. Those who had shifted into their wolves rushed passed her, making her hair and jacket fly up with their speed, and dug through the debris trying to sniff out Van. They were larger, stronger and could move larger bits of the building with little to no effort.

"We have oxygen and medical supplies for when they're out," Drake muttered as he moved over to where Jillian stood.

The cold beauty simply shook her head. "*If* we get them out in time."

Drake, although feeling just as hopeless as the rest of them, smiled. "We can get this done a lot faster if—"

"*Don't* even think about it, Drake. We're already front page news with Ronan's giant screw up," she growled. The last thing she needed was another headache if someone noticed a wolf the size of a house digging through the rubble like he was looking for a bone.

She didn't like that grin. She didn't like it one bit.

"Drake…" she heard her father warn. Her father was just as nervous as she was.

He wouldn't do it. He couldn't be *that* stupid. He was a doctor for heaven's sake… and yet, that cocky smirk told her otherwise. He was basically telling her he was going to pull a Van. He was going to do what he wanted, no matter the repercussions.

"Oh, I'm thinking about it," he smirked before Jillian was forced to take a step back. Although Drake was only a beta, he was still a very powerful Lycan and would likely tear her apart if she tried to stop him mid-shift.

There was nothing she could do as Drake's bones began to snap and reshape. "Drake, stop it!" she snapped, ready to beg if she had to.

"Drake!" she heard Emma scream. Drake's mate ran to him, keeping at a distance, begging him not to do it. "Drake, please, I'm scared to, but don't do this!"

It was far too late as his Lycan began to take control. The wolves digging stopped what they were doing and watched in awe as Drake began to shift, growing much larger than they ever would. He let out deep, heavy grunts as he formed out fully.

Staring up at him, Jillian sighed heavily.

Lucas was the first to show his displeasure. "He can be just as stubborn as his brother, if not worse," he growled.

Jillian stayed silent as she watched Akim lower his head for his mate, something most high-bloods did when in front of their other halves. She watched stoically as Emma smiled and touched his head gently, even moving in to place her cheek against his giant ear.

Akim's voice boomed through everyone's minds as he grunted, *"It is good to be free... and to see you again, moya dusha, my soul."*

Although Emma had just been sobbing, Jillian couldn't help but notice the tiny human smile through her tears. "I have missed you, Akim."

Emma's eyes, full of worry and a sadness Jillian could never comprehend, showed a small spark of hope as she stared into Akim's eyes. "Please find Aira and Van, Akim. Konstantin's in danger, and he needs help," she pleaded. Jillian wondered if that would help, given Akim and Konstantin's history.

Akim chuckled darkly. *"The great Konstantin needs my services? How droll."*

Jillian frowned. She was well aware that Akim was hostile towards Konstantin for what had happened in the past, which was why Van was nervous whenever Drake would let Akim out. The dark Lycan was eager to butt heads with Konstantin, and Konstantin was eager to knock back just as hard. No one ever dared to use Konstantin's name in the same sentence as Akim. That was just asking for trouble.

"Akim, our daughter is in there, and Van is our only hope. If you find him, you will find Aira," Emma snapped.

Akim's bright golden eyes seemed to darken. *"I will do it for the girl. As Aiden is my pup, she is also mine, something I will knock into Konstantin when given a chance,"* he growled before swinging around and heading towards the collapsed building.

Emma's face dropped as she watched Akim trot away. "Don't you dare lay a claw on Van while Aira's with him, Akim!" she screamed, obviously frantic that the human girl would see what they truly were.

Jillian stood close to her father as everyone held their breaths, not knowing what would be found. Jillian could hear Emma praying silently to all that it wasn't the body of her daughter Akim pulled from the rubble.

Just as Akim's paw pulled back, removing one giant load of bricks and drywall, Van was freed, pulling the human's body with him as he held her to his chest. Emma let out a horrified cry, but Aiden held her back. From the looks of it, Jillian knew that Aiden was sheltering his mother.

The human wasn't moving.

Chapter Forty-Seven

He kept holding on for Aira. He could feel his arms slipping and growled fiercely as he willed himself to keep fighting. He disregarded any danger to himself as he lowered his body just a little just so his mouth was down by Aira's ear. He needed her to come too. He needed to hear her voice. He needed *her*.

Panting heavily from that tiny bit of effort, he whispered, "Wake up." He didn't know what else to say. Van didn't know how to make her open her eyes.

As if she could feel him beside her, Aira's eyes fluttered open, although she looked as if she would go back to sleep any moment. He could feel her breaths on his cheek, giving him more than enough confirmation that she was indeed still breathing.

"Van…"

As soon as his name left her lips, the light started to stream in through the darkness. He watched eagerly as she took a deep breath of fresh air and coughed louder than she had the previous time. She was coughing so loudly he was afraid she would choke.

Van felt the weight on his body lift away and almost instantly his strength started to return to him as Konstantin came alive after being dormant. In one quick swoop, Van lifted himself and Aira up, pulling the girl up as fast as he could so that she wouldn't further injure herself.

She coughed violently she clutched his shirt, taking in as much air as she possibly could. Van held her close, letting her wrap her arms around his neck as she whimpered into him. However, he was too busy glaring up at the wolf that had saved them.

He had not expected Akim to be the one to save him although the alpha was fairly sure Akim had come to save the girl — Drake's daughter. Van never even said a word as he started to walk towards the group of shifters waiting in safety. He had expected that the humans would be sent away.

He kept hold of Aira's head as he gently held her face against him, knowing she would not have a very good reaction to seeing all these wolves surrounding them. Akim came closer as if to inspect the girl, and Van couldn't help the warning growl that erupted from his throat.

Akim looked displeased as he said, *"Let me check my pup before I rip your head off."*

Van couldn't help the dark scowl that crossed his face. He tried to keep his voice low as he replied, "For my brother's sake, I will let that slide, Akim." He kept his voice low so that the girl in his arms wouldn't stir to see what was happening.

It seemed he couldn't keep her in the dark forever as Aira forced her head back to see what was speaking. The voice was so low and so deep; he shouldn't have been surprised by her curiosity.

"Yob," Van swore as he felt the dark-haired girl stiffen in his arms as she stared wide eyed at Akim.

Van looked up as Emma came rushing over to them, cupping Aira's face as she kissed her forehead. "Oh Aira, I-I… Are you okay? No, are you *both* okay?" She sobbed hysterically, which only made Van more irritable as he noticed the girl's expression turn from horror to confusion.

It seemed a second glance at Akim was too much to bear as she promptly passed out in his arms, causing Emma to scream and Akim to nearly take his head off getting to the girl.

Van jumped back and sighed as he pulled her closer. They needed to get her to the hospital before he sprayed Akim's blood over the entire area.

Chapter Forty-Eight

The meaning of awkward: embarrassing, uncomfortable and unpleasant — three words that summed up this entire situation. Emma had left her to sit and stare at the three males that crowded the room. She wasn't even going to pretend she didn't remember this time. She was *not* going to pretend that she wasn't attacked by wolves three times the size of her own pet wolf nor was she going to pretend the giant wolf that nearly took Van's head off never happened either.

However, she was going to pretend that she didn't notice Van staring a hole through her head next to her hospital bed or that they didn't stare into each other's eyes for a good portion of time while buried alive. The awkwardness just kept coming wave after wave.

"I... what... *what* are you, exactly?" she finally asked. Years of living under the same roof and you'd think you knew a person — apparently not because she had no freaking clue about this Titanic-sized secret. Aira was four docks away from paddling up shit-creek at this point.

Drake and Aiden seemed to look every other way but in her general direction. The only one who had the guts to tell her anything was Van. Go figure.

He answered as if it was obvious. "Shifters... or your kind refers to us as werewolves. Degrading..."

Her rapid blinking should have been enough to tell them she had no clue what they were talking about. "Werewolves aren't real," she replied, matter-of-fact. She loved the men in this room with all her heart, but that was so far-fetched even Aira couldn't just sit back and believe it.

Van's hand crept up and squeezed her bandaged arm softly, catching her attention. Aira turned her head and gave him a puzzled expression. After a moment, she snatched her arm away as if it burned. She couldn't help but notice Van's face fall into a dark expression as he snatched her arm back, squeezing it in iron like grip.

Drake shot up out of his chair when he noticed his daughter flinch. "Van..." he warned.

Van flipped her arm and with a scowl, muttered, "You need to change this." He showed Aira the blood seeping through the bandages on her injury.

Aira frowned and tenderly took her arm back. "This is a mean joke," she muttered as she turned her head away from them.

The arm that shot out and grabbed her chin made Aira gasp in fright. Van's hand tightened as he pulled her face closer to his, his grip like iron as he stared into her eyes. Through the murky brown color of his iris, Aira could instantly tell these were nothing but contacts as the gold shined through.

Has Van always worn eye contacts? she thought to herself. Now that she really thought about it, the way the light often shines off of her father's eyes had always been odd. She always knew her father wore contact lenses, but Aira had thought it was because he had bad eyesight. She supposed that was just another lie she was told over the years.

Her face was inches from Van's. She knew her father was watching them carefully. She could almost feel the tension when Van's face tilted away from hers, giving Aiden a quick glance.

"Pup, show her," he commanded, leaving no room for discussion. Aira vaguely remembered Van calling her brother "pup" when they were kids, but that memory had been lost as she grew older.

Aiden's face paled. "Me?" he asked, visibly dumbfounded by the very notion of Van's demand. "Why me?"

Drake's body had visibly slackened from his angry stance when he realized what Van was trying to do. Shaking his head, he looked to Aiden and chuckled, "Well, considering you're the *least* scary version of us, I have to take Van's side." He stayed closed to Aira.

Van smirked when Aiden huffed in defeat. Aira wasn't sure what they were talking about, but she certainly wasn't thrilled to find out.

"Lock the door." Aiden's face showed defeat, and Drake moved to lock the door. They didn't need a nurse to come wondering in when they were in the middle of this little show, Aira supposed.

As soon as they heard the lock click, Van let go of her face, and she turned to watch Aiden. His eyes were closed as if he was concentrating on something and then she all but screamed in terror as she moved towards Van. The man caught her just before she fell out of the bed but put his hands on either side of her head to keep her focused on Aiden. His grip like before was like the Jaws of Life as she tried to look away. Her back was to his chest, and she could feel him chuckling softly at her reaction.

Aiden's teeth had sharpened into canines. His eyes turned to slits like cats. His nails grew into razor sharp claws, and even his skin seemed to look thicker, rougher and not... *human*. If that wasn't supposed to be as scary as what Van and her father could turn into, then she was grateful they had picked Aiden.

"The only difference with Drake and I is we can control what we want to change..." she heard Van mutter and tilting her head when his grip loosened, noticed his fingernails were now sharp, dangerous claws scraping against her temples. They looked even scarier than Aiden's if that were even possible.

She was thankful her father stepped in when he did. Otherwise, she might have passed out again. "Okay, that's enough," he snapped, eyeing Van more so than Aiden. "You're both scaring her."

Aira tried to push the thought away that Van was actually enjoying her reaction. She supposed this was some sort of sick payback for how she treated him over the phone days prior. If that were so, she was glad she had hung up on him.

After her father had stepped in everything was back to normal. They even looked human again, almost, anyway.

Aira had to regain her composure or risk stuttering when she muttered disdainfully, "Next thing you know, you're going to tell me you're a hundred years old." This was insane!

She almost hit the button and called for a nurse when Van and Drake swapped amused looks. "Two hundred, was it?" Drake asked, trying to hide a small laugh.

Van's tone was bored as if he were asked the same question often. "I thought you were keeping count?"

Aira watched in horror as they seriously tried to do the math, determining their age. She was too stunned to even register Aiden's voice as he said, "You know you're old when a doctor and a businessman can't calculate those numbers."

Van didn't find that funny. "Watch it, pup, or you won't live long enough to call yourself old."

Aiden made a zipping motion over his lips and sat back down with a grin. What really made Aira nervous was that they couldn't even remember the year they were born. She made a promise that if BC were in that number, she would make a run for it.

As Drake and Van argued between each other about the years they were born — they were tossing up between 1780 and 1812 — Aira felt Van absentmindedly place his hand on the crown of her head as if subconsciously trying to calm her down. She looked up and realized she was right. He was still talking to her father as if she didn't exist.

Aira didn't get the chance to think much more about the situation when an uninvited visitor stormed into her hospital room, breaking the lock on the door while they were at it. Her gaze was fully fixed on the gorgeous raven-haired woman as she moved to stand in front of Van, waving a newspaper in front of his face. The woman's frown and creased eyebrows let Aira know Jillian hadn't come to wish her a fast recovery.

Van didn't seem as thrilled to see her as he snatched it out of her hand and growled, "It's good to see you too, Jillian. I'm fine, thank you for asking."

Aira would have giggled at his sarcastic response if not for her brain still panicking about this... werewolf identity crisis with her family.

"Oh, yes, Van, it's great to see you, but pardon my French when I say, you are so far up shit creek right now that you better know how to fucking swim!" she spat, her chocolate eyes burning with annoyance at his nonchalant expression. "Look at that New York bestseller." She turned to take her fury out on Drake next and snapped, "And you! I warned you about shifting, but no, you decided to go rogue and get all our asses on a front page spread!"

Aira felt Van's hand snake away from her head to look at the newspaper he had snatched from Jillian. Aira knew why Jillian was so hostile when she peeked over and saw the cover. She determined that giant beast she had seen was no dream. The proof was staring at her like a hungry lion.

Unexplainable Oddity Hit's Washington.

The article was full of pictures ranging from the giant wolf that had almost chomped Van's head off, the wolves that had attacked her at the school, the destroyed school building, and lastly... her face as Van carried her from their tomb of rubble.

"You're very lucky my father made a deal with the editors to not show your face, Van. Other than that, they wouldn't budge from printing this... this... horror story!" Jillian was more than ready to slap him in the face as Drake tried but failed to calm the ticking bombshell down. Aira could tell this just by Jillian's shaking fists.

Van ignored Jillian as he stared at the article for some time and then, finally, turned the article to show it to Aira. His equanimity surprised everyone as he asked her, "Do you like that picture?" He pointed to the picture of her, disheveled, scared, and covered in dirt and a little blood.

Well, she couldn't deny it wasn't a front pager for *Seventeen Magazine*. The girl, barely surviving their earlier discussion, shook her head stupidly. "Um... not really?"

Jillian was about ready to shoot herself in the head. "Van, please... *please*, just for today, take this seriously. You can't threaten your way out of this one!" she begged.

"Well, people have already seen it, Jill. It's too late to get them to retract anything," Drake mused, trying to defuse the whole situation.

"You..." Jillian's blazing eyes had set their sights on Aira who had happily gone unnoticed up until this point. "What the *fuck* did you do to piss off Ronan? In fact, the last time I saw you, you were dumber than a doorknob and couldn't even speak without a damn stutter," Jillian hissed, her intentions clear that she simply wanted to point the finger of blame at everyone and anyone. "I knew you would cause us trouble and look what has happened!"

Her father was already in protection mode as he pulled Jillian back. "Hey, that's enough. She's just a kid," he snapped.

Aira was aware her father was much nicer with his words than the way his face darkened let on.

Aiden jumped up, ready to defend his sister. "Hey, chill out, lady. She didn't *do* anything."

The woman's face was anything but stunning as she spat, "You followed Van around like a lost puppy for years. He treated you well enough and now, look where it got him!"

She looked more than happy to go on with her rant; that is until Van stood from his seat. His face was a haunting swell of rage, but Aira had a feeling Jillian had been in the warpath of far worse when it came to Van. She ripped her arm from Drake's hold and stood tall in front of the fuming man.

Her smile was wicked as she calmly said, "Are you going to hit me, Van? Choke me, perhaps? Or, better yet, you'd prefer me on my back in your bed like all those other bitches you control?"

Her eyes were on Aira as she spat that last question, and Aira, although not certain, could have sworn a flash of jealousy darken Jillian's face.

Van's smirk was intimidating as his face turned cold, something Aira had remembered seeing when he busted into that classroom to save her, and growled, "Well... if you insist, *Jillian*."

Aira could have sworn her father was anticipating this reaction as he warned, "Van... don't..." He sounded nervous, and that made Aira nervous.

Van ignored Drake's warning as his hand bolted out, grabbing Jillian by the back of her hair, and spun her around. She let out a loud yelp as he then started to drag her out of the hospital room. Nurses and doctors in the hall got out of Van's way as he dragged the screaming and thrashing woman roughly down the hall. Aira could hear the thundering kicking sounds her legs made down the hallways.

His voice was filled with dark humor as he grunted, "If you wanted to be on your back, all you had to do was say so the first time."

Aira watched as her father flew out of the room, chasing after Van. Aiden was about to follow when Aira snapped, "Aiden, a little help here!"

She was halfway out of bed and couldn't walk on her own due to her sprained ankle, an injury that happened when she fell trying to escape out the window during the attack. Aiden, conflicted on what he should do, caved and went to aid her. Aira slung her arm around Aiden's shoulder as he helped her out of the room. Although the situation was chaotic, Aira couldn't help but notice that even though Aiden had grown, he still felt the same. He even smelled the same. She had missed that smell of fresh grass and summer mornings.

When they entered the hall, it was worse than she had thought. Van still had an iron grip on Jillian's hair, nearly ripping it out, while Drake had stopped his departure by grabbing onto the arm Van was pulling her with. They seemed to be yelling back and forth; Drake telling him to let her go while Van simply replied with growls and threats.

By this point, Aira had *enough* of this insanity. First, they had dropped an unbelievable bombshell of a secret on her, and then she was accused and her intelligence insulted by Jillian, and now, this? If this were a common occurrence between her hero and Drake, she wondered how her mother dealt with it.

Slipping away from Aiden, Aira winced as she limped towards the scene, overhearing a nurse call security as she did so. She had to do something fast before her father and Van were hauled off in a police cruiser.

As soon as she reached them, Aira grabbed hold of Van's shirt and stared up at him. Any rational girl would have slapped him, but Aira couldn't dream of mustering enough backbone to do that to a man she adored, so she did the next best thing — she yelled at him.

"Van, let her go!"

She felt his growl rumble through his chest. "Go back to the room."

He couldn't be serious? "No, you should never put your hands on a lady! My hero, the man I respect, would never do that!"

To her utter surprise and relief, Van let go of Jillian completely. She crawled away from him as fast as she could until her back hit the wall. Aira continued to stare up into Van's enraged eyes before he ripped his arm away from her father and used it to gently push Aira away.

Van pushed past her as he made his way down the hall, muttering, "I'm not your damned hero… get back to your bed," before making his escape.

Aira sighed as she watched him go, confused and baffled by what she had just witnessed.

Drake looked as if he were feeling the same way. "Aira—"

"I don't remember him being like that," she whispered sadly.

Her father frowned. "You idolized him. That's why. You were the only person he never... well, went crazy in front of. Even though he'd never admit it, I think he liked the respect and adoration you showed. But Van has always had problems with his temper, something Jillian knew," he finished with a compassionate look towards the nearly hysterical woman on the floor.

She was ashamed to say it out loud, but she still adored him. She was angry with him for leaving and for doing what he did to Jillian, but she still put him on that pedestal so high up that no one could even compare. Perhaps, now, that she was older, he didn't see her as this innocent little girl anymore. Perhaps, he wanted to show her what he was capable of.

Aira took a deep breath as she limped to Jillian and reached her hand out to help her up. The proud woman simply slapped Aira's hand away and laughed, but it was far from humorous.

"You think you can heal his demons? No one can fix Van Volkov. He's a monster with a handsome face. He's no hero, honey," she snapped, venom lacing her tone.

Aira's mouth formed a straight line as she let her father help her catch her footing. "I hope he didn't hurt you, Jillian."

She faintly heard Jillian say, "Yeah..." before her father led her back to her room.

However, before she entered her room, she looked back and smiled. "Jillian, I may be a lot of things, but I'm not dumb, not anymore, anyway." She added that last part; referring to her blindness when it came to a secret that was so obvious it basically slapped her in the face with hints and clues.

She asked her father if, after he had helped her back into bed, he could make sure Jillian was okay.

Just as Drake was about to help her to bed, she froze, feeling bile rise in her throat. "I'm gonna puke," she moaned.

Aiden barely made it to her with a vomit bag before she threw up the few contents she had in her stomach. Maybe their confession along with witnessing Van's temper for the first time had a much worse effect on her then she had originally thought.

Chapter Forty-Nine

Aira sighed as she finally had the chance to just relax in her own bed, in her own house, in her own bedroom. Despite her wolf, Vaughn, having a bit of a hurt paw, he was as good as new in the days she had been away. She was thankful for that. It seemed he was just as happy she was home as she was to be home.

However, Emma hadn't been too thrilled when she learned of Van's outburst. Actually, she hadn't been thrilled until Drake had explained what Jillian had said to set him off in the first place. Emma had been ranting for hours over Jillian's audacity and gall to accuse her daughter of bringing this upon herself. Aira had no idea who this Ronan was or what she had done to make him angry. For heaven's sake, she barely left the house as it was!

Van was different, *very* different from what Aira remembered. He looked rundown and tired, albeit still handsome. She still looked up at him and remembered seeing the strongest man she had ever known.

"You think you can heal his demons? No one can fix Van Volkov. He's a monster with a handsome face. He's no hero, honey."

Jillian's words continued to run through her mind on a repeated loop. Aira had remembered Jillian from when she was a child. The only times Aira had come into contact with her was when Van was around. Jillian was like Van and her father — a shifter. It made sense that she was always around Van; she must have been his girlfriend at the time or even still.

A pang of jealousy raced through Aira's chest as she thought about it. The sudden emotion startled her, as she'd never been jealous of women around Van before. For all she knew, he could have had many girlfriends back in Russia. He was a very handsome man after all.

"Or, better yet, perhaps, you'd prefer me on my back in your bed like all those other bitches you control?"

"If you wanted to be on your back, all you had to do was say so the first time."

A deep blush crept up onto Aira's face and chest as she threw herself into her pillow, screaming bloody murder into it as she thought more of what they had said to each other. "Bad thoughts, bad thoughts, bad thoughts!" she chanted, embarrassed.

True to her word, she was by no means dumb, and Aira knew exactly what they had meant. She knew exactly what sex was, but sex and Van in the same thought seemed to both tarnish her childish idolization and make her stomach churn in excitement. By now, her teenage mind had turned to thinking of Van with his shirt off and...

She screamed louder into the pillow, trying to wipe those thoughts completely from her mind. This was wrong on so many different levels, and she was already on level fifty. Fifty more to go until she was officially in Van Naked-Ville.

Van naked...

"Jesus Christ, brain, why?" she cried. She tried to block out the automatic Emma voice in her head that reprimanded her for using the lord's name in vain.

Thinking about Van with his shirt off — or everything off, more like it — and the fact he wasn't even human to boot made this all the more confusing. She was an awkward teenage girl living in a world that wasn't all it appeared to be. The only thing that kept her from puking from the stress once more was trying *not* to think about everything she had just been thinking about. Easier said than done...

The knock on her door made her jump and almost fall out of her bed. It was difficult to lower her voice when she answered, "Come in!" A cough at the end wasn't any less suspicious.

The person she had just been thinking about, well, more like drooling over, was the same person who stood at her door. Van looked hesitant to enter, but his face was stoic as always. His attire surprised Aira, as she was always used to seeing him in expensive fancy suits. Van always looked like he was going somewhere important, but today, he simply wore a pair of black denim jeans, black shirt and a leather jacket that looked just as expensive as his suits. She supposed he wasn't a businessman twenty-four hours a day, seven days a week, despite it seeming that way.

"You're not naked," she blurted out, giving him a once over. Then, it clicked.

God, I know you failed before, but it's okay, you can kill me now! she thought desperately.

His brow shot up as he leaned against the doorframe. "No, I'm not." He nodded, and after staring at her for a moment, he asked, "Should I be?"

She wondered if she could move fast enough to throw herself out the window. "No, no, clothes are good! I like clothes!"

Idiot.

She couldn't help but notice he looked a lot more relaxed today. She had always remembered him having a constant glare; always looking annoyed and never smiled. Since his return, he showed more emotion in his face. Perhaps, being in Russia had been good for him.

He kept his distance, much to Aira's gratitude. Finally, after a few agonizing minutes, he spoke, "Are you coping well?"

She nodded. "As well as I can, I guess," she laughed nervously. In fact, she most probably wasn't coping well at all. "At least, Halloween will be funnier this year..." she tried to joke.

It seemed he didn't find it as funny as she did because he turned around and started to head downstairs. "Come on, get your ass up, we'll be late."

Ah, there was the Van she remembered. Her embarrassment was replaced with curiosity as she shot up off of her bed to follow. "What? Where are we going?"

He didn't give any clues away as he said, "Human's shouldn't ask too many questions."

So now her nickname had been replaced with "human" instead of "girl." Lovely.

As she followed him down to his car, she instantly replied with, "I didn't know old men were so cocky."

He didn't miss a beat. "You should speak up. This *old man* didn't hear that little remark."

She gulped when he turned to look at her, his eyes instantly flashing with anger and amusement, something that caught her completely off guard.

She shook her head. "Nothing, just talking to myself..."

"Thought so," he muttered as he opened the driver's side door.

She got into the passenger side, instantly feeling giddy when the smell of his cologne hit her. She had never been in a car with Van before, and now, she knew why her parents never let her get into a car with Van. He was a speed freak.

She sat back into the leather seats as she held on for dear life. She was too busy concentrating on *not* dying when she asked, "Have you ever considered anger management?"

This question only seemed to make him drive faster. "I wonder if the garage fixed that airbag on your side," he said with a nonchalant tone.

If Aira was all red before, she didn't have to worry because she was certainly pale now. "Point taken..."

"About that," he muttered, eyes trained on the road as he swerved in and out of traffic, "I should speak to Jillian. It was inappropriate of me."

Aira couldn't help but get the feeling that that was as close as an apology she was going to get. He certainly didn't look remorseful.

"You have a choice, Aira," he suddenly said, a serious expression washing over his face.

Aira looked at him. "A choice?"

He nodded. "Drake and Emma are coming back to Russia with me, for their safety. You have a choice whether you'd like to stay or leave with them."

Her eyes widened as the car slowed down. Leave the only home she'd ever known? Go to Russia? "Russia…?"

The car had, by now, come to a complete stop on the curb of a little, quiet street. Looking around, she didn't recognize where they were until she spotted her mother, father, Aiden and even Susan standing in the driveway of a little suburban house.

"Van, where are we?" A sinking feeling in her stomach was all she needed to know that this wasn't right.

He was already getting out of the car when he answered. "You should know, you were born here, little one."

Chapter Fifty

There was something so familiar about this place. She didn't recognize it nor did she remember ever coming near this street, but it was familiar. It was a fair way from the upper side she had grown up in. The house had the white picket fence and a lovely front decking with potted plants decorating the little chairs and table outside. It was a simple single story home with a giant tree in the front yard — all set with a swing on one side and a tire swing on the other. However, years of neglect had turned the once green grass brown, and the flowers had either died or outgrown their potted homes.

As she slowly exited the car, a thought randomly fluttered through her mind. *I wonder where Daddy put my bike.*

Her eyes widened as she placed her hand on her forehead, mentally freaking out about that one little thought. She most certainly did not own a bike at her parent's house, well, not anymore anyway. Slightly perturbed, she made her

way to her parents, still staring up at the house as her mother
came and took her hand.

"Aira, sweetie, if you want to leave…" Emma started.

Aira shook her head. "No…"

Susan came up behind her with a soft smile and took
the girls free arm gently. "You've grown up so much, darling.
I'm proud of you. Just say the word, and we'll leave."

Aira was still staring with a vacant expression when
she asked, "Why are we here?"

Both Susan and Emma's mouths formed a straight line
as they watched her like a hawk.

"To help you grieve." Susan's eyes were hard and
determined as if she knew this is what Aira needed to see to be
able to come to terms with her past.

It was then that Aira finally realized where they were.
She remembered this place. She had lived here before *that* day.
All Aira could do was nod before untangling herself from the
two worried women and making her way up to the front patio.
She was hesitant as her hand hovered over the doorknob. She
went to pull back her hand before someone caught her wrist.

Looking up with glassy blue eyes, she smiled warily at
Drake. "Hey, Dad…"

Drake smiled back and placed her hand back onto the
door. "It's okay to be scared because I'm scared too."

Aira sniffled and shook her head. Next to Van, Drake
was the strongest person she had ever known. It was hard to
think he was just as scared as she was. She knew what they
were trying to do. Emma and Drake were giving her a gift, a
choice to remember and throw all that pain away for good. Aira
had known Van would have told them about her confession

about knowing the truth, but she hadn't expected them to go this far just for her.

With Drake's strength behind her, Aira felt that she was ready to venture inside. Turning the handle on the door, she pushed it open and peered into the home she had long ago forgotten.

Aira was met with a dark hallway and two open doors on either side. They were wide open, revealing two bedrooms. Slowly, she stepped inside the house and carefully looked into the bedroom to her left. It was obviously a young man's bedroom with just a single bed and a desk. The floor was barely visible under the piles of clothes scattered across the room.

"Ian…" Aira whispered. This was her brother's room. She had remembered her mother yelling at him to constantly clean his room. He never did.

Through the darkness, she could faintly see a calendar pinned to the wall. Walking inside and peering at the old and frayed paper, it was stuck on April. There were dates for random things written down, but one certain date stuck out to her the most — April 16th: camping with family and a line drawn through until April 23rd.

Closing her eyes, Aira took a deep, shaky breath. She was supposed to come home after seven days, but instead, she returned with Emma and Drake eleven years later.

Light filtered in through the dark as Emma and Susan opened the blinds and windows throughout the house. Aira barely noticed. She moved back into the hallway and moved into the other room, staring aimlessly around her as she did so. Aira remembered this room.

"Wake up!"

Her mother groaned as she twisted in the bed covers. "Aira, it's early. Go back to sleep," the woman muttered as she hid her head under the pillows. "Charlie, tell Aira to go back to her room."

Aira giggled as her mother sat up in bed, looking fairly irritated, before punching her "sleeping" husband on the shoulder. "I know you're not asleep. You're not snoring."

Her father chuckled as he sat up and tackled her mother, causing the poor woman to scream. "Well, I was asleep!"

Aira squealed playfully as her mother tried to get away from her father's hold, laughing hysterically.

Aira smiled as the memory vanished. She never did go back to bed that morning. This room was where her parents would nurse her when she was sick, cuddle her when she was scared and grumble at her when she would wake them up at six in the morning on a Sunday. She'd sit with her mother on that very bed and watch television while her mother napped. Aira would sometimes play with her mother's rings as she slept, trying to slip them off so that she could play dress up.

The television that sat on top of the dresser was still there, turned slightly so that Aira could see it when she snuck into their room. The bed covers were in shambles as if someone had just been sleeping in them, only to leave in a hurry. It was almost haunting that this house hadn't been touched since the morning they left, only to never return.

Towards the end of the room sat her mother's vanity table. Her makeup set was still out, and as Aira ventured further inside, she noticed the blush brush she had been obsessed with as a child was still out. She bent down to look into the mirror, only to be confronted with the image of her as a young child, sitting in her mother's lap while the woman applied some blush to her cheeks playfully.

From the size of the room, it suddenly dawned on Aira that her parents had most probably chosen the smallest bedroom in the house to sleep in. Their wardrobe was a simple pole strung up to the ceiling to save space. The room had lost her mother's sweet rosy smell over the years, but those clothes still smelled the same. Through the mustiness, she could smell her father's musky cologne and her mother's sweet, fruity perfume.

Breathing a deep sigh, Aira exited the bedroom and hesitantly made her way down the hall, leading her passed the bathroom and separate toilet, to the living room.

She ignored everyone standing around her as she gazed into the room her family had spent a lot of time in. The sofa was an eight-seater that curved around the room, with a wooden coffee table and a television cabinet. Pictures lined the walls and spaces on the tables. The VCR was still in its original spot with videos sitting on top of it and the television. In the corner sat a CD player, and that's when she remembered that her father would blast out Bob Seger every morning to wake them up.

"Old time rock and roll," she muttered fondly, remembering her father's favorite song was "The Famous Final Scene."

Emma smiled sadly when she heard what Aira had said. "Bob Seger was played at their—" She stopped before finishing that sentence, but Aira knew what she meant.

"Funeral."

She hadn't even been to their funeral. She never got to say goodbye. Aira wasn't sure why that hurt so badly. She probably wouldn't have even remembered the people who were being buried at the time, anyway.

The kitchen and dining room were only a few steps away to her right. The kitchenette in this house was very small compared to Emma's lavish design, but to Aira, it was warm and inviting. She had made cakes, gingerbread men, chocolates and other such treats in that kitchen with her mother and sometimes, even her father.

"Can-can I have some water?" she asked, feeling her mouth become dry from all the emotions and memories flooding through her.

It was almost comical how Susan and Emma seemed to scatter back to the car for a bottle of water. The house had no electricity, let alone any running water.

They soon came back, cold water in hand, and stared at Aira as if she were about to disappear. "Baby, we can leave right now if you—" Emma gasped, but Aira cut her off with a shake of her head.

"Mom, it's okay," she smiled. "It's good that I'm remembering and not... you know, fainting." She tried to joke, but no one laughed. It was strange referring to someone else as

"Mom" in this house with all these memories flooding back one by one. The human mind was truly amazing; it could shelter you from so much pain while giving you the information you had thought gone forever all at the same time.

Aira knew that Emma wanted to ask why she hadn't said anything about remembering sooner, but she also knew that this wasn't the right time to ask questions. Right now, they needed to take this as slowly as possible.

Looking around briefly, Aira noticed Van had stayed outside. She was thankful. She didn't want him to see how tormented she was by just being here. This whole situation had left her feeling emotionally weak.

There was still one more room she hadn't ventured into yet. The door was across from the living room and was staring her down. She didn't want to go into that room just yet.

That's when she noticed the black camcorder sitting in the kitchen. She had been gazing around, almost star struck when she had spotted it. She remembered that camcorder from her youth. Her father used to point it in their faces whenever he had the chance, driving her sister crazy in the process.

Her body seemed to move by itself as Aira quickly walked towards it, grabbing the object and flipped open the screen. She could feel her whole body tense up as she held down the power button. She didn't hold much hope that the thing would even turn on, and then, as if God had read her mind, the screen lit up, and the SONY logo was displayed.

Aira's mouth went dry again as she played the most recent video. The battery life was all but gone after eleven years, but there was still a chance that she could see for herself the people that had been lost to her.

That was when she heard her father's voice for the first time since she was six years old.

"Come on, Avery, smile! I know you've forgotten how to but just try!" her father joked.

Aira watched with wide eyes as her sister, her *real* big sister, scowled into the camera and slapped their father away. "Get away from me, you weirdo."

"Avery Renee, calm down and take a joke," her mother snapped from the background, throwing a glare at Avery as she walked by with a plate of food. "You better not talk like that in front of our friends."

"I wanna look! Daddy, let me look!" came a whiny little voice as the camera shook. Aira heard her father chuckle as he pointed the camera down to a little girl who didn't look very happy to be filmed either. "What's that?"

"It's a video camera, Aira," he explained as he bent down and pulled the child behind him. "See, it remembers everything it sees, just like you and I remember."

"Charlie, there's people at the door!" She heard the woman plating the food yell before the image scrambled, only to be replaced by Aira sitting at the large picnic table with kids and adults surrounding her singing happy birthday.

"I did have birthdays," Aira whispered.

Her brother's face suddenly filled the screen as he grinned and then turned the camera back onto Aira, who sat on her big sister's lap as they both blew out the candles. Aira couldn't help but smile at how beautiful her sister was especially when she laughed.

The image faded out once again as static ran through the screen and then slowly, a new image of her parents sitting at the table hovering over some bits of papers appeared. They both looked upset.

"Can we afford a car *and* life insurance?" her mother asked worriedly.

Her father simply nodded. "We gotta do it, Viv. We have three kids to think about. I'm not worried about Ian so much, but Avery and Aira…"

"Hey, for all you guys know, I could become a beggar." She heard her brother joke from behind the camera.

His parents didn't look too happy as they both snapped, "Turn it off, Ian," giving Aira the impression they had asked more than once at the time the camera had been on.

And that was when the battery finally died.

Even when the screen was blank, Aira continued to stare as if she had seen a ghost. In actuality, she had seen four ghosts, and it broke her up inside. She could feel her heart shattering by just hearing their voices. Aira didn't understand. She wanted to know *why*. Her biological parents were just normal people trying to get by with a family. They weren't rich, and they didn't do anything wrong.

She felt her sanity breaking as Aiden came up behind her and placed a hand on her shoulder. Without realizing, she had shrugged him off and stampeded for the bedroom she had been avoiding. *Avery and Aira's room* was marked in bright pink paint on the door.

Kicking the door open, she started to pull down fluffy stuffed toys and books. She threw everything around the beautiful pink room that it started to look like a cyclone had just run through it. The room was pink with two single beds on either side of the room and a desk and bookshelf. The bed covers, like the other rooms, looked as if they had just woken up that morning.

Aira couldn't take it anymore. She threw anything she could and grabbed any breakables, throwing them at the wall. It wasn't until someone had grabbed her by her wrists that she stopped and froze.

Looking up, Aira was met with Van's stern eyes glowering down at her. "Stop," was all he had to say.

In her hand, she clutched a little, stuffed rabbit doll. It was ironic how that had been the only thing to survive her wrath.

"Avery, wanna play pretend with me and Peter Rabbit?"

"Leave me alone, and I'll read you a story tonight," Her sister snapped while she continued to flick through her magazine.

That memory seemed to break whatever emotions Aira had been holding in as tears slipped down her cheeks.

Why?

Why?

Why?

Staring up at Van, Aira screamed, *"Why* did they leave me? Why'd they have to go?"

She felt her legs start to give way as she nearly collapsed onto the ground. Emma tried to get to her daughter, but Van shook his head.

"I needed them, and they just left! I was a little girl, and they left me to-to-to sit in that hole and watch them die for two days! We didn't do anything to anyone to deserve that!" She was crying hysterically as she clutched the rabbit to her chest, heaving and coughing as she tried to get out her words. "My mother told me it would be okay! She *lied*!"

Van kneeled as he lifted Aira's chin carefully. She was in her own world right now — a world that was breaking down little by little. "You're right," he suddenly said. "Your family didn't deserve that, but they did it to protect *you*."

Aira shook her head rapidly. "I hate that game," she muttered, her voice croaky and tired.

Drake bent down and put his hand on his daughter's head while Van still had her chin elevated. "What game, sweetie?" Drake whispered, almost at breaking point himself.

"The floor is lava. I hate that game." She said it as if it should have been obvious. "I don't want to remember anymore."

After that breakdown, Aira felt like a weight had been lifted. It was as if her soul had been grieving this whole time, but her body refused to feel the hurt.

She got to her feet, sniffling and hiccupping as she did so, and smiled sadly up at Van and her father. "Sorry... about that."

Her momentary lapse in sanity made her feel slightly embarrassed. It wasn't until Drake took her into his arms and hugged her that she realized she had nothing to be ashamed about. Aira hugged her father back, quietly sobbing into his shirt, secretly wishing that it was Charles Blight standing there in Drake's stead. Until now, she had no idea just how much she had missed them.

As Drake locked the house back up, Aira stood out on the porch looking dazed. It took her a moment to notice Aiden had grabbed her hand and given it a gentle squeeze to get her attention. Turning to look at him, she smiled.

He smiled back. "Air, no matter what happens, I love you more than anything in the world. I don't say it often enough. I know that." He fidgeted with her hand as he said this, looking a little embarrassed.

Aira laughed half-heartedly. "I love you too, Aiden. Let's go."

Aiden grinned and led her down the stairs towards their parents. Aira knew he was probably a little stressed out after seeing all that back in the house, but she also knew that Aiden had stayed strong for her sake. She wondered if Aiden ever thought about the people who gave birth to him.

Aira hugged Susan goodbye, and the woman took her face into her hands, smiling adoringly. "You did great, honey. Remember, if you need anyone to talk to, I'm just a phone call away."

Aira nodded. "No more sessions then?"

Susan laughed as she got into her car. "Oh, no, you're not getting out of therapy that easily."

"Wouldn't dream of it..." Aira muttered sarcastically but waved as Susan drove away. It was still a shock to think that Susan was also a shifter. Aira wondered if there was someone in her family besides Emma who was just a normal human. However, that didn't mean she had accepted it. It was still too hard to believe that they were actually beings that could turn into giant dogs at will.

Giant dogs.

For the majority of her life, she had been plagued with dreams of giant wolves chasing her through the forest. Perhaps, that had been a sign that things weren't exactly right with her family. Aira never mentioned anything, but she suspected Van and Drake might know what happened to her family that dark day in April, eleven years ago. Maybe, like today, she was scared about what she may find out. Maybe she was scared of *them*.

However, she wasn't scared of the memories that haunted her, not anymore. This wasn't her final scene, and this wasn't the last goodbye. To Aira, this was a see you later to the people who loved her with all their hearts. She had so much more to do and see, and Aira would take their memory with her even if she went all the way to Russia with Van.

"Goodbye…" she whispered softly, "I love you."

Just as Emma took Aira's hand to leave, a woman from the house next door cried out, "Avery?" She was standing on the porch, eyes wide, and came running down to get a closer look.

By the time she reached the two women, she gasped, "Oh my Lord! You look just like Avery, I'm sorry about—" She cut herself off as she took a closer look at the young girl, and her eyes seemed to widen even more so. "Aira…" she exclaimed. "Is that really you?"

Aira took a step back and hesitantly nodded. "Yes?"

Emma noticed Aira's unease and before Drake could step in front of them, let go of Aira's hand and reached out to shake the shocked woman's hand. "This is my daughter, Aira. You are?"

The light-haired woman didn't even bother to take Emma's hand as she glared. "Aira's *mother*? What sort of joke is that? Vivian's been dead for more than ten years!" It must have dawned on the older woman about who Emma was because her face flushed when she gasped, "Oh, you must be her *adoptive* mother. I'm terribly sorry!"

Aira almost fainted when Emma threw the woman a heated scowl. "Well, I'm her mother either way. Emma Volkov," Emma spat, still holding out her hand as a good gesture.

The woman's face dropped as soon as Emma said her name. Those gray eyes seemed to fly in the direction of Van and Drake before she realized the importance of the woman standing before her. It didn't take long for the lady to shoot her own hand out and give Emma's a good shake.

"I'm Mary Carder. Do you remember me, Aira? You used to play with my daughter all the time."

Aira shook her head. After knowing Mary for all of ten seconds, Aira knew that she already didn't particularly like this woman. "No," was her curt response. She could tell Aiden was getting just as annoyed with this woman's arrogance towards Emma.

Mary seemed to ignore any hostile responses by chirping, "You look so much like your sister that I almost fell off the patio! I thought I saw a ghost, and all those fancy, *noisy* cars that pulled up earlier, well, I was about to call the police. No one's been around here since Viv and Charlie passed away," she explained. Aira couldn't help but shiver.

Something deep down told Aira this woman had known exactly who she was the moment she stepped out of

Van's car earlier. Aira didn't know why this woman was lying nor did she care to know.

The woman reached out and grabbed Aira's hand, giving it a hard squeeze before she smiled and gushed, "I'm so happy I got to see you again. When your grandfather came around and told us what had happened, I cried for days. I couldn't believe this could happen to people I cared for so much." Her face turned solemn as Aira tried to escape her grip. "Sweetie, I tried to find you so I could take you in, but those officers wouldn't tell me where you were or who had you. I came to visit you at the hospital honey, but—" She gave Van a nasty glare. "By the time I told your grandfather where you were, you were gone!"

Emma visibly stiffened while eyeing this annoying female. "Grandfather?"

Mary finally released Aira and nodded. "Richard; hadn't seen him around here for years until Vivian died. She hasn't spoken to her mother or father for such a long time."

Judging by the disdainful look on Mary's face, it was obvious she didn't favor the man. She was singing out as much information as she could like a damn songbird. Aira frowned.

She had a grandfather? Her *biological* grandfather had been looking for her?

She could sense Van and Drake watching them, but they never stepped in. She was glad. Van's poisonous tongue could hit hard when someone showed any disrespect. She stood witness to that with her own eyes.

Aira could have sworn Emma sighed when she heard the name but ignored it as she smiled at Mary and said, "Well, we better go now, Aira's had an emotional day. It was nice meeting you."

Just as Aira turned to leave, Mary grabbed her hand once more and with her eyes clouding over with desperation, begged, "Honey, stay for dinner. In fact, why don't you stay the night? Your mother would have loved that."

"With all due respect," Aira muttered as she snatched her hand back. "I really don't remember you nor do I appreciate what you think my *mother* would have thought." In all honesty, she couldn't imagine someone like this being friends with Vivian. From the videos, it seemed like her mother would have kicked Mary to the curb the moment she met her.

Mary's gray eyes turned steely. "Your attitude hasn't changed, I see."

If Aira's puffy red eyes and flustered face didn't get the message across that she didn't want to stick around, she didn't know what would.

"Excuse me?" Drake asked, finally stepping in to deal with this intolerable woman.

"Well, she *was* a handful when she was a child. Always screaming and very rude. In fact, most of the kids back then didn't want to play with her except for my Marie," she shrugged as she said this. "Always crying as well."

Aira was flabbergasted at this woman's audacity. She had just returned, and now, this woman was filling her head with garbage. Granted, she may not have been a model child, but even Aira couldn't remember what she was like back then. However, from the video, she had to admit that she might have been rather demanding, perhaps, even pampered.

Drake's brows furrowed, and Aira knew that was a warning sign in itself. "Well, you hear that, Aira? Be glad she never found you," Drake said darkly, chuckling.

It seemed Mary didn't feel the same way as she spat, "Vivian would be horrified by the way you're speaking to me! I told her this kid needs special help. She stabbed a teacher with a pair of plastic scissors for heaven's sake!"

Whoa, whoa, hold up; this was escalating into a pretty bad situation from where Aira was standing. Her parents were both standing straight, and their arms were folded across their chests. Aira knew from previous experience they were getting defensive.

Come to think of it, Aira did recall a situation where a pair of scissors and blood was involved, but she couldn't quite pull that memory from the back of her mind.

"That child was always such a compulsive liar and so clingy to Vivian and Charles. I always said it wasn't healthy, and it took a kindergarten teacher being stabbed to really get the point across all because that poor woman wouldn't let Aira leave the classroom!" she spat, taking a step back as Aiden now hovered next to his father.

Emma looked apprehensive. "She *stabbed* a teacher, huh?"

Mary, now feeling trapped, turned her head to the side and nodded. "She was a strong kid. She once threw Marie off the porch by just picking her up," she stated, a matter of fact.

Aira was getting more and more upset by every word this woman said. Before she could plead to Emma and Drake for them to just leave, she had to take a step to the side as Van moved passed her. Mentally, Aira was panicked at what Van would say or do. Her panic wasn't directed at Mary's safety but at the thought of police being called to likely investigate a murder. This woman wasn't only being disrespectful to Emma but also to Drake, which she knew would cause Van to insinuate she was nasty to him as well.

Chapter Fifty-One

As soon as Van moved closer to Drake, he looked the woman up and down, sizing her up. Mary's eyes seemed to glass over with sudden recognition. "You-*you* should be ashamed of yourself for how you treated me at the hospital that day!" she screamed, anger and frustration washing over her face.

Van didn't feel the same way. "And you are...?"

"Oh no, *no*, you will not intimidate me again, Mr. Volkov," she growled as she pointed an accusing finger at the larger man. "You scared me away from that hospital, but you will *not* scare me away from my own front lawn! You're a dirty *liar*!"

It took a moment for Van to understand just what this vile creature was on about. After briefly looking her over, he remembered where he had seen this vulture before. It was the day Emma had first arrived at the hospital, and he had excused himself to get some coffee.

He growled low as he tapped on the damn machine. It was jammed, and because of Drake's pleads in the past, he couldn't even rip it open to see what was taking so long. The hospital cafeteria was closed, and upon further inspection, there wasn't even any milk in the reception office.

As if his day couldn't get any more irritating, there were two scarecrows chatting loudly in the seats across from him. At first, their attention had been set on Van until he had cleared it up by throwing them an annoyed glance. They soon shut up and started to whisper about someone's death and money. Van really couldn't have given a damn until a certain little girl's name popped up in their conversation.

"It's horrible what happened, I mean, wolves, really? They were ripped apart! Wasn't the ranger there at all?" one of them exclaimed. "How are you coping with all of this, anyway, Mary?"

The Mary woman sighed. "Well, as far as I know, she doesn't have anyone that will take her. I would, but that child is such a handful, and with this added trauma, well, I'd end up murdering her myself by the end of it."

The other woman, despite the situation, stifled an obvious giggle. "Well, I heard—" She ushered Mary to come closer and despite whispering, plainly stated, "That Vivian and Charles both had life insurance. Don't tell anyone, but my husband said that Charles told him their kids would each get over three hundred thousand dollars. The only one left is Aira, so she gets the house and over nine hundred thousand dollars!"

Although Van couldn't have cared less about these two morons, the fact remained that they showed no sympathy towards the situation when the topic of money was brought forward.

The older scarecrow, Mary, almost fell out of her seat. "Really? Holy— Well, now that I think about it, we do have more than enough room, and my brother is a lawyer," she gushed, and they both let out maddening giggles.

Van ignored them as best he could. He even ignored Konstantin pacing and growling at the pure topic of these arrogant women's conversation, but it was a losing battle. He couldn't stand money-hungry humans. Although he wasn't particularly fond of the child, he didn't think it was right to let her go to this money leech. After all, his brother had been throwing hints for days about adopting the girl himself, no matter how much Van disliked the idea. In fact, from the spike in his brother's energy from upstairs, he was fairly sure Drake had just talked Emma into it.

Well, he supposed he did need an outlet for Konstantin. Turning around, Van moved closer to the two women, scowling with his cup of coffee in hand.

Their eyes instantly widened and lit up at the mere sight of him. "Can we help you?" one of them asked, smiling like they'd just won the lotto. From their conversation earlier, Van guessed they thought they really had just won big time... but not for much longer.

"You were both just talking about a child named Aira, were you not? Aira Blight, by any chance?" He feigned

ignorance, averting his eyes as he did so — he was bored with this already.

Well, the way their faces paled he could tell this little mind game fun was already over.

"N-No?" one of them stuttered as she touched her face nervously. "Why would you want to know about her?"

This was far too easy. Van's cold smirk could have sent them running for their lives. "I'm here to visit her as her temporary guardian. Her father's contract was through my company." It was so easy to lie when you were the boss.

Their faces seemed to drop so low. Van contemplated calling over the janitor to pick them up off the floor, but he was far from done with these idiots.

"You see, I think you're a bit confused, ladies. Her claim isn't nearly as much as you seem to think it is — by the time she's twenty-one, as her guardian, I'll make sure her assets and net worth are ten times that amount. She'll be worth more than your own pitiful existence."

They were stumbling over their words as the older one tried to make a coherent sentence. "How-How dare you assume that we were—?"

Van chuckled ominously. There wasn't much in this world that amused him, but watching this two squirm in their own seats was most definitely humorous.

Van reached his arm out and dropped his coffee, watching as it splattered over the two ladies. They yelped and jumped from their seats, screaming like banshee's as they wiped the hot liquid away. "Are you crazy?"

"Well, some would say crazy, but most would jump at the word monster. Pick your poison," he answered, his tone *husky and ardent. He was truly at a stalemate between feeling amused and vexed.*

"I'm calling security," the younger one muttered as she made a break for it down the hallway, with that Mary woman following. They looked incredibly uncomfortable as they hobbled away with their dampened pants.

Van's amusement quickly dissipated as he realized what he had just done—for a human child no less. Growling in annoyance, it suddenly dawned on him that he was, yet again, in a bit of an incredibly exasperating predicament.

He had to get that shit-stain of a coffee machine to somehow spit out another cup of coffee without destroying it in the process.

"Damnit…"

The shit he did for that kid.

Ah, now, he remembered. He'd come back just as Emma and Drake decided that they were going to adopt the girl — and then proceeded to persuade *him* to do most of the dirty work soon after the kid was released from the hospital.

Before he could stop himself — he was never good at self-control with his words — Van asked, "Where's the other scarecrow you were with?"

The look on her face was enough to tell Van she was completely taken aback. "You are so much ruder than all those magazines made you out to be!" she shrieked. "I bet that girl hasn't got a cent left to her name thanks to you."

He ignored Aira and Emma's confused looks as he replied haphazardly, "Think what you want. I wasn't the one gossiping about blood-money when the wound was still fresh."

True to his word, he had rolled Aira's inheritance into his company stocks and other franchises. That kid's net-worth at this point trumped his by thousands. Aira would soon learn she had been a millionaire since she was ten years old. He just hoped Emma and Drake had drilled some business morals into her so that it stayed that way. He had been stuck with a lot of things concerning the girl, but being her financial savior when she was of age was *not* going to be one of them.

In a way, he had indeed taken his role as her financial guardian quite seriously. Van was no idiot when it came to money and how to handle it. Being alive for almost two centuries, you learned very quickly how to make money, and Van Volkov became quite good at it. He had over thirty shifter packs under his thumb, and with most shifters refusing to even correspond with humans, he had a lot of monthly allowances to hand out. The exchange rate wasn't helping in recent years, either.

Nothing came free in this new world, and that included land. What had once belonged to them now belonged to the Government, and that meant taxes and buying back land deeds that had once never existed. It was all a headache to his lawyers who cursed him to hell every day, among other things.

"But," he continued and grabbed Aira by her arm, pulling her to him and shoving her forward towards this old bat. "If you want the girl for the money, take her."

Aiden stood in front of his sister to catch her as she stumbled. "Van, what the *fuck*?" he hissed.

He ignored Aira's confused and sad eyes as she looked back at him and snapped, "But if you take her, I'll be riding on that Donkey-ass of yours the whole damn way. Originally, I had thought you were a simple vulture, but now, I see you're the carcass those vultures feed on."

"You... Go to hell!" Mary, despite her horrified expression, seemed to take the hint as she turned on her heel and stormed back towards her house. Van resisted the urge to boot her in the ass on the way up.

"Going there in a hand basket," Van muttered. People said a lot of things to him, and 'go to hell' had to be the politest so far.

At that reaction, Drake muttered, "I'm actually glad we don't talk to our neighbors now."

Emma huffed, "Women like that is the reason I didn't have many friends in college."

Aira didn't even let out a laugh as she stared sadly at the woman's retreating figure. Van simply turned and started to walk to his car. The small hand that caught his jacket sleeve didn't even make him bat an eyelash as he stopped and asked, "What?"

Now, the fact that Aira had actually made him stop didn't annoy him nor did it annoy him when she blatantly ignored his question, but what annoyed him was when she turned her head and asked, "Mom, can I go with Van?"

The last thing he wanted was an emotionally charged human riding home with him. Releasing pent up anger and sadness was one thing, sobbing in general turmoil was another. After all, Van had experience with anger and rage-induced rants. He couldn't even be around a crying female without saying something to add to their hysteria.

And, like always, he was left dealing with this fractured human when Emma hesitantly nodded. She was obviously confused by Aira's request, but Van knew better than anyone that the woman couldn't say no to this little creature when she was upset.

That make's two of us, he thought with a disdainful frown.

Moving to the car with Aira trailing behind, Van got in and waited as Aira waved to her mother. As soon as she was in the car, Van sped off, his wheels screeching as he drove over the gutter. He did it solely to annoy the vulture in the house next to them. That thing should count its blessings. She was lucky he didn't do a burnout on her lawn and leave the street up in smoke.

He drove slower waiting for Drake and Aiden to catch up. He didn't need Emma riding his ass about his driving with Aira in the car. Van also wondered if Emma and Drake knew that Aiden didn't actually have a license to drive when he borrowed their car to get to the house. Perhaps, deciding *not* to have any pups was the best idea Van ever had. Drake made them seem like more trouble than they were worth.

"Mr. Van?"

He mentally groaned. In the few days he had been back in America, Van had quickly learned that when the girl referred to him as "Mr. Van," she was planning on asking him some rather painful questions or wanted something. He wished she would revert back to being a snarky little brat. He, at least, *knew* how to handle that crap.

He didn't hold back as he snapped, "What?"

"That woman said something about money…"

"And?" He didn't like where this conversation was going.

It took a moment for her to gather her courage to ask, "How much did my parents leave me?"

Well, she caught on quick. Perhaps, Drake and Emma *did* do something right.

"The last time I checked, a little over three, but that was five years ago. I haven't checked the accounts lately," was his blatant answer.

He could tell she was staring at him incredulously. "Three hundred thousand dollars, you mean?"

The way she stared wide-eyed was almost laughable to Van. "Three *million*, little one."

Van chuckled when her eyes just about popped out of her head. Three million dollars would be a lot of money to a girl who only had to survive to earn it.

It bothered him that he wanted to ask if she was okay. It bothered him a damn lot, actually.

Her smile suddenly shined through those sad eyes. "I don't think I thanked you, Van."

"For?"

"Giving me this life. Giving me a second chance. Giving me a *choice* to come with you to Russia or stay here."

He tilted his head to look at her briefly before his eyes fell back on the road. "And what's your choice?"

Russia was a hard place to be with his pack. She would have to learn how to speak, how to act and how to stand up for herself if she wanted to survive among his kind. His brothers were all wild at heart and followed old traditions, including those of the animal they had close connections with. They were humans in form only. In their souls, they were as wild as the wolves that ran free and just as dangerous if *anyone* showed submission. Aira would have to learn to be a wolf while in a human's body. Truthfully, he hoped she would stay with Lucas Wright. His pack was more closely related to humans than the animal inside. Jillian would forgive him, as she always did.

And yet, deep down, he hoped she'd come with him. Van wouldn't admit it out loud, but maybe he would miss her. Perhaps, he would even worry about her. Or maybe he was afraid she wouldn't need them if she were to find her own path in the future. He refused to feel disturbed by the thought of this girl finding a husband and making a normal life for herself.

"It hurt a lot when you left and took Aiden with you. I don't think this time I could take it if I had to say goodbye to you two a second time as well as my parents. I mean, I just said goodbye to the parents I never remembered until now. I don't think my heart could take it." She placed a small hand on her chest and looked down. "So I want to come too… more than anything."

Van couldn't help but give a small, very unnoticeable smile as she said that. "If that's what you wish."

He was glad she didn't ask about her grandfather. He could have strangled that stupid human for even mentioning the old bastard. He was sure Emma was going to ask questions, and then he and Drake would be holding down the fort in his apartment for the night. That was a secret they had hoped to keep just that — a secret. That man was an annoying milestone in his very existence and checkbook.

Aira grinned and nodded. He could feel her sadness start to dissipate already. "One more thing, Mr. Van?"

He resisted the urge to sigh. "*Yes*?"

"I'm a little hungry. Can we go get something to eat before we go home?"

Now that she mentioned it, he could have sworn he heard her stomach rumble after they were both in the car. Chuckling softly, Van shook his head and said, "All the restaurants are in the other direction."

Aira flushed when she realized he was right. "Oh, well, don't worry."

Too late, Van found an opening in the island that separated the two cross lanes, and the car screeched as he made a sharp left-hand turn, his tires screeching the whole time. As soon as his car made it to the other side, it came to a jolting halt until he stomped on the gas and made a dash for the green light up ahead.

Aira didn't even piss her pants this time. She actually laughed as she held on to the side door. She was grinning as she looked at him and giggled, "You're either suicidal or crazy!"

Van ignored her but felt as if his whole body had suddenly been electrocuted when he heard her whisper, "But that's why I love you."

He didn't know whether it was Konstantin or his own being that drove his mind to near insanity from those few words. Nothing scared Van Volkov easily, but words like those made him both angry and terrified all at the same time.

Chapter Fifty-Two

Emma watched carefully as Van and Aira got into the car. She didn't believe this sinking feeling was caused by that horrid woman but instead, by something much darker, and it involved her daughter and Van, no matter how hard she tried to deny it.

Aiden was next to leave as he got into the car she had let him borrow and drove off. He had made plans, or so he had told her. Truthfully, Emma didn't believe he had *plans*. He was running home to call a certain someone back in Russia, though he had failed to tell her who this someone was or what they were to him. Her children needed to stop growing up *now*.

As she and Drake got into their own vehicle, she looked over at her mate and gave him a very odd look. This didn't go unnoticed as Drake looked over and asked, "Something wrong, hon?"

Everything. She shook her head and frowned as she buckled her seatbelt. "You knew about Aira's grandfather, didn't you?" she accused. She had felt him when the name was mentioned by Mary and knew that Drake had tensed up just as much as she had. It was as if he knew all along.

He started the car and paused for a moment as if thinking about his answer. "Yes, I knew."

Emma let out a deep sigh. "Van as well?"

Drake nodded solemnly. "I'm sorry, hon. I should've told you."

"Yes, you should have. I feel like we kept her from him now! We could have sorted something out, Drake. Perhaps, this whole thing could have been easier on Aira if she knew her family. We could have worked something out like weekend visits or even holidays and—"

She was cut off when Drake snapped. "He wanted to get full custody, Emma, and take her away."

It was as if someone had just dumped a bucket of ice water down her back. "What?" She was in shock. "Whe-when?"

Drake sighed heavily. "A year before Van and Aiden left. Van's lawyers got a call from his and slapped a custody case in their faces. Because of the law, our names were kept confidential, even Van. We had to pay a lot of people to keep it all quiet."

"That money that went missing… you…?" Emma was almost losing her mind. She almost was too afraid to even know the dirty details.

Drake averted his vision away from Emma. "Paying off favors. Van took the harder hit, though. I don't think his checkbook really recovered," he explained, his tone filled with contempt.

"B-but why? I-I mean; we would have been fine. Those documents were legally binding and... and Van made sure of that." She was desperately trying to make sense of the situation.

"Because we almost lost her, Em. The judge ruled that to protect Aira because of her memory loss and trauma, it was best to let her be where she was. We got lucky."

Emma closed her eyes, trying not to scream out and have a breakdown of what had been happening over the last few days. "Well, who *was* he to make you and Van so nervous that you couldn't even tell *me*?"

Who the heck was their daughter related to that would make Drake this secretive? They had a link where no secrets could be kept; yet, Drake had defied it for this long. Years ago, people had come to her house and did an inspection. Aira was taken to three different therapists besides Susan. Drake would leave work in the middle of the day for "meetings." Van paid for all of that and more.

Drake started to drive the car away from the premises and towards the highway following Van and Aira when he muttered, disdainfully, the name of the man that had caused him grief for a year straight. "Richard Croft."

Emma could have swallowed her own tongue for asking so many questions. No wonder Drake had gone so far as to keep their identities a secret. It couldn't be true. Aira couldn't be the granddaughter of Richard Croft.

Richard Croft was the man who covered up vampire and shifter related problems politically and in the media. He made sure anything in the news concerning the supernatural was downplayed and kept only a myth. He was a powerful man only because his *son*, Vincent Croft, was the previous Sargent Major of the United States Army. Now, she knew exactly why Drake decided to keep this from her. Van and Drake had known this man for a long, long time, and to think, they had been hiding his own granddaughter right under his nose.

"No, no, Drake please tell me you're joking," Emma pleaded, wishing more than anything that this was some twisted joke on her mate's part.

"Wish I was, Em..."

Emma sighed shakily. This was just the thing to break apart what they had built.

"But you don't have to worry. It happened years ago, and we haven't heard anything since then. Van isn't worried, so I'm not worried either. There was a reason Vivian kept him away from her kids — enough reason for Richard to just drop the case," Drake explained, smiling at Emma soothingly.

Emma nodded slowly. "Maybe she knew what Richard and Vincent were doing. This is just too crazy. Is that the reason Ronan's after Aira? Because he knows about Richard?" Nothing made sense anymore.

Drake sighed. "I don't know. Em, let's just drop it. It's in the past along with *that* day. Aira didn't ask about it, so we should just let it rest. I haven't even thought about Croft in years, and we haven't needed his help."

So, *that* was the reason Van never contacted Vincent to fix this media frenzy about the attack at the school. Emma relaxed, knowing that years had passed and that if he wanted Aira, he would have come for her a long time ago. Things just kept getting more complicated. But something else that woman had said made Emma uneasy.

"She was a strong kid. She once threw Marie off the porch by just picking her up."

Emma had thought she was just being a hypochondriac thinking that Aira was stronger than most girls and even men. There had been a couple of incidents where Aira had caught an object in mid-air without even batting an eye. There was also that incident in middle school where she...

"Drake, remember when Aira... threw that boy into the lockers when she was in middle school?" she asked hesitantly.

Drake grunted, feeling uneasy that all this crap was being brought up after his daughter had just confronted her own nightmares. "Why?"

"Mary, she mentioned Aira was pretty strong when she was a child. Drake, everyone we spoke to did say she was a lively, loud kid, but when she came to us, it was like she wasn't even there. She never spoke out of turn. She never asked for anything. We never had any trouble until now..."

Drake was becoming irritated as he snapped, "So what's your point?"

Emma flinched at his brash tone. Drake only ever snapped when anything negative about Aira was involved. He was a protective father and lived for his family.

She gulped. "Well, perhaps, there's something much more deep rooted in Aira than just the murders."

She knew Drake was rolling his eyes when he said, "You were strong as well before you met me. Remember when you put a crack in Van's office wall?"

Emma huffed and shook her head. *"Yes,* thank you. But that was because I had a shifter mate, and Susan explained that humans who have that certain fate, no matter how rare, are stronger so that they can survive long enough to find their—"

The car suddenly went quiet. Both occupants went stock-still. Drake slowed the car, his mind going crazy processing what Emma had just said. Aira's abnormal strength, her nightmares about wolves, and her intelligence — all that added up to something much, much bigger... and dangerous.

"Drake..." Emma muttered with a worried expression. "You don't think Aira has a—. You don't think there's a shifter out there, who is destined to be with Aira, do you?"

Drake was silent, thinking back to Aleksandra's warning years earlier.

"They came looking for the mate of Konstantin that day they attacked the humans. It's too bad the seer they have on their side is not very accurate, for they came a few years too early. It's ironic. Their attempt at changing the future really did set everything in stone, no?"

Drake growled as he punched the steering wheel in pure frustration, making Emma jump.

"Drake, are you okay?"

He nodded as he sped up, catching up to Van and Aira in the car ahead. "I'm fine."

Van's car suddenly swerved through the island separating the highways, making Drake slow down. Emma gasped from the passenger seat, eyes wide as she exclaimed, "What's he doing?"

Their handsfree started to ring, and Drake hit the button to answer. "Van!" he yelled, already thoroughly annoyed from the topic their conversation had ended on.

Van's monotone, gruff voice came over the speaker. "The kid was hungry."

Drake blinked as he did a double take. It almost sounded like Van was *laughing*?

Sighing heavily, Drake slammed on the brakes and followed suit, ignoring Emma's shouts as he spun around onto the other side. After all, Van always did what he wanted to do. There were no limits to what he would do to get what he wanted, and for the first time, that scared both Drake and Emma.

Chapter Fifty-Three

"Grandpa, do you want a burger?"

The old graying man shook his head with a smile. "No, Christine. Grandpa will just have a good ole' water," he chuckled.

The man, flipping burgers on the hotplate outside, rolled his eyes at his father. "Sure, Dad, 'water,' as in whiskey."

Richard shook his head as his family sat down on the backyard picnic table to eat. It was a special day today. Today was his late wife's birthday. Every year, they celebrated the day she was born and the life she lived. He only wished his daughter and youngest son were here to celebrate as well.

He chuckled sadly as he held up his scotch and whispered, "I miss you, Vivian."

Despite being surrounded by his remaining children and grandchildren, he felt alone. In times of war, he had learned that sons buried their fathers with honor and pride. He shouldn't have had to bury his daughter and his grandchildren. His wife's heart broke in half the day he buried his youngest son, Aither, and when his youngest daughter left, it nearly killed both he and his wife.

Richard smiled as he remembered how creative his daughter was when she named her youngest Aira. He would never forgive himself for not being there to save her — to save Avery and Ian, his first-born grandchildren.

He wanted Aira to come live with him and his wife but whoever had her, fought tooth and nail to keep her away. It made him angry that he couldn't even see her face. Sighing, he took another swig of his whiskey and watched as his grandson tried to entertain him with sports stories.

Mae would have enjoyed this, he thought sadly as he thought of his wife. She had died nearly six years ago. Sometimes, Richard thought that Mae had wanted to die if only to be reunited with her children — Vivian and Aither.

His oldest granddaughter suddenly took his arm, pulling him up with panicked eyes. "Grandpa, get up! There's something on TV!"

Richard sighed heavily. "There are lots of things on television, Christine." Perhaps, it was one of those silly soccer shows his grandson rambled on about incessantly.

"Dad, you come look at this!" Vincent called, his tone harsh and foreboding.

Richard finally got to his feet as he walked into the house. His three children, including Vincent, stood in the living room, staring wide-eyed at the television. It was a news program.

"The attack at Newport High School is still under investigation after giant 'wolves' invaded the facility and injured dozens of students, teachers, and officers. Following the buildings collapse, rescue crews were instigated to leave the premises following information that all students were evacuated. However, this picture has surfaced showing a student being carried from the debris, injured and frightened, before being taken for medical treatment."

Vincent hissed, "Shit. Dad, did you know about this?"

Richard shook his head. This was the first he'd heard about wolves being involved. As soon as the picture popped up on the screen, everyone seemed to look twice at the girl in front of them. The girl had dark hair — all matted up from the event — and bright blue eyes. She looked pale and scared as she stared up at something. The name that the news anchor declared made his blood run cold.

"Aira Volkov."

"Dad... that's..." his daughter gasped, but Richard simply nodded.

"I know... but how?" She had Vivian's eyes. He had no doubt in his heart that the girl on that screen was the only surviving child of his daughter.

Volkov.

Richard growled as he dropped his glass and ordered, "Vincent, do what you have to do. Find her."

His son nodded obediently. It seemed this family get-together had just turned into a manhunt.

Chapter Fifty-Four

It seemed that one minute; Aira was just lying in bed, listening to repetitive pop music with a book in her hand wishing Van and Aiden would return, and the next minute, there they were, right in front of her. Everything had just changed so rapidly that the poor girl thought she might have to check for whiplash. So much had happened in the past few weeks that she was sure this was all a dream. She was still deciding whether it was a good dream or not, however.

And now, she was back at the reserve where she had gotten lost on Emma's birthday more than five years before. Aira remembered this place so well because it was the place where she spoke normally for the very first time and where she found Vaughn, the little gray wolf cub who would later become her best friend, her only *true* friend.

Aira took a big, shaky breath as she looked down and smiled at the now adult wolf. It seemed he knew where they were as he raised his nose into the air and sniffed around. It hadn't been an easy decision. That was certain, but Aira knew it was the *right* decision.

Sighing heavily as she placed different items of clothing into her suitcase, Aira glanced over to her wolf friend who sat by the window, just staring out. He did that sometimes as if he were waiting for something. Aira smiled as she tread over carefully and petted his head.

"What's up, boy?" she asked as she massaged behind his ear. Usually, the beautiful animal would go crazy over this treatment, but tonight, he simply sat there, gazing out the window so intently that Aira had to look to make sure there was no one outside.

A low grumble erupted from Vaughn's throat as he started to howl. This was something he'd never done before. Even when Aira tried to shush him, he continued to howl loudly, as if crying out into the night.

"He's trying to call out to see if there are any other wolves around," came a smooth, deep voice from her doorway.

Aira looked at Aiden and frowned. "There aren't wolves anywhere around here."

Aiden nodded. "Exactly, but he doesn't know that. He's waiting to get a message back."

She looked back at Vaughn with a sad expression before kneeling down and wrapping her hands around the wolf's neck, nuzzling her cheek into his fur. Never had Aira even once thought that he might be lonely here. Perhaps, she had been the only one comfortable in the way things were.

"Are you taking him to Russia?" her brother asked as he moved to sit next to her on the floor. "He'll have to get vaccinated and chipped and all that sort of stuff before he'll be allowed on the plane. It doesn't sound so great to me, though. He'll never be able to go back to the wild after that. At least now, he has some chance."

Aira had a deep frown on her face as she looked at her best friend with worried eyes. She had wanted to grow up and become an adult—but Aira never thought about the adult decisions she'd have to make along the way.

She felt Aiden ruffle her hair as he made his way out of the room. "You'll know what to do, Air. You always do."

"Yeah..." she whispered as she stroked Vaughn's ear lovingly.

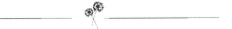

That was the night she realized that Vaughn needed more. He needed to be free — free to roam and find his own place in this strange world... just like her.

This wasn't the first time Aira had met Lucas Wright, but it was the first he had spoken to her. Aira didn't feel uncomfortable around the man like she did around his daughter, Jillian, but it was still awkward. Lucas didn't mention the incident concerning his daughter as he smiled at Aira.

"I'm happy to see you recovered well," he mentioned towards her still-bandaged arm. "It was quite a show."

Aira placed a convincing smile onto her face. "You could say that..."

Lucas was close friends with the people that ran this certain reserve, who made sure the "wild" wolves that occupied the area stayed away from the humans that populated near here. They had assessed Vaughn briefly and concluded that it wasn't too late for him to adjust back into the wild. The good side of all this was that this place technically wasn't out in the natural wild. It was monitored so that every living creature was safe.

"He'll do fine here, Aira. He *was* born here after all," Drake tried to make this transition easier on his daughter, but the look on her face said otherwise.

"I feel like I'm abandoning him."

She looked up as Lucas moved closer and placed a comforting hand on her shoulder. "You see that collar and leash?" he said as he mentioned towards the objects that were strapped around the young wolf. "Those are meant for *dogs*, my dear. He is not a dog. He is a part of us, and he belongs out there, with his brothers."

He pointed towards the neck of trees leading out to the hundreds of acres of land. Aira didn't know anything about shifters or their history — hell, their history was only in fairytales — but she did know *one* thing; their brethren were their heart. They held each other in the highest regards and would easily put themselves in danger for their pack or loved ones. Aira knew this from experience.

With understanding sweeping across her eyes, Aira kneeled and took off her friend's collar. He sat still, patiently watching her, before biting into the piece of material in her hands.

"No, boy, it's not playtime," she muttered, trying to keep her tears at bay. With a shaky breath, she wrapped her arms around his neck and hugged him, burying her face into his fur as she whispered, "Thank you for saving my life. Thank you for listening to me when I was sad. Thank you for finding me when I was lost."

Vaughn seemed confused as he tilted his head, watching as his master got to her feet. She was sad. He knew.

Aira suddenly put on a strong face as she snapped, "It's time to go, Vaughn. Go on." She pointed towards the neck of trees and Vaughn, still confused, moved away from her with his ears down. However, he never left.

Howling could suddenly be heard as Drake called out. Aira stared at her father in complete awe as he mimicked a wild wolf's call. Before she could ask what he was doing, a low, haunting howl could be heard in the far distance, almost as if replying to Drake.

Vaughn's ears suddenly perked up as he heard the call as well and with a moment of hesitation, bolted towards the trees. He stopped for a moment to look back at the human he was leaving behind. Aira waved a shaky hand, and that was all Vaughn needed to see before he was out of sight completely.

Aira remembered the first day they had met. She had once thought that she was the one to find him, but really, *he* was the one who found *her*. Her wolf had risked his own life to save hers when she was attacked at the school. He was there when she had cried for days after Aiden and Van had left for Russia. He was always there and now... he wouldn't be there anymore.

The thunder crashed down, and Aira whimpered as she hid under her bed sheet. Just as she was about to make a dash for Aiden's bedroom, she could feel something crawling on the

top of her sheets, right before a head popped under. Aira simply watched as the little wolf cub huddled under the sheet with her and jumped up to lick her face.

Aira giggled. "Go-go back to be-bed, Vaughn," she stuttered. He didn't listen and just kept jumping onto her. Aira laughed harder as she pulled a book out from her side table and asked, "Would-would you li-like to learn words wi-with me? I-I can't tal-talk very good, though."

He didn't seem to mind or care as his mouth formed what Aira thought was a big grin. They spent the rest of the night with a torch under some sheets learning words together. Aira had convinced herself Vaughn could understand her, and soon, the thunder and lightning were forgotten.

Her mother had found them huddled together the next morning and sound asleep, and from then on, Vaughn had always slept with her. Aira shivered as she realized her bed would be a very cold place from now on.

The arm that wrapped around Aira's shoulders almost went unnoticed until her father said, "You did great, sweetie."

Aira nodded as she tried to hide her tears and after muttering a quick thank you to Mr. Wright, she fled back to the car and waited for her father. It didn't take very long for him to come after her.

The car ride was silent until Drake asked, "You okay?"

No, nothing was okay, but she nodded absently, anyway. She didn't like how much was changing. Aira gripped the collar and leash in her hands, her thumb tracing over the nametag that dangled from the object. It read the name "Van" because Vaughn's spelling was too long. She had held on to the belief that she would at least have one friend in Russia, but now, he was gone. The further they drove from the reserve, the more Aira's heart ached. It took all of her willpower not to tell her father to pull the car over and go running back to find him.

"He wasn't my dog or my pet," she suddenly said, the tears finally spilling over her reddened cheek. "He was my *friend*."

Drake seemed to understand. "I know he was, hon. Vaughn saw us as a part of his pack, and I know he loved you." He grinned. "Albeit, he didn't see you as his equal... but he cared..." he joked.

A soft, sad giggle erupted from Aira. "You're lying."

Drake laughed and shook his head. "You'll see him again someday, Aira. I promise you that."

The tears didn't stop, but the aching of her heart did stop a little bit. As Aira gripped the last remnants of her best friend, she smiled. They would meet again someday, and even if Vaughn didn't remember her, she would always remember him. Van Volkov was the man who saved her life, and next to him, Vaughn, her pet wolf, was also her hero. To Aira, her wolf did his namesake proud.

Perhaps, it was destiny. Maybe he was supposed to find her and save her from Erik. Or maybe it was all just coincidence. Whatever it was; Aira thanked God for that special gift even if he did leave too soon. She wondered if he realized she had left.

"Thanks, Dad, for taking me home that day and for today. I don't think I thanked you properly."

Her father smiled a smile that let Aira know he would do anything for her. "Your mother and I would do anything for you, Aira. But..." He hesitated for a moment, "I feel like you're suppressing how you really feel about everything you've been through over the last couple of weeks."

Drake looked worried as his eyes momentarily glanced at her before going back to the road. Aira bit her lip as she thought about what he had just confessed. Perhaps, she *had* been suppressing her emotions about their visit to her *home*, but there really wasn't much she could do. She knew she would grieve heavily at some point, but she also knew her parents would be there to catch her when she fell.

"It'll come... in time. When it does, I promise I won't hide it like before," she whispered. She knew she had everyone's support. That was the only thing that kept her going. Today was just the first stepping stone into moving forward with her life.

Drake chuckled. "We'll always be there, Aira. Never forget that."

As his words sunk in, Aira grinned. She felt like the luckiest girl in the world. There was nothing that could break her down when she had her mother and father to pick her back up.

All that seemed to come crashing down when they pulled into her driveway, only to notice an unknown vehicle parked on the curb while Van's car was parked on the lawn.

As soon as the car stopped, Drake unbuckled his seatbelt and snapped, "Stay in the car, Aira."

She watched her father move towards the door, only to be greeted by a much larger man. Her father seemed to visibly pale as he briefly spoke to the stranger, almost trying to divert his attention back inside the house. It wasn't until the man's eyes locked with Aira's that she realized why her father was so nervous.

Those eyes seemed very, *very* familiar as they seemed to gaze into hers. He suddenly shoved her father out of the way as he marched towards the car, only to be pulled back and flung against the garage door by Drake.

Aira's breathing hitched as she watched the scene unfold, seeing more strange men come from around the side of the house and stab her father with what looked like a syringe.

All hell was breaking loose, and there was nothing she could do.

Chapter Fifty-Five

The room was silent, as the blonde woman looked him over with a horrified expression. It didn't take much to coerce her to let him in, but in the time she had gone missing while he waited in the kitchen, she had gone and contacted the very man he had wanted to speak with. It was almost turning out *too* well.

Van Volkov stormed into the room, the urge to kill almost seeping from his skin as he slammed one hand onto the kitchen bench. Richard didn't flinch; Volkov would not harm him, not with the media already so far up his ass. The wolf needed Richard.

The older man chuckled. "How good to see you again, Van." His greeting was flippant, and Van probably expected no less.

It seemed the beast already knew what Richard was after. "She's not here, and when she returns, I expect you to not

be here either." His warning fell on deaf ears as Richard simply smiled.

"*Eleven years*, you've hidden her for eleven years. I wonder how you have kept her so well behaved in that amount of time."

Van didn't look impressed as he growled, "What are you on about?"

Richard's expression fell into shock as he stared, baffled, at the Lycan. "That depends on what you're on about, Volkov? Eleven years and you truly haven't seen it?" he questioned, sincerely surprised. "I thought for certain that is why you fought so hard in court to keep her away."

At the time, Richard hadn't had a clue on who the people behind those God-forsaken lawyers were, but now, he understood. Only someone like Van Volkov could have thrown out money like that without a care.

It looked like he wasn't going to get an answer out of the woman or Volkov, so Richard quietly asked, "Has she had the dreams yet?"

The short gasp from the corner where the woman stood was the answer he needed. If she were having the dreams, then half his theory was at least correct.

"Emma, leave us," Van snapped, twisting his head to stare at human sneering in the corner.

Emma, although hesitant, nodded before exiting the kitchen. Van's attention swiveled back to Richard, asking, "What is it you want, old man?"

Richard seemed to know the questions Van would throw at him and answered almost instantly, "I want my granddaughter, Mr. Volkov. I've been searching for a long time, but now, I know why it was such a difficult task. What exactly would a *Lycan* want with a descendent of a L'ightat, I wonder?"

Van, just moments before, calm and tall, seemed to stiffen as his eyes glowed through his contacts. *"What...* did you just say?" he growled.

The graying man grinned at the wolf's reaction. "Well, I see that a shifter born of this world still has at least some knowledge of his roots back in Altholo. It shouldn't surprise a lowly human such as myself — Konstantin *is* one of the seven pureblooded Lycanthropes that were so cruelly cursed into purgatory on Earth, after all," he chuckled. His tone was haughty as he all but glittered with Van's realization. "Tell me, boy, is Konstantin serving his punishment well? It must be truly terrible, banished from one world, only to serve in another for the next thousand or so years."

Van looked as if he were about to rip the man to shreds. Richard wished he could have gotten a picture of the look on the beast's face. "My service to this world is none of your concern, human," he snarled.

"Your service? No, you were just the unlucky vessel Konstantin chose when he was thrown back like last week's stale bread."

Van's whole body seemed to shake as he snapped, "I see you've been in contact with the elders to know so much about me."

Richard huffed, "I have fixed your kind's mistakes for years, Volkov, and if I want to know something, there is little those degenerates can hide from me. You should remember yourself that shifters, vampires and the like are simply guests in this world."

Van chuckled as disdain seeped from his very being. Konstantin fought to come through; Richard could see this, but Van pushed him back down. There was little good letting the monster out on Richard at this point. He'd already made his intentions clear.

"I can assure you that the girl is no L'ightat." He tried to hold back the ferocious growl that grew in his chest, but Richard could see right through him. This monster couldn't hide his feral ways easily.

Richard's face seemed to soften. "You can't assure me of anything, Volkov. If she had the dreams, then she has seen the dead. Do not blame me. L'ightats were created by your people. They — *my wife* — were created to solely be a monster's meat shield." The contempt in his voice was painfully obvious as he spoke.

"They haven't been used for centuries, as you well know, Croft."

Richard shook his head. "They're still being used under the radar. They're drawn to shifters like a damn moth to light and if triggered, can be extremely dangerous to any aggressor threatening the shifter they choose to protect. Stop trying to convince yourself with lies. They're still being used under both our radars, and you damn well know it."

Richard was well aware that Van was powerful and that *if* his granddaughter were a L'ightat, her potential would stay dormant for as long as Van Volkov could defend himself or until he commanded her to fight.

"From what my son has found out about you, it seems the girl is fairly attached. Do not kid yourself into thinking her feelings are more than just her drive to serve you. It's in her blood to seek out the strongest shifter, and unfortunately, it was you who found her first," he explained, his expression riddled with derision. After seeing that news broadcast and catching the name Volkov, it had been easy to find out information on the child's life up until that point.

Van's expression seemed to mimic the old man's as he muttered, "If she's not a L'ightat, will you leave?"

With a curt nod of his head, Richard agreed. "If she is not a L'ightat, then I have no need to protect her. However, if she is what I suspect she is, then I do hope you understand why I need to take her away."

Richard Croft knew the Lycan would understand. Although they both felt equal disdain for the other, there was one person in the mix who would suffer the most from this: Aira.

"You better collar me up in case I decide to stop being so generous," Van grunted, looking in the direction of the kitchen window. His brother and Aira would return soon.

Richard chuckled and nodded as he pulled out his cell phone to call his son and some backup.

"If things work out today, we will take care of those problems in the news, Mr. Volkov, just as we always have."

Van didn't say a word and simply nodded, looking angry and sullen as he leaned against the kitchen counter.

Chapter Fifty-Six

The tears escaped her eyes as they did many days before, and Aira did nothing to wipe them away. No, not today — any day but today.

Aira stifled a frustrated and angry scream as she watched the chaos ensue from her comfortable place in the car. Mayhem had ensnared her life in the passing weeks, and she was sure this wasn't the end of it. But why did this have to happen today? She couldn't even begin to think about how God could let this happen. She had just said goodbye to one dear friend, and now, she watched helplessly as her family home was being intruded by these ghastly men.

Aira's breathing became haggard and still as her body tensed up. She could feel her muscles shake and convulse as she stared in absolute horror, watching as her father slumped to the ground from that *thing* the man had just stabbed him with.

Aira did indeed feel helpless, but beneath that horrible feeling was something else, she felt almost empty.

It wasn't until she saw Van, her hero and savior, calmly step out of the house and walk over to Drake that Aira, without much thought, threw the car door open, ran to the dark Lycan and grabbed hold of his shirt sleeve when she finally stumbled towards him. She stared up at him with pleading eyes, and he didn't even glance down or bat an eyelash at her disheveled appearance.

She shook his arm as her father kneeled, panting and grasping the area where he had been stabbed. "Van, what—?" she tried to ask what had happened, but Van seemed to already know the question her father was struggling to ask.

"It's a type of contagious bacteria that is deadly to humans but once injected on us, leaves shifters without their strength," was his blunt response. "After that, it then becomes harmless to humans even if it does spread."

The man that had injected her father stood off to the side simply watching Aira as she silently pleaded with Van to help. "What's going on?" she cried. Nothing made sense. Why was Van letting these men do this?

His eyes, hard and cold, looked down at her as if she were nothing but a nuisance. Slipping his arm out of her grasp, he suddenly turned the tables and grabbed her wrist, gripping it painfully. Aira winced as she tried to pry herself away. It was no use as her hero simply pulled her close, ripping her arm up, so she was almost dangling off the ground.

Aira let out a tiny, frightened squeak as she stared into his eyes, her face inches from his as Van whispered, "You will go with them, and you will *stay* with them."

What? What did he mean by that?

Her questions were never answered as she was thrown back, stumbling from the force as she tried to regain her balance, and stared in shock as Van simply grabbed hold of her father and helped him to his feet. It was then that she noticed Emma standing in the doorway, her face red from crying, staring sadly at her daughter.

The urgency of the situation suddenly dawned on Aira as she looked at Van once more. His face showed only regret rather than malice. His eyes, which dripped with cold rage, were not directed at her as she had thought previously. It was directed at someone else. Aira knew instantly that he was powerless to do anything at this point and was doing what he thought was best for the situation.

The sun glittered off of the silver collar around his neck, spooking Aira as she studied that cold, metallic object. Whatever it was, it was subduing him. For reasons unknown, she could almost *feel* his energy weakening.

"Aira, my sweet grandbaby," came an unknown voice from behind. Aira spun around just as a gentle hand touched her shoulder, and she was face to face with a man much older than Van or her father. "Please, don't be frightened."

She took a step back out of instinct, shrugging the man's hand off of her shoulder. "What have you done to them?" she snapped.

His body stiffened as he leaned more on his cane. Aira couldn't help but hear the low growls from Van and her father.

The old man shook his head and sighed heavily. "It's a shame, really it is. You were genetically bred for so much more than this, but Vivian did not listen. Now, look at the *things* you had to endure…" He eyed the two men behind her.

Aira couldn't help but let out an angered grunt, but before she could say anything, her father beat her to the punch.

"As soon as I recover, I'll rip your head off, Croft," he spat, using Van for support as he got to his feet.

Genetically bred; those words fluttered through her mind like tiny knives carving a window into a memory long forgotten. This old man, gray and withered, held Aira's gaze like a magnet.

Van's voice was what brought her back to reality. "You speak of the girl as if she was an item."

This Croft chuckled; as Aira's eyes seemed to glass over as if she had just faded off to another world. Nodding to the other man, he gave the signal to carry on with their plan. "It is time to show these creatures just what sort of *human* they have taken into their care, Vincent."

Vincent, not missing a beat, moved stealthily over to Van and Drake, pulling his gun from his pouch and pressing it against Van's temple. Although pure silver would do little to harm him on the outside, it would almost surely kill them if embedded *inside* their bodies. Aira knew this from the hundreds of questions she had thrown at her father shortly after her release from the hospital.

Aira supposed Croft had his answer, as she seemed to stare directly at the weapon against Van's head. Perhaps, he should have been more careful with his wishes. Aira stepped forward, her foot sliding across the cemented floor, and in an instant, her hand had shot out and grabbed Vincent's arm in a steel grip. Everyone stood in complete and utter shock as a loud crack resounded through the silence, and a wail of pure agony soon followed.

"Crap…" was all the old man could say as he raised his arm and his men thundered towards her, ready to pull her back. "L'ightats aren't that strong," he growled. "What have you done to my granddaughter, Volkov?"

Aira continued to hold onto the man's arm as he struggled. She was in a daze and completely ignorant to his grunts and cries. All she saw was Van and Drake in danger — that was all that registered in her mind. All she wanted to do was get the gun away. She didn't even notice the other men running towards her until she had finally let go, only to find her head buried into someone's chest, shielding her vision from this literal nightmare.

She didn't have to think twice about whom it was as she gripped her savior's shirt and pressed her body into his. Van pulled her closer, placing a hand on the back of her head as he growled low, warning everyone to stay away lest he rips their throats out. The men seemed to take the hint as they backed off, looking to Richard for a sign on what to do. Even he looked confused as to what to do, and that made Aira nervous.

Aira cried into Van's chest, shaking her head as she asked, "What am I?" For years, she had often wondered why she did the things she did, but no one could give her the answers, not even Van. "I want this to stop!" she wailed, crying heavily and soaking his shirt in the process. "I didn't do anything to anyone to deserve this!"

Van couldn't say anything as he held back his own rage at the situation. She could sense some sort of inner turmoil, but between her sobs, Aira couldn't concentrate on anything more than the situation at hand.

"There's nothing wrong with you," he grunted as he gripped her hair lightly, keeping her close to him. Turning to look at Richard, Van growled, "Get these idiots out of here."

There was a moment of hesitance before Richard nodded. Vincent slowly tread back to one of the cars to get first aid, and Emma stumbled out of the house to help Drake who was finding it hard to stay on his feet.

Van continued to stay with Aira for a moment longer before picking her up and carrying her into the house. He cursed when she hiccupped and continued to sob softly. Richard had gotten his damn answer, and Van could feel his body tense just thinking about this amazingly fucked up situation. This girl was both the bane of his existence and the sole reason he existed in the first place.

He knew now what he had to do, even if that was letting her go.

Chapter Fifty-Seven

Emma sighed as she came downstairs and with a curt glare to the two men sitting in the living room, said, "I gave her something to help her sleep. It's best *everyone*—" she eyed everyone in the room warningly, "—keep their voices down."

Richard cut through the silence as he coughed lightly. "I thank you for looking after her, but as per our agreement, I'll be taking her from this point on."

Drake almost choked on the water he had been sipping when the old men said this and exclaimed, "You'll be doing *what*, exactly?" Van instantly knew Richard would be lucky getting two steps out that door with Drake's "pup."

Drake looked at his brother for backup but was greeted by a man who seemed to be looking into space and ignoring everything that was going on around him.

Richard looked as if he had expected this reaction. "She needs guidance and to be with people who are biologically related to her. She can't be around Lycans, Mr. Volkov. As I've explained twice already, she displays temperaments of a L'ight—"

"Yes, we heard you, Croft, loud and fucking clear," Van growled, finally tuning in on the conversation. "Excuse my brother for his brash reaction to the thought of the girl being taken away. He *has* raised her from the time she was six years old if you recall."

"What exactly is a-a Light-what?" Emma asked, visibly confused.

Drake sighed as he answered, "L'ightats were created when the first Lycanthropes left *that* world," he explained, not even bothering naming the world his ancestors originated from before continuing, "They were originally created as gifts by the Wiccan covens who seemed to be infatuated with us. They would seek out human women and curse them to do any Lycan's bidding — including fighting for them. Over time, they became more powerful depending on the wolf they chose to serve. They were used as a meat shield."

Emma's eyes widened as she looked from Drake to Van. "A meat shield?"

Drake's lips formed a straight line as he too looked at Van. "We always made excuses for her devotion to Van. Maybe Croft's right; maybe she did choose him."

If Aira was a L'ightat, then this was wrong on so many levels. She would gladly die for Van, and Van would die without her *if* ever they did bond. It made Van's stomach churn in disgust just thinking about it. Even with these thoughts roaming around in his head, he refused to believe it. It was silly to even *think* that that was possible, but it was, and that made him burn up as the only emotion he'd ever known boiled inside of him.

Pure anger.

Van threw Drake a dark glare as his brother spoke about him as if he weren't even there. "Whether the *human* chose me or not, that doesn't draw away from the situation. She'll be staying with Mr. Croft."

Drake's head snapped around to stare at Van. "I didn't realize that that was your choice, *Alpha…*"

Emma fidgeted in her place in the corner. The way Van and Drake snapped at each other was making her nervous. They rarely fought or argued, but when they did, it was hard to break it up. She would often go out the next day and replace the furniture they broke…

Richard could sense the uneasy situation and stomped his walking cane down onto the floor to get both Lycan's attention. "I would never hurt my granddaughter if that is what you think… but don't think me as stupid for one moment. You two…" He pointed to Van and Drake. "Stop bickering and think reasonably about the situation. I know that stupid rogue Ronan is after her, and the last place he would ever dare to tread is on or near my compound. Think about it."

Ronan has no use for a L'ightat, Richard was well aware of that, but that certain Lycan had been giving everyone grief.

"It was only recently that I learned it was he who killed my daughter and grandchildren. The only thing I have left to offer is safety for my granddaughter — the last thing I have left of Vivian," he whispered.

"He killed them. She almost died," Emma squeaked from the corner, her head down and her eyes downcast looking at the floor. She rarely thought of Aira's time in the hospital, but when she did, it made her angry. Van supposed that was why Drake rarely mentioned the incident.

It didn't take Richard long to figure out Emma was referring to Aira and his family. "I know, and that's exactly why she will be better off with my family and me. I thank you for raising her, but I won't withhold my disdain for your husband keeping me away."

Emma didn't miss a beat as she replied, "There was a reason Vivian kept you away. What was that reason?" It had bothered her since that awful woman had mentioned it a week prior.

Richard didn't fuss as he answered, "We had our problems with Vivian. We lost our son, Aither, when she was a teenager. They were twins. She changed after that. She was never the same, and she left. It wasn't until my wife passed that I knew I had to find Aira and bring her home."

Van could tell that Drake and Emma were both uncomfortable with this conversation. Just from the looks on their faces, he could tell that they wouldn't give her up without a fight. However, the looks they gave Van as he hugged Aira outside couldn't compare to the looks they had at that very moment. Richard smiled knowingly as he asked the question that would send everyone over the edge.

"You wouldn't happen to be *in love* with my granddaughter, would you, Van?" he asked nonchalantly. That old bastard was stirring the pot, and he damn well knew it.

Van was well aware that, in the time Richard had come into contact with him, Van had given the impression humans were disgusting and vile despite living amongst them. It must have been amusing to watch the girl hug him and sniffle into his shirt.

All eyes were on Van as they waited for his answer. Drake and Emma both expected a curt huff and something along the lines of "The hell are you on about?"

His answer certainly sent them all reeling.

He smirked. "And what if I am?"

Richard's face fell so low it could have hit the floor. That was *not* the answer he had expected, but it certainly did help the bastard's cause when Drake, still weak, went to get out of his seat, a look of murder flashing across his face. Emma raced to hold her mate down, panic flashing across her face.

"Drake!" she snapped, pressing him back into his seat though Van was sure he could have thrown her aside if he wanted to.

Van eyed Drake carefully and gauged his reaction with uncertainty. He had expected Richard to react unpleasantly but not Drake. In truth, the old man was starting to irritate the crap out of him with this senseless chatter.

"I care little for the girl," Van admitted. "So, if you're all done wetting your pants…" He waved his hand as if to urge them to carry on with their conversation. Truthfully, that answer to Richard's question had left his lips before he even had the chance to think about the question. On the outside he was calm, but on the inside, he was going insane trying to find some reason behind his rogue tongue.

"You don't... care what happens to me?" came a soft, little voice from the staircase.

Van didn't even flinch when he realized the girl had heard him. His answer was cold, flat and direct as he snapped, "Don't put words in my mouth, girl."

It seemed Van wasn't the only one near breaking point as Aira snapped back, "But that's what you meant!"

With that, she took off back upstairs and the only other noise that could be heard was the loud slamming of her bedroom door. Emma visibly flinched from the boom, possibly not used to Aira displaying such behavior.

Drake sighed, as he went to stand up from his seat, but was left staring as Van stormed upstairs without a word. They all were left staring as the echo of a door slamming resounded back downstairs.

Chapter Fifty-Eight

As soon as she had reached her bedroom, she had started to grab any leftover clothing she had and threw them into her open bags. Aira had packed up most of her room previously for her move to Russia, but now, that seemed pointless. Van had made it clear he wanted her gone. If he wanted her to go, then she would go.

The slamming of her bedroom door made her jump as she kneeled on the floor over her luggage bag. Turning her head slowly, she visibly paled when she saw Van standing in the middle of her bedroom, eyes blazing and arms folded as he stared at her, possibly angered by what she was doing. Aira could safely say that that was the greatest emotion she had seen in his eyes *ever*.

It didn't take long before this one-sided staring contest turned into a battle of heated words. "If you needed help packing, you just had to ask," Van growled before he started to grab random pieces of clothing and items and shoving them into an open bag in the corner. Aira could faintly hear him cursing as he moved around, glaring at the air in front of his face.

Her lips tilted into a small smile as she tried to stifle the tiny giggle that was ready to escape but couldn't hold it in for long as she started to laugh. Her laughter was so heavy that tears started to build up before spilling over onto her reddened cheeks, and before she knew it, she was laughing and sobbing hysterically as she threw her torso to the floor and hid her face with her arms. For a brief moment, Aira actually considered that she might have just lost her marbles.

It wasn't until she felt the soft pressure on the back of her head that she looked up, hiccupping as she took in Van's candid expression. He had crouched down and placed his hand on the back of her head, as he had been doing the last few days when Aira completely broke down. This tiny action— something that *should* have made her uncomfortable — comforted her and brought her back to reality, no matter how tough the situation was.

"When I found you, I swore I'd wipe my hands of the problems that came with you," he mumbled, looking away when he realized what he had just said.

Taking his hand away and standing up, Van went to pace around the room as he picked up the clothing he had just been throwing around and placed them neatly back into the bag.

Aira gulped as she asked, "That man, he doesn't seem to like you or Drake very much. Why?"

Van's body stiffened as the walls he had let down seemed to reinforce tenfold. He turned slightly, his piercing eyes staring straight through her as he said, "You really want to know?"

Aira nodded from her place on the floor. She wanted to know more about Van.

His face visibly darkened as he looked away. "The human believes in a story that is only told to pups to scare them. They call the story *The Legend of the Lady and the Wolf*. The first shifters to come into this world were Lycanthropes — purebloods. Among them was a Lycanthrope named Konstantin, who was exiled from that world with six others."

"Why were they exiled?" she asked carefully.

Van continued to throw garments into the bag as he answered disdainfully, "Because they were *different*, stronger and smarter. They came here and were forced into purgatory, having to learn the ways of humans. They learned the hard way that humans also disliked anything that was different." His face was cold and guarded as he continued, becoming angry as he recounted the story he had been told since he was a pup. "One day, he was given a gift from the Wiccan Isadora. The gift was a human girl. He had come to resent humans and kept her locked away, but when you don't know something in poison, you won't know whether to toss it away or not."

"He began to care for the girl, and Isadora became jealous, and in her jealousy, she decided the best way to overcome her emotions was to request her brothers to kill the girl. Konstantin, clouded in rage and anger, killed anything and everything in his path. He murdered countless humans and shifters."

Aira didn't know why Van was telling her this when he had never told her much of his history before. Perhaps, he was trying to scare her, give her a reason to want to leave this place and never look back.

Or maybe he was trying to show her that he was no hero.

"What happened to Konstantin?"

He looked surprised when he turned and saw that she was concentrating solely on him. He looked as if he didn't know whether she was insane or simply an idiot for wanting him to continue such a story, but his face let it show he was seriously trying to figure it out.

Perhaps, he was the mad one for continuing. "He was destroyed by the ones he had sworn to protect. Konstantin's punishment was to serve humans and shifters alike for the next millennia as their protector," Van chuckled as he turned back to the girl. "But, he's not doing a very good job of that."

Aira turned her gaze from Van as she got up off the floor. "That girl… I think she would have been very sad to know he had died because of her."

Van looked slightly stunned with what she had just said. However, he hid it well as he raised a curious brow and said, "Well, it's just a story, but people like your grandfather seem to take it seriously. Because of that incident, humans are well prepared if anything like that should happen again. Richard, being one of those humans, prepared for any such trouble. You asked why he doesn't like us, and that's why, *malyutka*."

Aira's face reddened like a beet as she heard Van use Russian. His voice seemed to deepen with that one word, and it sent a chill up her spine. His voice was much nicer when he said it, though…

"The world I come from is a dangerous place. Maybe I forgot that when I asked you to come with us," he sighed.

A soft tap at the door caught her attention as she looked out at her father, who held a rather annoyed expression on his face. It seemed he had recovered as he looked from Van back to Aira and grunted, "Van, stop telling her stories…"

Van's earlier angry expression had all but disappeared as he threw Drake a bored look. "Yes, *stories*."

Aira took a step forward as she grabbed hold of Van's sleeve and looked up at him. "I'd like to meet him… Richard, I mean," she said hesitantly.

Van looked down at her, and if just for a split second, Aira could have sworn she saw a tiny smirk cross his face before it all but disappeared.

Aira kept close to her father and Van as they made their way down the stairs. The first person she noticed was her mother, Emma, as she sat awkwardly in the living room. The second person was the old man standing off to the side. It seemed this was the first time he was able to get a good look at her as he stared with wide eyes. Aira stepped forward with a little hesitance and said a little, "Hello…" Her smile was infectious as she continued, "I'm Aira."

Richard nodded slowly. "I know. I held you the day you were born."

Before Aira knew what was happening, Richard had dropped his cane and had taken her into a giant bear hug. Aira could feel the tense males behind her but ignored their presence as she awkwardly hugged this bear of a man back. It was then that she could have sworn she heard him quietly sob into her shoulder.

"I'm sorry," he whispered. Aira was shocked, wondering how long he had been holding his sadness in.

Aira closed her eyes as she patted his back gently. Lots of people had said they were sorry when she had eventually learned about her past. They had all been sorry for her, but this old, tired man had also lost people he loved. He was her grandfather whether she liked it or not.

Maybe that's why she could only respond with, "I'm sorry too."

Maybe this is what I need to do, she thought sadly. *Maybe he needs me more than they do.*

She knew what she had to do, even if it was facing a past she never wanted to find.

Chapter Fifty-Nine

Aiden huffed, "All the fun stuff happens when I'm gone."

Emma looked as if she could have kicked Aiden as she snapped, "It wasn't exactly *fun*, Aiden. Where were you, anyway? 'I'll be out for an hour,' my butt!"

Aiden feigned a hurt expression as he frowned. "I was doing some stuff for V—" he was cut off when Van threw him a nasty glare and put his index finger to his lips, basically saying, "Keep quiet or I'll rip your tongue out." Aiden gulped. "I had things to do," he muttered as he looked away from his mother.

Something was up, and Aira didn't like it one bit.

"So…" Aiden sighed as he jumped up and sat on the kitchen counter. "She's really leaving? *We're* really gonna leave without Aira?" he questioned. When he had come home, it was like a cloud of absolute misery had just washed through the house.

Emma simply nodded as she wrapped up some valuables with newspaper. She had been snapping at everyone for some time now, and no one questioned her sudden mood swing. Emma, as well as Aiden and Drake, were coming to terms with Aira's decision.

They were to leave in two days, and Emma had gone through the house like a tornado, packing and cleaning anything she could. Van and Drake were still adamant that when Ronan realized Aira wasn't with them, he would come after the people closest to her. Emma understood their concern and had accepted the move, but that was when she was sure Aira would be coming as well. Now, everything had changed.

Aira sighed as she slowly walked down the stairs, carrying two of her duffle bags over her shoulders. The rest of her items would be taken to Richard's home later that day. There was no room in the car he brought.

Emma timidly walked up to her daughter and placed a gentle, soft hand on her cheek. "I see you don't need me to pack your bag for you anymore," she whispered with a distant smile.

Aira smiled back and placed her own hand on top of Emma's. "I always need you. You're my Mom."

Emma took a step back as she looked around frantically. "I... I have to clean something..." She all but sobbed as she walked away with her hand covering her mouth. Aira frowned as she watched her mother's huddled form take off into the next room.

This was painful, but it was for the best. Aira was a magnet for trouble, and she wouldn't be able to live with herself if something were to happen to Emma or Drake.

Just as Aira went to take a step down from the staircase, someone had taken her duffle bag from her grasp and picked it up. Looking up, Aira smiled sadly as Van hauled the bag over his shoulder and, without even glancing at her, muttered, "I'll take this outside."

All she could do was nod and watch as he retreated outside. Even from that small encounter, Aira could tell Van had closed himself off. He was cold with the way he interacted with her as if he were detaching himself mentally, or perhaps, she was just over thinking everything.

However, despite the morbid circumstances, she plastered on a tortured smile and offered her hand out to Aiden who came walking towards her. With a soft chuckle, Aiden wrapped his arms around her and pulled her into him, tightening his hold just a touch when she hiccupped, a sign she was close to crying.

"Hey," he muttered as he pulled away and grinned down at Aira, "I have presents…"

She was confused as she tilted her head, much like a puppy would, and Aiden stifled his laughter as he pulled her towards the kitchen counter. Aira couldn't help but notice two satchels that obviously held documents sitting on the marble top. Her curiosity only sparked more so when Aiden handed one of them to her.

The envelope was addressed to Van, but on the other side, it had "Aira Volkov" clearly printed in bold letters. Opening it up, her eyes widened as she briefly read over the contents. It was an apology letter from the board of education, apologizing for the incident that occurred and the bullying that went unnoticed. The second document she pulled out almost made her fall over on the spot.

Somehow, Van had managed to convince *someone* on that panel to give Aira her High School Diploma. She was still a full year off of graduating for heaven's sake! How was this even possible?

"I didn't finish school, though?" she gasped, looking at Aiden as if he had all the answers that were swirling in her mind.

Aiden smirked before shrugging. "Really? Well, according to them, you did."

Aira smiled and took a deep breath as she clutched the piece of paper to her chest. "Is that where you were?"

"Well, when Ma called Van we were in the middle of something, so I took care of the other stuff. You can't open the other one until later on, though," Aiden said as he nodded towards the other envelope sitting on the counter.

Aira shook her head in disbelief. The thought suddenly crossed her mind that there was little Van couldn't have, and for some strange reason, that made her happy and terrified all at once. Looking up, she noticed Aiden staring off into the living room at the pile of blankets sitting on the ground atop a large dog bed. She looked away instantly.

"I asked him to look after you while I was gone, and he kept his promise," Aiden whispered, locking his sight on Aira as he turned to stare at his sister.

"I've been keeping my head busy and with everything going on..." She couldn't say that she missed her wolf. She couldn't say it out loud because then it became real that he was gone.

Aiden smiled and gently touched his sister's shoulder. "You did the right thing."

"Aira, they're here…" her mother called quietly from the front door.

Aira took a deep breath and turned to walk towards the door. Before she left, she turned and smiled at Aiden, shaking her head as she said, "Call me selfish, but if Vaughn had a voice and told me he wanted to stay, I would have been the happiest girl in the world."

Aiden watched carefully as she tread away before smiling back. "He did want to stay," he muttered. "But it wasn't worth you torturing yourself over his freedom."

The air outside was a mixture between bitter cold and almost muggy. Aira convinced herself that that was simply her own body sweltering from the inside out as she prepared herself mentally for the onslaught of, for lack of better words, culture shock. She even had never been to a sleepover before and was already silently choking back the heavy sobs that were ready to escape. Despite being within inches of Emma, she missed her mother terribly already.

It seemed it was only her family smothered in the tense air because as her grandfather and uncle stepped out of the black jeep, their smiles couldn't have been any broader. Aira winced slightly as Vincent stepped forward with his arm in a sling and cast.

"Sorry about that," Aira muttered.

He didn't seem to mind as he, himself, offered an awkward smile. "I can't say you should be the one apologizing."

Aira hadn't even realized she had been swaying nervously from side to side until her father came up behind her and steadied the nervous girl by gripping both her shoulders. Drake offered her an encouraging look, but it seemed Richard had already noticed her fidgety movements.

"Her mother used to do that. She'd rock or sway when she was nervous or shake her leg when she was seated. She was always a nervous girl."

Drake's expression looked forced as he tried to look sympathetic. "Well, Aira doesn't usually do this unless she's uncomfortable." It was a noticeable stab towards Richard with Drake making it no secret that he was not happy with the situation or the stress it was putting on his daughter.

"Dad…" Aira whispered, her eyes pleading with him to be nice. This was a side she had only recently seen her father, and quite frankly, it scared her a little.

Richard nodded and turned to head back to the car, a scowling Vincent following behind with her luggage. They were letting her say her goodbyes in privacy. Although Aira had expressed interest in staying with Richard, she had also told Drake and Emma that she was not certain whether she would stay or go to Russia. Aira was undecided about this whole situation. She was caught between her untold duty to her biological family and her love for the family who had raised her.

Aira turned and wrapped her arms around her father's neck. Drake squeezed her lightly and kissed the side of her head. From the way his body tensed, Aira knew that he was just as upset and anxious as her mother was although he tried very hard not to outwardly show his distress. Her dad was strong like that.

Next, Aira hugged her mother, who squeezed her so hard Aira was sure she heard her back crack. Emma sniffled as they pulled away from each other and cupped her cheek as she croaked, "Call me tonight and let me know how it goes. Remember to tell them you like a cup of water next to your bed at night. Don't be shy when you ask, either. Keep your belongings neat and don't leave your bed all messy like you usually do." Emma cleared her throat, but the tears spilled anyway as she said, "I love you so very much, sweetie."

Aira dived in and gave the only mother she'd ever really known a last, long cuddle. "I love you too, Mom. I'll talk to you later, okay?"

Emma nodded nervously but smiled her way through the hurt. "Of course you will."

After saying her goodbyes to her parents and Aiden, Aira nervously turned to Van, who had stood back and simply watched. He leaned against the patio as Aira stood in front of him and simply stared down at her.

"Thank you for convincing the school board to let me graduate. That's all I wanted." Her smile seemed to hurt as she tried to keep a strong front, but no one could fool Van, not even himself.

He nodded briefly before digging into his pocket and pulling out a small box. He gave it to Aira, who blinked confusedly as she took it from him, and opened it. It was then that the tears she'd been holding back for the friend she had set free started to come out as she peered down at the gift her hero had given her. It was the silver dog tag he had worn around his neck for all those years made into a necklace for Aira.

Ripping it from the box, Aira put the long chain around her neck, watching at the name **Van** glittered from the sun that peeked out through the clouds. They had used the name because Vaughn wouldn't fit on the dog tag.

Van gently took the tag in between his thumb and index finger and ran his thumb over the engraved name. "So you don't forget."

Before Aira could stop herself, she lunged into Van's chest, her arms wrapping themselves around his torso. Although she knew her father was watching carefully, she didn't care. This wasn't wrong. A *hug* wasn't wrong. She had picked up on her father's odd behavior early on, but today, she would ignore it.

She felt Van's arms slink up and around her, his hands holding the back of her head. After a moment of surprise, she smiled through her hurt. Aira didn't care if Van was confused as to why this simple gesture made her so happy.

After a moment, Van pulled away and gently pushed Aira back by her shoulders. He noticed she had the unopened manila envelope in her hands and her expression seemed to turn to that of unresolved solace.

"Open that tomorrow morning," he said, nodding towards the object.

Aira, forgetting she had been clutching it, nodded. "Why tomorrow?"

His brow lurched up in amusement. "You're questioning me?"

Aira was surprised but smiled. "Of course not, I would never question the great Van," she joked.

For the second time in her life, Aira witnessed Van chuckle with actual laughter as he tucked a piece of hair behind her ear. "Good."

Aira, shocked beyond belief, was about to stutter in absolute astonishment when a voice called her name. Looking back, Richard was calling her out and pointing at his watch. Aira hesitantly said another goodbye to Van and her family before rushing down to the car. As she got into the vehicle, she took one long look back at the family she loved so before waving goodbye and getting inside.

Looking back at the house she had grown up in, Aira couldn't help the sinking feeling that settled in the pit of her stomach. She tried to push back the feeling that something wasn't quite right, but she couldn't help but think that those goodbyes seemed so much more than just temporary.

"What is that?" Richard asked, nodding towards the necklace around her neck.

Aira, not used to this man's presence, answered, "A gift."

Richard huffed as he got comfortable in the back seat with his granddaughter. "It looks like something that belongs around a dog's neck."

Aira's lips formed a straight line as she held back a snarky reply to that comment. Sitting back in silence, she looked around the car awkwardly before finally asking, "Am-am I meeting people tonight, Richard?"

Richard nodded. "Yes, your *real family*, dear, and enough of this Richard nonsense. Call me Grandpa." It was more of an order than anything else.

Aira tried not to be visibly deterred by the steely mask that fell over the old man's face. She simply nodded and sat back, nervous and scared about what was to come when she got to Richard Croft's home.

Chapter Sixty

Aira's lips twisted into a nervous frown as she fidgeted in the back seat with her grandfather. She was nervous to meet her *family* members but at the same time, excited to see if any of them resembled her in personality or looks. She had always wondered what it would be like to have an aunt, a cousin, or even an uncle.

She inwardly flinched as that last word struck her straight in the heart. She had never ever associated Van with being an uncle or even a family member. He had always just been her hero. He was just Mr. Van, the man she had had a special bond with since she was a child. However, the thought still made her insides twist into something akin to shame.

Her *uncle*, Vincent, turned right which lead the vehicle up a long, steep driveway. They had been driving for some time, and to Aira's surprise, her grandfather had been in

Washington this whole time. It shouldn't have surprised her that her real parents had also lived here. As they drove, the dry dirt that dusted up around them shielded Aira's view. The dust soon cleared, and when they pulled to a halt, Aira could finally take in the sights of the property.

It was bigger than she had imagined with trees and lush grass cascading up and around the older style house that sat on a hill. The garden outside was beautiful, but the cold weather had left the flowers looking withered and forgotten. The house itself was made of timber that had been painted white. It looked about the same size as her parent's house and was dwarfed by the large scale of the grounds that surrounded it.

Aira was so busy gawking at everything around her that she failed to notice Vincent open the door for her. The overwhelmed teenager seemed to come crashing back down to reality and after throwing him an embarrassed smile, cautiously stepped out of the car. It was then that she noticed a large, broad woman standing on the veranda that circled the house, staring at her as if Aira had just butchered a kitten.

Now, Aira had only been terrified twice in her life — the day her parents died, and the day Eric tried to kill her. But today, she added a new "near death experience" to her life event list. All she could do was stare in utter fright as the woman stampeded down the steps and made a beeline for the girl shaking in absolute astonishment at this woman's speed. As soon as the unknown woman got within choking-feet of Aira, she simply stopped, looked the girl up and down, and nodded.

"I knew it! She's got that look Charles had. You know the one, Dad? The one where he would stand there and stare at you like an idiot?"

Oh, no. It took all of Aira's self-control not to run down that driveway and call her mother for help. She would rather face Van on a bad day than this woman.

Richard seemed to sigh. "My, you're looking incredibly bloated today, Elizabeth," he drawled, giving Aira a wink from the corner of her eye. All coldness he had been showing in the car seemed to have evaporated. Perhaps, he had been nervous just like her.

The woman's face seemed to fill with air as if she were either about to float away or pop like a balloon. Aira stifled a loud laugh at that thought, imagining Emma wouldn't have been able to contain herself if she had thought the same.

Elizabeth was a tall woman who was a little on the larger side but nowhere near overweight. Aira assumed it was muscle because she looked as though she could snap the girl in half like a twig. Hell, Elizabeth Croft looked as if she could even snap Van in half like a twig.

This time, Aira laughed out loud as she pictured that scene happening in her mind. Elizabeth didn't seem to see the humor in Aira's daydreams, however.

Besides birthdays, thunderstorms and dishwashers, Aira also hated being manhandled, which is exactly what this burly woman attempted to do. Eric's face flashed through Aira's mind as Elizabeth grabbed the girl's upper arm in an iron grip and pulled her so roughly that Aira stumbled forward.

Aira had always wondered why, if she was anything "special," she couldn't fight off Eric back at the school. She had felt so weak and powerless, and that scared her. It never occurred to her that Emma, Drake, and Van had protected her all her life from people exactly like him.

As Elizabeth went to pull her forward once more, Aira cemented herself to the ground as she pulled back just as hard, making the larger woman yelp as she was hauled back towards Aira, stopping just inches from toppling over the younger girl. Looking down, Elizabeth was momentarily stunned to find that the nervous eyes she had met earlier were now steely as Aira stared up at her.

Aira found her backbone as she muttered, "I don't like to be pulled around," and yanked her arm away.

Elizabeth brushed a dark curl behind her ear as she took a step back. Vincent, probably sensing his sister's unease, put his arm around her and pulled her towards the house. "We should go inside…" he whispered cautiously, but his eyes never wavered in their hidden message – *walk away*.

Elizabeth, finally breaking eye contact with Aira, nodded absently as she turned and walked with her brother. "She has the eyes of a wolf, Vincent," she whispered back, heat rising to her flushed cheeks as the anger started to work its way through her body.

Aira glared as she saw Vincent nod once. "She'll learn to be human again. In time, she'll forget those beasts."

"What makes you think she isn't human?" she asked, curious.

Vincent chuckled lightly as he pulled the front door open. "Those eyes are Vivian's one minute and the next, she will stare you down like prey. That is not human. That is a monster's influence."

Aira eyed them. They knew she could hear every word of their conversation as they stared back at her. Aira smiled and waved them off as she moved towards her grandfather, who looked about as happy as she did at that moment.

"Ignore them and their jealousy, Aira," he muttered as he ushered her to follow him towards the house. "They were always jealous of Vivian and what she had."

"Oh my, goodness! Look at her, John. She looks just like her mother!"

"Dear, do you want anything to drink? Are you hungry?"

"Oh, that was terrible what happened to you. If you want anything at all, sugar, just ask."

One after the other, the women in the house fluttered around Aira like flies as they asked questions and threw her looks of sympathy. Her grandfather was sitting on the outdoor decking, drinking some whiskey, and offered Aira little help from this awkward situation.

Smile and be gracious, that was a lesson Emma had drilled into her daughter time and time again. Aira did just that as she smiled as sweetly as she could, given the situation and thanked her newly found *family* for their concerns. The living room was filled with laughter and alcohol-fueled cheers, followed by the sound of cups clinking together. She wasn't used to the smell of alcohol and tried to block the stench as best she could without seeming rude.

"Aira, darlin', can you help me with these snacks?" a woman asked from the doorway of the kitchen.

Aira nodded as she walked towards the kitchen and helped her Aunt Dawn place chips and dips into bowls laid out on the table.

"You... do this all by yourself?" she asked hesitantly. Ever since she had entered the house earlier, she had noticed Dawn consistently in and out of the kitchen. No one seemed to offer any help or even ask if Dawn was okay doing all the hard work. It was almost as if the poor lady was expected to do the cooking and cleaning duties.

"Oh, darlin', I'm used to it. Don't worry too much about it. Besides, I don't see Vincent raising his hand and offering anything useful." Dawn giggled to herself.

Aira simply watched Dawn from the corner of her eye and nodded solemnly. It just didn't seem fair to her. Dawn Croft was the only person Aira felt comfortable with in this new environment.

"You look like your daddy; you know that?" Dawn suddenly quipped as she dragged a chicken roast from the oven.

Aira coughed nervously. "They seem to think I look like my mother," she answered, nodding towards the living room where family and friends laughed and topped up their drinks.

"The dead don't sleep when it comes to this family, sweetie. They'll sweet talk ya' cause you're Vivie's baby, but the second you turn your back, they'll be at your heels like hungry piranhas," Dawn warned, looking Aira dead in the eyes. "You got your daddy's kind soul. I can tell."

Aira brushed a strand of loose hair behind her ear as she pretended those words didn't scare her. "Right, don't turn my back," she whispered, slightly deterred with this whole conversation.

It's just for today, Aira tried to convince herself that this nightmare would end after today. Tonight, she was calling her mother and getting the hell out of this crazy environment.

At least, that's what she had thought would happen.

Chapter Sixty-One

Never in her life had she felt so awkward. She tried to play coy as her Uncle Vincent rambled on about his time as a sergeant and completely ignored Aira when she inquired about his involvement with shifters. Every time he looked at her, Aira swore she saw a flash of annoyance cross his face before it was wiped away with a very forced smile.

It wasn't until her cousin, Christine, came to Aira's rescue did the poor girl sigh with relief. She wasn't used to people swearing so openly nor was she used to the stench of booze flooding up her nose every time someone opened their mouth to speak. It was early morning the following day, and they were already at it again.

"Do they always drink?" Aira asked as she followed Christine down the hall.

Christine flicked a piece of dark auburn hair off her shoulder and giggled. "Not usually, they're just happy. We find any excuse to celebrate," she replied flippantly.

Christine Croft was a beauty in her own right. She was Vincent's eldest girl. With reddish auburn hair and bright blue eyes, Christine was certainly stunning. She wore lavish clothes with high waist jeans that fit her perfectly, and she never seemed to show her face without a mask of makeup covering whatever flaws she thought she may have had.

Christine breathed in heavily as she leaned against the railings outside, taking in the fresh air with a fond look. "It's so stuffy in there," she remarked.

Aira nodded absently. "It's certainly beautiful here," she said as she looked around and took in all the tree's that obviously weren't native to this land.

"Dad and Grandpa built this place from the ground up. It used to be a two-bedroom homestead when Dad was a kid. Your mom grew up here, you know."

Aira's eyes seemed to glass over ever so slightly at the mention of her mother. "I didn't know that."

Christine frowned as she looked over at the younger girl. Her eyes flew down to the diamond ring on her left finger, and she smiled sadly. "I sometimes wonder if Avery and I would have been engaged together at the same time. We used to talk about that when we were like, twelve. Grandma and Grandpa were the only ones Aunt Vivian spoke to after she cut ties with the family. She always was the favorite, as Dad says."

Looking up, Aira briefly caught the sight of tears glassing over Christine's eyes, but she wiped them away before Aira could say anything.

"I thought she cut Richard out of her life?" Aira asked, confused. That wasn't the story she had been told.

If Christine was insulted that Aira had referred to their grandfather by his first name, she never showed it as she replied, "It's not my place to say, but what I can say is that she didn't know her place when it came to the pecking order around here."

Aira held her breath and any remarks she may have had. Pecking order?

"It's still sinking in that you're alive — that you're standing here next to me," Christine suddenly exclaimed as she shook her head. She probably still thought Aira was nothing but a ghost at this very second.

Yes, Aira Blight was indeed alive although the trauma still haunted her from time to time.

Christine suddenly giggled, "And to think, you were literally raised by wolves. It's all so... *odd.*"

Aira tilted her head as she stared at her cousin in confusion. "Odd?"

"Aira, you were raised by a monster. Van Volkov is the literal Godfather of all things evil and... and crazy! Why he hasn't killed you yet is beyond me," Christine huffed. "Not even other shifters like to hear his name. Grandpa's worked with a lot of bad Joes, but Volkov was someone even he stayed away from until he found you, of course."

Aira shifted uncomfortably as she backed away from Christine. "Van's no monster," she stated as a matter of fact. "He saved my life." And she would always be grateful for that. Van was a hero in her eyes, and no one would ever say or make her think otherwise.

The beauty's soft expression suddenly turned malicious as she spat, "You think he cares about you? Do you think any of *them* care about you? They're nothing but beasts in human skin for God's sakes. Those things killed your mother and father!" Christine was on the verge of tears as she only screamed louder with her next sentence, "They killed my best friend! Avery and Ian didn't deserve to be ripped apart by those creatures!"

"Hey, hey, what's going on out here?" came Dawn's irritated voice as she walked outside. "Chrissy, why are you screamin' for God sakes?"

Aira was stunned as Christine's hurt expression flipped into a snarky smile. "Why don't you tell her, *Aira*?"

Dawn sighed heavily. "Tell me what?" she asked, exasperated and not in the mood for guessing games.

Aira stayed silent, her expression hardening as she braced herself for whatever was about to come. For some reason, she felt like she was getting ready for the battle of her life.

She couldn't have foreseen what came next as Christine went on to say, "She's defending those monsters, Momma. She said that *Van* was no monster. She doesn't care that they killed Aunt Vivian. She doesn't *care* about her brother and sister being ripped apart."

For a moment, Dawn, a woman Aira had admired not hours before, simply stared at the girl as if sizing her up. It had seemed like an eternity before the woman took Christine into her arms as if soothing her and said, "Don't blame poor Aira, dear. She's been brainwashed, and very soon, she'll learn that *we* are the ones she belongs with."

What the heck was going on? Aira was dumbfounded and angry at what Dawn had just said. What did they mean by brainwashed? Aira most certainly was not brainwashed. If anything, these people were the ones who did the brainwashing.

Aira couldn't contain her anger as she spat back, "You people are the ones who are brainwashed. You call my *family* evil, but you shouldn't judge others based on what you, yourself, are!"

Dawn's eyes nearly popped out of her head as she gawked at the girl in front of her, standing defiant and ready to fight for what she believed in.

"I was wrong," Dawn muttered as she held her daughter back from Aira. "You're not like Charlie at all. Elizabeth?"

Elizabeth had obviously been listening in on the conversation as she came through the patio door, having heard every single word from the look on her distasteful face.

"You selfish, spiteful little brat," the large woman hissed. The men in the back room could hear everything, but Vincent and two others simply sat back, including Aira's younger cousin who played with his phone as if nothing was happening.

Dawn held up her hand as she smiled almost sadly. "Do you remember, Elizabeth, how we punished Vivian for such disrespect?"

A sinister smile spread across this ghastly woman's face. "Can I?"

Dawn stepped back with Christine and nodded. "Do what you have to." She looked around nervously, "But do not let her make a sound. We don't want Richard hearing, or it'll be over."

Aira's senses started to go wild as she put her right leg forward, watching Elizabeth carefully as the beastly figure came forward, her arm outstretched and grabbed Aira's upper arm painfully — the same way she had tried to the previous day.

Aira's instinct was to fight back. She had had enough of this craziness. What she did next, not even Aira herself believed she had had inside of her. Thinking of Van, thinking of his strength and how — in her eyes — he was the strongest man she had ever known besides her father, Aira grabbed the arm Elizabeth had grabbed her with and twisted it. The strength she always knew she had but never used to hurt another being purposely seemed to twist Elizabeth's arm like a rag doll.

Vincent was now paying attention as he jumped up from his seat, stunned at what the smaller girl had just done. "Liz, she's not a normal human!" he had tried to warn, but it was too late.

Far too late.

Elizabeth was on the ground, struggling defiantly as Aira had her pinned down, and her knee digging in-between the woman's shoulder blades. Her arm was twisted in a painful way as Aira subdued her, the girl's hand planted firmly on the back of Elizabeth's large head to keep her face down.

"Touch me again and eating dirt will be the last thing you'll *ever* have to worry about," Aira growled with such maliciousness that she wasn't even sure if that was her voice or not.

"Vincent, what the hell *is* she?" Dawn squalled as her husband came rushing out, pulling a stun gun from his belt. Dawn pulled her daughter closer as Christine stared wide-eyed and astounded at the sight of her aunt struggling to breathe on the ground.

"Get off her!" Aira heard Christine scream as she tried to pull away from her mother.

Vincent cursed. "She's a L'ightat with some fucking unusual strength. That damn wolf has done something to her."

Dawn continued to stare as she eyed Aira up and down. Aira's eyes were a piercing blue as she watched all of them carefully while continuing to subdue Elizabeth.

"A L'ightat?" she whispered under her breath, "You always did want to outdo me, didn't you, Viv? First, Charlie, now this."

Christine seemed to do a double take as she yelled, "No, she can't be like Grandma! That was supposed to be *me*. You're lying, Dad!"

"I wish I was," Vincent muttered as he lifted his stun gun and two prongs shot out, hitting Aira directly in the stomach area. She convulsed as she collapsed to the ground, shaking and gasping as she tried pitifully to get those nasty things out of her.

Elizabeth, finally free, stood shakily to her feet and clutched her fractured arm. Growling low to herself, she stared hatefully at the girl writhing in pain on the ground.

"You okay, Liz?" Vincent asked, never taking his eyes off Aira.

Elizabeth grunted as she spat down at the girl. "I am now," she answered, a strange happy tone to her voice as she kicked the teenager in the side of her ribcage and watched her gasp in pain and shock. "Much, *much* better."

Chapter Sixty-Two

Now, she knew why her mother had cut ties with her family. Aira knew the truth. It was because Vivian had been abused and hated in a place she should have been able to call home. She was an outsider in a place she should have felt safe, just like Aira.

Aira now knew that the reason she wasn't handed over to her maternal grandparents was that Aira's parents had specifically requested that *none* of their children be given to them in the event of their death — with good reason. Richard was so drunk he hadn't noticed her limp body being carried down to this hell hole.

She hadn't spoken since she was stunned and thrown into this prison of a room and planned to keep it that way. She had formed a protective shell around herself, the same shell she had used to protect her heart and her mind after her family's tragic death. Without Emma or Drake there to protect her, this was the only other way she knew how to protect herself. She had to close herself down mentally for a little while.

Aira had one last little fleeting hope left inside of her. If she ever got the chance, she needed to call Emma and ask for her to come home. They were probably already in Russia by now. Aira held her head as she tried to remember her mother's cellphone number.

She had contemplated breaking the door down; it was simple enough. However, there was one little problem — Vincent had obviously assessed how strong she was and went the extra mile to assure that she would not try to escape. He had thrown her into one of the dozen or so cells under the house. They were military grade holding cells with large metal doors that were only accessible through voice control. All that separated her from the outside world was a tiny window and slot in the door where her breakfast had been thrown in.

Her breakfast was still festering on the floor just inches from the door where they had thrown it inside.

Perhaps, they had done this to scare her. They had converted the whole underground of this place into a block of cells, a steel prison. It was like walking into a mental facility and was obviously built by Vincent. He had brought in two military guards to watch the doors and had seen him talking to a woman in a doctor's coat. That woman's face was the first thing Aira had woken up to, leering down at her as if she were some sort of mutant.

Aira lightly pulled at the metal collar around her neck that was locked in place like some sort of choker. Whatever was inside of it pricked her like a tiny needle every hour or so and whatever it was inserting into her body made her feel weak and disorientated. It was the same sort of collar she had seen Van wearing when she and Drake had first pulled up to the house and encountered Vincent and Richard. She couldn't just rip it off. She was warned that any sort of trauma to the device would instantly electrocute her. Aira was certain she wasn't immune to being electrocuted to death.

However, none of that was the worst of it. Looking on either side of her cell, Aira looked through the heavy security glass that separated her cell from the two cells on either side of her. She had realized early on that she wasn't the only prisoner down in this dungeon of terror.

A little boy sat to her right, sleeping soundly after being sedated by that doctor earlier that day, just after Aira had woken up. He had been screaming and snarling for his mother and "alpha" to come rescue him. He couldn't have been any older than six years old. His hair was a beautiful shade of dark brown, almost black, and if he could smile, Aira was sure he'd have the cutest dimples. Aira had been watching him for some time, a tear slipping from her eye as she realized she had been that age when she had found herself alone in this world as well.

To her left, there was a man that had been napping against the wall for some hours now. He would awaken every now and again, look at Aira, frown, and close his eyes again. He had nothing but a pair of tattered cotton pants on and the same collar Aira had on around her neck. He was marked from head to toe, with obvious wounds that had only just healed recently.

Aira could tell, just from the look of his eyes, that he was a shifter as well. He didn't have golden eyes like Van and her father, but the way his pupils slanted like cats, she knew he was not human. He also seemed like he was on guard even while he rested.

"He's been here a few weeks. He was brought here by his own mother if you can believe it."

Aira's head snapped so fast to look at the man who had spoken to her that she winced when her neck let out a sickening crack. Stumbling over her words, she couldn't even form a coherent sentence, and the strange man laughed as he ruffled his golden brown hair.

He chuckled. "Am I that astounding to you? I can take my pants off if you like. Let's see your head spin from that *astonishing* sight," he joked. He quickly recounted his offer when her face turned beet red, and her eyes looked as if she were ready to pass out. "Take a joke. I didn't usually wear pants — it was fun to piss off that stupid human who put that collar on you earlier. But when River came, I decided to present myself with a little more," he paused as he thought of the word, "Decency."

Aira, forgetting her promise not to speak, stuttered, "Riv-River?"

God, it was like she was seven years old all over again. Despite getting over her debilitating and embarrassing stutter, she still managed to revert to it whenever she was surprised or scared. At that moment, she was a mixture of both.

The strange man nodded and pointed to the cell containing the sleeping child next to her. "The kid, and would you keep your damn voice down? He was crying for hours before you came. He needs to keep up his strength if he wants to live comfortably here," he muttered that last sentence, looking disdainful as he probably recounted his own experience.

"How long have you been here?" Aira asked. He looked young, probably around twenty-five, maybe younger

"Twenty-seven years, maybe longer. I haven't kept count."

Aira blanched for a moment before coughing lightly to cover the sputtering sound she was about to make. Twenty-seven was a pretty rounded number considering he didn't remember exactly how long he had been imprisoned here.

He folded his arms over his chest and yawned loudly as he went on to say, "I wasn't always here. I was held for ten years in another facility before Richard bought me. I may as well have been born in captivity, I suppose." He scratched the back of his head as he thought about it for a moment.

Studying this man and the way he moved and spoke, Aira smiled lightly. He looked tough and scary, but Aira could just tell that his personality depended on companionship and a yearning for freedom.

It seemed he was used to talking to himself as he completely forgot about Aira's presence and said, "Now, if Volkov would just get off his lazy ass and work out some sort of agreement with the damn government, I can finally get out of here."

Now *that* caught Aira's attention. "What?"

His eyes swung her way as if just realizing she had been there all along and muttered, "Oh, you're still there. *Spose* I can't complain too much. If Richard didn't buy me when he did, the government was gonna *humanly euthanize* me like some common dog. Peh," he spat on the ground as he said this.

He was indeed angry at the world, and Aira couldn't blame him.

She supposed all those years in captivity left him a little nutty as he flew entirely off topic. Aira didn't mind as she asked, "Why would the-the government euthanize you?" She didn't want to use the words "put you to sleep." That was just too cruel to even think.

"Whoa, you're still fresh outta the litter, ain't ya'?" he laughed.

Aira looked away as she realized he thought she was a shifter as well. They were separated by glass with only a few holes for breathing, and he was a few feet away. Drake had told her that a shifter uses his nose before his eyes to identify someone, so this man obviously couldn't smell her from his position.

"I'm classed as a danger to society," he chuckled darkly. "I was six, maybe seven, when I was picked up and taken to a holding area in Colorado. A shifter who isn't in a pack is classed as rogue, even if those stupid humans wouldn't know what a real rogue was if it came up and ripped their faces off. A real rogue would likely eat you before saying hello. I was raised behind a steel door and, according to those doctors, wouldn't be able to adjust back into pack life."

He looked so incredibly sad behind that angry front he put up. Aira, sitting on her cot-bed, threw him a look of sympathy as she asked, "The government knows about shifters?"

He laughed again as if slowly losing his sanity just by this conversation alone and snapped, "Course they do! They got tabs on every shifter pack in the country. If you got a pack, you bet your left ball sack, they got a file on it and everyone in it in a dusty cabinet somewhere. And if you *don't* get a family or pack, well, you end up like me... and him," he nodded towards the child in the cell beside her who flinched in his sleep, most probably having a bad dream. "They never even gave me a chance. That's all I wanted. I spose it could be worse. The old man upstairs, he keeps the peace between humans and us and gets rid of any information that's leaked. He saved me from being put down. I'll give him that."

Aira almost cried from the dejected look on his face but held her tears back as she carefully asked, "Did you mean Van Volkov by any chance?"

His eyes, glazed over in anger, suddenly cleared as he nodded. "Yeah, you know anything about what he's doin' out there? If oh holy *Alpha* Volkov is supposed to be watching over us, he's doin' a shitty job. I don't see him coming and saving my ass anytime soon," he muttered angrily, still talking to himself.

Aira frowned, and before she could think about her words carefully, she exclaimed loudly, "He'll come!"

His curiosity seemed to peak as Aira yelled this. She immediately clamped her lips shut and turned away, cursing herself for getting too emotional about what he had just said. She really had to stop getting so worked up and start putting her foot in her mouth.

"I don't get to talk to many people, so, sorry if I'm talking too much. What's your name?"

Aira thanked her lucky stars that he overlooked her outburst and smiled as best she could, given the circumstances. "Aira."

His eyes widened to the size of baseballs as he jumped from his seat on the floor and raced over towards the glass. He looked stunned as he raised his hand to the glass separating them and gasped, "You're—"

His sentence was cut off as both he and Aira heard the doors outside rumble open, and a resounding beep flooded the still air.

The man next to Aira was instantly on alert as his chest rumbled. "Not now…" he muttered and began beating at his cell door. "Hey! Don't you fucking dare!" he screamed, making Aira jump from the pure panic that filled his voice.

She wondered what in blazes was going on to set off *that* sort of reaction. It wasn't long before it was very clear why he was panicking.

Two people barged through the hall. One was that woman doctor Aira had woken up to, and the other was a larger male in uniform. He looked like a soldier. Her eyes widened as she tried to gather the thoughts that seemed to be floating every which way in her mind. She knew Vincent was in the army but had seen no other man in uniform on the property. Until today, that is.

"Hey!" Aira called out to them, but they just marched right passed her holding cell without so much as a glance her way. It was like they were robots programmed to reject any sort of distraction.

It dawned on Aira just what the angry shifter had meant earlier when the woman spoke into the machine up the hall and asked it to open cell door six. To Aira's horror, the cell the boy was sleeping in on her other side opened, waking him from his sound slumber.

"What are they doing?" she exclaimed as the two stone-faced humans made their way towards the pup's cell.

"Taking him for testing," was all she got as a reply as he banged on the glass. "These damn collars left me almost human. It's no use fighting."

His voice sounded so dejected, so lost, that it set off a nerve in Aira. She stepped towards the glass that separated her and the boy and shouted, "He's sleeping. Leave him alone!"

Finally, she got a response from the woman. "Jarret, have you taken your medicine today?" she asked, completely ignoring Aira.

He simply snarled in response, flashing his deadly canines as a warning. "Screw. You."

Her smile was cold and filled with maliciousness as she replied, "Behave yourself. You know what happens when you became cranky," and went back to doing what she had originally come here to do.

The soldier — armed to the tee — rolled in a metal tray with towels and a syringe sitting on top. It sent a cold chill down Aira's spine as the objects clattered around. She could feel her anger rising as the woman pulled the needle from the tray and asked the man to hold the pup down. When the boy started to whimper, and fight back, he decided to hold him down by his throat, and that's when Aira couldn't stand it anymore.

With one, hard punch, she slammed her fist into the glass. *That* seemed to grab both of their attention, including Jarret's, as their heads snapped around to see what had just made that booming sound.

"I told you," she snapped, "To leave… him… alone…" Her words were dripping with anger and disgust. She never in her life felt this sort of rage before.

The man seemed to size her up as he spat, "Keep quiet, or I'll put a gag over that mouth of yours."

The doctor noticeably stiffened as she hurried to put on her rubber gloves. "Don't talk to her. She's a Code Four detainee," she hurriedly explained this as a nervous look crossed her face.

That seemed to shut him up as he nodded and turned back to the squirming boy. The doctor was almost done with her prepping when Aira heard a soft chuckle from Jarret. Turning around, she threw him a seriously confused look as he mumbled, "A code four. *Now* it makes sense."

"What?" Aira whispered low so that the people next to her wouldn't hear.

He didn't reply to her question. Jarret only went on to explain to her what they were going to do to River once they got him out of the cell. "They're gonna throw him in a transport van and take him to a facility where they'll do experiments on him, just like they did to me, just like they did to her." Jarret nodded towards the female shifter in the cell opposite him.

Aira looked out carefully as she noticed the girl was missing a leg and gasped.

"They cut off her leg to see if it would regenerate when she shifted. The answer? No, no it didn't." Jarret growled low in anger as he watched the cell holding the girl.

The female doctor growled, "We'll have to sedate him to if he keeps stirring her up." To which, the man nodded feebly.

The only thing keeping her from stepping over the edge was the knowledge she couldn't escape even if she tried. Turning her head away, Aira couldn't watch the scene any longer. It wasn't until Aira heard the pain-filled screams of the boy after the needle broke off in his arm from moving around did something snap.

And it snapped hard.

Aira threw herself against the glass, making a loud boom as she did so. The doctor and soldier seemed to jump back as she pummeled her fists over and over again against the solid wall.

"Get away from him!" she screamed, punching the glass after each word.

Aira was surprised she didn't break her shoulder as she stepped back each time she threw herself at the wall that separated all of them. She threw herself against the glass with such force she knew she was bound to get them to at least come into her own cell and sedate her, giving her an opening for escape.

The commotion Aira was making seemed to catch the attention of the other shifters held captive. They had been relatively silent or napping until then, but as soon as they heard River's screams and the loud bangs, they knew something was terribly wrong.

"What's all that fuckin' noise, Jarret?" asked a gruff tired voice from beside Jarret's cell.

Jarret turned to see a larger than average shifter rub his eyes as he awoke.

He chuckled lightly as he replied flippantly, "She's a code four, Rion."

Rion froze mid-eye rub and stared knowingly. "Dangerous when angry…" he stated as he looked towards the girl throwing herself at the glass as if her life depended on it. He had to admit; it was pretty damn sweet watching the doctor and her lapdog visibly pale as they tried to get the girl to stop. "Doesn't matter. She won't get out."

Rion looked over to the cell directly opposite his and frowned when he noticed his mate, Lara, looking out her tiny box window at the display. Rion growled low as his green eyes glowed dangerously, and he slapped against his own window, telling her to sit back down. She shouldn't have even been walking when her leg, recently removed, was still healing.

Her eyes immediately flew to her mate before she frantically pointed towards the other irritated female. Rion was ready to ignore her and instruct her to sit back down when a sudden, ear piercing sound caught his attention.

Crack.

To others on the outside, this sound might have been alarming, but to Rion and Jarret, it was the sweet sound of freedom.

Rion turned slowly as his eyes went back to this strange girl who continued to punch, scream and hurl herself again and again at the glass. Once again, the sound echoed throughout the underground complex.

Crack.

The glass separating her from River was cracking all around the area she was trying to break through, and the look of absolute terror in the doctor and soldier's eyes gave Aira a sick sort of satisfaction she'd never felt before.

"My God, she might actually be able to do it!" Jarret gasped, the shock evident on his face.

"*What* is she?" Rion asked.

Jarret looked at his friend and threw him a serious look. "She said her name's Aira."

The brooding male nearly fell over backward as Jarret said her name. He knew that name. Rion knew that damn name very well. "The last time I had ever *heard* that name was the happiest day of my life," he growled. "Ronan killed the old man's daughter, and I fuckin' hope Richard suffered."

"Are things so messed up in the world that they would throw their own down here?" Jarret wondered out loud.

"Was she bitten by a radioactive spider or something?" Rion growled, secretly shitting his pants at the damage this girl, barely five-foot-six, was doing to a wall even they couldn't bypass.

It wasn't long before Jarret spotted the deadly sparks that started to flutter from the collar around her neck, something Aira hadn't noticed until she heard his voice. "Hey!" he screamed and banged a heavy fist against the glass that separated them. "The collars gonna burn out and kill ya'! Stop!"

He was suddenly regretting stirring Aira up as her collar was almost burnt out and sent sparks flying. Aira ignored him, just a little more, and she'd be in the next room. She couldn't give up now. She ignored the painful burning from the collar around her neck, but the needles that stabbed into her and injected her with whatever was inside of it was getting harder and harder to just disregard.

Alarms were going off left and right indicating a breach in security. With all the commotion, Aira shouldn't have been surprised when her cell door flew open and in popped Richard, a scowl on his face and looking not too happy.

"That's *enough!*" he roared, but it wasn't towards his irritated granddaughter.

The doctor and the man in uniform took a step away from River all while under the watchful glare of their higher up.

"Get that thing off my granddaughter and bring her upstairs," he demanded. "You two," he turned to the doctor and her sidekick, "I expect a report about who sent you down here. We do not and will not harm children, no matter the background."

Aira panted heavily as she watched her grandfather storm off, confusion covering her face and the many others in the area.

Chapter Sixty-Three

"You two are as stupid as each other!" screamed Susan over the car's loudspeaker. "How dare you take her to that place and not consult me about it first? You could have sent her to a mental asylum for all we damn well know!"

Van grunted, "It's for the best." Besides, he had done some looking into Richard's background. Nothing indicated she was in any danger.

Susan huffed, which usually meant she was getting ready to give him an ear lashing he'd never forget. "Then why are you going back for her, pup? You think you know everything. Good, guess what? I have about three hundred more years of experience than you, my boy, and believe me, I'll come down there and slap you in the face if I have to!"

Van was at his breaking point when Drake took over the call, noticing the terrible reddening of the man's face. It was certainly an angry red. That was for sure.

"Susan, calm down, please. We should be there within the hour, and we'll collect her. Emma has already landed in Russia and is getting everything sorted out. I bet when we get to Aira she'll be fine and shoving us out the door."

Susan let out a taut little laugh filled with sarcasm. "You think Aira is fine? Explain to me this. Why are you two even bothering checking up on her in the first place if you think she is fine? She is your pup, Drake, and you're on your way there because you know something is very wrong. Admit it."

Van felt a sudden tiny pang at his chest as Susan finished her sentence. Yes, he and Drake had both felt something was a little off but nothing to be concerned over. They had simply decided that checking on her before leaving for Russia was the best way to calm their nerves. If there was so much as a hair missing from her head, Van knew Drake had no qualms about demolishing the entire complex.

"I've done my research on these people, Van," Susan said seriously. "I spoke with that woman, Mary. She seemed to know a lot about Vivian. She gave me information that led me to another source close to Vivian and Charles, or who had once been close. It's not good."

Van covered the growl that was threatening to rumble in his chest and snapped, "*What's* not good?"

Drake looked just as worried as he leaned in closer. "Susan, I'm losing my hair enough as it is."

"Vivian didn't cut Richard out of her life. In fact, she had nothing but good things to say about her parents. Her brothers and sisters, however, she confided were the reason she cut her family out of her life. Vivian was a L'ightat, and they made her suffer for that."

Van suddenly slammed on the brakes and skidded to the emergency stopping lane. Drake barely seemed to notice as he glared at the car's dash and growled low, shaking his head at the situation.

"What are you boys doing? Don't do anything crazy! He's probably got a whole SWAT team of guys waiting there for you two," she exclaimed, trying frantically to ease her alpha's temper. Even from the other side of the state, she could feel his anger rising. An angry Van always meant trouble.

Susan was met with a dial tone as Van shut off the car and threw his door open. Drake followed, removing his jacket and unbuttoning the top two buttons of his dress shirt. He didn't want to be strangled if a branch caught him at the wrong angle.

"Think Susan will be mad?" Drake asked, a slight smirk gracing his face.

Van chuckled darkly, a menacing energy surrounding his body as he crouched to get a running start. "Let's bring her home," he muttered, and with a quick sprint, jumped into the nearest tree, taking off towards Richard's base.

Drake followed suit, just as eager to have his daughter back with them. He was so focused on getting to her that he failed to notice his brother rub the red, welting ring that formed around his neck... as if he'd been burned.

Chapter Sixty-Four

This place was cold.

She hadn't noticed it before. Perhaps, she had tried to avoid thinking that this place was anything but pure and welcoming. This wasn't what Aira had expected. She had expected open arms with love and warmth, not a pair of steel boots cementing her in place.

"There you go, sweetie," a strong voice muttered as he removed the fried collar from around her neck. Aira looked down, turning her head away.

Don't call me sweetie.

"Her neck?" Richard asked, concern marring his aged face as he looked at the welts blistering over her neck.

Don't act like you care.

The man that came to care for Aira's wounds stared at her long and hard before answering, "They should heal quickly.

Cream and some ice should stop it from getting any worse. Then again, I'm not exactly a doctor, Dad."

Richard sighed heavily as he ran a hand through what graying hair he had left. "You're the best we have right now. Patricia won't come near her after what happened in the cells."

The man with no name chuckled as he applied some cream on Aira's neck, making her jump away from his touch. "Whoa, whoa, whoa! I'm not going to hurt you."

Head down, hair covering her face and slumped in her seat, Aira whispered, "I want my mother, please."

She needed to get to a phone and call her mother. Emma was probably worried sick, not having any contact with Aira for days now.

A dark silence fell over the room as if she had just been covered in a blanket that had been soaked in gasoline. What Richard said next almost made Aira wish someone had thrown a match on her.

"We can't allow you to contact them, Aira. I'm sorry."

Somehow, that "sorry" didn't seem as sympathetic as Richard had tried to make it sound. Looking around, Aira blanched for a moment before letting out what seemed like a humorless laugh.

"I've asked nicely for a phone so that I can contact my mother. Don't make me ask again," she snapped, her eyes darkening as she looked from Richard to the other man. She was warning them. The next time she asked, she wouldn't be so nice. She was done with being nice.

Richard stared for a moment while the other man simply shook his head as if saddened by this whole situation. She couldn't take this anymore. She couldn't just sit here with these people. Getting out of her chair, she made a dash for the door but was caught by the man she didn't care to catch the name. His eyes, so much like hers, stared down at Aira as if seeking some sort of acceptance or forgiveness.

Shifter, she thought, shocked by this revelation.

He realized his mistake instantly when Aira narrowed her eyes, and with one small shove, he went flying across the room, hitting the far wall with a dreadful thud. Richard stood to the side; his face drooped into a shocked expression as he watched his son slide down the wall, obviously winded.

It took Aira a moment to realize what she had done and immediately took a sharp breath. "I-I did warn you," she stuttered, wide-eyed as she looked down at her hands. What exactly was happening inside of her body was a mystery, but Aira felt frightened of her own strength after what had happened in the cells.

The hand that gently grasped her shoulder made Aira jump a mile high, and she had to force herself not to kick Richard away.

"It's okay," he soothed. His voice held sincerity Aira had yet to hear in her time here. "We can help you, Aira. We can help you control it. That's why you're here. People will do terrible things to use the gifts you have. That's what Van was afraid of. That's why you're here."

Control *what* exactly? She had been successfully controlling her strength since she first realized that something was wrong with her body in her early teens. It was only since her arrival here that everything was going haywire inside of her mind. Aira needed to get away if she wanted to *control* it.

"My parents would want me to contact them. They'll start to get nervous if they don't hear from me." Her eyes narrowed angrily in Richard's direction and completely disregarding the man struggling to pick himself up over in the corner.

Richard sighed as he pointed his walking cane over towards his desk, and that's when Aira noticed that oddly familiar manila envelope. Keeping her eyes glued to her "grandfather," she shuffled over towards the desk and picked it up. With a lopsided frown, she carefully opened it up and took out the contents.

Aira immediately froze as she read over the titles. No, this was all some kind of sick joke. He wouldn't do this to her. He *couldn't* do this to her.

Richard's voice boomed through her mind as he said, "Do you understand now?"

In her shaking hands were the titles and deeds to copious amounts of land, all signed over to Aira by Van. It was as if, along with her inheritance, he was setting her up so that she'd never have to worry about money for the rest of her life.

Why?

"In our agreement, it was discussed you would have no further contact with shifters or Lycans, including the Volkovs. You may contact Emma, but they can't come for you, Aira. I promise you this." He took a step forward. "What happened today will never happen again. What happened to Vivian went under my nose because I preferred my drink to my family, and I will spend the rest of my life making it up to her. I love you, just as I loved your mother."

The sound the paper made as she tore it up ripped through the silence that filled the room. She didn't want any of this. If Aira accepted these, then it was set in stone that she would never see her family again. She didn't want Van's money or his assets. She wanted her freedom — freedom to choose where she belonged, and she most certainly did not belong here.

"After the accident, I couldn't remember what had happened or where I was. I remembered my name, and that I had a mother, but everything else was dark. I was in the dark for a long time until... until Emma showed me it was okay to feel happy, because I was ashamed to feel happy. I couldn't talk, or scream, or cry. I was in a body I couldn't fully control." She dropped the pieces of torn up paper to the floor, her eyes downcast as she spoke.

Aira didn't know why she was explaining herself to Richard. Perhaps, this was her last chance to let him know that *those* people he referred to as monsters were actually her guardian angels.

She remembered how hard it was to communicate without the use of her voice. Aira knew how to speak; she just couldn't make her voice work. She felt so frustrated until Emma told her that it was okay and that she had all the time in the world to let them hear her voice.

She looked at her grandfather and gave him a confident, proud stare. "All I had was my little whiteboard, my words, and my trust in Van and my *parents*. I could write the simplest word, and they would know what I meant. They believed I could use my voice again, and I did *because* of Van. Van Volkov gave me a second chance at life, and I believe you're giving him very little credit for that — he saved my life twice, and expected nothing in return."

Richard looked as if he were trying to swallow a lump that was stuck in his throat as he took a step back. "Those eyes that remind me so much of Vivian. How can I say no to those eyes?" he asked softly. "I couldn't protect Vivian then, and I can't protect her own daughter now. I'm a rather pathetic excuse for a father, aren't I?" His smile was sad as he remembered a memory Aira was sure he had tried to drown out for many years. "I didn't know."

The old man shook his head to get rid of those sad thoughts and turned to his son who was now standing shakily on his feet. "This is your uncle, Damon. He works with the government in getting paperwork for the shifters and vampires we acquire here. He's going to help me keep River away from the labs." He turned to Aira and sighed heavily. "And he's going to get you a phone."

Aira's eyes widened slightly as she processed what Richard had just told her. "Thank you."

Aira couldn't help but look into the man's blue eyes and smile. His eyes were not like Vincent's — they were kinder.

"I'd like to leave this place with River and Jarret and the others that are down there. Van can help them. He'll find them a home and he'll—"

Damon shook his head again, but this time, there was no smile on his face. "No, I'm sorry, but that isn't possible. All shifters brought into lockup are put through to Van straight away, and then it's his decision whether he takes them under his protection. All the shifters you see down there are the shifters he rejected."

Aira visibly stiffened. "No, Van would never do that. Van protects everyone!"

Richard shook his head sadly as he sighed, "We take in the ones he rejects, Aira. We, as humans, care little for the ones out there struggling in our own world. What makes the world of shifters any different? There is one thing you should know. Van and Drake Volkov will take in those with the power to help them in their own war, and those that offer nothing will be left in our hands. *We* are the ones who clean up *their* mess."

"If oh holy Alpha Volkov is supposed to be watching over us, he's doin' a shitty job. I don't see him coming and saving my ass anytime soon."

Aira gawked for a second as she thought about what Jarret had said to her. It dawned on her that Jarret had once held hope in Van to come and rescue him, but that had never happened. She had never thought about it before, but after everything had come to light about whom her family really was, it seemed Van was someone very important. He had the power to save lives, so, why didn't he?

She never did get the chance to ask that question as the door to Richard's office flew open. Vincent barged in, grabbing Aira's arms as he pulled out his stun gun and quickly zapped her in the side of her neck. With a loud scream, Aira's knees buckled, but the brazen man held her up.

Richard attempted to come to her aid but was held back by his own astonishment as he recognized the two men that had come in with his son. "You? Why are *you* here? Vincent, what the hell are you doing?" he snapped.

Damon stiffened as his eyes almost seemed to glow in anger. The way his eyes shifted were not human. It was as if something inside of him were raging to come out.

Aira, disorientated, lifted her head to look at her attacker, only to have a new collar strapped around her neck making her cry out in pain.

One of the men that had barged in with Vincent circled her like a shark before grabbing her chin and roughly yanking her head to look up. Instantly, Aira knew that he was a shifter. His claws sunk against her pale cheek, leaving a trail of deep bloody scratches. She let out another pain-filled scream as she gasped, pleading that he stop.

"So this is the *thing* whose death will bring us all to our knees? Pathetic. We had ordered you and yours long ago to do away with its mother, but you let her live. Now, we have Volkov on his way to retrieve her!" he bellowed.

Richard was glaring daggers as he yelled, "What in Christ's name are you talking about, Lanark?" He took a step forward, but the other man held his hand up, claws extended. Richard knew if he took one more step he'd be sliced to shreds. "What you're doing is against our agreement," he warned.

Lanark snapped his head to look at Richard, glaring back with just as much heated fury. "Our agreement was to help each other keep the peace between humans and us. I serve under Konstantin's law, and under that law, anything threatens the peace between the humans and his brothers is to be destroyed immediately."

Richard froze instantly. "What? *What* exactly is my granddaughter threatening? She *is* a Volkov, you idiot!" He then went on to say something Aira thought he would never say. "Her father is Drake Volkov!"

His smile was almost sinister as he threw some papers at the heated old man. "According to these, she's a Blight again."

The blood rushed from Richard's face as he looked at the documents signed by a judge. Looking up, Richard stared at his son and shook his head. "Why, Vincent?" was all he could ask.

Damon seemed to already know that answer. "Because he's the one who told Ronan where Vivian would be that day, didn't you, *brother*?"

Vincent couldn't look at his brother or father as he shook his head. "She wasn't supposed to die. It was just supposed to be the little one. He swore he'd leave humans alone if he had her."

Richard was in shock at his son's admission. Damon growled low as he went to lunge at his brother, only to be held in a headlock by Lanark. The fair-haired shifter chuckled as he threw Damon to the floor.

A soft, broken voice seemed to halt all the commotion. With a light whimper, Aira lifted her bloodstained face and glared. "You'll get what's coming to you," she growled out, eyeing Vincent like an animal would its prey.

Aira watched as the man named Lanark moved over to her and with a smile of his own, lifted his knee right into Aira's stomach. She gasped as the air instantly left her lungs, and she slumped down, not able to hold herself as Vincent held her arms behind her.

Richard couldn't hold it back any longer as he pulled a gun from his desk and held it up to Lanark, ready to shoot. The shifter simply chuckled as he stared the old man down. "I hope Volkov tears you apart," Richard growled.

Vincent pulled Aira towards the door but stopped when Richard said, "And you-*you… murdered…*" he found it difficult to continue his sentence as the gun shook in his hand.

Vincent held little remorse as he muttered, "I'm sorry Dad," before dragging his niece out of the room and back down to the cells.

Lanark smiled as his friend moved towards the door, nodding. The shifter sighed and went to leave.

"What are you doing with her?" Damon demanded to know.

Lanark refused to answer and instead said, "You're wrong, Richard. Konstantin will not be killing me; he'll be thanking me."

"For *what* exactly?" Richard barked.

Aira's face paled as she heard exactly what Lanark had said as she was dragged down the hallway.

"For retrieving the body of Aira Blight."

She gasped as Vincent shoved her forward. The beeping was murder to her ears as he entered the code to move through the door back to the cells. On the outside, Aira was beaten and bruised, but on the inside, she seethed with an emotion she never even knew she could feel. Sadness and anger for the murdered family she never had the chance to know flowed through her like a raging river. This man carried on with his life while she remembered what had happened over and over again like a never-ending nightmare.

"Murderer," Aira spat as they passed through the door. "You sent Ronan after them, *knowing* my mother would rather die than let him have me."

Aira's world suddenly spun as Vincent slammed her head into the white wall beside them. His hand held her arms back while his other hand gripped at her matted hair. "Hard-headed like your mother," he replied flippantly before steadying her and forcing the wobbling girl to keep moving.

Her vision was blurred, but she knew he wasn't taking her to her original cell as she briefly saw the outline of Jarret as he pressed himself against his cell door. When her vision returned, she could see that the shifters caged like animals watched her carefully as she passed them, the shock evident on their faces.

Although the cells were sound proof from the outside, she could have sworn she heard Jarret's voice echo through her head, telling her to fight. Thundering bangs suddenly resounded around her as she noticed the shifters were banging on their cell doors, yelling words neither she nor Vincent could hear.

It wasn't until she saw the little pup, River, look at her as if he'd seen a ghost that she realized it wasn't yet time to lay down and die. Summoning the same strength she had used previously and ignoring the stabbing pain of that collar, Aira threw her pounding head back, straight into Vincent's forehead. A crack echoed through the corridor as he let her go, staggering back and gripping his forehead.

Looking back just in time to see him pass out, Aira threw him a look of disgust and spat, "You're right. I *am* hard-headed like my mother."

Giving a shaky sigh, Aira bent down and grabbed the set of blue ovals attached to a key ring from her uncle's pocket. Disappointment quickly clouded her face as she realized they weren't what she needed to get the cell doors open. That was when she noticed the stun gun poking out of his belt. The gears started to roll in her head as she looked from the stun gun and over to the little box she had seen people speak into and type numbers to get the doors open.

Taking it carefully from the unconscious man, Aira pointed it point-blank at the control box. Even if this failed, she could at least sleep at night knowing she tried to free Jarret and the others, or at least, died trying.

Ignoring the panicked bangs from the shifters around her, Aira took a deep breath and pulled the trigger, watching as the electrified nozzle hit the control box. Thinking quickly, she dropped the gun instantly and watched as the box exploded, covering her ears as sirens started to blare all around her.

The doors to the cells immediately flew open one by one, and for the first time since her arrival, Aira laughed with joy. Rushing to Jarret, Aira quickly swiped one of the blue ovals on the key chain over his collar as she'd seen her grandfather do with hers earlier and then undid her own. Before she could move to River's cell, Jarret gently took her wrist, making her turn and frown.

"We need to leave," she warned, looking back towards the entrance uncomfortably. Swarms of them could come down at any moment.

He paused for a moment before shaking his head and letting her go. "You-you're different than the other humans. Why?"

Aira shook her head, confused, but smiled when it suddenly dawned on her. "I was raised by wolves, so that means I can't let my family die down here, right?"

Jarret chuckled before throwing her a cheeky grin. "Let's get the fuck outta here then."

It didn't take much time to get all the collars off. As Aira went to get one of the female shifters collars off her neck, the big guy — Rion — gently pushed passed and mumbled, "I'll do it. Go help the old girl."

Aira nodded as she moved to let him in. She watched for a moment as he gently took the girl's cheek into his palm and kissed her forehead. It was then that Aira knew that just, maybe, maybe she'd changed something for them both.

Sighing, she moved to help an older shifter and put her arm around her shoulder. The older woman was obviously hurt from an ailment that had probably been happening for years.

Just as they were about to move out, Aira gasped, "No!"

Rion stopped just as he was about to stomp on Vincent's head. He and the girl he was carrying looked directly at Aira, surprised. "He deserves it," he snapped.

Aira was unwavering as she snapped back, "The cycle ends today. We aren't murderers like him. Let's just get out of here."

Rion grunted and spat down at the unconscious human. "He'll have his day in hell whether I send him there or not," and moved towards the exit.

She never said it out loud, but for a moment, she had actually contemplated harming Vincent when that stun gun was in her hands. That thought alone scared her.

"Let's move it."

Chapter Sixty-Five

He stared down at the little man in uniform quivering in front of him. The gun he was armed with shook in his hands as he, yet again, tried to explain to Van why he couldn't enter the compound.

"Sir, shifters can't enter the property without special authorization, and-and I don't have permission to let you in," he explained, for the *third* time. Van was just pleased the idiot didn't stutter as much this time.

As this repetitive conversation played out, Drake was in the background, looking around the large wired fence and gate curiously before carefully touching it. The soldier quickly turned, and before he could give any warning, Drake watched as his hand started to smoke and burn.

Without so much as a peep, Van smiled. The soldier was up in the air, screaming in fright as Van lifted him by his shirt. "Could you be a dear and please tell us why that gate is doused in silver?" he asked, willing the corners of his mouth to tilt up into an obnoxious smile. Why Richard had gone through so much trouble to melt down silver and coat his gates in it was a mystery that he was going to find out.

It wasn't long before the cat was out of the bag. "I-I have orders not to let any Volkov's in!"

There was a loud thump on the ground as Van dropped the human, amused by the way he whimpered like a little girl. He scrambled for his gun, pointing it point blank at Van, who simply stared at him with a nonchalant expression.

"They have something that belongs to us, so I suggest you get onto that little Parker Brother's Walkie-talkie of yours and tell Richard to get his ass out here before I make his house my new stomping ground," Van threatened. He was sure if he growled this human would wet his pants, and honestly, the smell of urine on a scared human was one of the few scents that made him want to evacuate his stomach.

"I couldn't get those gates opened even if I tried!" he yelled, the gun still shaking as he pointed it at Van. "They can only be opened from the inside!"

Van glared as he looked towards the grounds. If they tried to jump it, they'd be classed as a national threat and no amount of talking could make the human government think otherwise. Van growled in frustration as he tried to think of a way around this headache.

Then he heard the sirens.

"*What* is that?" Drake asked, feeling just as annoyed as his brother.

The officer scattered to his feet as he moved back to his station. "We're going into lockdown."

"And *why* would you be going into lockdown?" Drake asked again. A feeling of panic was slowly seeping into the pit of both their stomachs.

After a moment of talking on his radio, the officer sighed and cursed under his breath. "There's an escape in progress."

Chapter Sixty-Six

The heavy thud that hit the floor made Aira wince. She had to remind herself again and again that the person Rion had just thrown without mercy against the wall wasn't dead, but they'd certainly be in a lot of pain when they awoke later.

"Every fucker comes out to stop us 'cept the ones I want. Makes me feel uneasy," he growled as he slapped his hands together to get off some form of imaginary dust. Aira knew he deserved to get back at the ones who caused him pain, but this wasn't the way to do it.

She pulled the older female shifter upright next to her and frowned. "Fighting hate with hate never works, Rion."

He threw her a deadpanned expression before shaking his head and pulled his mate, Lara, into his arms.

"If he doesn't say it, I will. *We're sorry*," came a tiny little voice from Rion's arms.

Aira blinked twice as she tried to think of what the girl could have been sorry for. "You're sorry?"

She was hesitant, but Rion didn't say anything as she continued, "We wished death on these humans for so long that when we heard that Richard's daughter had been murdered by Ronan, we were so happy. We thought he deserved it, and for that, we're sorry. We didn't know that one day her daughter would come and save us." Tears prickled Lara's eyes as she tried to keep calm. She refused to look at the human girl.

There was a moment of silence before Aira smiled sadly and said, "The only people I will ever want an apology from are the people responsible for their deaths. Now, let's go."

Surprise clouded their expressions before following the girl who had risked everything to save their lives. Lara watched Aira as she carefully pulled Malinda, the eldest shifter in captivity in Richard's cells, through the back patio door. "Will Van really come for us?" she asked. She had heard Aira say it at some point but didn't believe it.

How on earth did a young human girl know Van Volkov after all? Aira could have laughed at this but given the situation, kept that to herself.

Aira nodded. "He'll come, and he'll take you home. I promise."

Jarret huffed as he held River close to him. "Yeah, that's what we said to ourselves for years, and he never came."

Aira had just about had enough of their doubt when she snapped, "I swear to you, before I step one foot out that gate you'll all be free again. He's here. I *know* he's here. I don't know how I know but please, just trust me?"

It wasn't like they really had a choice in the matter. It was either believe that Volkov was coming to save them, a hope they'd held onto for years prior, or come to the horrid realization they may just die before they step foot outside those gates. Even if Aira was wrong, it was still nice to have some hope shine through even for just a little while.

Gently, Aira handed Malinda over to another younger shifter who gladly took her. They were out of the house now, and it was a straight run for the gates. Those big electrified fences had scared Aira when she had first entered the property, but now, they called her name — they called her to freedom. She had never been contained before. Everything was so messed up she didn't know what to do except run.

Jarret and Rion were still getting used to not being collared and having their strength and wolves suppressed. They were still considerably weakened, and that was a setback for all of them.

As Aira caught her breath, a small twinge of light sparkled from the trees that surrounded the house and property. She looked up, focusing on where the light had come from and felt herself freeze in absolute terror.

The sniper in the tree to her right took aim at Rion. Aira couldn't say a word as she watched in horror as the man kept his target on lock. Without thinking about it, her feet suddenly came unglued from the hard ground, and she sprinted to move behind Rion and Lara. That was when they heard the muted click and the object fly through the air.

Aira gasped and clutched her side; leaning to her left as she covered whatever had hit her. Although they seemed more shocked than worried, Rion asked, "Hey, did they get ya'?"

Aira winced but let out a smile to try to ease them. "It wasn't a bullet. I'm fine."

Just as Jarret went to walk towards her, River in his arms, they heard the sound of feet shuffling towards them. Aira could feel her breath begin to get shaky as she stared at the newly freed shifters in fear.

"Run!" she shouted. "Run, go!"

Hesitance stopped them, but Aira ushered Rion to move, and after he glanced at Lara, he closed his eyes to take a deep breath before sprinting with inhuman speed towards the far paddock. Jarret soon followed with River, and the others took note to also run.

Aira clutched her side, not wanting them to see what was temporarily immobilizing her. Looking down, she pulled the oval shaped syringe out of her side, wincing as the long needle escaped her skin forcefully. It didn't take long before she was shaking off the slight head spin that plagued her before running after them, only looking back to see that Vincent had now recovered and was exiting the compound with around a dozen armed men. She knew he'd kill her if he caught her.

Her breathing was much heavier than before as she made a mad dash for freedom. It confused her why Vincent wasn't in a hurry to catch her. That is until she caught up with the others and realized one of two little obstacles. The shifters, having had their strength and agility contained for such a long time, could not jump the fence nor could they climb after Jarret clutched his hand with a sweltering burn.

"What do we do now?" Lara asked, looking absolutely terrified and inconsolable at this setback. "Aira?"

Clutching her forehead, Aira felt her eyes prickle with tears as she too started to panic. "I-I don't know."

"Aira?" came a shocked, hardened voice she knew all too well. It was a voice she had grown up with, a voice that soothed her when she was frightened — the voice she knew would protect her.

Looking up, she knew she probably looked like something out of a nightmare. Her head was covered in dried blood, a cluster of it forming in the place Vincent had tried to cave her head in earlier. Her arms were littered with bruises. Bits of her hair had been ripped from her scalp, and her cheek was shredded from Lanark clawing her.

But her father didn't look at her any differently. He hadn't even bothered to hide his golden eyes that seemed to shine as he realized who she was. Drake moved to the metal fence, grabbing it, and Aira watched in stunned silence as his hands seemed to burn and smoke. He never even flinched.

It wasn't until his eyes shifted to her obvious injuries that his eyes turned hard. The hues of his eyes turned to slits as he growled viciously — a sound she'd never heard her father make, and he lurched his body against the steel fence that separated them.

This broke Aira out of the best dream of her life as she gasped. "Stop! It's hurting you!"

This seemed to break Drake out of his own trance as he sighed heavily and stopped for a moment. Aira felt the tears well in her eyes as she watched her father with a sort of broken expression. The tears finally streamed down her cheeks, and a hiccup escaped her throat as she saw someone she, herself, wasn't even completely sure would show up.

Van walked carefully over towards Drake, but his attention was on Aira. His face was pulled into an expression Aira had never seen before, but that didn't matter. He had come for her. She knew he'd come for her.

It seemed Aira wasn't the only stunned one as Rion and Jarret stared at Van as if he were some sort of god. Rion, as tough as he was, looked as if he was also about to cry out in absolute joy.

Lara was the first to break the silence. "She said you'd come. She never doubted that."

Rion's voice was gruff as he said, "He still has to accept us, Lara. He didn't before."

The hope quickly dashed in her eyes as she realized that, yes, Van Volkov had turned them away when they were first brought into captivity. Aira knew that he hadn't met them personally, but she was sure they had felt his rejection to take them under his protection. From then on, their fates were sealed to Richard and his band of psychopaths.

Aira expected guards at the gates waiting for them but after a moment of inspection, noticed the pile of slumped men in the background.

Before Aira could breathe a sigh of relief, she heard the distinct sound of clicking from behind them. Turning slowly, Aira paled when she saw that Vincent and Elizabeth had lead a small army of armed men in uniforms, their guns pointed at her and the escapees.

She was dizzy, she was tired, and she felt as if this was it. That this was what she had survived to do. It was a rather morbid thought, but she was okay with that. Perhaps, being sent here was destiny. Maybe she came to save River and Jarret and be done with all this pent-up anger towards someone she didn't even know.

The panic in her father's and Van's eyes when she took a timid step back nearly made her crack. She was smiling as the tears streamed down her cheeks. Emotionally, she was crumbling.

A hand stopped her as Jarret grabbed her wrist. River, the little pup in his arms, looked at Aira with wonder and confusion. He didn't know who she was; she didn't know who he was. But somehow, in that very second, they connected. He looked at her with all the light of the world shining back, and she looked at him knowing she had at least guaranteed one safe future.

She was seventeen and ready to accept that maybe her own future wasn't as bright as her parents had always promised.

"You look after him," Aira whispered.

Jarret looked at her, confused, before saying, "What do' ya think you're doin'?"

She ripped her arm away from him and shook her head. She was aware that the small army behind her was ready to attack the moment they saw a threat. There wasn't much time. "I said that you would all be free before I took one step outside those gates. I'm keeping my promise."

His expression was that of shock. "You're *what*? We're here! We can all get out!"

"Jarret... you don't know me. You don't owe me anything; so, don't try to convince yourself that you do. This, all of *this*, ends today." She moved away from Jarret and looked to Van and Drake one last time.

They came back for her. She had made a choice to leave, but still, they came back to save her. Aira blew a kiss to them. With one last look, she turned and started to walk towards the onslaught of guns aimed in her direction. "Try to get those gates open!" She knew that she was the one these people wanted. They wanted her head, and she would give them what they wanted if it meant more time.

She stopped dead in her tracks when a crashing bang sounded against the fence. She never turned around but knew that Van was seething as he growled, "Girl, you get back here… *now!*"

With a slight smile, Aira tilted her head and glanced at him. "As I have said before, I'm not your *dog*, Mr. Van," she replied, throwing him the same insult she had months prior when he tried to order her around before making a run down the hill. She heard threats and yells coming from both her father and Van — mostly Van — but ignored them. She tuned out of their desperate cries as she came closer to where Vincent was standing.

Her head was heavy, and her vision was beginning to blur. She didn't have much time before that tranquilizer took effect. She knew they wouldn't kill her on the spot, not with Drake and Van watching on. The memory of their panicked conversation earlier when they realized her real family was coming to save her convinced her of that fact.

The yells and pleas were nothing but distant voices in her head as she wobbled and struggled to stay standing. Falling back on her backside, she was breathing heavily when her vision began to darken.

The last thing she heard was a deep, throaty howl. Whether it came from Van or not, she couldn't stay awake long enough to find out.

Chapter Sixty-Seven

"You've been sitting there for a long time, little one."

She didn't even acknowledge his presence, and that irked him in a way he found both amusing and irritating all at once.

Her head tilted towards him as she pulled her knees to her chest, balling herself up into a sort of protective cocoon. "You look like Van, but you're not Van, are you?"

She watched carefully as he slowly shook his head, a frown playing on his incredibly handsome face. "No, little one, I am not, but we are in fact the same person. He protects me within him, and I protect him when the time calls for it. He is my master, the body I was put in after my death many, many years ago."

"What's your name?" she asked, her voice tense, scared... broken. She was afraid of the answer. "How can you be here with me if you're inside Van?"

His frown turned into a smile — a tender and kind smile that made her cold body instantly warm with light. "Where Van cannot reach you, I will always be there. He did not lie when he said that no matter where you are, he would always come for you. He cannot reach you within your dreams, but I can."

She turned her head, not wanting to look at him as he inched closer and closer before he was finally kneeling in front of her. There was no light in this place; there was only darkness, the kind of darkness you see when you close your eyes just before you drift off to sleep. There was nothing to look at or to hope for. It took her a moment to realize that this abyss she had thrown herself into was, in fact, her own mind.

"Do you think I'll ever be me again?"

He looked a little puzzled by her question. "You will."

"How can I come back from something like this? I'm tired. I don't want to fight anymore. I don't want to go back to the nightmares, the sadness, or the heartbreak." A tear slipped down her cheek as she thought about Vincent's confession. Did her mother even suspect Vincent held so much hate in his heart to do such a thing?

Yes, he knew Vivian would sooner die than let anything happen to her children. He knew... he knew...

A little gasp escaped her lips as the stranger grabbed her chin, gently turning her face to look at him. His words, deep and filled with years of regret and wisdom, hit a nerve on her as he said, "You will come back from this. When you fall, we will always be there to pick you up. That light in your eyes, the one that's always been there to help my master through his darkest days, is fading fast, but if you stand up right now, you can take back what has been taken from you."

It was a fleeting hope, but what had been taken from her so long ago could never be brought back, no matter how hard she wished it.

And then, as if some deity from up above heard her somber thoughts, a shadow moved from behind the man. It took a moment for Aira to realize a light had been slowly growing, lighting the space around her and the stranger.

That was when she saw her.

"Mom...?"

The smiling face of Vivian Blight stared back at her, warming Aira's heart. She had thought she had let them go when Emma and Drake had taken her back to their family home, but it seemed she was still holding onto that demon inside that told her she had caused this. Susan called it survivor's guilt, but Aira thought of it more like torture.

Through the shadows, more figures started to appear — two men and a young girl. It didn't take long for Aira to realize she was staring into the haunted faces of her dead family. She cringed and turned her head, sobbing hysterically into her forearm. She couldn't look at them. Aira couldn't face them after so long of forgetting their sacrifice.

"I forgot you. I'm sorry... I'm sorry..." she sobbed.

Two hands encased her face as the man slowly turned her head back, making her focus on the little figure clutching at her father's waist. The little girl looked scared and just as tired as she did. Her hair was matted, and her clothes, pajamas, looked dirty and forgotten.

"You never forgot," he muttered, his face leaning down closer to hers until his eyes were just centimeters away from hers. "You've been here with them this whole time."

Now, it all made sense. Aira had forgotten them, yes, but in forgetting them, a part of her stayed. All this time, the little girl she once was had been clinging to the family she lost all those years ago as if her life depended on it.

"It's time to take back what is yours, little one," the man muttered as he stood up. His hand stretched out, offering Aira the chance to stand up with him and take back that little girl she had once been.

Aira reached up and took the man's hand. His hand tightened around hers almost instantly, and with one hard pull, Aira was launched to her feet. Images started to appear before her, images of a life she could have had if that day had never happened — her brother graduating from college and going to medical school. Her sister went off and traveled the world with men falling at her feet before Aira saw her sister with two children of her own, smiling and so very happy. Aira was going to a normal high school, becoming a cheerleader, surrounded by friends and eventually meeting a boy she would later fall in love with. The last image was Aira, dressed in white, her father beside her as he walked her down the aisle. She was getting married.

This life — a life she could have had — was filled with endless opportunities. It was a life she was meant to have, but there was something missing, something very important to her.

In this life, there was no Aiden there to tease her or make her laugh. There was no Emma there to teach her right from wrong, respect, or courage. There was no Drake to encourage her to speak her mind and help those who needed it, and there was no Van...

No Van.

No, she never would have met Van if that day had never happened. Perhaps, she couldn't have the best of both worlds. She and Van would have had no reason to meet. Perhaps, he wouldn't have even looked her way, to begin with. Her life would have been so very different. And then it all made so much sense. This strange man was giving her a choice — stay in this wasteland that was her own mind with the family she had lost so very long ago, or...

"Take back what's mine," she whispered.

That little girl clinging to Richard was the part of Aira stolen the day her family was killed. That part of her that held so much confidence and trust had been hiding here this whole time, not ready to let go or forget. In that child was the girl Aira was supposed to be. Inside that little girl's heart held the key Aira needed to get through that final door she had been banging her head against for years.

Reaching out her hand, she was aware she probably wasn't the most approachable person at that very moment. Even in her own mind, she was cut up and bruised but most certainly not as broken as she'd thought she had been.

The little girl turned her head away, simply rejecting the hand Aira held out. She didn't want to leave, and Aira couldn't blame her, after all, that little girl was her.

"It's okay," Aira cooed. "It's time to come home."

The little version of herself shook her head no. "Don't wanna. Staying here with my daddy," she mumbled as she nuzzled into her father's shirt.

The strange man who had welcomed her here, standing tall next to Aira, seemed to sigh as he said, "You'll have to do better than that."

Frowning, Aira moved closer, but her family seemed to only take a step back. Her mother's face looked saddened as if she wanted to say something but couldn't.

Aira had to remember that the apparitions of her family in front of her were not real. They were simply a memory lost long ago, a memory she had apparently been holding onto since she was six years old.

Sighing heavily and trying not to crack, Aira kneeled down and held out her arms, beckoning the child to come closer. "I don't know if you know this, but I need you. I can't do this alone." Her tone was cracking, her voice tired and beaten. This was her last chance. "Van can't do this alone..." was the last thing she said.

That seemed to get the little girl's attention as she finally turned to look at Aira. It took a moment for Aira to realize that this little version of herself knew exactly who Van was despite hiding here for so long.

"Mr. Van... Hero..." she murmured. The man she clung to, their father, looked down at her and smiled.

Aira grinned. "That's right. Our hero needs us, and so do Drake and Emma and Aiden, even Jarret, and River. You've been watching, haven't you?"

The girl nodded solemnly. "Hmm," Looking up, she smiled and slowly let go of her father. "I think I'm ready to go now."

Their father nodded and with a sad smile, let the little girl walk towards Aira. The moment their hands touched, Aira *felt an instant wave of relief, as if a pile of bricks had just been lifted off of her shoulders.*

Looking up at the man Aira had first met in this strange place, the little girl frowned. "This means they'll know now." She sounded concerned, more concerned than a little girl should have sounded.

"Know what?" Aira asked, confused. Who would know what?

A sudden jolt rippled throughout Aira's body. She staggered back, grasping at her head. Everything was blurring, and this world seemed to shake uncontrollably.

She looked up, expecting something to happen. The little version of herself grasped her hand as they prepared to head back to the real world. Before everything completely faded, Aira gasped loudly and shouted, "Who are you?"

The handsome man with the golden eyes smiled as he replied, "My name is Konstantin. Call my name, and I will always be there to fight for you." By the end of his sentence, another voice seemed to overlap his as he repeated, "Always."

Van — that was Van's voice. She just knew it.

The light seemed to race towards her at unimaginable speed, and after a moment, she felt herself crash back down into the world she had wanted to escape.

Air — she needed air.

Her eyes opened wide almost instantly as Aira took in a giant gulp of air. She spluttered and coughed as she rolled onto her side, moaning from the pain that shot through her entire body.

As the ringing in her ears began to fade, she could hear the distant growling from behind as both Van and Drake shouted at her to stand up. It wasn't long before she realized what had them so panicked.

Vincent was only steps away from her as he strutted up to her pathetically fragile form. With one look, his face dropped into a disappointed expression as if he had hoped she was dead.

"She's not human; she can't be. She should be knocked out!" Elizabeth growled as she came up behind her brother, gun out and aiming at Aira.

"Relax," Vincent muttered as he nudged the gasping girl with his foot, "If it gets back up after the first shot, you just shoot it again." He wiped some dried blood from his face with a piece of his sleeve before huffing and kicking her in her side.

Aira screamed in agony, but she refused to let anymore tears fall. Sitting up, she resembled a wounded animal giving one last fight, and this was a fight she would win. Using her hand to hold her torso off the grass, she smiled up at her *aunt* and *uncle* and whispered, "Konstantin."

She glanced back and saw that Van stood stock still as he heard her whisper the name of the demon dog he held at bay. She saw his face twitch slightly as his golden eyes brightened. Drake looked just as astonished.

Van was quick to act as he calmly shouted, "If you want me to protect you, say that name again!"

The pieces started to come together. She was asking for Konstantin's protection, and then the fight would really begin.

A sudden clattering of metal broke everyone from their attention on Aira as the gates separating them clambered open.

Elizabeth was the first to realize as her pudgy face turned white. Stepping back, she swore under her breath.

"That stupid old man! Get the gates!" she ordered, turning to her crew, as they too seemed to lose color in their faces. "Vince, Dad's gone senile! He's opening the gates!"

If those gates opened, there was nothing separating Van Volkov and them.

Vincent, however, was too concerned with Aira as he pointed the gun at her forehead. Aira never even seemed to flinch. She just continued to smile as if she *knew* just how screwed they all were.

Jarret and the others were ushered through the fence by her father, and Aira smiled as she ignored the steely coldness of Vincent's gun against her forehead. She could have laughed at the way his hand shook, as he demanded she repeat what she had just said. Repeat it, and he'd blow her brains out.

Aira's lip twitched into a bigger smile. She would win this. She now knew what she had to do. Aira knew that Van was also catching on. She could feel him—he was so close.

"Konstantin," she said loudly, tilting her head back to look at him, "Take this idiot out!" She needed her hero and the demon he withheld.

The ground seemed to shudder as the giant gate slammed open. The army of men raised their guns, ignoring the thumping sounds, as their hearts jumped into their throats. Vincent's hand visibly seized up. Everyone fell silent as they watched in horror as the man at the gate almost *smiled*. Van Volkov did not smile.

And then the silence was swiftly broken as Drake all but ran to the rescued shifters. "Get down!" he shouted.

He moved them just as the ground started to rumble, and Van began to change. Jarret looked on in absolute horror as River clung to him, watching as Van's bones started to change and grow. The growling alone was horrifying enough as his body twisted and morphed, growing triple that of a normal sized shifter. Before he knew it, he was looking up and into the face of what most never lived a hundred years to see. Yet, he had been free a couple of hours and saw the most remarkable thing in his life.

Konstantin, the black Lycan, stood tall and proud, but his attention was solely on the girl whose life hung between him and a stupid human with a trigger finger.

The wind was devastating as it nearly blew them off their feet when Konstantin took off towards Aira. Vincent was all but frozen as he watched helplessly. Aira was much the same as she looked at the giant wolf hurdling towards them, but she was not frightened. No, she was oddly calm. Whatever Van had just turned into; she knew he would never hurt her.

Taking the chance, Aira kicked Vincent away, sending him skidding across the grass. Using the last of her energy, she sprung to her feet, letting out a tiny yell as the pain seared through her body. By the time she even thought to take a step, Konstantin was by her side, making the ground beneath her shake violently.

Before anyone could think to use their weapons, Konstantin let out a thundering roar, making any within his warpath drop to their feet, hands over their ears. However, the ringing was the least of their worries as the angry Lycan hovered over the human he was most eager to rip apart.

Vincent cowered, nearly crying as he shakily tried to steady his gun.

But a tiny voice stopped him as she cried, "No, don't kill them!"

The surprises kept coming as Konstantin spoke, *"You defend this human, little one?"*

Aira held her side as she stuttered, "I-I don't want any-anymore people to die!"

"I've killed many for less than what this creature has done," he replied nonchalantly in a thundering voice. Although his mouth did not move, his words were passed through to everyone within their minds. Some of the humans hid and covered their ears, slowly going mad from the deep, hate-filled voice.

Huffing, the god-like creature turned away from the cowering humans. With one look at the tiny human girl, they both seemed to come to an agreement as they went to walk away.

"No!" Vincent screamed as he scrambled to his feet that his pants was wet after the fright Konstantin had given him.

Konstantin, having had enough of the human's foolishness, turned and let out a thunderous growl, making the man stumble back.

Elizabeth stood frozen in place. Turning briefly to look towards the house, she saw Dawn and Christine staring horror-struck as they huddled together on the balcony.

The only thing she could think to say was, "It's over, Vincent." She turned as she spat on the ground, disdain covering his face. "Rest in fucking piece, Vivian. I bet you're happy now."

Aira sighed as she pulled the last of her bags out and threw them into the car her grandfather had organized. Drake watched her like a hawk, not letting her out of his sight for more than three minutes at a time. She scratched the back of her head as she wondered if that was everything she had brought.

As she went back into the house, Drake went to follow until Aira held up her hand. "I'm going to talk to Richard for a moment, Dad. I'll be okay, I promise."

Her father looked apprehensive but took a step back and nodded. "Five minutes."

Aira smiled and gave him a quick salute. "Yes, sir."

She ran up the stairs and moved quickly through the house. She ignored the heavy sobs of Dawn as she passed the living room and the soft voice of Christine consoling her mother. Aira knew Vincent would be locked up for a while because of his confession regarding Vivian's murder. Lanark, however, had run off, probably terrified of what Van would do to him once he found him.

As she came to her grandfather's study, she gently knocked on the door and smiled. "I'm leaving now," she announced quietly.

Richard looked up at Damon and nodded to the door. "Can you give us a moment, Damon?"

The man nodded and as he passed Aira, gently put his arms around her and gave her a light hug. "Good luck, kid."

Aira hugged back and waved as he walked away, leaving her to speak with her grandfather alone.

"How are you feeling?" he asked as he stood from his desk.

Aira sighed, "I've felt better, but my father's a great doctor."

A look of sadness washed over the old man's face. "I wish it didn't end this way. I wanted a piece of Vivian home, but I know now that Vivian was safer far away from this place."

"Why did Elizabeth and Vincent hate her so much?" Aira asked. She needed to know why they hated her mother, why they justified having her slaughtered.

"I don't know why Ronan wants you dead my girl, but I do know that jealousy is what brought my children to this point in their lives. Did you know your mother had a twin brother?"

Aira shook her head. No, she didn't know very much about her mother at all, and during the chaos of things, she hadn't had much time to ask any questions.

Richard chuckled. "I suppose you were too busy fighting for your life," he sighed. "Aither was a good boy who turned into a very confused man. That happens when you have two halves of yourself that are natural enemies. Vivian was Mae all over, but Aither was half Mae, half his father. It was like those wolf-dogs; they don't know whether they're wild or man's best friend, but the wild always comes out in the end."

Aira stared in complete shock, confused as to what he was getting at or trying to explain. "What are you saying exactly?" she asked as she wrung her hands together, her body swaying nervously from side to side.

"I'm telling you the truth, something you're probably not accustomed to." His eyes were glassy, giving Aira the impression he hadn't told anyone what he was about to tell her. "Elizabeth and Vincent's mother passed away when they were very young, and after that, I took Mae in to help me raise them. Mae wasn't my wife although that's what I had always wished, and Vivian and Aither weren't my biological children. I was asked to keep her safe for as long as her life allowed it, and I kept that promise until the day Mae died. I just pray I'm not alive when the day comes *he* comes back from Altholo, and I have to tell him his mate, children and grandchildren are dead."

A tear slipped down Richard's face, but he quickly wiped it away. Aira was in complete and utter shock as she stared at him, her head shaking back and forth. "Altholo? Wait, you're not my grandfather?" She had so many questions and very little answers.

Richard grunted, "He's in Altholo, the same place Akim and Konstantin were born, the same place *he* was born, the same place they all tried to escape, and ultimately failed in one way or another."

Chapter Sixty-Eight

"Aira. Aira, wake up."

Her eyes slowly opened from the backseat of the car. After being released from the hospital for a quick checkup, she was given the all clear to make the flight to Russia with her father and Van. However, she had at least wanted to see River, Jarret, and the others again before she made that journey.

The smiling face of her father greeted her as she woke up, making the injured girl sigh with relief. For a moment, she had thought she would have seen the sneering expression of Vincent. She knew, in time, she would learn that she was now safe. She didn't have to fight anymore.

"Where are we?" were the first words out of her mouth. From the looks of things, it would have appeared they were in the middle of nowhere.

Drake chuckled as he gently released her of her seatbelt. "A special place."

Aira smiled and tried to stifle a wince as she moved from the car. "I think I've had enough of 'special places,' Dad."

However hard she tried, she just couldn't seem to get that panic stricken feeling out of her chest. After everything she had been through, she felt on edge all the time now. It was a terrible suffocating feeling Aira wished would just go away. She didn't feel safe anymore, and that was a nightmare in itself.

As soon as she staggered out of the car with her father's aid, that was when she saw them, and by God, there were a lot of them.

Dozens upon dozens of people filled the shaded grassy area around her. They easily made up a large crowd. Aira stared in absolute shock as they all stared back at her. There was a moment of tense silence before clapping and cheering resounded, their faces lighting up when they realized who she was. She was the girl who had saved their loved ones from captivity.

Aira watched, bewildered, as a large wolf wandered up to her. Now that she looked a little closer, there were many wolves of all shades of colors standing or lying around lazily. The wolf that slowly came up to her easily tripled her in size but was far smaller than the wolf she knew as Konstantin.

The dark gray wolf moved closer until he was face to face with Aira. However, intimidating as he might have seemed to others, Aira felt no threat and reached out her hand to gently stroke his snout. He seemed pleased with this and lowered his head.

Seeing she was confused, Drake chuckled and whispered, "He's submitting to you."

"Me? Why?" she asked. Her eyes widened as she tried to think of a reason he would want to submit to her.

Drake already knew the answer. "You saved his mother," he answered and looked towards the elderly woman Aira had helped shoulder out of Richard's cells. She smiled from a distance, holding hands with another lady.

It was then that the other shifted wolves also lowered their heads, respecting the young human who looked on in complete astonishment.

Drake gently nudged his nervous daughter forward. "Go on. Say hello."

Taking a couple of steps forward, Aira shook her head, terrified as to what she had to do. Nerves quickly set in as she looked back. "But-but I don't know what do to exactly?"

The gray wolf had now moved out of her way, and a giant bear of a man came thundering up to her. Aira blanched as she almost fell backward, but his arms caught her in a hard embrace. She was shocked as he hugged her all but crying on her shoulder.

"I never thought I'd see them again. I gave up hope so long ago. Thank you! Thank you!"

He rambled, "Thank you" again and again, and all Aira could do was pat his back awkwardly. She had no idea who he was talking about before a familiar face came pushing through the crowd of shifters.

"Dad, let her breath!" Rion hollered, placing a hand on his father's shoulder.

Sudden realization dawned on the man, and he instantly let the teenager go. Aira coughed lightly but smiled all the same. Looking at Rion and his father side by side, she could see the resemblance almost instantly.

Her smile only broadened as she saw Lara hobble up behind the two men. Aira grinned from ear to ear when she noticed Lara's prosthetic leg. "That's amazing!" Aira quipped.

Lara blushed slightly as she held on to her mate. "Thank Alpha Volkov; he got it for me a couple of days after we left that terrible place. I can walk again on my own for the first time in a long time."

Looking to Rion, Aira felt a warmness sweep through her chest as he looked down at Lara, brushing some hair from her eyes and wiped his own.

Rion's father seemed just as happy as he chuckled, "We're under Konstantin's protection now. No one can take my family or brothers again, thanks to you."

"Konstantin's protection?" She had heard Jarret talk about this before.

Drake put his hand on Aira's shoulder. "An old law — very old. Humans can't touch shifters if they're under Van's leadership, but under Konstantin, no other shifter can touch them either. John, his pack and the other packs you see here are under both those laws now. They'll be safe for as long as they need Van."

It suddenly dawned on Aira just how important Van was to these people — to the shifters who lived in fear every day. He was doing so much for so many, all on his own.

Many more shifters moved forward to thank Aira and hug her, albeit awkwardly. Looking around, she suddenly noticed the two people she had wanted to speak with. Smiling as she moved closer, she giggled when she saw Jarret's attire.

He shifted uncomfortably in his button-down shirt and dress pants, a sullen expression washing over his face as he fumbled with a loose button.

Aira shook her head and fixed it for him although the expression on his face never faltered. "I suppose you'll be going home," she casually stated.

Jarret's eyes seemed to shift away from her. "Nah, don't have a home to go to, anyway."

Aira looked up at him, frowning at his answer. "What about River?" she asked, looking down at the pup who looked up at her in amazement. It was the first time they could actually meet properly.

"Rion and Lara wanna take him, but we're both on our own now, 'spose." Jarret looked upset at himself as he rubbed the back of his neck and paid very close attention to the grass beneath his shuffling feet.

Aira kneeled as she pulled her shirt sleeve and used it to wipe some dirt from River's chubby cheek. "My name is Aira," she said, smiling.

River smiled back but never said a word. Instead, Aira decided to do most of the talking. "Russia's going to be very lonely. I won't know anyone besides my family, and I'm a little scared." She suddenly snapped her fingers after a moment of thought and tilted her head to look up at the gruff looking shifter. "Hey, I could always bring a friend to keep me company. We're friends, aren't we?"

It took a moment for it to click in Jarret's head as to what she was getting at. After a moment of stunned silence, a giant grin spread across his handsome face. "Yeah, yeah, guess we are friends."

Chapter Sixty-Nine

It was an odd feeling watching the girl prance around greeting the shifter's families of those she saved. Van couldn't help but chuckle at the irony of the situation. She held no hatred in herself for the species that killed her parents and nearly took her life away. Since she was just a young girl, she had always held her hand out to those she should have wanted to stab with a vengeance.

"How's that debt of yours, Mr. Volkov?"

Van paid no mind to the flippant insult. "Your courage is either remarkable or remarkably stupid. You're very close to over fifty shifters who would like nothing more than to castrate you and serve your balls up for afternoon supper."

Damon simply laughed as he shoved his hands into his large overcoat. The cold wind seemed to wail through the trees, muting the noise below them and their conversation.

"You have a way with words, I'll give you that." Damon paused for a moment before asking, "You're taking her to Russia, then?"

Van could have laughed well and truly laughed if he could remember how to. "You expected me to hand her back to you and your family with good wishes for the future? I may as well send a get well card to Vincent while I'm at it," he sneered.

Damon looked away, sighing. "I just thought—"

"Stop thinking then," Van interrupted, his voice disdainful and agitated, "I left her with people I had thought were safe. Never again will I put her in that situation. You and yours would do best to keep away." Lest he felt the need to rip a throat or two out.

Damon felt his body tense as he tried to stay calm; Van could sense it. "I would rather kill myself than hurt Vivian's daughter. But I had taken a backseat when it came to her safety, and for that, I am sorry. Vincent is being detained with maximum security. Elizabeth is getting it a little easier, but I can assure you she would be safe this time—"

Van, this time, actually laughed. It was a cold laugh filled with malice and anger. "You can't assure me shit, but *I* can assure *you* that you are a moment away from being thrown into that group of shifters just itching to have their revenge for the torment their loved ones went through."

Damon leered at the alpha with contempt. He was indeed the product of a human and a shifter, but he was no half-caste. "Better to be a half-caste than a murderer serving his sentence in a world he can't stand. How does it feel

Konstantin? Altholo doesn't want you, but neither does this world."

Damon cracked his neck as he faced the Lycan. Van knew that he had no power over Damon. It was a shame he didn't just lay down and accept this verbal ear-lashing like the good mutt he was. "You're nothing but a liar, Mr. Volkov. You sit on that perch of yours like you're some kind of god. You look after that girl because I can guarantee she will be your only salvation when you face the people you've slaughtered."

Van didn't seem to even flinch at the words. "Is that a threat?"

"No," Damon spat. "If you wish to keep your dirty little secrets to yourself, I *will* keep them for you. Just know that when Aira finds out you knew Ronan's whereabouts the day my sister was killed and that you *knew* there were humans in that vicinity, there will be no one there to take that fall for you."

Damon seemed so sure of himself as he said, "And I know for a fact that you will crumble when she looks at you, just the same way as she looked at Vincent — as a murderer."

As Van went to walk away from this mundane conversation, he looked back briefly and did something Damon did not expect. He smiled. "And who, exactly, said that *isn't* what I want?"

The man was left stunned as Van walked off towards the crowd of shifters. He couldn't truly deny Damon's accusations. The truth was, he had known full well what Ronan was up to that day he destroyed the life of the girl who was now in his care. He had simply put it down to not enough resources to protect them, and well, he just didn't care what happened to a handful of humans. He did, however, care when the time came for clean-up of the bodies.

He *did* care when ten years later, he would be picking up the pieces of a life he was partly responsible for destroying.

In Aira's eyes, he knew the wounds were still deep, and that the nightmares would never truly disappear, but she hid it behind a smile. It annoyed him that the girl wouldn't just come out and say what she wanted to say. But as he ventured closer, all annoyance left him instantly as she walked up to him and took his arm into her hand as if it were the most natural thing in the world.

The shifters around them stepped back, respecting Van's space, and all he could do was tuck a piece of hair behind her ear. It had been bothering him, though he didn't know why. She was asking something about Jarret and River coming to Russia with them. Looking up, he acknowledged the two standing off to the side and nodded.

He would give her this wish if that was something that would make her happy.

She beamed as she ran back to them and ushered them towards the car. Goodbyes were said, and hugs were made, but Van wasn't paying attention. He was too busy having a battle within himself. Half of him denied what he was seeing while the other half fought to let it be known loud and clear. He supposed this feeling he had been having for years is the reason for his inner torment. Aira was his mate. He could see that now so very clear.

But he would never tell her. He wouldn't put that burden on her shoulders, not with his debt and the hatred of those he betrayed.

"Are you ready?" he asked, opening the car door for the injured girl.

She simply nodded. "I'm ready for anything now."

His eyebrow raised slightly. Van was curious. She answered without him having to ask. "You helped me take back a part of me I didn't know was missing, Van. I can stop searching now."

She never failed to surprise him... *never.*

Chapter Seventy

The clouds in the sky looked dark and moody, ready to let it rain at any moment. She stared up at them as the scenery around her whizzed by as if she were still in a dream. She had to keep reminding herself that she was safe now — that no one could harm her. Aira wanted to believe that more than anything, but the dread in the pit of her stomach continued to stir.

"Will they like me?" she asked carefully.

Van kept his eyes trained on the road in front of him as he answered, "It's hard to say."

That didn't seem to give her the confidence she craved. Searching the road in front of them, she spied out the car her father drove. He had taken River and Jarret while Aira had opted to go with Van.

"What's my father's role in your pack? It's called a pack, right?" If she were to hold her head high, she needed to know what roles there were within this new world. She would never say openly that she was frightened.

She could tell Van was getting irritated as his left brow seemed to twitch, but he answered her anyway. "Beta, my second in charge. Although he likes to think he is of a lower rank," he finished with a slight disdainful tone.

"And you take care of other packs as well?"

He nodded slowly. "I take care of any who ask to be under Konstantin's law. That's never changed." He didn't sound very proud or happy about that fact.

Sighing heavily and ignoring her gut instinct to jump from the car and run, Aira smiled. "I'm not weak, Van, not anymore. Maybe I could help you one day."

His blank expression didn't hide the surprise in his eyes as Van momentarily glanced at her. A sly smirk crossed his face, but it was gone before Aira could really take it in.

It seemed this was all becoming real as she looked around with wide eyes. The cars passed through the massive gates that seemed to surround and preserve the area. The second they started to speed up the dirt road Aira could hardly believe what she was seeing.

Half-built houses lined the drive with more and more coming into view as they went deeper into the brush of thick trees that seemed to just entangle the entire area. If she didn't know any better, Aira could have sworn they had just driven into a decently sized town. The houses only grew bigger and more "together" as they came closer to their destination. By the time they came to a stop before a house that could have easily outsized even her grandfather's complex, Aira was taken aback by the swarms of people and *wolves* that seemed to be bustling around as if they were in a marketplace.

Her leg seemed to shake uncontrollably as her nerves kicked in when some spotted the two cars and came over, big smiles on their faces. They first stopped at her father's vehicle and stared inside with a confused expression. It took a moment, but they seemed to relax as a nervous Jarret exited the car with River wrapped around his side.

Females ran to the pup, trying to take him into their arms but backed off when Jarret gave them a stern glare. He wasn't ready to let go of River just yet, and Aira couldn't blame him.

"He's doing well," Van commented as he took off his seatbelt.

Aira looked at him, confused before he explained. "He's showing them dominance. That's how you show your rank here. Starting sooner than later will mean the difference between an easy life or a life of constantly defending what's yours; food, water, and shelter." He said this as if it were commonplace. It probably was where Van and Drake came from, but not for her.

It wasn't until she saw two other males walk towards the car she was in that she saw the true horror of the situation. Her father swooped around the car and growled viciously at the two males, showing his inhuman canines as if to warn them away. They backed off almost immediately, but that drew the attention of others. Aira was truly terrified as she ripped off her seatbelt and tried to push herself towards Van's side of the car.

Van didn't try to comfort her. He continued to exit the car as if none of this were happening. "We're still animals, girl.

My brother is warding off the others and telling them you are his pup and to keep their distance. It's something the mother would usually do, but given the circumstances regarding Emma, she is unable to do that." He sighed and gently pushed her towards her own door. "Go. They're waiting to see what Drake is protecting."

"But-but I'm a human, not a shifter," she stuttered, her face growing whiter by the second.

Van opened his door and didn't even look back as he all but spat, "Yes, you *are* human. I'm very aware of that fact."

His face looked contorted in anger as he exited the car. Aira was shell-shocked, not knowing what she had done exactly to cause that sort of reaction in him.

Gulping back her fear, she slowly opened the door and with trembling legs, got out of the car to stand behind her father. Whatever chatter was going on around them soon stopped, and a deafening silence filled the air.

She could practically hear her own breathing as her eyes locked with several people. The looks she gathered were not kind, nor were they hostile. Eyes were moving from her to Van before his glare sent them back to what they had been doing before her arrival. It was as if a light had been switched, breaking them out of whatever trance they were in, all because Van looked at them.

"They don't like me," she stated abruptly, making her father finally look at her. His tense body seemed to relax as he tried to smile without showing his fangs.

"No, they're scared of you. In time, you'll be accepted."

"Why would they fear me?" she asked.

Drake just shook his head. "People fear what they don't understand. The people you just saw haven't ever seen a human before. Emma is still working out her place. There are a lot of new faces here that haven't been a part of our pack before. Don't worry."

"Aira…?"

The voice behind her almost made her faint. Aira turned, looking at her teary-eyed mother. Her own eyes teared up as she smiled and Emma ran to grasp her in a hug. Aira hugged her back, fighting back the urge to just crumble into a sobbing heap.

"I'm so sorry," Emma repeated over and over again before she let go to get a good look at her daughter. What she saw horrified and made her stomach turn.

Aira's head was still bandaged up, and Emma could faintly see more bandages lining just below her shirt. She gently touched her daughter's head, her lip trembling as she asked, "What happened to you?"

Aira's smile suddenly seemed forced as she stepped away and shook her head. "Just… people…" She didn't know what to say. She couldn't tell her mother that a man had nearly caved her head into a wall, that she had been spat on, kicked and made to live like a dog for three days. She just couldn't say that — not out loud.

Emma was about to say something when an older man walked towards her with a very pretty but older lady latched on to his arm with a smile on her face. Aira backed up but not before the man placed two gentle hands on either side of her face, his own smiling down at her. All fright she might have had instantly vanished as she stared into his kind gray eyes.

"We've waited so long to meet you, my dear." His voice was filled with pride and happiness as he let go, only for the female next to him to grab Aira's cheeks and give her a kiss on her forehead.

Aira certainly wasn't used to this sort of greeting, but oddly enough, it made her incredibly happy to know they knew who she was.

"Oh, Emma, she is beautiful! You did well. My name is Darya, and this is Kasimir." Her voice spilled nothing but complete acceptance.

All Aira could do was nod and watch as Darya gave Drake the same welcoming. Her father chuckled as he gave her a kiss on the cheek.

The man named Kasimir grinned as he nodded to Aira. "Welcome home, where you should have been long ago." He eyed Drake as he said this. "We've been waiting a long time to meet her, Drake. Thank you for bringing her home."

Walking along Kasimir ushered her forward where her brother waited patiently. He instantly hugged Aira and patted her back softly. Staring past him, Aira looked curiously at the stunning female that had just been draped around her brother. Feeling a little more welcomed, Aira smiled as she went to move forward, her hand outstretched to shake the girl's hand.

A loud crack sounded, and all went silent once more. Aira skidded across the dirt, her cheek red and her clothing dirtied as she landed about three feet from where she had been standing. Looking up, the blonde beauty looked down at the human in disgust.

The girl protected her hand as she spat, "I don't touch filthy humans."

As she lay on the ground and ignoring the sting of her new wounds, Aira watched helplessly as others rushed towards her, growling.

It was then that she remembered what Drake had warned her about earlier.

"If one attacks, get up and fight back until I can save you. We have a pack mentality, Aira. When one attacks and you're on the ground, you're the Omega — the weakest link. You will be attacked by others."

Van. *"We're still animals, girl."*

As Aira remembered her father's warnings, another thought went through her brain; her face — why was it that they always went for her *face*? Was it something about her face that people didn't like? If they wanted her to be cross-eyed for the remainder of her life, they were doing a damn good job at making that happen.

Her vision shifted from the shifters coming straight for her to her father, who was currently being held back by the older man, Kasimir. Her eyes widened when she realized no one was coming to save her. This wasn't good. It was as if everyone were standing stock still, wanting to help but not able to.

That made her angry. Promises of safety were made when she agreed to come here, yet she was being thrown to the wolves *literally*.

Her own thoughts were interrupted when she heard Jarret's familiar voice call out, "Get up, ya idiot!"

Idiot, she most certainly was not an idiot. Grunting, Aira saw a hand come out to grab her, and she used it to her advantage. She yanked at the arm to pull herself up and twisted around to behind the disadvantaged shifter. He grunted in obvious pain and surprise as Aira pulled his arm painfully, her free hand splayed out onto his back for added pull.

A crack echoed out as the other shifters backed off, and Aira turned her head, smiling at Lillya as she said, "Don't worry, this won't take long."

Aira swung her arms as she tried to unstiffen her shoulders. She walked towards Lillya, who ultimately backed up, eyes wide. Aiden had been stiff with shock but snapped out of it as he got between his mate and his sister — at least; he thought it was his sister.

"Aira, please, calm down! Come on, it's me. You don't need to hurt anyone. What happened to you?" he pleaded. Still worried with the mark Lillya had left on her face, his only focus now was that this didn't escalate any further.

Aira cracked her knuckles as she continued to walk towards the pair. Anger seemed to cloud her mind as she replied, "*Me*? Retaliate with violence? Never. Now, if you'd get out of my way, this can go a lot quicker."

Aiden stood his ground. He looked as if he were fighting something within him, but the look on his face was priceless when Aira came face to face with the girl who had slapped her to Norway and back. "Now, apologize," Aira demanded.

Both Aiden and his friend stood there in stunned silence. The girl blinked twice, obviously not knowing how to respond. Aira glared. "You can't just slap people," she explained.

The girl whispered something in Russian to Aiden. Aiden, looking between both females, sighed heavily. "I guess you haven't changed," he said with a small grin spreading across his face.

It was Aira's turn to blink this time. "Well," she looked down at herself, "Not to my knowledge, I haven't."

Aira eyed Aiden when he suddenly groaned. They both turned and noticed the shifters who had come for her before were right behind her now. He moved instantly as he jumped over Aira, blocking the closest male that was about to wring her neck. Aira seemed to come out of her confused daze as she threw the other girl a scathing look before moving to help Aiden. It was then that a big, burly man with a wispy dark haircut went in front, stopping two of the shifters dead in their tracks.

Another held the last one back, taking him into almost a bear hug. The only way this man stood out to Aira was because of his striking red hair and big grin.

"*Ivan, drop him,*" the man in front of her demanded in a language she couldn't quite understand. It must have been Russian like Aiden had spoken earlier. Only, this man was fluent and less choppy. Whatever was said, the redhead obliged and dropped the helpless, much smaller shifter. "*All of you get back!*"

Blinking back her shock, Aira spluttered as the dark-haired man came up to her and grabbed her chin, nearly yanking her up off of the ground.

"Nikolai!" her father called out, near panic-stricken, but Aira could feel this man meant no harm, as he looked her over carefully.

"You fight like week old pup, but I will help you," he said as he let go of her chin. With a flick of his head, the redhead followed as he stormed off. Aira was left wondering what had just happened, and why the shifters that were so hell bent on ripping her head off two seconds ago seemed to just calm down and submit.

Looking over towards her father and Van while ignoring her horrorstruck mother, Aira could have sworn she felt as if Van had asked that man to help her without saying a word. Was that even possible?

As Van looked right back at her, Aira swore she saw a tiny smile cross his lips. In that second, she knew Van had helped her even if he had thrown her to the wolves. If she had something within reach, she would have thrown it at his head. He had literally just used her for amusement purposes.

She would get him back, one way or another.

Chapter Seventy-One

"Am I some sort of monster?"

Kasimir looked up at her as if she had grown a third head. "No, my dear, in time, you'll learn more about yourself."

"Before, I could control myself, but now, when I get angry, I just lose it. I don't know what to do." She looked down, but the old man lifted her head back up as he wiped some blood from her chin. He didn't say a word as she continued to speak, "Where's my father? Why isn't he here?"

Kasimir finished mending her face as he rolled back on his stool to dispose of the bloodied swabs. "He's out helping with some of the events. We use any excuse to celebrate, and tonight, we welcome home our alpha and Drake. I'm certain he's also trying not to let them see how much your attack affected him. Weakness is death when you're as high up like your father."

Her smile was forced as she muttered, "You guys sure do get over fights quickly."

Kasimir heard this and chuckled softly. "Much alike to canines, we fight to know our place in the pecking order, and then we return to being brothers. We do not fight to kill nor do we intend to seriously harm. Lillya initiated that attack by challenging you, and we will automatically protect our females. At the time, you were not one of us."

"And now?"

"You'll find your place in time. In a pack, there are no secrets. Only our alpha's mind is closed off, but we can hear each other's thoughts and emotions. Humans are quite scary to us because we cannot form a link to their minds nor can we sense what they are going to do before they do it. Humans are a mixture of emotion and feelings, something we are born knowing how to control. You scared them, and that's the only answer I can give you." He sighed and slapped his hands down onto his knees. "Do not blame Lillya, please. She is wrong for what she did, but she doesn't know any better."

Aira glared slightly as she touched her jaw. "Seems she knew exactly what she was doing to me."

His expression softened as he said, "A long time ago, Lillya's mother was taken by humans and killed in the worst imaginable way. Her father had his revenge, but a deep hate grew in Lillya's heart. It's just Lillya and Olya now. They're alone and have been taught to hate regardless of who the human is."

Aira's face seemed to sink as she thought this over. In a way, she could relate to Lillya, but she didn't hold anyone accountable for her family's murder. She didn't even know who did it. "She's special... to Aiden, isn't she?"

Before Kasimir could answer her question, Aiden came into the room, a sheepish little smile on his face. He grimaced when he saw the bruise and cut across Aira's jaw. Kasimir smiled before nodding to Aiden and quietly leaving the room. It was best they had their moment in privacy.

"Your face isn't in pieces. That's great!" he cheered before groaning and slapping his forehead. "No, no... I had this whole speech worked out in my head, and I say that. Stupid."

Aira couldn't help but turn away as she laughed. However, that action caused her to wince as her jaw ached. Great, she couldn't even laugh.

Aiden rubbed the back of his head as he sighed and grabbed the stool Kasimir had just been sitting on. Rolling closer to his sister, his face drooped into a sad expression as he said, "That's not how I wanted you to meet my-my mate, but..." he couldn't find the words he wanted to say. Nothing could really fix the situation. His father was all but shunning Lillya, and everyone seemed to be keeping their distance from both of the girls.

Her nose crinkled in confusion. "Mate? What's a mate?"

"Well, uh, when a shifter meets *someone* they find *special*, they connect on a very, very different level to humans. It's like a bond forms, uh, like you've known that person your entire life without even meeting them." He cringed throughout that entire explanation.

Her eyes seemed to shift from annoyance to instant excitement as if forgetting she had just been angry a moment before. "Like, instant love?"

"No, not even close. It's much deeper than that. I just, I can't, Aira. I've never had to explain this before, and it's—" He couldn't even finish his sentence.

Aira tilted her head, a sign she was very much confused. "It's what, Aiden?"

"It makes me really see how different we are. You won't understand, and that kills me because I never want you to feel insignificant or stupid. It terrifies me that by the time I see my first wrinkle, you'll be nearly five-hundred years old and more than likely gone."

Her face said it all as she nodded. "I see…" She had no idea how strongly Aiden felt about this. She hadn't given much thought to the fact her father and Aiden would outlive Aira and their mother, but it obviously weighed on Aiden considerably.

"You scared me today. Aira, it's always been you and me in a world filled with insanity. Wc talked about everything. We didn't have any secrets, and I hope we can still do that." He laughed as he looked down and swiveled around on the stool like a child. "We're kind of like twins when you think about it. I remember the day you came home with Mom and Dad, and I hated keeping this secret about what we were, but you know, I guess I didn't want you to hate me."

"Why would I hate you?" she asked. Her brows shot up, surprised that Aiden would ever think she hated him. She could never hate him, no matter what he did.

Whatever was on his mind, it was obviously hard for him to say it out loud. He took a deep, shaky breath as he said, "Because it was our kind who killed your family — shifters."

"You didn't kill them, did you?" she asked seriously as if it were a genuine question.

Aiden was a little surprised but shook his head, a small smile crossing his lips. "No."

"Aiden, no matter what happens, I'll never hate you. You taught me how to write on my little whiteboard. You taught me how to tie my shoelaces. You taught me sign language. You made me laugh when I was sad, and you came for me when I needed you the most. It doesn't matter that we're different. You'll always be my brother."

His face clouded with sorrow as he got up off of the chair. Aiden paced for a moment, his hands tucked into his pant pockets as he thought about what she had just said. "I never got to meet my parents. I don't even know who they are or where they are or if they even care that I'm alive or dead. But I do know one thing, Aira, I know that I'm very lucky to have what I have now, and if it came down to it, I'd choose my human mother and sister over my mate."

Although happy, Aira didn't want Aiden to have to choose between anyone. It wasn't fair to him. However, before she could state her opinion, Aiden ran through the door and out into the hallway. For a moment, Aira sat in confused silence until her brother came rushing back in, an old tattered board game in his hands.

"Mom actually packed our old Monopoly?" she asked, laughing quietly.

He jangled the game around and grinned. "I gotta do a few things, but I thought you could find someone to play with; maybe that Jarret guy. He seems nice but, yeah, a little hesitant to be best friends right now."

Aira snorted as she shook her head. She supposed he was somewhere around, hiding out with River. She should probably go and find him and let him see that she wasn't a bloody mess.

"Oh… about Mom…" Aira muttered as she took the game from Aiden's hands.

Aiden knew exactly what Aira was getting at as he winked. "I'm keeping her busy, don't worry. She thinks you're napping. You really know how to upset her, Air. I never saw her want to actually harm another person until I saw Darya holding her back."

As Aiden went to leave, he turned back and said, "Stay inside tonight. You'll get to meet more people in the morning. No one will hurt you, I promise. Despite what happened today, you're in the safest place you could be right now. We're family here, and soon, you'll be loving it."

Yeah, right? She nodded and waved slightly as her brother left. She supposed this giant house was where Van lived. When her father led her inside before he left her for Kasimir, she noticed a room that had her mother's things inside of it. She wondered if she got a room as well. That would be nice.

Aira trundled down the hallway in a sort of daze, wondering if her things had been brought over and if she'd ever get to drive the car Van had bought for her. It was a vain thought, she had to agree, but it *was* a very nice car.

Her shoulder collided with another, and Aira fumbled to keep hold of the old board game. If the box fell open, she'd have the time of her life picking up all the pieces that flew out. She always hated it when Aiden would throw the money everywhere whenever he'd lose.

So many useless thoughts floated around in her head that she nearly forgot about the person she had just walked into. Looking up with slight hesitation, Aira made eye contact a beautiful brunette. The girl stared Aira up and down before a sly smirk spread across her face.

Aira tried to smile, but the way this woman seemed to just ooze distaste put her off having any sort of happy greeting. All that came out of Aira's mouth was a simple, "Hello…"

The dark-haired girl didn't look exactly pleased as she backed up. "It's not polite to look a shifter directly in the eye. You could get your face slapped off."

It was strange how these sorts of interactions really had become commonplace in her complicated life. Aira couldn't help but shake her head. She had put up with worse from human girls in high school. "Well, I'll make sure to not to look at you at all then…" She left her sentence hanging as she waited for a name.

That reply didn't seem to sit well as the other girl's blue eyes hardened. "Innochka."

Aira only nodded before turning on her heel and trotting off. Her feet came to a standstill as she heard Innochka mutter something under her breath, making the human cringe.

"Too bad, I would have hit you so hard you'd still be picking bone up off the floor."

Why? Was it something she did? No one liked her. But she didn't do anything wrong. Was this just a mistake? Maybe she should have stayed in America. An overwhelming sadness suddenly came over her as reality set in. She wasn't welcomed all because she wasn't like them.

Dazed, Aira dropped the board game and watched as everything scattered across the floor. It wasn't fair.

"Always crying about something. You do a lot of that, don't you?"

Aira jumped as the deep, familiar voice filled her head. Looking up, she saw Van standing in front of her, that same bored frown playing on his lips. Before she could respond, he had already kneeled to start picking up the contents of the game.

He gave a confused glare at one of the pieces before grunting. "I always hated this game."

Aira's reply was almost instant as she responded, "It's my favorite. I like games where you have to think."

He looked as if he were in thought as he studied some colored bills. "Is that so? Should we play?"

Looking down at him, Aira was stunned. He looked up at her, waiting for a genuine answer. It suddenly dawned on her that he was trying to make her happy. That Van Volkov was trying to do something nice.

"You don't have to play out of pity, Van. I'll be fine."

Van stood up and placed the game under his arm, nodding down the hall. "If you like it as much as you say you do, you shouldn't have a problem kicking my ass."

Chapter Seventy-Two

She stifled a little giggle as she watched Van study the playing pieces. It was somehow satisfying watching him slouch over his chair. His normally perfect button down was wrinkled, and he seemed awfully relaxed given the situation he was in.

"Why aren't you with everyone else?" she casually asked as she started to work out the colorful pieces of play money.

His eyes swiftly diverted from the race car in his hand to her. "You've always been an odd girl when it comes to your silly questions."

Aira blanched for a moment, not sure how to reply to that flippant remark. She quickly looked around, trying to change the subject, when she noticed the hundreds of books that lined the walls. "You've... read many of these?" She mentally punched herself. He had just mocked her about her question asking, and here she was, asking another question.

It seemed she was more frazzled than he was as he responded, "Every one of them."

"My favorite book is The Secret Garden," she whispered, staring longingly at the shelves of dusty old books. It saddened her that they looked so ill kept.

He actually looked interested as he asked, "Is it now?"

She nodded. "I understood Mary to an extent and what it was like to be alone. I was by myself a lot of the time after Aiden left. I used to pretend our backyard was a magic garden and that you—" She left her sentence hanging with a soft gasp. She couldn't possibly tell Van that she would pretend he had made that garden for her, just like Archibald had made the garden for his beloved wife. "But-but I'd much rather be Lois Lane," she corrected, giggling softly as she hid her embarrassment.

After a moment's thought, she nearly fell out of her chair as she realized admitting she wanted to be Lois Lane was just as bad, considering she called him her hero. She needed to get some duct tape and keep it permanently over her mouth. She had to give herself credit, though. It wasn't as bad as the naked comment she had made.

The smirk that crossed his face seemed to make her stomach drop as he got up from his seat. He moved towards Aira as if he weren't walking on solid ground at all — it was as if he was marching his way towards a mission. She was as still and as pale as a ghost as the man seemed to tower over her.

His golden eyes — eyes he no longer had to conceal — pinned her down as his hands trapped her in her seat. His face suddenly turned sour.

"I'm no hero, little one, and you'll never be what I want."

Eyes wide and blood running cold through her veins, Aira watched as Van retreated to his seat. He knew. Of course, he knew. Van Volkov knew everything. There was no secret she could keep. She was so stupid.

Before she could stop herself, Aira snapped, "But maybe I could be what you *need*, Van." Her blood started to warm up as anger coursed through her veins. It wasn't fair that he could make her feel like an idiot and get away with it.

Now, he was the one surprised as he took in her sharp remark.

"You don't scare me, Van Volkov. You may not be Superman, but you'll always be my hero. You're the man who saves me from my worst nightmares, and one day, I'll save you from whatever demons you're running from."

A creek of the floorboards snapped both of them out of their staring contest. Kasimir and the two men who had helped Aira earlier stood just outside the doorway. It seemed they hadn't been there long, their faces showed no surprise nor guilt if they had overheard Aira and Van's heated "discussion."

Brushing back the awkwardness of the situation, Aira smiled and got up from her seat. "Thank you both for earlier. Ivan and...?"

Kasimir ended up answering, "Nikolai. He doesn't speak much English."

Aira couldn't help but stare up at Ivan. He towered over her and every other male in the room. She had no idea someone could grow to be that big of a size. However, as daunting as he seemed, the big grin that spread across his face reminded Aira of a little boy who had just been caught with his hand in the cookie jar. She already knew she liked this giant of a man.

Her eyes widened as an idea came to mind. Aira pointed towards the game that was somehow set up during her conversation with Van and asked, "Come play with us?"

Nikolai grunted as he pushed passed a surprised Kasimir. "Alpha," he stated, ignoring Aira's question altogether. It sounded as if they had something they needed to discuss with him urgently — *away* from her.

"Scared, Nikolai?" Van teased, that same sly smirk spreading across his face. "*She asked you to play, so play.*"

"*I have no time for games,*" the shifter snapped. Aira still had no idea what he saying.

"*Sit down, shut up, and play. Worried I will destroy you as always, Nikolai?*" Van snapped, a small smile playing on his face. Whatever was said, Aira was sure it was quite nasty as Nikolai's face turned three shades of red.

Van speaking Russian was quite nice on the ears, though.

Nikolai calmly waltzed over to the table and threw back a chair, almost falling into it as he growled, "Bring it, Alpha."

Aira simply stared on, confused by their conversation, before Van flicked his finger towards Kasimir and Ivan. "You two, play as well."

Van left little room. Kasimir chuckled awkwardly as he moved to sit by his alpha. Looking over the human's game, it puzzled him as to how something so vain could be any fun whatsoever.

After Aira quickly showed them the rules, it wasn't long before he realized this game came straight from the depths of hell itself.

By the end, Nikolai had broken the table, and Van was inches away from wringing Ivan's neck. Everyone was on edge as Kasimir stacked hotel upon hotel on his properties. Tensions were high until the unexpected happened.

Nikolai started to laugh, and laugh, and laugh. It wasn't long before Ivan followed suit. Even Van had a wry smile on his face as he lounged in his chair. It was the most comfortable any of them had been, given their history when in the same room. Aira smiled.

Aira quietly began to pack up the game as everyone made their way towards the door. Van lingered, staring at her, probably curious as to why she was hovering and nervous. He leaned against the door frame and advised the Kasimir he would be out in a moment.

Aira coughed lightly. "I need to ask you something," she stated. She had been thinking about what Richard had admitted to her about her grandmother and mother. It was bothering her, not knowing who her grandfather was. She needed to ask Van. If he knew about Altholo, he could possibly know what had happened.

"I thought as much." Van nodded for her to continue.

She took a deep breath, ready to ask him when Nikolai came back and stood behind Van. He muttered something in Russian, and Van's face dropped slightly as he listened. Aira bit her lip lightly and shook her head. "It can wait. It's not important."

Van eyed her for a moment. After she smiled and waved him off, he walked away without another word. Aira knew he didn't have time to wait for her to make up her mind.

Aither, her mother's twin brother had struggled with some sort of wildness inside of him. In the end, it had killed him, driving him to the brink of insanity.

Aira wondered if the same thing was happening to her.

Chapter Seventy-Three

News always traveled fast, and when it was about Van Volkov, any news was bad news. The elders certainly wanted to keep track on their prize and paying a visit was just what was needed. Van couldn't help but groan miserably.

"You'd think they'd be dead by now," Van muttered. Kasimir pretended he didn't catch that flippant remark and chuckled nervously.

"They're just making sure you're keeping up with your duties, son. After the Ronan incident, they don't need another Lycan going rogue." He saw the look of frustration that crossed his Van's face and corrected himself, "Not that you would, but you understand their concerns."

No, he didn't understand. All his life he had been watched and trained like some circus monkey by those old dogs and not once had they ever given him so much as a thank you for his years of service. However, it wasn't like he had had much of choice, he was born into this role, and he would die protecting people he didn't care much for.

Konstantin's debt was ultimately Van's debt as well.

"It's not their concerns I'm worried about," Van muttered as his mind turned to Aira. If those old dogs found out she was a L'ightat, they'd want to know more about her, even use her. He couldn't let that happen.

Kasimir seemed to know exactly what plagued Van's thoughts and sighed. "She'll just have to stay out of sight. Everything will be fine. They'll come, they'll drink, they'll eat, and then they'll leave us be."

Van didn't respond as he leaned against his desk. There wasn't much he could do for the human girl except keep her locked in her room. There would be so much going on he was sure they wouldn't sniff her out without thinking it was Emma.

Kasimir looked at Van with a solemn expression. "Whether you keep the girl here or send her away, that is your choice, pup, but just remember — she's human... and you're not."

Van didn't even look up as he responded, "I knew it wouldn't take long for you to figure it out, old man. You figured it out a lot quicker than I did."

Kasimir smiled sadly. "When someone enters your life, you get this feeling, and I know what she is to you. I know you don't like it and you might even hate it, but you have a choice, and you can ignore that feeling, son. You always have a choice; you know that, right? You know the consequences of rejecting her."

Van knew what Kasimir meant. "I've made my choice. I made it the second I realized what she was to me, Kasimir. I'll watch over her, as I always have, but the girl will always be just the human I saved all those years ago. I owe her nothing more than that."

No, she would never be anything more to him. In truth, she was still just a child and nowhere near strong enough to stand beside him. Fate was cruel, but that didn't surprise him. He had always been dealt the wrong cards in life. He wouldn't drag her down into the dirt. It wasn't as if he thought she deserved more. He just knew that in the long run, they came from different places and they would go down different paths in life. It was just how things were.

He would die, Aiden would take over, and Aira would go on to live a normal, human existence — without them.

Chapter Seventy-Four

"Ah, Mer—"

Olya simply tightened her lips. She wasn't playing ball, and that made things difficult for Aira. She sighed heavily as she scratched her head. The only word Aira could get out of the she-wolf before her was her name. Jarret sat in the corner of the room; River curled up next to him and chuckled.

"Come on, Olya, you can do it," he cheered; giving her some much-needed praise.

Aira wondered for a moment how she had gotten herself into this situation. One moment, she was walking to the living room, and the next, Jarret was dragging her into one of the guest rooms.

"Help me! She's been following me and doesn't speak a lick of English," he had pleaded. Aira, not exactly comfortable with the situation, told him to learn Russian and tried to escape.

No, go — she was trapped. Apparently, her former "speech problem" made her the perfect candidate to teach Olya how to speak English. She didn't know whether to be angry or insulted. Besides all that, Jarret didn't know how to read, so using a book to translate wouldn't have helped.

Fortunately, Aira had picked up a book at the airport before she arrived. It was how she had the slightest clue on what Nikolai was screaming at her most days. She had read it a couple of times and caught the gist of sentence structure and wording; and so, tried her hand at Olya's native language.

"Hello, my name is Aira, and this is Jarret. How are you?"

Oh, God, that probably sounded horrible.

An awkward silence filled the air as Olya stared at Aira and promptly proceeded to laugh hysterically.

"You sound worse than I do when I speak English," she laughed, nearly rolling over.

Aira's face fell when she realized Olya could indeed understand what she had been saying earlier. "So you *do* speak English?"

Olya simply nodded, her brown curls bobbing with her nods. "I hate the way I sound, but I do speak a little," she confirmed.

Jarret seemed to perk up as he asked, "So then tell me why you've been followin' me?"

Olya's whole face seemed to go red as she seized up and refused to say anything more. Jarret, already aggravated, stood up and went to the door. He had had enough of these mind games. River refused to leave, after sharing a look with Aira, understood he would be safe with her and stormed out.

River instantly came to Olya and patted her sleeve. He could see the tears welling up in her eyes, and Aira smiled as she realized just how sweet River was.

"He hates me…" Olya whispered. She looked broken.

Aira's eyes widened as she finally realized what was going on. Olya had a crush on Jarret. She looked from Olya to the door and frowned, knowing how much that must have hurt her. She knew exactly what the poor girl was going through.

"No, no, Jarret's just a little dense when it comes to emotions. He's… never really been around so many shifters before now."

That was probably something she should have kept to herself, but Olya never asked any questions about Jarret, and Aira sighed with relief. She didn't know if Jarret would appreciate her delving into his history with a stranger.

Olya smiled. "I thought humans were barbarians, but you are no barbarian."

Aira smiled and brushed off Olya's controversial comment. A slight knock on the door made both of them turn, only to see Emma, a surprised look covering her face. Aira was about to ask her what was wrong before Emma let out a soft cry.

"You're making friends!" she squealed, "Oh, oh, I'm sorry. Olya, isn't it? Oh, my goodness, I'm so sorry. I'm just so happy!"

Aira's face turned beet red as she waved her arms to try to calm her mother down. "Mom, calm down and breathe."

Emma seemed to realize her overreaction as she laughed, embarrassed, and asked Aira if she could speak to her privately. Olya took the hint and nodded, leaving the room briskly, making sure not to make eye contact with Emma.

"What a nice girl," Emma whispered, smiling after Olya. Aira kept her awkward, lopsided smile as Emma came to sit next to her. "There's something happening tonight," she started. The way her demeanor went from excited to nervous made Aira twitch in anticipation.

"Should I get ready? Do I even have any dresses? Is it an important event?" Question after question spilled from Aira's lips. She was excited. Emma wouldn't be here explaining if it weren't important. There had been many events happening over the last few nights, but those were just gatherings from what she could tell.

Emma seemed to strain to keep the smile on her face. "Well, some very, *very* important people are coming tonight. The Elders—"

"Who?" Aira asked, her face scrunched up in confusion. Elders? What was an Elder?

It was now that Emma looked saddened as she let Aira down the best way she could. "They're people who hold more social power than even Van. They're watching him very closely, and they're coming to see how he's doing tonight. Aira, you have to stay in your room until they leave."

The look of shock that crossed Aira's face was expected, but it still ripped Emma in half. "Why? Did I do something wrong?" she asked. Had her outburst when she came here made her not party worthy?

Emma was about to explain things a little bit more when her name was called from outside. Sighing heavily,

Emma kissed Aira on the forehead. "We'll talk more later. I promise," and left the room quickly.

Aira just sat there, dumbfounded, confused and hurt. She was so bewildered that she didn't even realize River had scuttled over and into the corner the moment Emma had entered the room. He came over and gently touched Aira's hand, his golden eyes staring up at her. Aira looked down, not even bothering to force a smile and petted his hair.

"We, ah, should go find Darya so you can get dressed for tonight. Or maybe you'd prefer Jarret?" She wiped some tears from her eyes and stood up to lead River out.

Just as she did, River wrapped his tiny arms around Aira's waist and said, "Don't worry. I like you."

Shocked but touched, Aira smiled. "You might just be the sweetest boy I've ever met, River."

Later came and went, and Emma never came back. Aira sat in her room, staring solemnly out the window and watching as different people showed up. She was entranced at how happy everyone seemed to be — everyone but her.

A soft knock resounded at her door. She didn't get the chance to tell them to come in when, to her surprise, Van stepped inside the room. He looked like his usual self, but tonight, Aira couldn't help but think he looked almost handsome.

He looked a little angry, perhaps annoyed. It nearly made her laugh.

"They'll be gone soon," he mumbled, fixing a button on his dress shirt.

That one sentence carried more words than he let on. "They'll be gone soon. I'm sorry" was what Aira could imagine him meaning. Did Van feel bad she was cooped up in this room while everyone else was outside having fun?

Her smile was an obvious lie as she said, "It's okay. I'm fine."

He seemed to move closer, slowly but surely. "I'll come back when they're gone, and we can have dinner together."

She seemed to instantly perk up. "Really?" That question came out with a high-pitched squeak. Aira forced back an embarrassed groan and carried on with her embarrassed smile.

His lips turned up in a smile — a real smile — as he nodded. "Really."

"Van, they're waiting," a voice came from the door, and there stood Innochka, smiling brightly.

Van didn't seem to really care much as he moved to exit the room, only to be stopped by the dark beauty as she pulled at his dress shirt, fixing some crinkles. Van sidestepped her; seemingly aware of what she was doing.

Before she left, Innochka looked back at Aira, still smiling as she said, "We'll save you some scraps." And closed the door behind her.

Aira blanched. It took all of her self-restraint not to follow the girl and shove those "scraps" down her tiny throat. She threw herself down onto her bed and huffed.

"This sucks."

Chapter Seventy-Five

121, 122, 123, 124, 125...

Had she been reduced to a dog now? Give her a ball, and she'll be fine, Aira thought disdainfully. One hundred twenty-five times she had thrown the ball into the air, catching it inches from her reddened face.

She was angry.

Later came and went, and Emma never came back to talk. There had only been a handful of times Aira had been angry at her adoptive mother, and this time would be one of them. The laughter and chatter that echoed from downstairs and outside just made her blood boil with contempt. Why should she stay up here? Why should she be contained to this prison?

"They said I couldn't come downstairs. They never said anything about *upstairs*..."

A sly smile spread across Aira's face as she chucked the ball into the corner and got up of her makeshift spring bed.

The ball, however, had other plans as it crashed into an unpacked bag and *somehow* sent some of the contents sprawling out onto the hardwood floor. Aira sighed.

She supposed this was the universe's way of keeping her contained just like everyone else had. Well, the universe be darned.

But all rebellion left her as she noticed a photo frame sprawled out amongst the contents. Aira moved closer to the mess and picked up the photo, thinking she must have missed one while unpacking a couple of boxes.

Oh.

"Did Emma bring this...?" she whispered as she traced her finger over the old glass protecting the image inside of it.

Her body tensed as she looked over the image. A man crouched behind a little girl as she stood in front of him, holding the arms that encircled her.

Daddy...

Her late father, Charles, looked handsome but aged with worry as he smiled into the camera. Aira seemed to be too preoccupied with what was off to the side of them to really look at whoever was holding the camera.

Why did she have to find this now?

Tears pricked at her baby blue eyes just thinking about him and her mother. Could they see her now? Were they proud? She would never stop thanking them for the sacrifice they made all those years ago. Avery and Ian should have been here with her, but destiny had a cruel way of playing out.

Loud chatter and laughter outside her window burst Aira's thought bubble. She needed silence. Somewhere she could think and just be by herself with no one else to bother her. She just wanted to think.

"But I wouldn't be completely alone."

Slinking away from her quarters, Aira quietly assessed whether anyone was lurking around upstairs. She wasn't surprised when she saw no one. Up on the second floor was usually pretty desolate. The only occupants up here were Jarret, River, Drake and Emma.

And Van.

Coast clear, Aira made her way down the hall, turning left as she reached the end. When she came to her destination, she slowly pushed open one of the double doors. They stood tall and proud — stained glass welcoming her — and headed inside the room. She had found this place only a few days earlier. It was sort of like her own little retreat, a place she could read, think and even talk to herself without someone interrupting her.

Clutching to the photo, she tenderly touched the dog tag around her neck, sighing. She wished her companion were here. Vaughn, her wolf dog, would have loved the grand open spaces of this place. But he wasn't here. He was finding his own path in life, just as she was. But why was it still so hard to accept when it was the right thing to do?

Moving further into the massive hall, Aira opened the glass balcony doors to let the soft, cool breeze flutter through the open area. It was empty in here, all for two old steel chairs and a dusty piano.

Who played the piano? she wondered. Music didn't seem to exist in this place, well, besides the soft humming of her music player when she cared to use it.

Sitting at the piano, Aira sat the picture of her and her father on top of it. A comfortable silence fell over her as she smiled, just thinking quietly to herself. She pressed a key down on the piano, giggling quietly as she thought of someone coming in here and catching her playing an off-tune melody.

"I thought this place was still locked up. It seems I was wrong," came a gruff voice from the doorway.

Aira jumped, letting out a scared yelp as she spun around to see who had walked in on her peace and solitude.

A man, looking as if he were in his late sixties or seventies, looked around the room, almost as if in a trance. His hair was completely white and slicked back. His face showed his age, and years of worry marred his cool pale eyes. He was dressed immaculately, wearing a black suit that looked like it took years to make. If he didn't need his walking cane for balance, Aira could tell this man would have been standing tall, shoulders straight and head held high.

Even age didn't hold back its wrath on a shifter. She could tell immediately what he was. He didn't radiate mortality. He didn't look at her the way a human would. Funny how, now, she could tell a shifter from a human simply by just looking at them.

Aira stood up immediately. "I'm sorry if I'm not supposed to be in here! I just thought, well, I-I'll go now." Head down, she went to grab the photograph when the cane the older man used to walk with tapped her hand away.

Shock registered in her eyes as she snapped her hand back, grasping it as if she'd been burned. He didn't notice as he looked at the photo.

A small, genuine smile spread across his face. "You must care about those people very much. I could tell from the way you looked at this picture when I first stepped in."

She still looked shocked as she said, "That's my father and me..." Why had she responded so willingly? Was it because of his gentle smile? Or the fact she just sensed he meant her no harm?

His smile faded and a look of knowing replaced his expression. "Drake and Emma raised you well. You told the truth when I was sure you would have lied and told me Drake was your father."

"Drake *is* my father," Aira confirmed. "But I'm—"

"Human?"

Just like she could sense he was a shifter, he could sense how very human she really was. With a slow nod, Aira confirmed what he already knew.

"Why are you not downstairs with everyone else?" he asked, looking to his left and then his right, making sure no one else was in the room with her.

His question caught her off guard. "I-I don't know. Maybe it's because I'm a human?"

Somehow, it looked as if he didn't believe that answer.

He looked up wistfully as he leaned on his cane. "It's funny how people like to push away what is different. Van should be ashamed of himself. He should know better than anyone what that's like."

"Van?" Who would push Van out? She couldn't imagine anyone treating Van as if he were some sort of leper, not like she was treated.

The man looked awfully tired and wary. Aira's eyes popped as she hastily moved the piano chair towards him. "You should sit down!"

At first, he looked shocked, but then, his lips turned into a smile as laughter rang through the air. "My, you are polite. Thank you."

He sat down, and Aira pulled the old steel chair from the corner to take a seat herself. "Why aren't *you* downstairs?" she asked, her tone teasing. She felt oddly at ease with this old man. Old would probably be an understatement — he was probably thousands of years old for all she knew.

His chuckle was music to her ears. It was nice to be able to sit down and just *talk* to someone who didn't slink away as if her touch would burn.

"Far too loud, dear. All those people trying to get on this old man's good side as if I were already on the ground! I wish they were all like Van. No, sir, he would likely tell me what he really thought rather than kiss my wrinkled ass!" His laugh grew heavier before he started to cough. Perhaps, from too much excitement? Aira didn't know what could be so amusing just talking to her.

But she to let out a loud giggle. Yes, that did sound like Van.

"And I take it you have no idea who I am?" he asked. She shook her head. "Aren't I rude? My name is Aemilius, Head Elder."

She nodded as if she knew what that meant. "I'm Aira, but I guess, you already knew that."

"Oh, dear, everyone knows who you are. Van doesn't save just anyone."

Was that a good or bad thing? She didn't bother to ask. She just smiled and nodded.

Looking around, a cloud of sadness washed over his face. "Samiul would have loved to still be here and watch Van grow into such a good leader. I suppose he is still here in a way. He's still watching over his sons." He leaned in close, and Aira leaned forward to meet him. "I can sense it," he whispered with a broad grin.

Aira couldn't wipe the smile off of her face. "So, Samiul was Drake and Van's father?"

His face turned solemn. "Drake's father, yes…"

What did that mean?

He could see the question on her face. "My goodness child, do they tell you anything? I would have thought Drake would have explained."

She shook her head, and he sighed. "An old man is usually the one to spill the beans, yes?" he chuckled. "Better you know than not. Van wasn't born a Volkov; he was born a Dimitriev, a very powerful shifter community long feared. But that was many, many years ago."

So, that meant Aleksandra wasn't his mother? Van had another family?

"Van was just a small pup when it happened. Shifters were naturally scared of Lycans and went after him. His whole pack was killed, but his father managed to escape with him." His sadness was evident. This was a story he probably cried over. "But his father died on the journey to get Van to Samiul and Aleksandra. I remember he was such a cold pup, but that was expected. He had lost everything."

Aira held back her shock. Van had been through the same hell she had been through. Why had he never told her?

"Tell me, dear, have you ever heard Van say goodbye?"

Come to think of it, she had never heard Van say goodbye... *ever.* "No, I haven't."

He nodded. "Because goodbye to Van means forever. He had said goodbye to one person, and that was his father. I believe he's afraid of goodbyes when it comes from his own mouth."

Is that why Van hated people hanging up on him? Is that why he needed a goodbye to be able to put the receiver down? He had written the word goodbye in their letters, but he had never said it out loud.

She thought Van wasn't scared of anything, let alone one simple little word; one word she never had to opportunity to say to her own parents the day they died.

That was why Van never pitied her. Was it because everyone had pitied him at one point?

"Let me give you some advice — keep at it. Never let him stumble because just like he judges others, he judges himself just as harshly."

This man truly cared about Van and Drake as if they were his own sons. Aira smiled and nodded.

"Just because you're human doesn't mean you're weak my dear. Samiul always said that one's greatest weakness would always come to be their greatest strength."

"He sounded like a great man. I wish I could have met him," Aira smiled sadly. Samiul Volkov sounded a lot like her father — kind and wise.

Aemilius chuckled and threw his head back as if going back to a place from the past. "Oh, Samiul was my dearest friend. He had this house built when he met Aleksandra. He had gone to the human's domain and saw the places they lived in and loved it! It didn't help that Aleksandra was raised within human society, so she was adamant she wouldn't sleep out in the wilderness!" He laughed and laughed. It must have been a very silly situation.

Well, that explained why this house was shaped and laid out like a castle. "Aleksandra grew up with humans?"

"Oh, my goodness, yes! Her family were completely human. In fact, this was the first pack she had ever been around."

It felt like she and Aemilius sat there for hours just talking about everything and nothing. It was one of the best conversations she had ever had in her life. He gladly told her about the history of shifters, about Lycans, and about the wars he had seen over the centuries he had lived. It was absolutely amazing.

"Aemilius, you old bastard, is this where you ran off to?" came a new voice Aira didn't recognize but Aemilius did.

He laughed and said, "Guess I've been caught. They don't trust me wandering off on my own. Lucus! No ball and chain, I see?"

Aira went bright red as another old man came over to them. "Don't let my mate here you call her a ball and chain," he chuckled before nervously looking around. "She might just rip your nose off."

They joked back and forth before this Lucus fellow finally noticed Aira. "And who is this beautiful creature? My, humans sure know how to make them!"

He must have been going deaf because he didn't talk without yelling. Aira slapped her forehead. "Thank you?"

These Elders didn't seem scary at all. In fact, they seemed like regular old men that you'd find at a casino playing bingo. They also made some of the dirtiest jokes she had ever heard.

As Aemilius chatted with his friend, Aira shot up, surprising them both, and offered Lucus her chair. Had he been drinking? He looked as if he were about to fall over himself.

He gratefully took the seat, groaning as he rested his sore back. "My," he muttered as he looked around the room, "I haven't been in here since Van, Drake, and Ronan were just pups. They used to run around and get under your feet. Remember when Drake nearly burnt the place down, Aemilius?"

Aira covered her mouth to keep from laughing. Leaning against the piano, she bit her lip and let her laughter loose when Aemilius grumbled, "How could I forget? I had to jump out the window and roll in the snow when my shirt caught fire."

Lucus howled with laughter as he slapped his knee hard. "Samiul punished all three of them since Van was the one who taught him how to start a fire, and Ronan had broken the only usable bucket so we couldn't even bring any water inside to put you out."

Aemilius visibly flinched but still smiled at the memory. "Yes, I was just saying how Samiul would have loved to have been here."

Lucus sighed and shook his head. "May the spirits look after him, and he watch over us. We damn well need it."

Aira again joined in on their conversation and laughed at all of their memories of this place. This is the most fun she had in months. She quickly learned that her father was no angel growing up. In fact, it sounded as if Van and Drake were regular demons as children.

Again, another old man seemed to find his way into the room, followed by two more. Her space of solitude had turned into a regular old folk's home.

Soon, their attention had turned on her. They asked how life was in America, where she'd grown up and if Drake had taught her about their history. For the first time, Aira felt almost appreciated. They talked to her as if she were an old, dear friend they had known for years.

"Oh!" She noticed they didn't have anything to sit on and moved towards the door. "I'll get you some more chairs!"

Before Aemilius and Lucus could protest, Aira was out the door, running from room to room looking for seats.

This was going to be a long night.

Chapter Seventy-Six

It was tempting, but sticking a knife in his chest probably wasn't the best etiquette during something like this. The Elders seemed to flock to him like flies to cow dung. The object of discussion? Whether or not he would find a mate. He nearly growled with annoyance. He had found his mate, though he would never say it out loud.

"Van! How have you been?"

Markus made a beeline straight for the alpha. Van kept up charades as he nodded in acknowledgment.

Van didn't bother to return Markus's greeting as he stated, "I see Savelij isn't here. Your lapdog must be chewing at his collar to get back to you."

Markus, a shifter Van wished death upon daily, didn't even flinch as he replied, "Something about you trying to kill him the last time he was here, if I remember correctly."

Ah, now, it was all coming back. It took all his willpower not to chuckle. "I can't recall."

Markus, as high up as he was, didn't intimidate Van. He could start a fight right in the middle of this damn room, and no one would be able to stop Van from ripping his throat out. It was something Van often dreamed about, only to wake up and suffer from some severe disappointment when he realized the idiot was still alive and kicking.

His thoughts drifted, however, and they always drifted back to that one person. His vision moved to the stairs, which didn't go unnoticed by Markus.

"Distracted, are we?" he asked knowingly.

Van's eyes swiftly flickered to Markus. He glared at the shifter, ignoring the way Konstantin pleaded to rip his face off. Van shook his head and tried to offer a small smile. "Nothing at all, now, what do I owe the occasion? Will my soul be enough offering for you to leave me the fuck alone? Or will I have to rip off my own leg?"

Markus grunted. Van was well aware that he had a particular distaste for a certain F-word.

"If you're done with your tasteless jokes, I came as a sort of peace offering," Markus explained.

Van snorted, nearly letting out a small laugh. "Peace offering? You certainly aren't very bright if you think plopping your ass in front of me and making idle conversation is a tempting peace offer."

His eyes narrowed, and Van wished — *honestly wished upon a fucking star* — that Markus would just sign his death certificate and get it over with. "I see I'm still not welcomed here."

Van smirked. "You're a smart one, Markus. I was starting to think your brain had deserted you as well, just as your common *fucking* sense had the day you sided with Ronan."

Markus put on a forced, painful smile as people passed by them. "Lower your voice, Kostya, people might assume we're not on friendly terms," he exclaimed quietly, still wearing that frightful smile.

Van didn't miss a beat. "I wasn't aware we *were* on friendly terms. You should really lower the intensity of that smile, Markus. You're scaring people."

The man huffed loudly as he glared. With one turn, he muttered something about not standing here childishly arguing and stormed off. Van smiled.

"I win."

He couldn't take this charade of good will for much longer. People that he didn't care much for mingled around and his pack behaved at best they could, anyway. Nikolai was passed out in the living room, sleeping off that bottle of premium Vodka he had managed to sneak in from Ivan.

Van sighed. Idiots, the lot of them.

His mother was talking to as many people as she could, probably hoping the time would pass as quickly as he wanted it to. She was always a social piranha, digging her teeth into any form of bad news she could. For once, the bad news wasn't about Van.

Drake and Emma never separated. Van knew it was because of all the males lurking around. It was instinct to protect one's mate, no matter if he and Van were in the same room. Van, however, had no such urge, and if he did, he was suppressing it well.

Van's ears pricked as he heard loud shuffling coming from upstairs. That was odd, *very* odd. The only one upstairs should have been Aira. Which reminded him...

Where the *fuck* had Aemilius and Lucus run off to? In fact, quite a few Elders were missing and after Markus's departure — which Van had most certainly wished upon a star for — there seemed to have been a good chunk of his guests unaccounted for. Not that he was complaining, having been old-geezer free for most of the night was satisfying.

But still, *where* had they run off? And what part of the house would he have to destroy to find them?

This night was becoming more and more frustrating. Not only had he deliberately placed Inna in the living room to help Elina sober up that idiot Nikolai, but it also seemed Jarret and Aiden were having a field day riling up some of the female shifters. He was just happy he didn't have Lillya screeching in the background.

Darya should keep her on a leash more often, he thought.

Van stalked over to Aiden and Jarret before growling, "I need you to find me some old dogs. They're probably as wrinkled as the furniture, so don't confuse the two."

Before Van went to talk to Drake, he turned and took the glass of tequila Aiden had in his hand. "I'm not picking you idiots up off the floor tomorrow. I may just throw you off the balcony instead."

Besides, he needed this more with how this shit was turning out. Old men going missing, his mother riding his ass and Markus being a damn brownnoser had him on the brink of throwing *everyone* in this house off the balcony, and by God, he would do it.

Jarret leaned in, chuckling as he asked, "Is he *always* like that?"

Aiden laughed just as hard, staggering slightly as he nodded, "Only when it's a good day."

"Suppose we should check on Aira while we go on a wolf hunt."

Just as they turned towards the stairs, Aiden nearly fell over completely when he saw Aira sneaking around the banister and kneeling as she beckoned them closer. She had been there the entire time, trying desperately to get their attention.

"Think you can steal me a few chairs?" she asked, a sly grin spreading across her face. From the lines on her mouth, it seemed as if she had been laughing not too long ago.

Aiden, still wobbly, asked, "Why? And *why* are you sneaking around?"

That nervous look said it all. Aiden nearly fell over laughing, but Jarret steadied his newfound best friend. "*You're* the one stealing the old men?" This was just too funny.

Aira waved her hands to calm him down. "I didn't steal them. Technically, they stole me. I need chairs so they can sit. They look tired."

Jarret was the one to burst out laughing this time. "Cause they're what, a thousand years old? I'd be tired too!"

Aira groaned as she shooed them to go get what she asked for.

Jarret whined as Aira took his drink away from him. "You don't need to try to balance chairs with this in your hand."

Defeated, they both turned to go and get what Aira needed, mumbling something about "damn party-poopers stealing their drinks."

Well, it didn't take Jarret long to have a *bromance* with her brother. Aira laughed.

Staring down at the nasty smelling liquid, Aira shrugged. May as well put it down the hatch. After all, she needed it more after tonight.

Chapter Seventy-Seven

Aira had been through a lot in her short life. Some events no human would ever get to experience, but tonight would have to be the strangest event by far.

Aemilius laughed as he danced with Aira. Lucus played the piano like he had been a concert pianist his whole life. More shifters had gathered upstairs, and Aiden and Jarret were showing a couple of the Elders how to mix cocktails.

And then, as quickly as it had started, it abruptly ended. Aemilius had a sly smile spread across his face as he looked to the doorway. Her parents and Van stood there. Van was particularly looking none too happy. Her mother, however, was trying to keep herself upright as she laughed in the doorway.

It was looking like all the fun and games were over until Drake moved passed Van and took Aira's hand. With a soft smile, he chuckled and told Lucus to keep playing. His eyes seemed to shine as he looked around the room.

Everyone went back to his or her business, laughing and talking and dancing. All chatter revolved around how it was nice to be back in this room, laughing as if nothing had changed as if Samiul were still here. Even Aleksandra looked as though she were happy and had even thrown Aira a casual nod of acceptance.

"I'm not even going to ask how you did this," Drake chuckled as he hugged Aira. "You're a magnet for all sorts of trouble. Did you know that?"

Aira snorted, "As if. I just thought if I couldn't join the fun downstairs, I'd bring the fun up here."

Aemilius came up behind them and grasped Drake's shoulder. "She's a special girl, Drake. You did well."

Drake nodded, gently shaking off the man's hand. "Emma and I didn't do anything special. Aira did that on her own."

Aira looked from Aemilius and back to her father. Although they looked friendly, there was a sense of past conflict. The way her father shook Aemilius away made her wonder just what sort of history they had together.

As Aemilius and her father made idle chit-chat, Aira's eyes moved to Aiden and Jarret, who were about to give Lillya a rather questionable blend of alcohol. She rushed over, snatching the beverage away. Lillya glared. Aira didn't care as she snapped; "She's probably never had a sip of this stuff in her life!"

It appeared that rational thinking came back to both the young men as they realized that was probably true. The last thing they wanted was a drunken she-wolf trampling all over the place. Lillya didn't say a word to Aira as she huffed and dragged Aiden away. Aiden smiled apologetically.

Jarret laughed, "Guess he's got himself a ball and chain."

Aira let out a loud sigh before looking towards the balcony. She just managed to catch a glimpse of Van leaving the room and turning the corner, out of sight.

This was her chance. There were no more excuses.

She shoved the martini glass into Jarret's chest, splashing it all over him, before waltzing towards the balcony. She ignored his annoyed yells as she poked her head outside.

Standing there and looking out over the grounds, she couldn't help but think that Van had never looked so handsome. She sucked in a deep breath before slowly moving towards him. They were out of sight from everyone, and she prayed no one came outside.

"Are you mad at me?" she asked timidly. Her hands encircled the railing of the balcony. Looking out at the night sky, she wondered why she had never realized how beautiful it was.

He didn't answer as he looked at her with a slightly raised brow. Aira knew instantly that he wasn't mad at her — he could never be mad at her. She grinned before they fell into a comfortable silence.

"Why didn't you tell me about...?" she cut herself off as she realized what she was asking may have been too personal. She quickly looked away when Van's head snapped around to stare at her.

"About?" He looked at her, a serious expression falling over his face. "What did those old mutts tell you about me?" he growled.

She probably should have retreated right there and then, but she didn't. Aira wouldn't back down.

"Your pack before you came here and became a Volkov." Her eyes glowed with a yearning for an answer. She wanted him to tell her the truth — to say they were exactly the same.

It was one of the few times she saw surprise wash over his face. His mouth twisted as if he were trying to find the right words to explain.

"It happened a long time ago..."

Sadness filled her chest. The loneliness that clouded his eyes was absolutely heartbreaking. Van was... sad. He reacted the same way she did whenever her parents were brought up.

Grabbing onto his arm, Aira nuzzled into his side. She felt him stiffen, not expecting that sort of reaction. He didn't pull away, and she was glad.

"Goodbye isn't forever, Van. Goodbye is just until we meet again." There wasn't such a thing as forever, and she knew this. Goodbye was just a word. It was a symbol that meant you would meet again, someday, somewhere, and everything would be okay.

"What are you doing to me?" he murmured under his breath. To Aira, it almost sounded like a question he often asked himself.

Aira pulled away, looking up at him and smiled. "Thanks to you. I've had an amazing life. I've met so many people and have so many stories to tell. I could die right now and be happy, truly happy—"

"You won't."

Aira, surprised, looked up as Van looked down at her, his face masked with seriousness and... fear?

Did the thought of her death scare him?

"You won't die, not while I'm still here."

The way his voice bounced from annoyed to almost panicked made butterflies dance in her stomach.

She nodded and looked down. "You wanna know a secret? I'm scared of death..."

Well, everyone was afraid to die, but she felt guilty knowing her family had died and that she was scared to take that plunge. "I had been ready to die at Richard's home. I didn't care anymore. I was so tired and—" She turned to look her hero in the eyes, a soft look falling over both of their faces as she whispered, "But you saved me like you always have... like you always will."

It was now or never. She was going to take the plunge without any fear of the repercussions. She was going to show him loud and clear just what she felt and had been feeling for some time now.

"I love you, Van."

With that last sentence out and in the open, Aira threw her self-doubt to the wind and leaned up, inches away from his face. Van's face twisted into a confused scowl until the girl wrapped her arms around his neck and, after a moment of hesitation, placed her lips against his.

Aira couldn't believe she was doing this — that this was actually happening. After a still and very awkward moment, she went to pull away, but Van's arms circled her waist, pulling her closer instantly. That was all the confirmation they both needed as his lips moved against hers, holding her close to his warm body.

She hadn't been sure on what exactly to do, but Van seemed to take over as he gripped her, pulling her up and sitting her on the edge of the balcony's railing.

Aira let out a tiny gasp, but any fear of him throwing her over the edge dissipated as he whispered between kisses, "I've got you."

At that moment, she knew that Van would never let her go. That even if he didn't say it out loud, his actions spoke louder than words ever could.

He wanted her as well.

Chapter Seventy-Eight

Aleksandra sat with Kasimir, watching as old friends mingled and talked about old times. Every time Samiul's name came up in conversation, she flinched with hurt. Oh, how she missed that man.

She tried to ignore the fact her son had disappeared outside and that the human had followed. She tried to ignore the horrible sinking feeling in the pit of her stomach. It was getting harder to accept that fate had given Van yet another tragedy.

"He made his choice, do not worry," Kasimir tried to sooth, but Aleksandra wasn't having it. "Do you dislike the girl so much?"

Her head snapped to the side as she glared. "Do not put words in my mouth," she snapped. "Don't judge me for worrying about his life… and hers."

A look of confusion crossed his face. Aleksandra sighed.

"Fate is tricky, and her time is limited. She can love without reason and forgive without thought — that is her curse and her gift."

Kasimir nodded in agreement. "Forgiveness and love are something we're not used to, I suppose."

She shook her head. "Be that as it may, the wolf will remain by Red Riding Hood's side for all eternity. She is his curse, the one thing that Athea created to be Konstantin's downfall, and inside, Van holds a monster who is falling for it."

"Aleksandra, you don't have to fear for him. The Lady and the Wolf is a legend. Unless Kostya confirms anything himself, we do not know for sure if history will repeat itself," Kasimir sighed as he took another sip of his drink.

"I hope you are right," she whispered. "I really do."

A storm was coming, a terrible storm that would see her son fall into Aion's grasp and that girl throwing herself into the throes of it to save him. It would tear them both apart, and Aleksandra would have to stand back and watch.

She did warn him after all.

The End

Can't get enough of Van and Aira? Make sure you sign up for the author's blog to find out more about them!

Get these two bonus chapters and more freebies when you sign up at http://sa-cross.awesomeauthors.org/!

Here is a sample from another story you may enjoy:

MATED TO THE ALPHA KING
JENNISE K

Prologue

Dear Reader,

It is with great pleasure that I present to you a brief introduction to the new world you have decided to enter; a new life you have decided to live. Let it be that it will only last for some chapters, but I hope you enjoy it until it lasts.

Let me introduce myself, first.

Hi, I am Theia Anderson. I am just like any one of you, human, alive and breathing. (Unless you are a zombie, in which case I *am not*, and I especially *do not* have brains!)

Just putting it out there!

I am eighteen, and currently a senior in Rosenberg High. (I'm what they call, a nerd. But let us face it. Nerds nowadays are hot!) I have also, only recently moved from the sunny state of California to a city called Peidmond, just beside Seattle. Needless to say, it rains here a lot.

When I moved here, I imagined finally living in a cold state and thought that it would be an amazing experience. Although, the fact that it was in the middle of the year, and I would have to settle in as the "new girl" was very well placed in my mind.

New friends, new teachers, a new environment—everything was new. But that all was well-known and understood. I had expected those.

However, what I certainly didn't expect was to meet the man who owns the castle I gazed upon from my window every morning and night. Yes, a castle… A castle I am now living in.

This is my story. A story I am now willing to share but only if you can keep a secret.

Do you remember the stories your Grandma used to tell you every night about cursed beasts, village beauties, girls in red capes and wolves in disguises?

Well, maybe, just maybe... they actually do happen. Maybe, beasts do exist.

They do. I would know. I am bound to one.

Whom, you may ask?

Well, I am mated to the Alpha King

How?

You will see

You will live through it with me.

I hope you enjoy the ride.

Best wishes,
Theia.

Chapter One

Done finally!

Packing had never been my forte. In fact, I absolutely detested packing. Maybe it was because the amount of books and other things I possess seemed impossible to place in tons of boxes.

Slapping duct tape across the box, I picked up a marker and marked it as *Theia's Books #3.*

When the box was pushed aside carefully, I finally let out a sigh of relief as I wiped away a layer of sweat that had accumulated on my forehead. I lived in the warm state of California. It was summer. So naturally, the heat was killing me.

A single thing one should always know about me— I am not much for heat.

When my dad came home one afternoon and declared that we were moving from California to a cold city just near the outskirts of Seattle called Peidmond, I was actually very excited.

Well, that was until I realized that I had to attend a new high school in the middle of the year and leave my best friend, Casey, behind. And since it was senior year, with prom and all, well, it sucked.

Had I been in my old school, Stinson High, I would have at least had my best friend to accompany me. The thought of being home, all alone on prom, only helped me sweat more.

We were a small family— my dad, Arthur Anderson, a professor of History and Literature; my mom, Maia Anderson, a designer and entrepreneur, and me, Theia, currently a senior student in high school and hoping to become a criminologist or psychologist— whatever came first. I also had a very strange fascination with history.

I guess dad's genes rubbed off on me that way.

Another soft huff of sigh left escaped me as I lazily picked myself off of the floor and dragged myself towards the bathroom. I only had two hours before we were to load everything and leave, and I knew, in this heat, I would need every minute of it.

Minutes later, as I stood under my cool shower and slowly observed my bathroom for the last time, I let a few stray tears flow with the water as I washed the tiny ache in my chest away.

It seemed like a day had passed when I found myself scrubbed and fresh, walking out into my bedroom in a towel.

A loud yelp left my lips when I suddenly found myself on the floor and a heavy weight on me.

"Don't go!" Casey cried hysterically against me. I would have cried too, but the fact that I was currently sprawled on the floor with a towel on and my hundred *something* pound best friend was on top of me was a little... suffocating. Especially in my part, I was merely five feet after all.

"Need... to... breathe, Casey!" I managed to gasp as I writhed under her, trying to escape her deadly grip. Immediately, Casey stilled above me.

"Oh, I'm sorry!" she apologized hurriedly, blushing beet red as she got off of me, and stood. She gave me her hand and helped me stand up.

On my feet, I sighed as I brought her in for a hug, "We will talk every night on Skype or FaceTime, and then there is Messenger! We will always talk. It'll be like I'm not even away, I promise," I assured her as I pulled away. Losing my towel, I pulled on my clothes.

Casey sighed a little heavy and a little scared. "What if we don't?"

I smiled a small, broken smile. My hand found Casey's again, and I gave it a comforting squeeze. "No matter what happens, whether we talk every day or not at all for months, when we do talk or meet, we will always be the same best friends."

A small tear dropped down Casey's cheeks, and she nodded, chuckling against the moisture on her face.

"You better tell me everything when you get there!" she blurted out, smiling a bit as she folded and placed my towel inside a plastic before packing it into my suitcase. My room was nearly empty. It was literally stripped bare except for the built-in bookshelves and a few boxes and suitcases that were still lying around waiting to be hurled into the moving truck.

Smiling, I nodded and pulled Casey in for a final hug. "We'll visit each other during breaks. I'll miss you, you know."

Casey nodded. "I'll miss you too, Thi."

The loud stomping noises alerted us both of someone coming up the stairs, and soon enough, there was a knock on the door. "Theia, are you done?"

"Yeah, dad, come in!" I replied as I picked up my jacket— just in case it got cold— and slipped into my flip-flops, which seemed like an irrational choice considering the two contrasted each other, but I wouldn't need my shoes in the car, anyway. I'd probably just tuck them under me throughout the ride.

The door opened instantly and in walked my dad with two bulky men. Smiling at me softly, they strode towards the boxes and picked them up.

Again, Casey and I stood in my empty room— a room we had had dozens of sleepovers, a room we played doll in, a room we gossiped, planned and plotted in, and a room we did our homework and fangirling in. I sighed.

"I think we should go now…"

"Uh-huh."

Casey and I walked downstairs hand in hand. I took a deep breath as I stood in the living room.

The place had a lot of my memories. I grew up in this area. Well, that was until I turned sixteen and got the television set up in my own room. My eyes are closed. I let out a deep breath and whispered, "I'll miss you, home. Goodbye."

"Theia, sweetie!"

My Mom's voice rang out to me like a fire truck's siren. I instantly opened my eyes and walked out of the threshold, letting Dad lock the door and hand over the keys to our real estate agent, who had managed to sell our home for a very, very reasonable amount.

The day outside was bright and happy, vibrant and warm, yet the heat suddenly didn't bother me anymore. I looked around my neighborhood and smiled. I would be taking all the good memories as I went. But as much as I was sad, truth be told, I was also secretly excited.

I didn't know what it was, but I felt like something was waiting for me in Peidmond. An adventure was waiting to be lived; maybe, a mystery waiting to be unraveled. The little knowledge about the new feeling in me was all the more alluring, and somehow, secretly, I couldn't wait to reach Peidmond.

"Bye, Cas. I'll call you when I reach there okay!" I muttered, suddenly holding back my tears as I was pulled into a hug.

"Uh-huh, we will always talk! And if we can't, we will at least message when we can," Casey assured me as she hugged me back.

Smiling slightly, I pulled out of the hug and with a final wave, climbed into our SUV, watching my best friend stand in my yard and my neighborhood for the last time as my Dad drove off.

It felt like I was leaving a part of me here. But then again, I was going whole.

"Are you excited, darling?"

Mom suddenly asked me, cutting the silence that had been building up since we left seven hours ago. The ride from California to Peidmond was fifteen hours and thirteen minutes, and already in these seven hours, we had stopped twice to fuel up the SUV and buy some snacks for along the way.

"Yeah, Mom, are you?" I murmured back, knowing well that both my parents were extremely excited for this "new chapter" in their life. Dad would not stop talking about the amount of brilliant literature his new university had, not to mention the immense raise in wage and position. He was ecstatic. For Mom, her boutiques and salons around California were still running. And although she would have to fly back and forth occasionally, her excitement with opening a new boutique and salon in Peidmond was especially overwhelming.

"Oh, I am so excited!" She squealed, clapping her hands together before turning towards Dad and placing a loving kiss on his cheek.

It was normal for me to witness their weird romance, so I just rolled my eyes and looked at the passing views.

"The new house is bigger, Theia," Dad chuckled and looked at me from the review mirror.

I knew he was trying to make me feel better about moving, leaving my old friends and life behind, so I just grinned at dad and spoke the first thing I thought would make him worry less. "I get the room with the best view!"

Dad chuckled and nodded, making my grin widen. It was not hard to notice that I was a papa's girl. And with me being the only child, he doted on me. I was his little *Fuzzybottom*— not that my bottom was fuzzy, but... just because— well, he was my hero.

"One of the best things about the house is that it has great views all around the rooms. But you'll receive the one with the best view, we promise. We should be settled by tomorrow. Hopefully, the day after, you and I could go shopping!" Mom said as she turned to look at me. Not excited at all, I somehow managed to produce a fake smile and plaster it across my face.

Nobody messed with Mom when it came to shopping... *nobody*!

Once her attention was elsewhere, I turned around to see how far off our moving truck was behind us. Before turning around, I brought out a book from my backpack and plugged my earbuds into my iPod before playing "Davy Jones Music Box and the Rainy Mood." Somehow, the rumbles of thunder together with the soft sound of the tune playing together created a more reading mood for me. Shoving the iPod inside my pants pocket, I flipped through the pages of my newest read, *Indiscretions*, slumped back into a more comfortable position and began journeying once again into a different time and a whole different world; this time, into the world of Lord Lockwood.

"Thi, we are here!"

I mumbled a few incoherent words before turning in my bed. *Need sleep.*

"Thi, Wake up!" Dad's voice urged before I was shaken on the shoulder and lightly tapped on my face. *What the heck?*

"Alright, alright!" I grumbled as I sat up on my bed and peeped my eye open.

I gasped. My face becoming warmer by the second as I finally realized that I was in our SUV and a couple of people were staring at me, smiling like a bunch of weirdos. My folks included.

My cheeks burned as my eyes rested on a blond-haired guy smirking at me, an axe in his hand as he rested it on his shoulder.

What was he? A huntsman? I rolled my eyes in my mind as I pushed any budding crush away. I was more of a Beauty and the Beast girl, anyway.

Finally managing to look away, I smiled at the rest of the folks smiling at me, two slightly elder couples.

"Oh, she's so beautiful!" The red-headed one gushed as I shoved my iPod and book into my backpack and got out of the SUV.

"Thanks," I mumbled back, knowing full well that the blond was still staring and smirking at me.

"Hello, dear, welcome to Peidmond! I'm Jane, and this here is my son, Alex and my husband, Hugh. We live just there beside your house. That one there is Mary and her husband, Grant. They have a son too, Matthew. He is good friends with Alex here," Jane told me excitedly, and I smiled back brightly mirroring her excitement.

"It's nice to meet you all. I am really excited to be here," I replied back happily as I extended my hand towards each one of them, shaking their hands softly but waving awkwardly at the smirking blond, Alex.

That boy seemed as beautiful as he seemed arrogant... beautiful, nonetheless. But then, arrogance trumped beauty any day.

My new home stood tall and proud— red bricks and a posh-looking French door. It seemed to have at least three floors, including the small attic on the third floor. Even the front yard seemed beautifully cultivated. I waited for Jane and Mary to start talking to Mom and Hugh and Grant to start helping my Dad and the movers place all our stuff into the house before picking up one of my smaller book boxes. I made a run for it.

Making a dash into the house as quickly as I could, I stopped only to grab Dad and drag him away, begging him to show me my room.

He grinned excitedly and exchanging a knowing look with both Hugh and Grant led me upstairs until we came to a stop on the very end of the hallway. He unlocked the room and opened the doors, motioning me to walk in.

I walked in and froze.

There, in front of me was the most amazing view of a castle perched on a mountain, surrounded by pine trees and fog. Beyond it, I could see water, maybe a lake. Maybe a sea… It was actually hard to say through the fog.

I turned around, already readying myself to leap on dad but frowned when I noticed that I was now alone in my room. The blond Alex was standing in the doorway with the usual smirk on his face and his axe missing.

I frowned. The urge of just smacking his smirk away seemed quite strong now, and it would be easy too.

"That is the castle Dovelore, owned by His Grace, Alexander Whitlock. 'His Grace' because some say his grandfather was a Duke, and that has now been passed over to him. He is also very rich if the castle isn't proof enough. But not by heritage, most of it is self-made and all. We are supposed to visit that castle this year, you know. Mr. Whitlock is providing one lucky student with a full-time scholarship to any university he or she wishes to attend and another lucky student a chance to stay in his castle for the breaks with the full usage of his library and a full tour around the castle if he or she wanted to, that is." Blond spoke, but his gaze did not once shift from the castle which although looked quite brooding, looked equally inviting as if charming me into visiting. There definitely was something about that castle.

Suddenly very curious, I turned towards Blond and asked, "What would you like?"

He turned his attention towards me, and for the first time since the fifteen minutes that we had known each other, he smiled at me... a real smile.

"Although the most brilliant of literature are available in the castle library, and I would love to roam the dungeons and secret pathways where the Pirates were slain and beasts held hostage, I want the scholarship." I nodded and turned back to look at the castle.

What beasts was Blond talking about?

The feeling of my feet pushing itself forward registered slowly before I found myself staring at the castle and my hands, sliding the window open.

Is someone living there right now? How many rooms could there be?

I swept my gaze along the windows of the castle but stalled when I saw someone staring back at me. It seemed a *he*. His bulky built made sure of showing no confusion even if he was so, so far away. It was quite distinguishable that he was wearing a white shirt, but that was all that could be made sense of. The rest was a blur.

"Hey, Blond, come here!" I whispered, motioning Blond to move forward.

"Blond?" he asked quite confusedly and sounding outraged as he made his way to me.

The man was still staring. His stare seemed so intense it made hairs stand at the back of my neck. I turned towards blond, wishing he could see the strange man just as I did. Castles were always haunted. But the one I would see day and night could not possibly be haunted, could it?

"Can you see the man?"

"What man? I see no man," he whispered back, scrunching his eyes as he looked in the direction of the castle.

I turned towards the castle, and the man was gone.

"He was just there! I promise!"

He looked at me frowning for a second before his smile came back.

"I can help you decorate your room," he offered, looking as if he really were interested in sorting out my mess.

I smiled as I brushed a stray of brown hair behind my ear. Silently thanking God for his sudden offer to decorate my bedroom. It would have taken me all day and night, otherwise.

"Let's do this."

If you enjoyed this sample then look for **Mated to the Alpha King**.

Other books you might enjoy:

Break Me, Mate
Nique Joaquin
Available on Amazon!

Other books you might enjoy:

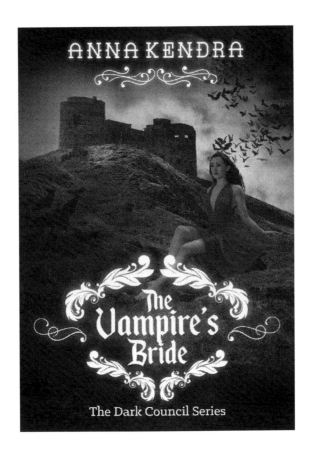

The Vampire's Bride
Anna Kendra
Available on Amazon!

Introducing the Characters Magazine App

Download the app to get the free issues of interviews from famous fiction characters and find your next favorite book!

iTunes: bit.ly/CharactersApple
Google Play: bit.ly/CharactersAndroid

Acknowledgements

In the end, there are so many people that deserve thanks for making this happen. My agent, Le-an is one of these people that will never know just how grateful I am. The thought I would ever be published was always just a dream, a dream I put on the backburner because I was so sure it would never happen. Thank you to Le-an and the staff at BLVNP. You made this real, and I will always be grateful for that.

A big thank you to my family, without my mother and father there to push me, I wouldn't have typed a single word. Without my family, Lady and the Wolf would have never come to be. Whether you love it or hate it, this story brings the good out in people, and shows them blood is not always thicker than water. Thank you to my Aunty Alli for teaching me that a good book can change your life. Thank you to my Nanny, Diane, for showing me guidance and patience.

Lastly, thank you to the millions of Wattpadders who read Lady and the Wolf. You gave my book a shot, and without that, I wouldn't be here, writing this sappy thank you note. Never forget that without you, I wouldn't be where I am. You gave me my confidence back. I had given up writing at one point, and five years later, look where I am now. Aira and Van were just character's in my head, but you made them real. You gave them life, something to look back on and forward to, and that's something no one else can give.

Some Special Mentions

My Partner, **Callum**. Without you, Nikolai wouldn't be awesome. Thank you for your help in Russian and your non-convententional plot idea's.

My best friend, **Shannen White**. Without you, my sanity would have been lost. I love you forever and always.

The new girl at work who turned into one of my closest friends, **Rachel Evans**. Without you, I wouldn't have survived work and writing. I'm so glad to have you in my life. I can't wait to meet your little man!

To my boss, the person who guided me and showed me true kindness. **Jen. K**, you are one of a kind. I hope you know how very special you are. Thank you for everything you have done for me.

Ash, without you, I would have never known my true potential. You showed me that I was worth so much more. I don't think I can ever repay that.

To **Brooke** and **Maxine**. You guys were the dream team, and your friendship is one of a kind. You two taught me so much, and I hope I can teach other's the same.

To my **Wattpad Biffle, Kelly**. You've been there from the beginning. Continue to write darling, because you have a talent, and I can't wait to see your name in a book store one day, because that is the day I'm kicked out for causing a public disturbance. (Haha).

To **Katie** and **Licia**, without you two, I wouldn't have found my happy place. We may be an ocean away, but I know you're right there with me whenever I need you. You two are the reason I write such amazing female characters. (LOL!)

To **Kiora**, my baby cousin. Thank you for shining and your continued support. You told me I could be something, so I did. Now it's your turn.

To my **Uncle Malcolm**. While Matt, Brett and Poppy may be gone, I knew you would always be there. You were always on my side. I love you.

And last, but not least, to **Mum, Dad and Sienna**. Everything I do, I do for you. Thank you.

Author's Note

Hey there!

Thank you so much for reading Lady and the Wolf! I can't express how grateful I am for reading something that was once just a thought inside my head.

I'd love to hear from you! Please feel free to email me at sa_cross@awesomeauthors.org and sign up at http://sa-cross.awesomeauthors.org/ for freebies!

One last thing: I'd love to hear your thoughts on the book. Please leave a review on Amazon or Goodreads because I just love reading your comments and getting to know YOU!

Whether that review is good or bad, I'd still love to hear it!

Can't wait to hear from you!

S.A. Cross

About the Author

I grew up in the Land Down Under, in a big city where you lived on other people's watches. When I was 4 years old, my mother gave me a giant book filled with fairy tales. I made her read it to me a thousand times before I could finally read it for myself. When I became a teenager reading much of anything was the last thing on my mind, until my grandfather gave a book that changed everything. After that, I wanted to read more, and before I knew it, I was begging my mother to take me to the second hand store every afternoon after school so I could check out their rejected books bin. After finding the internet, I realised I could write my own books, and before long, I was writing novels I never knew would even see the light of day.

Printed in Great Britain
by Amazon

60499750R00333